WASHOE COUNTY LIBRARY

3 1235 0110 9

8/13

P9-CJI-767

SPARKS BRANCH
WASHOE COUNTY LIBRARY

NOV 2 0 1996

The Best
AMERICAN
SHORT
STORIES
1996

GUEST EDITORS OF
THE BEST AMERICAN SHORT STORIES

The Best AMERICAN SHORT STORIES 1996

Selected from
U.S. and Canadian Magazines
by JOHN EDGAR WIDEMAN
with KATRINA KENISON

With an Introduction
by John Edgar Wideman

WASHOE COUNTY LIBRARY
RENO, NEVADA

HOUGHTON MIFFLIN COMPANY
BOSTON • NEW YORK 1996

Copyright © 1996 by Houghton Mifflin Company

Introduction © 1996 by John Edgar Wideman

ALL RIGHTS RESERVED

No part of this work may be reproduced or transmitted in any form or by any means, electronic or mechanical, including photocopying and recording, or by any information storage or retrieval system without the prior written permission of the copyright owner unless such copying is expressly permitted by federal copyright law. With the exception of nonprofit transcription in Braille, Houghton Mifflin is not authorized to grant permission for further uses of copyrighted selections reprinted in this book without the permission of their owners. Permission must be obtained from the individual copyright owners as identified herein. Address requests for permission to make copies of Houghton Mifflin material to Permissions, Houghton Mifflin Company, 215 Park Avenue South, New York, New York 10003.

ISSN 0067-6233
ISBN 0-395-75290-6
ISBN 0-395-75291-4

Printed in the United States of America

QUM 10 9 8 7 6 5 4 3 2 1

"Complicities" by Alice Adams. First published in *Michigan Quarterly Review.* Copyright ©1995 by Alice Adams. Reprinted by permission of Alfred A. Knopf, Inc.

"Fires" by Rick Bass. First published in *Big Sky Journal.* Copyright © 1995 by Rick Bass. Reprinted from the collection *In the Loyal Mountains,* by permission of Houghton Mifflin Company.

"Driving the Heart" by Jason Brown. First published in *Mississippi Review.* Copyright © 1995 by Jason Brown. Reprinted by permission of the Melanie Jackson Agency.

"Jealous Husband Returns in Form of Parrot" by Robert Olen Butler. First published in *The New Yorker.* Copyright © 1995 by Robert Olen Butler. Reprinted by permission of the author.

"The Eve of the Spirit Festival" by Lan Samantha Chang. First published in *Prairie Schooner.* Copyright © 1995 by Lan Samantha Chang. Reprinted by permission of the author.

"Fitting Ends" by Dan Chaon. First published in *TriQuarterly.* Copyright © 1995 by Dan Chaon. Reprinted from the collection *Fitting Ends and Other Stories,* by permission of Northwestern University Press.

"The Silver Screen" by Peter Ho Davies. First published in *Harvard Review.* Copyright © 1995 by Peter Ho Davies. Reprinted by permission of the author.

"Ysrael" by Junot Díaz. First published in *The New Yorker.* Copyright © 1995 by Junot Díaz. Reprinted from the collection *Drown,* by permission of the Putnam Berkley Group, Inc.

"Sleep" by Stephen Dixon. First published in *Harper's Magazine*. Copyright © 1995 by Stephen Dixon. Reprinted by permission of the author.

"Paper Lantern" by Stuart Dybek. First published in *The New Yorker*. Copyright © 1995 by Stuart Dybek. Reprinted by permission of the author.

"The Incredible Appearing Man" by Deborah Galyan. First published in *Missouri Review*. Copyright © 1995 by Deborah Galyan. Reprinted by permission of the author.

"Intertextuality" by Mary Gordon. First published in *The Recorder*. Copyright © 1995 by Mary Gordon. Reprinted by permission of the author.

"Past My Future" by David Huddle. First published in *Story*. Copyright © 1995 by David Huddle. Reprinted by permission of the author.

"Bright Winter" by Anna Keesey. First published in *Grand Street*. Copyright © 1995 by Anna Keesey. Reprinted by permission of the author.

"In Roseau" by Jamaica Kincaid. First published in *The New Yorker*. Copyright © 1995 by Jamaica Kincaid. Reprinted from the novel *The Autobiography of My Mother*, by permission of the Wylie Agency.

"Shades" by William Henry Lewis. First published in *Ploughshares*. Copyright © 1995 by William Henry Lewis. Reprinted from the collection *Speak My Name: Black Men on Masculinity and the American Dream*, by permission of the author and Beacon Press.

"A Stand of Fables" by William Lychack. First published in *Quarterly West*. Copyright © 1995 by William Lychack. Reprinted by permission of the author.

"Ghost Girls" by Joyce Carol Oates. First published in *American Short Fiction*. Copyright © 1995 by Joyce Carol Oates. Reprinted from the collection *Man Crazy*, by permission of E. P. Dutton.

"Sculpture 1" by Angela Patrinos. First published in *The New Yorker*. Copyright © 1995 by Angela Patrinos. Reprinted by permission of the author.

"Some Say the World" by Susan Perabo. First published in *TriQuarterly*. Copyright © 1995 by Susan Perabo. Reprinted by permission of the author.

"The Trip to Halawa Valley" by Lynne Sharon Schwartz. First published in *Shenandoah*. Copyright © 1995 by Lynne Sharon Schwartz. Reprinted by permission of the author.

"If You Sing Like That for Me" by Akhil Sharma. First published in *The Atlantic Monthly*. Copyright © 1995 by Akhil Sharma. Reprinted by permission of the author.

"All Shall Love Me and Despair" by Jean Thompson. First published in *Mid-American Review*. Copyright © 1995 by Jean Thompson. Reprinted by permission of the author.

"Xmas, Jamaica Plain" by Melanie Rae Thon. First published in *Ontario Review*. Copyright © 1995 by Melanie Rae Thon. Reprinted from the collection *First, Body*, by permission of Houghton Mifflin Company.

Contents

Contents

Foreword

THE WRITER works alone, in silence, endeavoring to put down on paper something that will touch and engage others. Thus a story conceived and born in solitude stirs to life only when it is brought out into the world — published, read, and shared. Each year, writers and readers are brought together and introduced to one another in these pages. Invariably, the volume seems larger than the sum of its parts, for the twenty or so stories chosen provide not only a testament to the vitality of the form, but also — in the contributors' notes that follow the stories — a window through which we may briefly observe writers at their craft.

Joyce Carol Oates, writing about her literary magazine, the *Ontario Review*, has said, "It appears to be a *thing*, but in fact it isn't a *thing* at all. It's a symposium. A gathering. A party. Open the cover and look inside. . . . The artist creates a single, a singular thing out of his solitary labor; but the editor creates a small unanticipated community that has never existed before and will never exist again."

So too is a volume of *The Best American Short Stories* a symposium, a gathering that reflects the tastes, the concerns, and the overriding passions of the editor assembling that year's collection. With the guest editor serving as host, the "unanticipated community" takes shape: this new writer appears alongside that established one; one story plays off another; themes emerge; connections are drawn. Writers meet one another through their stories; readers discover new voices and are reacquainted with familiar ones.

John Edgar Wideman read this year's stories blind — that is, with the author's name blacked out on each page. In one early telephone conversation, when I revealed that a story he had chosen was a first publication by a new writer, Mr. Wideman replied, "Yes, it feels like a first story. But you see, I like to watch NBA basketball, and I also like to watch college basketball and high school basketball, for different reasons." Mr. Wideman's wide-ranging pleasure in the short story is much in evidence in the selections he has made. Here are luminous new works by such masters of the form as Alice Adams, Mary Gordon, Joyce Carol Oates, and Lynne Sharon Schwartz. They are offset by a chorus of new voices, and there is, of course, an altogether different kind of pleasure to be derived from the debuts of Jason Brown, Junot Díaz, Deborah Galyan, Anna Keesey, William Henry Lewis, William Lychack, and Akhil Sharma.

Lionel Trilling once observed that while we are reading a work of literature, it is also reading us, locating the kinds of experience that interest us, the styles and tones to which we respond, our specific areas of educated feeling, as well as the blind spots and dead spots in our taste, sensibility, and competence to judge. As I read the nearly three thousand stories published in 1995, I was also read, in Trilling's sense — that is, provoked, enlightened, surprised, and at times left cold or impatient. John Edgar Wideman acknowledges in his introduction to this volume that "the stories I've chosen tell you more about me than I could ever tell you about them." So, too, do the stories that stood out in the course of this year tell all of us something about ourselves.

As grants and endowment funds continue to evaporate, as literary magazines struggle to obtain the funds necessary for survival, as publishers place their bets on known commodities, and as leisure time becomes increasingly devoted to and defined by technology, writers nevertheless continue to produce short stories, and readers continue to seek them out, knowing that there are reaches of the human soul that cannot be addressed on the Internet. In a culture that places high value on information — the factual, the explicable — there remains for those who wish it a deeper emotional truth, which can perhaps be articulated only in the stories we tell ourselves and each other. This collection includes stories from nineteen different magazines committed to publishing fiction, only four of which have circulations over several thousand.

It features as many unknown names as established ones, and the final contents were not set in stone until the very last moment; another whole handful of stories were hard to part with. (Indeed, breaking with convention, Mr. Wideman squeezed a couple of them in.) These stories have an urgency; they bear messages that need to be heard. Their very existence in this fast-paced, high-tech world testifies to the enduring value of the story as a continuing cultural resource, a unique vehicle for passing on the warnings and the wisdom of the age. These, then, are the stories that have read us — and marked us indelibly — in the past year. There is indeed a community within these pages; it is made up of people who agree that stories matter.

The stories chosen for this anthology were originally published in magazines issued between January 1995 and January 1996. The qualifications for selection are (1) original publication in nationally distributed American or Canadian periodicals; (2) publication in English by writers who are American or Canadian, or who have made the United States or Canada their home; (3) publication as short stories (novel excerpts are not knowingly considered). A list of magazines consulted for this volume appears at the back of the book. Publications that want to assure that their fiction is considered each year should include the series editor on their subscription list (Katrina Kenison, *The Best American Short Stories*, Houghton Mifflin Company, 222 Berkeley Street, Boston, Massachusetts 02116-3764).

K.K.

Introduction

MORNING, middle of February. Streets clear down the center, three-foot-high drifts along the edges. In my study, white piles of stories everywhere. Like the snow, the manuscripts have been the object of some heavy-duty plowing. A semblance of order, if you know how to look for it, among the scattered papers. Though they didn't disappear as quietly, naturally, as the white stuff evaporating outdoors, fewer stories now than when the storm hit. Three stacks I don't need to consult anymore shoved out of view. In descending order of interest, sprays of live stories on desk, countertops, a chair.

Okay, enough already of scene-setting, trying to make an introduction sound a little like a story. It's the middle of February. I'm near the end of the process of selecting for the 1996 volume of *The Best American Short Stories*. On my desk are twelve keepers I'm sure about. Twenty others, in two fan-shaped arrangements, are maybe yes, maybe no. Quota for the volume: approximately twenty, with two alternates. In spite of their intimidating collective bulk, reading the hundred-and-twenty-odd candidates for inclusion has been fun and informative. Sitting in the driver's seat brought its own particular kind of rush, the illusion of power and control as each story competed for my attention, tried to entertain, instruct, break my heart.

Now I'm floundering, unsure how to finish the task. Not so much a matter of standards and judgment deserting me as finding myself forced to acknowledge that if I began the selection again, I'd probably end up with a different batch of winners. Reading the stories in a different order, at different times of day, in different moods, would certainly affect my choices. Or reading them all again, two or three times again, or teaching them would change how I feel. Or I could decide to impose some rationale — thematic, stylistic, political — so the volume would reflect my vision of the contemporary literary scene. In each case a different story collection, not necessarily better or worse, but definitely different.

Also, I feel squeamish about making the final cut. No matter what my choices, plenty of good writing, good writers, will be left out. The mask of objectivity wears thinner and thinner as I fabricate reasons for whittling this last lot of twenty down to ten. Of course, the mask has been a fiction all along. Now it's a useless fiction. If I went back and subjected my keepers to the same sort of tight-lipped scrutiny I'm leveling on these stories still in contention, would the whole project sink in a slough of relativity, equivocation, second-guessing?

Once the protective mask of objectivity is scuttled or scuttles itself, a simple truth remains: the stories in this book are stories I like. Though the final shape of the volume will result from a cooperative effort among various readers and editors, I've been allowed plenty of rope — for instance, my push to include more than the usual twenty stories, my insistence on "In Roseau" though it has already appeared as part of a published novel — and if I wind up swinging in the wind, I have nobody to blame but myself.

Every time I give a public reading and open the floor to questions afterward, someone asks, in one fashion or another, the "audience question": for whom do you write? The answer I've settled upon lately is *me, myself, I'm my audience.* Then I go on to explain that I don't mean "me" in the narrow, solipsistic, self-important way my response might seem to imply, but a "me" in the more expansive, Whitmanesque sense of being always and inevitably many in one, all the voices I've heard and can speak and wish I could speak — my mother's, T. S. Eliot, Reverend Frank Felder of the Homewood A.M.E. Zion Church, Sam Cooke, Thelonious Monk, the voices conscious and unconscious, inherited, cultivated, instinctive, trained, me, myself the polyvocal microcosm, one whose experience is particular, unique, but who also and always bears a communal, historical experience of language and culture.

So the stories I've chosen tell you more about me than I could ever tell you about them. Reading them, I don new masks. They fit a lot better than any disguise of objectivity, let me breathe freer, explain myself better.

If you've read or written a great story in the past year and it doesn't appear here, relax. I certainly don't want to invest the collection with any of the pernicious authority of rankings and hierarchies that are a sure sign of intellectual exhaustion, dishonesty, chaos. What you'll read in this volume are not the best stories of 1996 but twenty or so stories distilled from a group submitted to me by the editor of this series, a group itself drawn from the pages of approximately seventy journals that somebody has deemed as serious and national. Of course, the stories that appear in such journals are a small sample of thousands of submissions received by the journals. Circles within circles within circles. A sort of roundabout way of saying that the stories reprinted here must survive multiple ambushes and interventions. Not the least of which is the current reigning idea of what a story is or should or can be. Surviving to this stage — publication in a respected series purchased by tens of thousands of readers — deserves applause and a prize, but it also depends nearly as much on accident as on intrinsic merit.

In a nation shamefully lacking in outlets for serious fiction, it's a minor miracle, and one much to be praised, that in spite of the haphazard, commercialized, politicized process by which stories break into print, stories like the ones gathered here — exhibiting craftsmanship, courage, emotional power, and commitment to excellence — continue to be written, let alone published. Mainstream culture systematically trivializes fiction by opposing it to other modes of representation deemed "true." We co-opt and corrupt the art of storytelling by enlisting it in the service of journalism and the big lie of advertising. Our fear and distrust of fiction reflect America's unfinished business of coming to terms with difference, our national reluctance to give full and equal credit to the *other* story — the woman's story, the black story, the immigrant story, the homeless story, our own story reimagined, the daunting freedom and responsibility that a reimagined self would demand.

As I read the selections culled from the seventy A-list publications, I was disappointed not to hear more African American voices. I felt an even deeper dissatisfaction in not finding more of what African American voices emerging in the sixties seemed to promise — reinvigoration, renaissance, an alteration of what generally was conceived as literature. Minority voices, voices the majority perceived as marginal, by their very definition carried immense potential to vary the script. Aside from but certainly not discounting problematic issues of ethical and moral fairness, political empowerment, self-identity and self-preservation, a place at the table and in the pecking order, the most exciting promise and raison d'être for reformulating the canon was the opportunity it presented to identify and reconnect with the multicultural vitality of the many strands that constitute our nation's literary heritage.

Given our country's history, our history before it was a country, you'd think the most American theme would be the inevitability of difference, the pain and consolation difference confers. But when you get past the lip service paid to individuality, get right down to the nitty-gritty, difference is abhorred, treated as a glitch in the cosmic scheme. Some of us are told we must endure this malfunction that sets us apart. Others seem driven to repair it (segregation/integration) or, if all else fails, to obliterate difference through denial or violence. The realm of art is marked just as distinctly by fear of difference as electoral politics and courts of law. To remain afloat, publications that feature fiction must compete not only in the marketplace of profit and loss but in the marketplace of ideas. America's dominant conservative ideology preaches conformity, and conformity buttresses capitalism. Capitalism depends on control, commodification, monopoly — a formula for conformity that permeates the entire culture. Will this closed circle define the closed American mind? James Baldwin warned us that fear and denial of difference would impoverish, shrink our collective imagination.

Our stories, their form and view of reality, are implicated by the reigning cultural imperatives. Entertainment has broken its traditional boundaries, become an alternative mode of consciousness, pervasive, immediate, and continuous, punctuated by hard-sell spurts of sex and violence, generating in its audience — us, from the moment we awaken and begin to be beguiled by the goods and services arrayed for our use — a kind of floating, seductive inattention to the serious business of our lives. TV dramas and a typical story printed in *The New Yorker* (the source, by the way, of several stories printed here and a large percentage of the stories reviewed for inclusion) are embedded in a collage of advertisements, news stories, simulations, editorial voice-overs, station breaks, logos, appeals subtle and not so subtle for direct audience interaction with the medium (phone numbers to call, perfume to sniff, calendars, coupons). Story is fractured, infected, less and less distinguishable from the marketing collage.

Page-turners, bestsellers, Muzak, commodify this mode of consciousness. The familiar endlessly repackaged, reproduced. Desire is objectified, materialized; a "piece," a "hunk," "number one," are paraded before us, seemingly upon demand. Striptease is the archetype governing the ritual of entertainment. Striptease seduces us into believing it's taking us somewhere we desire to go. It achieves this affect paradoxically by withholding, transforming a desired destination into an ever-receding horizon. Striptease plays on the tension between the familiar and the unknown. Our attention is seized, riveted to the moment. Striptease suspends our knowledge of what's going to happen next, the inevitable consequence of the last veil's removal. Desire fuels our attention, relieves us of the burden of the familiar. Which is not to say that, somewhere in our minds, we don't know how the dance will end. We know all too well. Yet for the moment it doesn't matter. What does matter is the excitement of tease and foreplay. And for this hype, these distractions (from death, boredom, repetition, the alienation of our work, the postpartum blues of sex), we're willing to pay almost anything. In this age of nonstop advertisement, the only business is the entertainment business.

Good writing teases us with the possibility/impossibility of sharing the intimacy and power of someone else's invisible vision. Mediocre writing works similar turf but compromises the invisibility, the mystery, the distance, the integrity of the "other" with the promise and pretense of delivering a final revelation: the last veil discarded. Exotic locales, an extraordinary chain of coincidence, drastic reversals of fortune, intricately convoluted plots, the impossible task, the unresolvable conflict, tragic accidents, virtue unrewarded, evil triumphant, turn out not to be what they seemed. We find ourselves at the conclusion of a docudrama or in a melodramatic story's epiphany exactly where we knew we were going all along. A familiar place. No surprises. No necessity to change ourselves. Difference resolved, dissolved. What had been hidden beneath the veil becomes commonplace, unthreatening, valueless the moment it's revealed.

Most of what passes for art, particularly narrative art, advertises mainstream values and culture. An ad for itself. Product endorsing product, creating a seamless web of resemblance and reinforcement. This art tells us that other peoples' lives aren't actually invisible, not intrinsically unknowable. We learn that anybody's story can be reduced to familiar terms, *our* terms, the terms our way of living prioritizes. Black people are just white people in darker skins, aren't they? In such art, disguise, illusion, technique, trickery, are deployed as delaying tactics, mystification that deadens our awareness of mystery.

Stories that don't acknowledge the mystery at the center of things, don't challenge the version of reality most consenting adults rely upon day by day, are stories that disappear swiftly into the ever-present buzz of entertainment. Stories that do mount a challenge to our everyday conventions and assumptions stir my blood. Not only because they are exciting formally and philosophically, but because they retain for fiction its special subversive, radically democratic role. The Ibo of West Africa put it this way: "All stories are true." Their proverb declares the value of storytelling, the value of every storyteller's unique access to the world.

Working hard, taking chances, having fun, failing, suffering, the storyteller through the tale makes us aware of a larger, unfinished story, the collective, collaborative utterance never completed because there's always another voice worth hearing.

I was seeking and found in the stories I've selected some hint that imagination can change the world, that the world is unfinished. A hint that we are not always doomed to make copies of copies but possess the power to see differently and the guts, skill, and good fortune to render accessible to others some glimmer of what our souls experience.

Stories after all are gifts. I'm grateful for the generosity that produces them, especially grateful for these fine stories that impel me to read more and write more.

JOHN EDGAR WIDEMAN

ALICE ADAMS

Complicities

FROM MICHIGAN QUARTERLY REVIEW

THE YOUNG GIRL, Nan, who has come to stay with the Travises, Jay and Mary, on their farm in southern New Hampshire — Nan is so thin that when she goes swimming in the pond deep indentations show between her small ribs. Her finely downed cheeks are hollow, her eyes the enormous eyes of a famine victim, or perhaps a sufferer from some lengthy and wasting disease. It is for this, from a desire to "build her up," to put some flesh on those bones, that her parents have sent her to the Travises for the summer. Also, there is an unspoken wish to do good to Mary and Jay, who are known to be "up against it," as the phrase went.

This was all some time back, before any talk of eating disorders, and Nan's parents, a kindly small-town druggist and his wife, in western Pennsylvania, distant cousins of Mary Travis, do not think in terms of neurosis, rejections of love — although it does seem to them that Nan eats a fair amount and is still morbidly thin.

Nan, at thirteen, is a fairly silly, unnaturally devious, and potentially bright girl (highest IQ in the local eighth grade). She thinks she looks wonderful; she feels herself possessed of vast and thrilling secrets. How powerful she is! and how private; no one knows anything about her, really, not even her lover. She does not use that word in thinking about Dr. Thurston, the minister whose babysitter she occasionally is; the man who is out of his mind, deranged with love for her, she says, and certainly he acts that way, following her everywhere in his car just to look at her as she walks home from school with friends, meeting her in that same car for rendezvous on the edge of town. Removing her clothes to cover her body with his mouth, kissing everywhere, breathing as though he might die.

Dr. Thurston (impossible to think of him as Bill, the name his fat wife uses) is one of Nan's secrets; the other is what she thinks of as "losing food," something she does in the bathroom with her fingers, after meals. Fingers down her throat, which if she has waited too long do not feel good. But it works, she can eat all she wants to and still have nothing on her bones but skin. Nothing to pinch, anywhere. "I adore your pale thin body," says Dr. Thurston. "I would never profane it."

Jay Travis is a failed painter; it is hard otherwise to make a sum of his life. Once a successful advertising man, he left his wife and married his assistant, Mary, and retired to the country to paint in a serious way, as he had always intended. Periodically he takes slides and sometimes canvases down to New York, but nothing has ever panned out, and they live mostly on the foolish articles that Mary writes (she knows they are foolish) for various "ladies' magazines." For editors who are old friends, from Mary's own single New York days.

Acerbic, melancholy, and exceptionally smart, Jay often feels that he may have been better off in a commercial venture at which he could constantly scoff; he fears that he is not doing well with this serious dedication to his talents — "such as they are," as he himself would be the first to add. And this has been an especially bad year for Jay; prostate surgery in January ("Some New Year's present for a tired old cock" was his terrible joke) left him weak and further depressed. Nothing sold, and the long wet spring wore on, and now they have this skinny nymphet in the house, watching everything as fixedly as a cat.

What he truly loves, though, what Jay Travis literally adores is this farm, this lovely hillside acre with its meadows and pond, its stands of birches and hemlocks and Norway pines, its surrounding low stone fence. And the falling-down red barn, with its population of busy, half-tame cats, its bats and a family of owls. And he loves the house, low-lying, weathered to silver, its long rooms smelling of apples and of lavender. On a cane, which is half affectation, Jay paces his house and his land; he inspects the fences (for what? he wonders, whatever could happen to a very old small stone fence?). He takes dishes of milk and tuna out to the barn for the cats, and he squats there, hoping and watching for some feline form of affection, or even notice.

He watches almost translucent Nan, as she walks gingerly across the tender meadow grass and down to the pond in her childish skimpy bathing suit — as, removing the towel from her shoulders, she shivers in the summer morning air. Occasionally Jay goes into his studio, unveils the canvas, and stares at it for a while.

Always, from his window, he is hoping for a sight of Mary, whom he loves truly more than his land or his house, or his cats, or anything in life that he can imagine.

Mary Travis, in early middle age (she is Jay's third wife; as she herself puts it, some men just never learn), is plump and beautiful and kind and very restless. She doesn't move about a lot, as Jay always does, but she sits and stares at books and windows, occasionally getting up to polish something. She has found some wonderful lavender-smelling wax.

Or to cook. Mary likes to cook. What she serves up is in fact exceptional, great culinary triumphs, often. Even just for Jay, and recently for Jay and Nan, she makes lovely foam-light soufflés, beautiful fresh vegetable terrines, and mysterious rich soups. And magnificent cakes; she is perhaps at her best with cakes.

Having been told by Nan's parents, her cousins, of their worry over their daughter's weight, Mary watches Nan's breakfast consumption of blueberry muffins, her noontime intake of meat and cheese and fruit, her adult-sized dinners. Pleased and flattered by this new consumer, Mary feels her own views of her cooking confirmed (this is her not-so-secret vanity). But then, further observing Nan, and with greater attention, she sees no change whatsoever in the almost transparent flesh stretched over those delicate ribs. And she notes too the alacrity with which Nan heads for the bathroom after each meal, a compulsion at first excused by murmurs about her dentist: "He's an absolute maniac about post-meal brushing."

Observant and wise, Mary thinks, Can that silly little bitch be making herself throw up? How entirely disgusting, not to mention the waste.

Though poor, the Travises are fond of giving parties, on Saturdays, generally. Around six in the evening people start to arrive in their shabby cars, seemingly from everywhere, bearing casseroles or bags of fruit, boxes of cookies. Or bottles: these parties involve an enormous number of bottles, Nan has observed. As she plans to say to her mother, they all drink like fish. An abstemious ghost, Nan hovers at the edges of these parties; she is often in white, as though to emphasize her difference.

They eat and they drink and they dance, these middle-aged hedonists.

They dance close together, mostly to old slow scratched records, old songs that Nan has barely heard of. Squinched down in an ancient leather chair with a heavy book, in a barely lit corner of the living room, Nan, who is not really reading, looks up from time to time at whatever is going on — which is not much, usually.

Until the night that Mary sings.

More absorbed than usual in her reading (it is *Gone With the Wind*), Nan has come to what she thinks of as the good parts, Rhett kissing Scarlett. She looks up with surprise at the sound of the piano, which no one ever plays; someone is playing a song she knows, "Honeysuckle Rose," a favorite of her father's.

And then suddenly Mary is standing right there by the piano. And Mary is singing.

"Don't — need — sugar —
You just have to touch my cup —"

She is singing and laughing, embarrassed, but still her voice is rich and confident and sexy — oh, so sexy! Mary is wearing a new blue dress, or maybe it's old. It is tight, some shiny material, stretched tight over those big breasts and hips. Nan, watching and listening ("— it's so sweet when you stir it up —"), experiences an extreme and nameless, incomprehensible disturbance. She feels like throwing up, or screaming, or maybe just grabbing up her knees so that her body is a tight-knit ball — and crying, crying there in her corner, in the semidark. Is this falling in love? Has she fallen in love with Mary? She thinks it is more that she wants to *be* Mary. She wants to be out there in the light, with everyone laughing and clapping. She wants to be singing, and *fat*. Oh, how wildly, suddenly, she yearns for flesh, her own flesh. Oh, fat!

"Were your other two wives as beautiful as Mary?"

None of your fucking business, is what Jay feels would have been the proper answer to this question. But Nan is only a child, he reminds himself. Also, she is their paying houseguest. And so he contents himself with saying, as vaguely as possible, "No, not exactly."

They are walking very slowly around the edge of the pond in an August twilight, Jay with his cane and Nan in her tiny white shorts, a skin-tight T-shirt. He had not realized before that she had breasts — or does she? Those small protuberances look a little unreal, as though she had stuffed something into a tiny bra — and it comes to Jay, with the sureness of a vision, that she must have done exactly that; she stuffed her bra, but why? Why on earth? And why has she come out after him like this, interrupting his solitary stroll?

"Thin or fat?" this terrible child persists. "Your wives."

"Uh. On the plump side. I've always liked a little flesh."

But with great eagerness she has interrupted. "There's this man at home, you know? I babysit for him and his wife. He's a minister, can you believe it? And he is absolutely crazy about how thin I am. Just crazy! He follows me."

"Nan, you must avoid this man. Tell him to go away. Tell your father."

"Oh, I will. The very idea of him right now makes me — makes me want to throw up." Nan laughs immoderately at this disgusting remark.

"It's quite a puzzle," says Jay to Mary at dinner one night, about three weeks after that walk, that conversation with Nan. It is in fact the next-to-last night of Nan's visit, but she has gone to bed early, leaving Mary and Jay to finish what has been a celebratory feast: they are not so much celebrating her imminent departure (not explicitly, that is) but rather the fact that after years of professional drought, Jay's agent has sold a large painting, a landscape (in fact Jay's own landscape, the meadow and stand of trees next to his studio). Not only was the painting sold, there is also a commission for four more large landscapes. And that was their conversation at dinner: without Nan present, Jay was able to speak joyously of his good fortune, plans, and eagerness for work.

In terms of festivity, feasting, Mary quite outdid herself, with an oyster soufflé, and something that she calls her twenty-vegetable lamb stew, and an orange salad and a chocolate mousse. Nan, protesting fatigue, went off to bed before the mousse was served ("I may come down for a little later on, will you save some for me, Mary?") — and it is this recent shift in Nan's eating habits that they now discuss, and that Jay has just described as a puzzle.

He continues, "I'd swear she's eating less now, and at the same time she's putting on some weight."

This has been expressed more or less as a question to Mary, which Mary accepts, but she only says, "I think I understand," and she smiles.

And then, simultaneously, they lose all interest in Nan; they turn to each other as though they had been separated for some time. They look at each other with a sort of pleased surprise — and then, because it strikes them funny, they begin to laugh.

"Shall we dance?" Jay is still laughing as she says this, but that is what they do; they put on some old Glenn Miller records, from their own era, and Jimmy Lunceford and Tommy Dorsey — and they dance. Laughing and dancing, very happy with each other, they end up necking on the sofa, exhaustedly, like kids.

And that is how Nan finds them, asleep on the sofa. Mary is snoring lightly as Jay, asleep, breathes heavily into her breast.

Giving them first a quick, disgusted look, Nan goes over to the cluttered table, which it does not occur to her to clear. There is a large, dissolving plate of chocolate mousse, all of which she spoons slowly into her mouth — ah, delicious! She will have to get the recipe for her mother, Nan thinks; they could have it at least once a week, which should mean two or three pounds right there.

Slipping back into bed without even brushing her teeth, Nan continues with what has been a waking dream, a plan: next summer, when she is sleek and fat — as fat as Mary is! — she will come back up here, and Jay will fall madly in love with her. He will follow her everywhere, the way Dr. Thurston used to do. But she will say no, no kissing even. You belong to Mary. And Mary, finding out what Nan has done, will say what a wonderful girl Nan is, how truly good, as well as beautiful, and fat.

And then Nan will leave, probably off with some boyfriend of her own by then, and Mary and Jay will mourn for her. Always. "If only Nan were with us again this summer," they will say, for years and years.

RICK BASS

Fires

FROM BIG SKY JOURNAL

SOME YEARS the heat comes in April. There is always wind in April, but with luck there is warmth too. There is usually a drought, so that the fields are dry, and the wind is from the south. Everyone in the valley moves their seedlings from the indoors to the outdoors, into their old barns-turned-into-greenhouses. Root crops are what do best up here. The soil is rich from all the many fires, and potatoes from this valley taste like candy. Carrots pull free of the dark earth and taste like crisp sun. I like to cook with onions. Strawberries do well too, if they're watered.

The snowline has moved up out of the valley by April, up into the woods, and even on up above the woods, disappearing, except for the smallest remote oval patches of it, and the snowshoe hares, gaunt but still white, move down out of the snow as it retreats to get to the gardens' fresh berries and the green growing grasses; but you can see the rabbits coming a mile away, coming after your berries — hopping through the green and gold sun-filled woods, as white and pure as Persian cats, hopping over brown logs, coming down from the centuries-old game trails of black earth.

The rabbits come straight for my outside garden like zombies, relentless, and I sit on the back porch and sight in on them. But because they are too beautiful to kill in great numbers, I shoot only one every month or so, just to warn them. I clean the one I shoot and fry it in a skillet with onions and half a piece of bacon.

Sometimes at night I'll get up and look out the window and see the rabbits out in the garden, nibbling at whatever's available, but also standing around the greenhouse, all around it, just aching to get in: several of them dig at the earth around it, trying to tunnel in — dirt flying all through the air — while others just sit there at the doorway, waiting.

The hares are only snow-white like that for a few weeks, after the snow is gone; then they begin to lose the white fur — or rather, they do not lose it, but it begins to turn brown, like leaves decaying, so that they are mottled for a while during the change, but then finally they are completely brown, and safe again, with the snows gone. But for those few weeks when they are still white, the rabbits sit out in my garden like white boulders.

I haven't had a woman living with me in a long time now. Whenever one does move in with me, it feels as if I've tricked her, have caught her in a trap: as if the gate has been closed behind her, and she doesn't yet realize it. It's very remote up here.

One summer my friend Tom's sister came up here to spend the summer with Tom and his wife, Nancy, and to train at altitude. Her name was Glenda, and she was a runner from Washington, and that was all she did, was run. Glenda was very good, and she had run in races in Italy, in France, and in Switzerland. She told everyone when she got up here that this was the most beautiful place she had ever seen, told all these rough loggers and their hard wives this, and we all believed her. Very few of us had ever been anywhere else to be able to question her.

We would all sit out at the picnic tables in front of the saloon, ten or twelve of us at a time, half the town, and watch the river. Ducks and geese heading back north stopped in our valley to breed, to build nests, and to raise their young. Ravens, with their wings and backs shining greasy in the sun, were always flying across the valley, from one side of the mountains to the other. Anyone who needed to make a little money could always do so in April by planting seedlings for the Forest Service, and it was always a time of relaxation because of that fact, a time of no tempers, only loose happiness. I did not need much money, in April or in any other month, and I would often sit out at the picnic table with Glenda and Tom and Nancy and drink beer. Glenda would never drink more than two. She had yellow hair that was cut short, lake-blue eyes, a pale face, and a big grin, not unlike Tom's, that belied her seriousness, though now she is gone, I think I remember her always being able to grin because of her seriousness. I certainly don't understand why it seems that way to me now. Like the rest of us, Glenda had no worries, not in April and certainly not later on in the summer. She had only to run.

I never saw Glenda in the fall, which was when she left; I don't know if she ever smiled like that when she got back to Washington or not. She was separated from her boyfriend, who lived in California, and she didn't seem to miss him, didn't ever seem to think about him.

The planters burned the slopes they had cut the previous summer and fall, before planting the seedlings, and in the afternoons there would be a sweet-smelling haze that started about halfway up the valley walls and rose into the highest mountains and then spilled over them, moving north into Canada, riding on the south winds. The fires' haze never settled in our valley but would hang just above us, on the days it was there, turning all the sunlight a beautiful, smoky blue and making things when seen across the valley — a barn in another pasture, or a fence line — seem much farther away than they really were. It made things seem softer too.

There was a long zippered scar on the inside of Glenda's knee that started just above her ankle and went all the way up inside her leg to mid-thigh. She had injured the knee when she was seventeen, long before the days of arthroscopic surgery, and she'd had to have the knee rebuilt the old-fashioned way, with blades and scissors, but the scar only seemed to make her legs, both of them, look even more beautiful, the part that was not scarred, and even the scar had a graceful curve to it as it ran such a long distance up her leg.

Glenda wore green nylon shorts and a small white shirt when she ran, and a headband. Her running shoes were dirty white, the color of the road dust during the drought.

"I'm thirty-two and have six or seven more good years of running," she said whenever anyone asked her what her plans were, and why she ran so much, and why she had come to our valley to run. Mostly it was the men who sat around with us in front of the saloon, watching the river, watching the spring winds, and just being glad with the rest of us that winter was over. I do not think the women liked Glenda very much, except for Nancy.

It was not very well understood in the valley what a great runner Glenda was.

I think it gave Glenda pleasure that it wasn't.

*

"I would like for you to follow Glenda on your bicycle," Tom said the first time I met her. Tom had invited me over for dinner — Glenda had gotten to the valley the day before, though we had all known that she was coming for weeks beforehand and had been waiting for her.

"There's money available from her sponsor to pay you for it," Tom said, handing me some money, or trying to, and finally putting it in my shirt pocket. He had been drinking and seemed as happy as I had seen him in a long time. He called her "Glen" instead of "Glenda" sometimes — and after putting the money in my pocket, he put an arm around Nancy, who looked embarrassed for me, and the other arm around Glenda, who did not, and so I had to keep the money, which was not that much anyway.

"You just ride along behind her with a pistol" — Tom had a pistol holstered on his belt, a big pistol, and he took it off and handed it to me — "and you make sure nothing happens to her, the way it did to that Ocherson woman."

The Ocherson woman had been visiting friends and had been walking home, but never made it: a bear evidently charged out of the willows along the river road and dragged her back across the river. It was in the spring when she disappeared, and everyone thought she had run away. Her husband had even gone around all summer making a fool of himself by talking badly about her, and then hunters found her in the fall, right before the first snow. There were always bear stories in any valley, but we thought ours was the worst, because it was the most recent and because it had been a woman.

"It'll be good exercise for me," I said to Tom, and then I said to Glenda, "Do you run fast?"

It wasn't a bad job. I was able to keep up with her most of the time, and we started early in the mornings. Some days Glenda would run just a few miles, very fast, and other days it seemed she was going to run forever. There was hardly ever any traffic — not a single car or truck — and I'd daydream as I rode along behind her.

We'd leave the meadows out in front of Tom's place and head up the South Fork road, up into the woods, toward the summit, going past my cabin. The sun would be burning brightly by the time we neared the summit, and we'd be up into the haze from the planting fires, and everything would be foggy and old-looking, as if we had gone back in time — as if we were living in a time when things had really happened, when things still mattered and not everything had been decided yet.

Glenda would be sweating so hard from running the summit that her shirt and shorts would be drenched, her hair damp and sticking to the side of her face, and the sweat would wet her socks and even her tennis shoes. But she was always saying that the people she would be racing against would be training even harder than she was.

There were lakes up past the summit, and the air was cooler. On the north slopes the lakes still had thin crusts of ice on them, crusts that thawed out, just barely, each afternoon but that froze again each night; and what Glenda liked to do after she'd reached the summit, her face as bright as if sunburned and her wrists limp and loose, sometimes wavering a little in her stride finally, so great was the heat and her exhaustion, was to leave the road and run down the game trail leading to the lakes — tripping, stumbling, running downhill again, and I would have to throw the bike down and hurry after her — and pulling her shirt off, she would run out into the shallows of the first lake, her feet breaking through the thin ice, and then she would sit down in the cold water, like some animal chased there by hounds.

"It feels good," she said the first time she did that, and she leaned her head back on the ice behind her, the ice she had not broken through, and she spread her arms out across the ice as if she were resting on a crucifix, and she looked up at the haze in the sky with nothing above us, for we were above the treeline.

"Come over here," she said. "Come feel this."

I waded out into the pond, following her trail through the ice, and sat down next to her.

She took my hand and put it on her chest.

What I felt in there was like nothing I had ever imagined: it was like lifting up the hood of a car that is still running, with all the cables and belts and fan blades still running. I wanted to take my hand away; I wanted to get her to a doctor. I wondered if she was going to die and if I would be responsible. I wanted to pull my hand away, but she made me keep it there, and gradually the drumming slowed, became steadier, and still she made me keep my hand there until we could both feel the water's coldness. Then we got out — I had to help her up, because her injured knee was stiff — and we laid our clothes out on rocks to dry in the sun, and we lay out on flat rocks ourselves and let the wind and the sun dry us as well. She said that she had come to the mountains to run because it would strengthen her knee. But there was something that made me believe that that was not the reason, and not the truth, though I cannot tell you what other reason there might have been.

We went into the lake every hot day, after her run, and there was always the thinnest sheet of ice back in the shadows. It felt wonderful, and lying out in the sun afterward was wonderful too. After we had dried, our hair smelled like the smoke from the fires in the valley below. Sometimes I thought that Glenda might be dying and had come here to live her last days, to run in a country of great beauty.

After we were dry we walked back, and as we went back over the crest of the summit and started down toward the valley, we would slowly come out of the haze and would be able to see all of the valley below us, green and soft, with the slow wind of the Yaak River crawling through the middle of it, and on the north wall of the valley midway up the slopes the ragged fires would be burning, with wavering lines and shifting walls of smoke rising from behind the trees, sheets of smoke rising straight into the sky.

The temptation to get on the bike and just coast all the way down was always strong, but I knew what my job was, we both did, and it was the time when bears were coming out of hibernation, when everything was, and the safety of the winter was not to be confused with the seriousness of summer, with the way things were changing.

Sometimes, walking back, we would come across ruffed grouse — males — courting and fanning in the middle of the road, spinning and doing their little dance, their throat sacs inflated bright and red, pulsing, and the grouse would not want to let us past — they would stamp their feet and spin in mad little circles, trying to block where it was we were going, trying to protect some small certain area they had staked out for themselves. Glenda seemed to stiffen whenever we came upon the fanning males and shrieked when they rushed at her ankles, trying to peck her, as we tried to hurry around them.

We'd stop by my cabin for lunch on the way back into the valley.

I'd open all the windows — the sun would have heated all the logs in the house, so that when we came inside there was a rich dusty smell, as it is when you have been away from your house for a long time and first come back, but that smell was always there in my cabin — and we would sit at the breakfast room table and look out the window, out at the old weedy chicken house I'd never used, which the people who'd lived in the cabin before me had built, and we'd look at the woods going up onto the mountain behind the chicken house.

I had planted a few apple trees in the back yard that spring, and the place that had sold them to me said that these trees would be able to withstand even the coldest winters, though I was not sure I believed it. They were small trees, and it was supposed to be four years before they started bearing fruit, and that sounded to me like such a long time that I had to really think about it before buying them. But I had just bought them without really knowing why I was doing it. I also didn't know what would make a person run as much as Glenda did. But I liked riding with her and having coffee with her after the runs, and I knew I would be sad to see her leave the valley. I think that was what kept up the distance between us, a nice distance, just the right-sized distance — the fact that each of us knew that she was only going to be there a certain amount of time, that she would be there for the rest of May and June and all through July and on through most of August, but that then she would be gone. We knew what was going to happen, it was a certainty, and therefore it seemed to take away any danger, any wildness. There was a wonderful sense of control. She drank her coffee black. We would snack on smoked whitefish that I had caught the previous winter.

I had a couple of dogs in the back yard, Texas hounds that I'd brought up north with me a few years ago, and I kept them in a pen in the winter so that they wouldn't roam and chase and catch deer, but in the spring and summer the sun felt so thin and good and the hounds were so old that I didn't keep them penned up but just let them lie around in the grass, dozing. There was one thing they would chase, though, in the summer. It lived under the chicken house. I don't know what it was; it was dark, and ran too fast for me ever to get a good look at it, and it's also possible that even if I had been able to see it, it would have been some animal that I had never seen before — some rare animal, something from Canada perhaps — maybe something no one had ever seen. Whatever it was — small and dark, with fur, but not shaggy, not a bear cub — it never grew from year to year but always stayed the same, though it seemed young somehow, as if it might someday grow — anyway, it lived in a burrow under the chicken house, and it excited the dogs terribly. It would come ripping out of the woods, just a fleet dark blur headed for the burrow, and the old dogs would be up and baying, right on its tail, but the thing always made it into the burrow just ahead of them.

Glenda and I would sit at the window and watch for it every day. But it kept no timetable, and there was no telling when it would come, or even if it would. We called it a hedgehog, because that was the closest thing it might have resembled.

Some nights Glenda would call me on the shortwave radio, would key the mike a few times to make it crackle and wake me up, and then, mysteriously, I would hear her voice in the night, floating in static as if it were in the night, out with the stars — her voice: "Have you seen the hedgehog?" she would ask sleepily, but it would be only a radio that was in the dark house with me, not her, not her real voice. "Did you see the hedgehog?" she'd want to know, and I'd wish she were staying with me, I'd wish she were with me at that moment. But it would be no good — Glenda was leaving in August, or September at the latest.

"No," I'd say. "No hedgehog today. Maybe it's gone away," I'd say — though I had thought that again and again, dozens of times, but then I would always see it again, just when I thought I never would.

"How are the dogs?" she'd ask. "How are Homer and Ann?"

"They're asleep."

"Good night," she'd say.

"Good night," I'd say.

On Thursday nights I would always have Tom and Nancy and Glenda over for dinner. Friday was Glenda's day off from running, so she could drink, could stay up late, and did not have to worry about any after-effects the next morning. We would start out drinking at the Dirty Shame, sitting out front watching the river, watching the ducks and geese headed north, and then before dusk we would go back down to my ranch, and Glenda and I would fix

dinner while Tom and Nancy sat on the front porch and smoked
cigars and watched the elk come out into the dusk in the meadow
across the road.

"Where's this famous hedgehog?" Tom would bellow, blowing
smoke rings into the night, big, perfect *O*'s, and the elk would lift
their heads, chewing the summer grass like cattle, the bulls' antlers
glowing with velvet.

"In the back yard," Glenda would say, washing the salad or rinsing off the carrots, or even the trout fillets. "But you can only see
him in the daytime."

"Aww, bullshit!" Tom would roar, standing up with his bottle of
Jack Daniel's, and he'd take off down the steps, stumbling, and
we'd all put down what we were doing and get the flashlight and go
with him to make sure he was all right, because Tom was a trapper,
and it riled him to think there was an animal he did not know,
could not trap, could not even see. Tom had tried to trap the
hedgehog before but had never caught anything, and he did not
believe there was any such animal. Out by the chicken coop, he
would get down on his hands and knees, breathing hard, and we'd
crowd all around and try to shine the flashlight into the deep, dusty
hole to see if there might be a patch of fur, the tip of a snout, or
anything, and Tom would be making grunting noises that were, I
supposed, designed to make the animal want to come out. But we
never saw anything, and it would be cold under all the stars, and
we'd be able to see the far-off glows that were the planting fires,
burning slowly even into the night but held in check by back-fires;
they were in control.

We had one of those propane fish fryers, and we'd put it out on
the front porch and cut the trout into cubes, roll them around in
sweet mustard and flour, then drop them in the hot spattering
grease. We'd fix more than a hundred of the trout cubes, and there
were never any left over. Glenda had a tremendous appetite, eating
almost as many as Tom and licking her fingers afterward, asking if
there were any more. We'd take whatever we were drinking up on
the roof — Tom his Jack Daniel's, Glenda and I rum and Cokes,
and Nancy vodka — and we'd sit high on the steep roof of my
cabin, above the second-story bedroom dormer. Tom sat out on the
end of the dormer as if it were a saddle, and Glenda would sit next
to me for warmth as we'd watch the far-off fires of the burns, a

flaming orange color as they sawed their way across the mountain-
side, raging but contained. Below us in the back yard, those rabbits
that had still not turned brown would begin to come out of the
woods, dozens of them, moving in on the greenhouse and then
stopping, just lining up all around it, wanting to get into the tender
young carrots and the Simpson lettuce. I had put sheets down on
the ground in the back yard to trick them, and we'd laugh as the
rabbits moved nervously from sheet to sheet, several of them hud-
dling together on one sheet at a time, thinking they were protected,
and all the time moving in on the greenhouse.

"Turn back, you bastards!" Tom would shout happily whenever
he saw the rabbits start coming out of the woods in the moonlight,
and his shouts would wake the ducks down on the pond, and they
would begin clucking to themselves, quacking, and it was a reassuring sound. Nancy made Tom tie a rope around his waist and tie the
other end around the chimney in case he fell. But Tom said he
wasn't afraid of anything, that he was going to live forever.

Glenda weighed herself before and after each run. I had to remember that I did not want to grow too close to her, as she would be
leaving. I only wanted to be her friend. We ran and rode in silence.
We never saw any bears. But she was frightened of them, even as the
summer went on without our seeing any, and so I always carried the
pistol. We had been pale from the long sunless winter but were
beginning to grow brown from lying out by the lake up at the
summit. Glenda took long naps after her runs, we both did, Glenda
sleeping on my couch, and I'd cover her with a blanket and lie
down on the floor next to her, and the sun would pour in through
the windows, and there was no world outside our valley. But I could
feel my heart pounding.

It turned drier than ever in August. The loggers were cutting again.
It was always dry and windy and the fields and meadows turned to
crisp hay. Everyone was terrified of sparks, especially the old people, because they'd seen the big fires rush through the valley in the
past, moving through like an army — the big fire in 1901, and then
the monstrous one, in 1921, that burned up every tree except for
the very luckiest ones, so that for years afterward the entire valley
was barren and scorched, smoldering — and the wind in our faces

was hot, and we'd go down to the saloon in the early afternoon, after we had stopped off at my cabin, and we'd drink beer.

Glenda would lie on her back on top of the picnic table and look up at the clouds. She would be going back to Washington in three weeks and then down to California, she said. We were both as brown as nuts. Almost all of the men would be off in the woods, logging. We would have the whole valley to ourselves. Tom and Nancy had been calling us "the lovebirds" in July, trying to get something going, I think, but they stopped in August. She was running harder than ever, really improving, so that I was having trouble staying up with her near the top of the summit on the days that Glenda ran it.

There was no ice left anywhere, no snow, not even in the darkest, coolest parts of the forest, but the lakes and ponds and creeks and rivers were still ice-cold when we leaped into them, hot and heart-hammering; and each time Glenda made me put my hand on her breast, her heart thumping and jumping around as if about to burst out, until I could finally feel it calming and then almost stopping as the lake's cold waters worked on her.

"Don't you ever leave this place, Joe Barry," she'd say to me as she watched the clouds. "You've got it really good here."

I'd be stroking her knee with my fingers, running them along the inside scar, and the wind would be moving her hair around. She would close her eyes after a while, and it was hot, but there would be goose bumps on her brown legs, on her arms.

"No, ma'am, I wouldn't do that," I'd say and take a swig of beer. "Wild horses couldn't take me away from this place."

I'd think about her heart, jumping and flapping around in her small chest like a fish in a footlocker after those long runs; at the top of the summit, I'd wonder how anything could ever be so alive.

The afternoon that she set fire to the field across the road from my cabin was a still day, windless, and I guess that Glenda thought it was safe, that it would be just a grass fire and would do no harm — and she was right, though I did not know that. I saw her standing out in the middle of the field, lighting matches, bending down and cupping her hands until a small blaze appeared at her feet. Then she came running across the field toward my cabin.

I loved to watch her run. I did not know why she had set the fire, and I was very afraid that it might cross the road and burn up my hay barn, even my cabin — but I was not as frightened as I might have been. It was the day before Glenda was going to leave, and mostly I was just delighted to see her.

She came running up the steps, pounded on my door, and then came inside, breathless, having run a dead sprint all the way. The fire was spreading fast, even without a wind, because the grass was so dry, and red-winged blackbirds were leaping up out of the grass ahead of it, and I could see marsh rabbits and mice scurrying across the road, coming into my yard. An elk bounded across the meadow. There was a lot of smoke. It was late in the afternoon, not quite dusk but soon would be, and Glenda was pulling me by the hand, taking me back outside and down the steps, back out toward the fire, toward the pond on the far side of the field. It was a large pond, large enough to protect us, I hoped, and we ran hard across the field, with a new wind suddenly picking up, a wind made from the flames, and we got to the pond and kicked our shoes off, pulled off our shirts and jeans, and splashed out into the water, and waited for the flames to get to us and then to work their way around us.

It was just a grass fire. But the heat was intense as it rushed toward us, blasting our faces with the hot winds.

It was terrifying.

We ducked our heads under the water to cool our drying faces, and splashed water on each other's shoulders. Birds were flying past us, and grasshoppers, and small mice were diving into the pond with us, where hungry trout were rising and snapping at them, swallowing them like corn. It was growing dark and there were flames all around us. We could only wait and see if the grass was going to burn itself up as it swept past.

"Please, love," Glenda was saying, and I did not understand at first that she was speaking to me. "Please."

We had moved out into the deepest part of the pond, chest-deep, and kept having to duck beneath the surface because of the heat. Our lips and faces were blistering. Pieces of ash were floating down on the water like snow. It was not until nightfall that the flames died down, just a few orange ones flickering here and there. But all the rest of the small field was black and smoldering, and still too hot to walk across barefoot.

It was cold. It was colder than I had ever been. We held on to each other all night, holding each other tightly, because we were shivering. I thought about luck, about chance. I thought about fears, all the different ones, and the things that could make a person run. She left at daylight, would not let me drive her home, but trotted instead, heading up the road to Tom's.

That was two years ago. The rabbits have changed, and then changed again: twice.

The hedgehog — I have never seen it again. After all these years, it has left. I wish I knew for sure that was what it had been; I wish I had a name for it.

Will it be back? I do not think so. Why was it here in the first place? I do not know.

Just the tame, predictable ways of rabbits — that is all I have left, now.

Is Glenda still alive? Is she still running? It is mid-February. It hurts to remember her. Things that should have been said, things that should have been done. The field across the road lies scorched and black, hidden beneath a blanket of snow.

JASON BROWN

Driving the Heart

FROM MISSISSIPPI REVIEW

TRAVELING BETWEEN Danvers and Natick yesterday I saw a man in a flower truck drive by at eighty mph with his eyes closed. I turned to Dale, a guy the hospital hired for me to train, and said, Nothing, not even someone's liver, is that important. He put his hand on top of the metal case marked *Liver* and nodded.

Most of the day jobs involve eyes, livers, morphine, or spleens traveling to or from the airport. Tonight we are driving way out to Lebanon Springs, to the town where I was born, with a heart for a woman about to die from some accident or some disease. Hearts travel at night.

Dale sits next to me holding the metal box marked *Heart*. His eyes droop. His head leans to the right. Next thing he'll be sleeping, dreaming down the highway. I know what it's like.

When the weather is foul like tonight and the airplane can't make it, they send us. We're the only choice they have for reaching a small town in an out-of-the-way place. Cellular phone service is out and in many places the power is out, but most of the regular pay phones still work. We stop every hour at designated places and call the hospital to make sure the patient in Lebanon is still alive. The hospital is in contact with Lebanon. We are not allowed to stop for food or drink or, if we can help it, even urination on this six-hour journey. We make the call, and if she's still alive we rush on. If not, then we can pause briefly for food and bathroom before we turn around and drive without stopping for Worcester, where a plane will take the heart to some other person in a city with a major airport. This heart, however, is getting old. There probably won't be time to take it anywhere after Lebanon.

Hearts are packed in ice. But even a frozen heart will last for only twenty-four hours on the outside, unofficially. That's why if we have to take it to Worcester, there will be time only to fly the heart to a major airport, then rush it from there by helicopter to a hospital in the same city. There is always a patient. Driving to Lebanon, we shoot for six or seven hours at the most. Tonight we have to hurry through the high winds and beating rain in order not to waste this heart.

I stop the car and have Dale run out through the rain to the pay phone with the number I gave him.

"What's her name?" he asks.

"You won't be talking to her," I say, "and it doesn't matter. Just give the hospital the job number. They'll say drive on if she's still alive, or turn around."

A few minutes later he comes running back, gets in the car, brushes the rain off his sleeves, and nods his head. After a few more minutes he says, "I'm hungry," even though I've already explained the rules.

Hospital delivery often attracts people like myself, who have cared very deeply about the wrong things. Who, in less than half an average life span, have been born, born again, arrested for armed robbery, and born once more. A person can be born only so many times before even the Christians don't want to take you seriously. The second time I was born I was twenty years old and lying in a donated suite on the floor of a jail in Sturgis, Michigan. I remember one of the officers brought me a bowl of stew and suggested I eat something before going into court, but I shook my head. I was being charged with driving under the influence and assaulting a police officer, although I didn't remember doing those things. The judge informed me that I had drunk ten ounces of 151 in a few hours. He lowered his head after this announcement, not because I was a startling case but because I was the same kind of case he saw day after day and he was tired. I asked what I could do to show him that I had finally gotten the picture, that all I wanted was one more chance. He looked at me and laughed, which was to say: That's what everybody says. He didn't know that I was reborn, that over in Grass Lake, where I wanted to go after I was released, people believed.

We drive all over New England, sometimes to New York, but mostly we stay around the Boston area. If you know the Wenham-

Woburn-Needham-Braintree route, then you know that the place to live is Belmont, Weston, Concord, or beyond, but not so far out as Lowell. All the names up and down the coast — Weekapaug, Quonochontaug, Naquit, Teaticket, Menauhaunt, and Falmouth Heights — remind me of the life I could have had if things had been different. I have a friend living that life over in Sakonnet right now. I go over and visit him once in a while — from his second-floor bathroom window a sliver of ocean can be seen.

Dale reaches over and turns up the radio; he leans on his right elbow against the window. He slumps in his seat. I turn the radio back down. No amount of training will make a kid like this understand his job. Even as the passenger you should sit alert. Someone else's life sits in your hands. His head nods against the passenger window as I flick off the radio. "No more radio," I say. That wakes him up. Dale straightens himself and asks what happened to the woman who needs the heart, but I can tell by the way he fiddles with the buttons on his coat that he doesn't really care. I tell him I don't know, that the woman could be thirty, could be seventy. Could be heart disease, could be anything, that they never tell me. Usually they take the heart from someone who is alive but brain-dead and transport it to someone whose thoughts are clear but whose heart is dead. And in truth, I explain, they usually give preference to the young. The moment the heart leaves the body of the donor, it is cross-clamped and the clock starts ticking. In the Lebanon hospital they are standing there in the operating room right now, smocked and ready, waiting for us. Dale nods and we drive on in silence.

I roll down the window for a moment to let in some air and then roll it back up again. I turn to Dale: "A man in Abilene, Texas, gets drunk and drives his car through a 7-Eleven. Three hours later his heart travels on a plane bound for Logan Airport. Six hours later his heart sits next to you in a large silver case marked *Heart,* and we are driving down the highway at the speed limit toward some prostrate client in a hospital room asleep or possibly in a coma who will not live another day without this heart. This," I say to Dale, "is the importance of your job." He nods, furrowing his brow. No matter how many times I explain, I don't think he will understand.

"What if something goes wrong?" he asks.

"Nothing will go wrong if you don't get any ideas. Now go make the call," I say, pointing at the variety store.

*

I live in a so-so neighborhood. The people there smell and never take out the trash. I look out my window at a funeral home, and for four months each year the sun rarely shines in this part of the country. Some mornings I consider the consequences of quitting my job and doing nothing for the rest of my life. People will still get their organs and their drugs, driven here and there by someone like myself. A replacement. The hospital has them. The only thing that will happen differently in the world if I quit my job is that I will not be able to eat.

I ask Dale if he has ever donated an organ. He shakes his head, looks at me in silence, and then we sit there, ahead of schedule, thinking. I feel like telling him to keep his eyes open.

I've seen some strange things. A woman from Nova Scotia once came into the hospital and offered to sell two kidneys. She said she had four. The doctor on duty was interested in such a claim, but he had to tell her that it was the hospital's policy, the law in fact, not to accept such offers.

I know what it's like to want things. I've always wanted to travel the world but probably never will. I've seen pictures. I've always wanted to date a very beautiful woman. To these things I say: So what.

Only once have I flown in an airplane, crossing the water to London with a case of hospital files to be signed by a man there. I remember that somewhere out over Labrador the pregnant woman across the aisle started to scream. The husband started running up and down the aisle while his wife was pulling on her seat and pushing with her knees against the people in front, her stomach seizing with contractions. The man suddenly whipped around, focused on me, and yelled, "I need a doctor! Is anyone a doctor?" A woman sitting in back came forward saying she used to be a nurse. The man stepped aside, pointing at his wife in her light cotton floral dress, the makeup washing down onto her neck. "She's only seven months — not even," the husband said. When he stepped aside a little more to allow the nurse to move in, I could see liquid from between the pregnant woman's legs pouring off her seat and onto the floor. The woman who used to be a nurse looked directly away, holding her head with her hand. She was looking at me and through me. "How much time before we land?" the man blurted at the stewardess who had just arrived. "Too much time," the ex-nurse looking at me said.

The most exciting thing that can be said about me is that I delivered pizzas in dangerous neighborhoods when I lived in New York. How I can be both obsessed and relaxed at the same time is a mystery to me, but I consider it one of my greatest accomplishments. I'm not very old, but I would say that so far nothing has gone according to plan, that people have been unpredictable, and that's about the extent of it. I would also say that certain ideas seem basically true to me: you cannot serve two masters well. Our thoughts are of little consequence. Live cautiously. You have to in my family. Back when I was twelve, for instance, I was traveling down Capisic Street in Lebanon when a woman traveling thirty, forty miles an hour hit the rear tire of my bike. I rolled over the hood and the roof, bounced off the trunk, and landed standing on my feet. She screeched to a stop and broke out weeping on the steering wheel, afraid to look. I walked up and tapped on her window. Her fingers danced on the dashboard. She looked at me. "Are you all right?" I asked. "I don't believe it," the woman said, resting her head back down on the wheel. "I don't believe it."

The road we're traveling down tonight feels familiar, the rhythm of the bumps and ruts against the tires, but in the dark nothing looks familiar. Dale fumbles with the map, turning it toward the window so he can read with the help of an occasional streetlight. "Where is this place we're going to?" he asks.

"Lebanon Springs." I don't tell him I was born there. One of the first rules with new employees is not to share unnecessary information.

"It's not on the map," Dale says.

"What?" I ask.

"Lebanon."

"Turn it over, it's on the other side." Dale turns over the map and brings it up close to his face. "Find the green line I made. It starts in Boston; follow to where it ends."

"I found it," he says. "It's tiny. There can't be much to this town."

"There's a woman who needs a heart," I say. "That's all you need to know."

Some people say I was thinking too much and some people say I wasn't thinking enough, but I probably just wasn't thinking about the right things. Don't take advice from yourself, don't leave your apartment without a good reason, don't have a telephone, don't own too many things, don't own too few. Live on the first floor. Watch out for people.

Dale lets out a long sigh. He runs his hands through his slicked-back hair, then rubs the back of his neck. Dale is wrong for the job. There's no use even getting to know him, because I'll just be training someone new next week and asking all the same questions, explaining all the same rules.

Dale asks if he can look at the heart, to see how it's kept alive. He thinks it might be helpful for the job, but I think otherwise. Does he think I haven't sat alone in this seat next to a case marked *Heart* and not looked inside? There's nothing to look at. It either works or it doesn't.

I turn to Dale. "You've read the manual?"

He nods, but I'm not sure he even knows what manual I'm talking about.

"You get to one of the designated stops only to find that the phone is out. What do you do? Stop at the next phone along the road or drive on? No time to think. Page fifty-two of the manual, right?"

"Stop at the next phone," he says. "The next phone along the road, I mean."

"I know what you mean and you're wrong. You drive on." I let him fiddle with the glove compartment handle and crack his knuckles. "When in doubt," I tell him, "always drive on. Just remember that one thing, all right? All right?"

"All right," he says.

He looks out the window. I look briefly where he's looking, but the shape of the hills on the horizon depends on the phase of the moon. I don't recognize a thing. On a night like tonight, when the moon is hidden by the storm, we can only recognize the windshield wipers, the sheets of rain, and the vague shape of the white road-sign letters. We could be headed anywhere. The last time I traveled down this road I was hitchhiking home and ended up in a car accident. I told a guy and a girl who picked me up on Route 302 somewhere that I would go as far as they were going. He told me that they were headed for her parents' house in a little town out where 302 turns into 89 called Lebanon Springs. I nodded, and he drove faster than the speed limit. I had been outside in the snow for too long, and my feet were numb. I took off my shoes in the back seat and rubbed each toe, worried that they might not come back. Suddenly there was a thud, breaking glass, and we slid into the guardrail. The head of a large buck had smashed against the windshield, spraying glass shards onto the driver, whose head rested against the steering wheel. I crawled out the back door. The tiny glass fragments melted into the bottoms of my bare feet. The guy's girlfriend had to crawl out her window and over the hood. She walked toward me, swaying her hips like a model, rubbing her head. The deer stood in front of the car watching us. Then he closed his eyes. I didn't make it back to Lebanon that time.

In the dawn haze I start to recognize sections of forest from the last time I was here, eight years ago. We will probably drive over the spot where I was born, and I must remember not to say anything to Dale. He does not need to know. But now that I think about it, we'll enter from the east side of town, so we won't have to use the Thurman bridge, where I was born crossing over from Stockton in a Chevy, my father behind the wheel and my mother sprawled out in back. The story goes that my mother said she wasn't going to make it and my father said she had to wait. She said she couldn't and there was screaming. She wanted something to kill the pain. He told her just to think about something else and hold it in and then before she knew it they would be there. But all she knew was that she couldn't wait another second, and I was born at 11:42 P.M., before we even crossed the river.

Staring through the rain-splattered windshield into the dark gray forest, I am reminded of the same forest twenty miles from here, where I lived with my parents at the end of a long dirt road. We lived there for five or six years, but one morning it was so cold that the storm pane cracked down the middle and fell into the back yard. I woke up and wandered into my parents' bathroom, waiting for them to wake, stepped up on a stool, opened the medicine cabinet, and pulled down a box of razor blades hidden from me behind the shaving cream. Taking out two, I placed one in the palm of my right hand, then squeezed my fingers shut. With my left hand I ran the other blade lightly, painlessly, up and down my arm from the shoulder to the palm. The little slits remained dry for a second, as if caught off-guard, before red lines appeared and eventually washed together like flooding rivers. I walked into their bedroom, groping my hand along the wall for the light switch. Her head bolted up. Then I found the light switch.

Several years later — I can't remember how many; we must have lived there for more than seven years — I was ten years old standing at the same window, my father having been gone from the house for quite some time, and I heard my mother's faltering footsteps climbing the stairs. I locked my bedroom door, pushed one of the chairs up against the knob, and then returned to the window. I heard the floorboards creak as she crept up to the door and carefully, trying not to wake me, turned the doorknob and pushed forward. When the door would not open, she pushed more frantically and cursed under her breath. The rain splashed against the window.

It has stopped raining now and the sky has started to lighten. Dale runs off into Ken's Variety, twenty miles east of our destination, to make our last call. Twenty minutes to go. I decide that when Dale returns I'll ask him some questions about his life, about the letter "D" sewn onto his high school jacket, about what he wants to do with his life after this. I should try to be nice.

Maybe he wants to live over in Wayland or Lexington and summer down at Marion or Pocasset, slightly off the beaten path, where it's warm and the grass comes right down to the ocean and the beaches keep going. It sounds like a good life to me.

I hear a car engine gearing down behind me and then the grumble of the braking wheels against the gravel of the shoulder. Two guys pull up beside my window in a pickup. The truck weaves a little as it comes to a stop. The driver rolls down his window, spits out some of his chew, and moves his hand in a circle, signaling me to roll down my window. When I do, he raises his upper lip and asks me what time it is. I look down at the blank face of my digital watch, tap it a couple of times, and tell him my watch is dead. There is a clock on the case, but I would have to get out of the car and walk over to the passenger's side to check it. I'm not about to waste time doing that. The guy says he thinks I'm lying about not knowing the time, so I show him the watch. "The watch is dead," I say. Then he asks how much money I have and I tell him. "Nothing." He says he knows I'm lying and I say, "Is that so?"

"We're hungry," he says. "We're driving all the way down from Elmira with no food. We want to buy some food at the store."

His partner raises a shotgun and hands it to the driver, who points it at me. "How much for your life?" he says. He turns back to his buddy, then back to me. "My friend here says ten dollars. Fair price, huh? Ten dollars and your life is yours."

I put my hand over the wallet in my pocket and thumb through the bills inside, thinking about the heart. "I don't have a dime," I say.

"Not a dime," he says.

"Not a cent."

The driver squints and releases the safety on the shotgun. "I know this isn't true," he says, closing one eye and lowering his head down next to the stock. "My friend says shoot you before someone comes along, but I'd rather have the ten dollars, so I'm waiting another couple seconds to see what happens."

I look down the double barrel, stop breathing, and wait to see what happens. For a long time I listen to the unsteady rumble of their truck's engine like it's my own breath.

Suddenly he opens his eyes wide. "Bang," he says, pulling the gun back in but leaving his eyes pointed at me. His lips move up around his teeth. "Guess you're hungrier than we are," he says, and they drive away. I fall against the steering wheel, my chest heaving, my right hand on the silver case.

Dale comes out of Ken's, trips on the steps, picks himself up, and keeps running. He climbs in the car, sucking in a mouthful of air, and says, "I couldn't get through." I throw it into drive and pull forward, knowing perfectly well what the situation is and what we have to do. "I don't know," Dale says. "The phone lines around here are fine, but Ken said the storm is worse back in Boston. Maybe the lines are down there."

"No matter," I say.

"Hey," Dale says, sitting up in his seat as if remembering an important message. "When I was on the phone, Ken looked out the window and mumbled something about your being in trouble. Anything happen?"

"It was nothing," I say. "Now in this situation, what do we do?"

"What situation?" Dale says, rubbing his forehead.

"You made the phone call and were not able to get through."

"Oh. We drive on, right?"

"You tell me."

"We drive on," Dale says, and we sit there in silence. After a few minutes a police car approaches from behind and flashes its blue lights. I pull over to the side of the road and roll down my window. The officer parks his car, pulls some papers off the dashboard, opens his door, closes it carefully, and starts walking toward us. He stops halfway, removes his cap, smooths back his gray hair, and puts the cap back on before continuing forward. Dale looks at the floor.

"How are you this morning?" the old officer says.

"Fine, sir," I answer.

"Glad to hear it," he says. "The reason . . . I've seen you before, haven't I? I know you."

"It couldn't be," I say. "I'm afraid you must be making a mistake."

"Well," he says. "I stopped you because old Ken gave the dispatch a ring saying you were having some trouble out in front of his store."

"It was nothing," I say.

"Ken said that some guys in a pickup . . ."

"Officer," I say, "I hate to interrupt, but we are on an urgent job, delivering a heart to the hospital just across town. We're coming all the way from Boston through the storm and every second counts. We have to drive on. After we deliver the package I will be happy to answer any of your questions."

"A heart, you say?" The officer rubs his head. "I've never heard of such a thing. Is that what your partner has there in that case?"

"Yes, it is."

"And you're taking it over to Community?"

"Yes, we are."

"Then I won't hold you up."

"Thank you, officer."

"Well. I won't hold you up," he says again, staring down at me. "But please stop down at the station when you're done. We'd like a description."

"Certainly."

"Thank you," he says and backs away from the car.

I drive on, spinning the wheels a bit in the gravel and holding the pedal all the way down as the speedometer slowly climbs back up to fifty-five. After ten minutes of silence, passing swiftly over Washington Avenue, down Winthrop Street, and across Thorton Avenue, we stop outside the electric doors and the lighted sign,

EMERGENCY. "Here," I say, grabbing the case. "Follow me." Holding the case in front of me, I walk swiftly, without running, for the doors of the emergency room. Dale takes several leaps to keep up with me. I walk right up to the glass booth where a woman behind a desk is filling out forms. Someone else, an enormous woman, sits in one of the waiting chairs with no obvious injuries. The man next to her holds a rag clamped over his bloody hand. They both stare at the opposite wall.

I tap nervously on the glass. "Can I help you?" the woman says without looking up.

"I'm here with the heart from Boston General. Here are the forms," I say, shoving them in front of her face. She takes the forms but does not look at them.

"A heart?" she says, looking at me and my metal case.

"Yes," I say.

She takes a deep breath and shifts her behind on the swivel chair. "What do you mean, you're here with a heart?"

"Look," I say. "It's an emergency. We've been delayed. There is a woman here who needs this heart. This heart will not last much longer." The woman stares at me, looks at the forms. "Didn't anyone tell you?" I ask.

"I just came on," she says. "I haven't heard anything about this."

I set the case down and grab the edge of the partition separating this woman from myself. I stare down, fixed on her lower lip. "Look," I say. "The heart is here."

"I'll have to go back and check with one of the doctors," she says, smiling faintly and disappearing down a corridor. I lean against the glass and close my eyes. I can hear the large woman in the chair shift from one hip to the other. The man with the injured hand coughs briefly and then starts tapping his foot. He taps it out of boredom, not pain. Once every couple of seconds he lets the toe hit the floor. Then he stops and I feel his eyes on me and the silver case. The fluorescent lights lining the ceiling buzz like insects, becoming louder with every moment, until in the distance I hear the clicking heels of the receptionist and the squeaks of a doctor's rubber heels coming down the corridor. I turn around suddenly, wondering what has happened to Dale. And just as the doctor comes up behind me, I see Dale appear from around a corner and pause next to a black sign with an arrow that says CAFETERIA. The doctor puts his hand on my shoulder and rests it there, waiting for me to turn toward him.

"I'm sorry," he says when I don't turn. "Boston General should have told you on the last call."

He removes his hand and waits patiently for me to respond. The receptionist returns to her desk and picks up the next form off the enormous stack. Dale has stopped to unwrap the rest of a sandwich he just bought down the hall. He leans over, allowing the lettuce strands to fall on the floor instead of his jacket, and then continues toward me. A sliced tomato hangs over his bottom lip. He swallows and keeps walking. After a few steps he stops to take another bite, this time scooping up the strands of lettuce with his free hand and pushing them in the corner of his mouth. The doctor picks up the case and, placing it against the wall, says a few words to the receptionist, who opens a drawer and shuffles through a bunch of papers. It is too late for Worcester, I think. When Dale sees that I am staring, he stops walking and tries to swallow what's left in his mouth.

The doctor steps up beside me again, carrying a clipboard. "We need to have you sign these," he says. I take the clipboard and the pen without looking at him.

"I was hungry," Dale says, shrugging his shoulders. "I figured we were here. I couldn't wait any longer."

"That's no excuse," I say and lower my head to the forms resting in my hands. I sign my name. *Time of arrival*, it says. I turn my wrist and look down at my blank watch. I look at the doctor. "Time?" I say.

He raises his naked wrist. "Forgot to wear it today." He smiles, dark circles under his eyes.

Dale shoves the rest of the sandwich into his pocket. "It's seven o'clock," he says, pursing his lips in an effort to take our job more seriously. He walks over to the silver case and picks it up. "What do we do now? I thought we were here."

I walk over to him, take the case out of his hand, and lay it down next to the wall. "It's too late," I say, but he furrows his brow and stares at the case. It is a good sign when a trainee doesn't understand how a job can fail. I remind him as we head for the door that a heart, once removed from the body, will last only twenty-four hours. There is nowhere left for us to drive. At the door he turns away from me, looking for the silver case, which a nurse is carrying down a long yellow hallway. I give just a light tug on his arm, but he won't turn around until the nurse has disappeared down another corridor. I understand this is the hardest part of the job; there is no way for me to explain how we could have driven all this way with a heart for which, in the end, there is no life.

ROBERT OLEN BUTLER

Jealous Husband Returns in Form of Parrot

FROM THE NEW YORKER

I NEVER CAN QUITE SAY as much as I know. I look at other parrots and I wonder if it's the same for them, if somebody is trapped in each of them, paying some kind of price for living their life in a certain way. For instance, "Hello," I say, and I'm sitting on a perch in a pet store in Houston and what I'm really thinking is, Holy shit. It's you. And what's happened is I'm looking at my wife.

"Hello," she says, and she comes over to me, and I can't believe how beautiful she is. Those great brown eyes, almost as dark as the center of mine. And her nose — I don't remember her for her nose, but its beauty is clear to me now. Her nose is a little too long, but it's redeemed by the faint hook to it.

She scratches the back of my neck.

Her touch makes my tail flare. I feel the stretch and rustle of me back there. I bend my head to her and she whispers, "Pretty bird."

For a moment, I think she knows it's me. But she doesn't, of course. I say "Hello" again, and I will eventually pick up "pretty bird." I can tell that as soon as she says it, but for now I can only give her another "Hello." Her fingertips move through my feathers, and she seems to know about birds. She knows that to pet a bird you don't smooth his feathers down, you ruffle them.

But of course she did that in my human life as well. It's all the same for her. Not that I was complaining, even to myself, at that moment in the pet shop when she found me like I presume she was supposed to. She said it again — "Pretty bird" — and this brain that works the way it does now could feel that tiny little voice of mine ready to shape itself around these sounds. But before I could get them out of my beak, there was this guy at my wife's shoulder, and all my feathers went slick-flat to make me small enough not to be seen, and I backed away. The pupils of my eyes pinned and dilated and pinned again.

He circled around her. A guy that looked like a meat-packer, big in the chest and thick with hair, the kind of guy that I always sensed her eyes moving to when I was alive. I had a bare chest, and I'd look for little black hairs on the sheets when I'd come home on a day with the whiff of somebody else in the air. She was still in the same goddamn rut.

A "hello" wouldn't do, and I'd recently learned "good night," but it was the wrong suggestion altogether, so I said nothing and the guy circled her, and he was looking at me with a smug little smile, and I fluffed up all my feathers, made myself about twice as big, so big he'd see he couldn't mess with me. I waited for him to draw close enough for me to take off the tip of his finger.

But she intervened. Those nut-brown eyes were before me, and she said, "I want him."

And that's how I ended up in my own house once again. She bought me a large black wrought-iron cage, very large, convinced by some young guy who clerked in the bird department and who took her aside and made his voice go much too soft when he was doing the selling job. The meat-packer didn't like it. I didn't either. I'd missed a lot of chances to take a bite out of this clerk in my stay at the shop, and I regretted that suddenly.

But I got my giant cage, and I guess I'm happy enough about that. I can pace as much as I want. I can hang upside down. It's full of bird toys. That dangling thing over there with knots and strips of rawhide and a bell at the bottom needs a good thrashing a couple of times a day, and I'm the bird to do it. I look at the very dangle of it, and the thing is rough, the rawhide and the knotted rope, and I get this restlessness back in my tail, a burning, thrashing feeling, and it's like all the times when I was sure there was a man naked with my wife. Then I go to this thing that feels so familiar and I bite and bite, and it's very good.

I could have used the thing the last day I went out of this house as a man. I'd found the address of the new guy at my wife's office. He'd been there a month, in the shipping department, and three times she'd mentioned him. She didn't even have to work with him, and three times I heard about him, just dropped into the conversation. "Oh," she'd say when a car commercial came on the television, "that car there is like the one the new man in shipping owns. Just like it." Hey, I'm not stupid. She said another thing about him and then another, and right after the third one I locked myself in the bathroom, because I couldn't rage about this anymore. I felt like a damn fool whenever I actually said anything about this kind of feeling and she looked at me as though she could start hating me real easy, and so I was working on saying nothing, even if it meant locking myself up. My goal was to hold my tongue about half the time. That would be a good start.

But this guy from shipping. I found out his name and his address, and it was one of her typical Saturday afternoons of vague shopping. So I went to his house, and his car that was just like the commercial was outside. Nobody was around in the neighborhood, and there was this big tree in back of the house going up to a second-floor window that was making funny little sounds. I went up. The shade was drawn but not quite all the way. I was holding on to a limb with my arms and legs wrapped around it like it was her in those times when I could forget the others for a little while. But the crack in the shade was just out of view, and I crawled on till there was no limb left, and I fell on my head. When I think about that now, my wings flap and I feel myself lift up, and it all seems so avoidable. Though I know I'm different now. I'm a bird.

Except I'm not. That's what's confusing. It's like those times when she would tell me she loved me and I actually believed her and maybe it was true and we clung to each other in bed and at times like that I was different. I was the man in her life. I was whole with her. Except even at that moment, as I held her sweetly, there was this other creature inside me who knew a lot more about it and couldn't quite put all the evidence together to speak.

My cage sits in the den. My pool table is gone, and the cage is sitting in that space, and if I come all the way down to one end of my perch I can see through the door and down the back hallway to the master bedroom. When she keeps the bedroom door open, I can see the space at the foot of the bed but not the bed itself. I can sense it to the left, just out of sight. I watch the men go in and I hear the sounds, but I can't quite see. And they drive me crazy.

I flap my wings and I squawk and I fluff up and I slick down and I throw seed and I attack that dangly toy as if it were the guy's balls, but it does no good. It never did any good in the other life either, the thrashing around I did by myself. In that other life I'd have given anything to be standing in this den with her doing this thing with some other guy just down the hall, and all I had to do was walk down there and turn the corner and she couldn't deny it anymore.

But now all I can do is try to let it go. I sidestep down to the opposite end of the cage and I look out the big sliding glass doors to the back yard. It's a pretty yard. There are great, placid live oaks with good places to roost. There's a blue sky that plucks at the feathers on my chest. There are clouds. Other birds. Fly away. I could just fly away.

I tried once, and I learned a lesson. She forgot and left the door to my cage open, and I climbed beak and foot, beak and foot, along the bars and curled around to stretch sideways out the door, and the vast scene of peace was there, at the other end of the room. I flew.

And a pain flared through my head, and I fell straight down, and the room whirled around, and the only good thing was that she held me. She put her hands under my wings and lifted me and clutched me to her breast, and I wish there hadn't been bees in my head at the time so I could have enjoyed that, but she put me back in the cage and wept a while. That touched me, her tears. And I looked back to the wall of sky and trees. There was something invisible there between me and that dream of peace. I remembered, eventually, about glass, and I knew I'd been lucky; I knew that for the little, fragile-boned skull I was doing all this thinking in, it meant death.

She wept that day, but by the night she had another man. A guy with a thick Georgia-truck-stop accent and pale white skin and an Adam's apple big as my seed ball. This guy has been around for a few weeks, and he makes a whooping sound down the hallway, just out of my sight. At times like that, I want to fly against the bars of the cage, but I don't. I have to remember how the world has changed.

She's single now, of course. Her husband, the man that I was, is dead to her. She does not understand all that is behind my "Hello." I know many words, for a parrot. I am a yellow-nape Amazon, a

handsome bird, I think, green with a splash of yellow at the back of
my neck. I talk pretty well, but none of my words are adequate. I
can't make her understand.

And what would I say if I could? I was jealous in life. I admit it. I
would admit it to her. But it was because of my connection to her. I
would explain that. When we held each other, I had no past at all,
no present but her body, no future but to lie there and not let her
go. I was an egg hatched beneath her crouching body, I entered as
a chick into her wet sky of a body, and all that I wished was to sit on
her shoulder and fluff my feathers and lay my head against her
cheek, with my neck exposed to her hand. And so the glances that I
could see in her troubled me deeply: the movement of her eyes in
public to other men, the laughs sent across a room, the tracking of
her mind behind her blank eyes, pursuing images of others, her
distraction even in our bed, the ghosts that were there of men
who'd touched her, perhaps even that very day. I was not part of all
those other men who were part of her. I didn't want to connect to
all that. It was only her that I would fluff for, but these others were
there also, and I couldn't put them aside. I sensed them inside her,
and so they were inside me. If I had the words, these are the things
I would say.

But half an hour ago, there was a moment that thrilled me. A
word, a word we all knew in the pet shop, was just the right word
after all. This guy with his cowboy belt buckle and rattlesnake boots
and his pasty face and his twanging words of love trailed after
my wife through the den, past my cage, and I said, "Cracker." He
even flipped his head back a little at this in surprise. He'd been
called that before to his face, I realized. I said it again, "Cracker."
But to him I was a bird, and he let it pass. "Cracker," I said. "Hello,
cracker." That was even better. They were out of sight through the
hall doorway, and I hustled along the perch and I caught a glimpse
of them before they made the turn to the bed and I said, "Hello,
cracker," and he shot me one last glance.

It made me hopeful. I eased away from that end of the cage,
moved toward the scene of peace beyond the far wall. The sky is
chalky blue today, blue like the brow of the blue-front Amazon who
was on the perch next to me for about a week at the store. She was
very sweet, but I watched her carefully for a day or two when she
first came in. And it wasn't long before she nuzzled up to a cocka-

too named Willy, and I knew she'd break my heart. But her color now, in the sky, is sweet, really. I left all those feelings behind me when my wife showed up. I am a faithful man, for all my suspicions. Too faithful, maybe. I am ready to give too much, and maybe that's the problem.

The whooping began down the hall, and I focused on a tree out there. A crow flapped down, his mouth open, his throat throbbing, though I could not hear his sound. I was feeling very odd. At least I'd made my point to the guy in the other room. "Pretty bird," I said, referring to myself. She called me "pretty bird," and I believed her and I told myself again, "Pretty bird."

But then something new happened, something very difficult for me. She appeared in the den naked. I have not seen her naked since I fell from the tree and had no wings to fly. She always had a certain tidiness in things. She was naked in the bedroom, clothed in the den. But now she appears from the hallway, and I look at her, and she is still slim and she is beautiful, I think — at least I clearly remember that as her husband I found her beautiful in this state. Now, though, she seems too naked. Plucked. I find that a sad thing. I am sorry for her, and she goes by me and she disappears into the kitchen. I want to pluck some of my own feathers, the feathers from my chest, and give them to her. I love her more in that moment, seeing her terrible nakedness, than I ever have before.

And since I've had success in the last few minutes with words, when she comes back I am moved to speak. "Hello," I say, meaning, You are still connected to me, I still want only you. "Hello," I say again. Please listen to this tiny heart that beats fast at all times for you.

And she does indeed stop, and she comes to me and bends to me. "Pretty bird," I say, and I am saying, You are beautiful, my wife, and your beauty cries out for protection. "Pretty." I want to cover you with my own nakedness. "Bad bird," I say. If there are others in your life, even in your mind, then there is nothing I can do. "Bad." Your nakedness is touched from inside by the others. "Open," I say. How can we be whole together if you are not empty in the place that I am to fill?

She smiles at this, and she opens the door to my cage. "Up," I say, meaning, Is there no place for me in this world where I can be free of this terrible sense of others?

She reaches in now and offers her hand, and I climb onto it and I tremble and she says, "Poor baby."

"Poor baby," I say. You have yearned for wholeness too, and somehow I failed you. I was not enough. "Bad bird," I say. I'm sorry. And then the cracker comes around the corner. He wears only his rattlesnake boots. I take one look at his miserable, featherless body and shake my head. We keep our sexual parts hidden, we parrots, and this man is a pitiful sight. "Peanut," I say. I presume that my wife simply has not noticed. But that's foolish, of course. This is, in fact, what she wants. Not me. And she scrapes me off her hand onto the open cage door and she turns her naked back to me and embraces this man, and they laugh and stagger in their embrace around the corner.

For a moment, I still think I've been eloquent. What I've said only needs repeating for it to have its transforming effect. "Hello," I say. "Hello. Pretty bird. Pretty. Bad bird. Bad. Open. Up. Poor baby. Bad bird." And I am beginning to hear myself as I really sound to her. "Peanut." I can never say what is in my heart to her. Never.

I stand on my cage door now, and my wings stir. I look at the corner to the hallway, and down at the end the whooping has begun again. I can fly there and think of things to do about all this.

But I do not. I turn instead, and I look at the trees moving just beyond the other end of the room. I look at the sky the color of the brow of a blue-front Amazon. A shadow of birds spanks across the lawn. And I spread my wings. I will fly now. Even though I know there is something between me and that place where I can be free of all these feelings, I will fly. I will throw myself there again and again. Pretty bird. Bad bird. Good night.

The Eve of the Spirit Festival

FROM PRAIRIE SCHOONER

AFTER THE BUDDHIST CEREMONY, when our mother's spirit had been chanted to a safe passage and her body cremated, Emily and I sat silently on our living room carpet. She held me in her arms; her long hair stuck to our wet faces. We sat as stiffly as temple gods except for the angry thump of my sister's heart against my cheek.

Finally she spoke. "It's Baba's fault," she said. "The American doctors would have fixed her."

I was six years old — I only knew that our father and mother had decided against an operation. And I had privately agreed, imagining the doctors tearing a hole in her body. As I thought of this, and other things, I felt a violent sob pass through me.

"Don't cry, Baby," Emily whispered. "You're okay." I felt my tears dry to salt, my throat lock shut.

Then our father walked into the room.

He and Emily had become quite close in the past few months. Emily was eleven, old enough to visit my mother when it had become clear that the hospital was the only option. But now she refused to acknowledge him.

"First daughter — " he began.

"Go away, Baba," Emily said. Her voice shook. She put her hand on the back of my head and turned me away from him also. The evening sun glowed garnet red through the dark tent of her hair.

"You said she would get better," I heard her say. "Now you're burning paper money for her ghost. What good will that do?"

"I am sorry," our father said.

"I don't care."

Her voice burned. I squirmed beneath her hand, but she wouldn't let me look. It was between her and Baba. I watched his black wingtip shoes retreat to the door. When he had gone, Emily let go of me. I sat up and looked at her; something had changed. Not in the lovely outlines of her face — our mother's face — but in her eyes, shadow-black, lost in unforgiveness.

They say the dead return to us. But we never saw our mother again, though we kept a kind of emptiness waiting in case she might come back. I listened always, seeking her voice, the lost thread of a conversation I'd been too young to have with her. Emily rarely mentioned our mother, and soon my memories faded. I could not picture her. I saw only Emily's angry face, the late sun streaking red through her dark hair.

After the traditional forty-nine-day mourning period, Baba didn't set foot in the Buddhist temple. It was as if he had listened to Emily: what good did it do? Instead he focused on earthly ambitions, his research at the lab.

At that time he aspired beyond the position of lab instructor to the rank of associate professor, and he often invited his American colleagues over for "drinks." After our mother died, Emily and I were recruited to help. As we went about our tasks, we would sometimes catch a glimpse of our father standing in the corner, watching the American men and studying to become one.

But he couldn't get it right — our parties had an air of cultural confusion. We served potato chips on lacquered trays; Chinese landscapes bumped against watercolors of the Statue of Liberty, the Empire State Building.

Nor were Emily or I capable of helping him. I was still a child, and Emily didn't care. She had grown beyond us; she stalked around in blue jeans, seething with fury at everything to do with him.

"I hate this," she said, fiercely ripping another rag from a pair of old pajama bottoms. "Entertaining these jerks is a waste of time." Some chemists from Texas were visiting his department and he had invited them over for cocktails.

"I can finish it," I said. "You just need to do the parts I can't reach."

"It's not the dusting," she said. "It's the way he acts around them. 'Herro, herro! Hi Blad, hi Warry! Let me take your coat! Howsa Giants game?'" she mimicked. "If he were smart he wouldn't invite people over on football afternoons in the first place."

"What do you mean?" I said, worried that something was wrong. Brad Delmonte was my father's boss. I had noticed Baba reading the sports page that morning — something he rarely did.

"Oh, forget it," Emily said. I felt as if she and I were utterly separate. Then she smiled. "You've got oil on your glasses, Claudia."

Baba walked in carrying two bottles of wine. "They should arrive in half an hour," he said, looking at his watch. "They won't be early. Americans are never early."

Emily looked up. "I'm going to Jodie's house," she said.

Baba frowned and straightened his tie. "I want you to stay while they're here. We might need something from the kitchen."

"Claudia can get it for them."

"She's barely tall enough to reach the cabinets."

Emily stood up, clenched her dustcloth. "I don't care," she said. "I hate meeting those men."

"They're successful American scientists. You'd be better off with them instead of running around with your teenage friends, these sloppy kids, these rich white kids who dress like beggars."

"You're nuts, Dad," Emily said — she had begun addressing him the way an American child does. "You're nuts if you think these bosses of yours are ever going to do anything for you or any of us." And she threw her dustcloth, hard, into our New York Giants wastebasket.

"Speak to me with respect."

"You don't deserve it!"

"You are staying in this apartment! That is an order!"

"I wish you'd died instead of Mama!" Emily cried, and ran out of the room. She darted past our father, her long braid flying behind her. He stared at her, his expression oddly slack, the way it had been in the weeks after the funeral. He stepped toward her, reached hesitantly at her flying braid, but she turned and saw him, cried out as if he had struck her. His hands dropped to his sides.

Emily refused to leave our room. Otherwise that party was like so many others. The guests arrived late and left early. They talked about buying new cars and the Dallas Cowboys. I served pretzels and salted nuts. Baba walked around emptying ashtrays and refilling drinks. I noticed that the other men also wore vests and ties, but that the uniform looked somehow different on my slighter, darker father.

"Cute little daughter you have there," said Baba's boss. He was a large bearded smoker with a sandy voice. He didn't bend down to look at me or the ashtray that I raised toward his big square hand.

I went into our room and found Emily sitting on one of our unmade twin beds. It was dusk. Through the window the dull winter sun had almost disappeared. She didn't look up when I came in, but after a moment she spoke.

"I'm going to leave," she said. "As soon as I turn eighteen, I'm going to leave home and never come back!" She burst into tears. I reached for her shoulder but her thin, heaving body frightened me. She seemed too grown up to be comforted. I thought about the breasts swelling beneath her sweater. Her body had become a foreign place.

Perhaps Emily had warned me that she would someday leave in order to start me off on my own. I found myself avoiding her, as though her impending desertion would matter less if I deserted her first. I discovered a place to hide while she and my father fought, in the living room behind a painted screen. I would read a novel or look out the window. Sometimes they forgot about me — from the next room I would hear one of them break off an argument and say, "Where did Claudia go?" "I don't know," the other would reply. After a silence, they would start again.

One of these fights stands out in my memory. I must have been ten or eleven years old. It was the fourteenth day of the seventh lunar month: the eve of Guijie, the Chinese Spirit Festival, when the living are required to appease and provide for the ghosts of their ancestors. To the believing, the earth was thick with gathering spirits; it was safest to stay indoors and burn incense.

I seldom thought about the Chinese calendar, but every year on Guijie I wondered about my mother's ghost. Where was it? Would it still recognize me? How would I know when I saw it? I wanted to ask Baba, but I didn't dare. Baba had an odd attitude toward Guijie. On one hand, he had eschewed all Chinese customs since my mother's death. He was a scientist, he said; he scorned the traditional tales of unsatisfied spirits roaming the earth.

But I cannot remember a time when I was not made aware, in

some way, of Guijie's fluctuating lunar date. That year the eve of the
Spirit Festival fell on a Thursday, usually his night out with the men
from his department. Emily and I waited for him to leave, but he sat
on the couch, calmly reading the *New York Times*.

Around seven o'clock, Emily began to fidget. She had a date that
night and had counted on my father's absence. She spent half
an hour washing and combing her hair, trying to make up her
mind. Finally she asked me to give her a trim. I knew she'd decided
to go out.

"Just a little," she said. "The ends are scraggly." We spread some
newspapers on the living room floor. Emily stood in the middle of
the papers with her hair combed down her back, thick and glossy,
black as ink. It hadn't really been cut since she was born. Since my
mother's death I had taken over the task of giving it the periodic
touchup.

I hovered behind her with the shears, searching for the scraggly
ends, but there were none.

My father looked up from his newspaper. "What are you doing
that for? You can't go out tonight," he said.

"I have a date!"

My father put down his newspaper. I threw the shears onto a
chair and fled to my refuge behind the screen.

Through a slit over the hinge I caught a glimpse of Emily near
the foyer, slender in her denim jacket, her black hair flooding down
her back, her delicate features contorted with anger. My father's
hair was disheveled, his hands clenched at his sides. The newspapers had scattered over the floor.

"Dressing up in boys' clothes, with paint on your face — "

"This is nothing! My going out on a few dates is nothing! You
don't know what the hell you're talking about!"

"Don't shout." My father shook his finger. "Everyone in the building will hear you."

Emily raised her voice. "Who the hell cares? You're such a cow-
ard; you care more about what other people think than how I feel!"

"Acting like a loose woman in front of everybody, a streetwalker!"

The floor shook under my sister's stamp. Though I'd covered my
ears, I could hear her crying. The door slammed, and her footfalls
vanished down the stairs.

Things were quiet for a minute. Then I heard my father walk

toward my corner. My heart thumped with fear — usually he let me alone. I had to look up when I heard him move the screen away. He knelt down next to me. His hair was streaked with gray, and his glasses needed cleaning.

"What are you doing?" he asked.

I shook my head, nothing.

After a minute I asked him, "Is Guijie why you didn't go play bridge tonight, Baba?"

"No, Claudia," he said. He always called me by my American name. This formality, I thought, was an indication of how distant he felt from me. "I stopped playing bridge last week."

"Why?" We both looked toward the window, where beyond our reflections the Hudson River flowed in the darkness.

"It's not important," he said.

"Okay."

But he didn't leave. "I'm getting old," he said after a moment. "Someone ten years younger was just promoted over me. I'm not going to try to keep up with them anymore."

It was the closest he had ever come to confiding in me. After a few more minutes he stood up and went into the kitchen. The newspapers rustled under his feet. For almost half an hour I heard him fumbling through the kitchen cabinets, looking for something he'd probably put there years ago. Eventually he came out, carrying a small brass urn and some matches. When Emily returned home after midnight, the apartment still smelled of the incense he had burned to protect her while she was gone.

My father loved Emily more. I knew this in my bones: it was why I stayed at home every night and wore no makeup, why I studied hard and got good grades, why I eventually went to college at Columbia, right up the street. Jealously I guarded my small allotment of praise, clutching it like a pocket of precious stones. Emily snuck out of the apartment late at night; she wore high-heeled sandals with patched blue jeans; she twisted her long hair into graceful, complex loops and braids that belied respectability. She smelled of lipstick and perfume. So certain she was of my father's love. His anger was a part of it. I knew nothing I could ever do would anger him that way.

When Emily turned eighteen and did leave home, a part of my

father disappeared. I wondered sometimes, where did it go? Did she take it with her? What secret charm had she carried with her as she vanished down the tunnel to the jet that would take her to college in California, steadily and without looking back, while my father and I watched silently from the window at the gate? The apartment afterward became quite still — it was only the two of us, mourning and dreaming through pale blue winter afternoons and silent evenings.

Emily called me, usually late at night after my father had gone to sleep. She sent me pictures of herself and people I didn't know, smiling on the sunny Berkeley campus. Sometimes after my father and I ate our simple meals or TV dinners I would go into our old room, where I had kept both of our twin beds, and take out Emily's pictures, trying to imagine what she must have been feeling, studying her expression and her swinging hair. But I always stared the longest at a postcard she'd sent me one winter break from northern New Mexico, a professional photo of a powerful, vast blue sky over faraway pink and sandy-beige mesas. The clarity and cleanness fascinated me. In a place like that, I thought, there would be nothing to search for, no reason to hide.

After college, she went to work at a bank in San Francisco. I saw her once when she flew to Manhattan on business. She skipped a meeting to have lunch with me. She wore an elegant gray suit and had pinned up her hair.

"How's Dad?" she said. I looked around, slightly alarmed. We were sitting in a bistro on the East Side, but I somehow thought he might overhear us.

"He's okay," I said. "We don't talk very much. Why don't you come home and see him?"

Emily stared at her water glass. "I don't think so."

"He misses you."

"I know. I don't want to hear about it."

"You hardly ever call him."

"There's nothing to talk about. Don't tell him you saw me, promise?"

"Okay."

During my junior year at Columbia, my father suffered a stroke. He was fifty-nine years old, and he was still working as a lab instructor in the chemistry department. One evening in early fall I came home from a class and found him on the floor near the kitchen telephone. He was wearing his usual vest and tie. I called the hospital and sat down next to him. His wire-rimmed glasses lay on the floor a foot away. One half of his face was frozen, the other half lined with sudden age and pain. "They said they'll be right here," I said. "It won't be very long." I couldn't tell how much he understood. I smoothed his vest and straightened his tie. I folded his glasses. I knew he wouldn't like it if the ambulance workers saw him in a state of dishevelment. "I'm sure they'll be here soon," I said.

We waited. Then I noticed he was trying to tell me something. A line of spittle ran from the left side of his mouth. I leaned closer. After a while I made out his words: "Tell Emily," he said.

The ambulance arrived as I picked up the telephone to call California. That evening, at the hospital, what was remaining of my father left the earth.

Emily insisted that we not hold a Buddhist cremation ceremony. "I never want to think about that stuff again," she said. "Plus, all of his friends are Americans. I don't know who would come, except for us." She had reached New York the morning after his death. Her eyes were vague and her fingernails bitten down.

On the third day we scattered his ashes in the river. Afterward we held a small memorial service for his friends from work. We didn't talk much as we straightened the living room and dusted the furniture. It took almost three hours. The place was a mess. We hadn't had a party in years.

It was a cloudy afternoon, and the Hudson looked dull and sluggish from the living room window. I noticed that although she had not wanted a Buddhist ceremony, Emily had dressed in black and white according to Chinese mourning custom. I had asked the department secretary to put up a sign on the bulletin board. Eleven people came; they drank five bottles of wine. Two of his Chinese students stood in the corner, eating cheese and crackers.

Brad Delmonte, paunchy and no longer smoking, attached himself to Emily. "I remember when you were just a little girl," I heard him say as I walked by with the extra crackers.

"I don't remember you," she said.

"You're still a cute little thing." She bumped his arm, and he spilled his drink.

Afterward we sat on the couch and surveyed the cluttered coffee table. It was past seven but we didn't talk about dinner.

"I'm glad they came," I said.

"I hate them." Emily looked at her fingernails. Her voice shook. "I don't know whom I hate more, them or him — for taking it."

"It doesn't matter anymore," I said.

"I suppose."

We watched the room grow dark.

"Do you know what?" Emily said. "It's the eve of the fifteenth day of the seventh lunar month."

"How do you know?" During college I had grown completely unaware of the lunar calendar.

"One of those chemistry nerds from China told me this afternoon."

I wanted to laugh, but instead felt myself make a strange whimpering sound, squeezed out from my tight and hollow chest.

"Remember the time Dad and I had that big fight?" she said. "You know that now, in my grownup life, I don't fight with anyone? I never had problems with anybody except him."

"No one cared about you as much as he did," I said.

"I don't want to hear about it." Her voice began to shake again. "He was a pain, and you know it. He got so strict after Mama died. It wasn't all my fault."

"I'm sorry," I said. But I was so angry with her that I felt my face turn red, my cheeks tingle in the dark. She'd considered our father a nerd as well, had squandered his love with such thoughtlessness that I could scarcely breathe to think about it. It seemed impossibly unfair that she had memories of my mother as well. Carefully I waited for my feelings to go away. Emily, I thought, was all I had.

But as I sat, a vision distilled before my eyes: the soft baked shades, the great blue sky of New Mexico. I realized that after graduation I could go wherever I wanted. Somewhere a secret, rusty door swung open and filled my mind with sweet freedom, fearful coolness.

"I want to do something," I said.

"Like what?"

"I don't know." Then I got an idea. "Emily, why don't I give you a haircut?"

We found newspapers and spread them on the floor. We turned

on the lamps and moved the coffee table out of the way, took the wineglasses to the sink. Emily went to the bathroom, and I searched for the shears a long time before I found them in the kitchen. I glimpsed the incense urn in a cabinet and quickly shut the door. When I returned to the living room, it smelled of shampoo. Emily was standing in the middle of the papers with her wet hair down her back, staring at herself in the reflection from the window. The lamplight cast circles under her eyes.

"I had a dream last night," she said. "I was walking down the street. I felt a tug. He was trying to reach me, trying to pull my hair."

"I'll just give you a trim," I said.

"No," she said. "Why don't you cut it?"

"What do you mean?" I snapped a two-inch lock off the side. Emily looked down at the hair on the newspapers. "I'm serious," she said. "Cut my hair. I want to see two feet of hair on the floor."

"Emily, you don't know what you're saying," I said. But a strange, weightless feeling had come over me. I placed the scissors at the nape of her neck. "How about it?" I asked, and my voice sounded low and odd.

"*I don't care.*" An echo of the past. I cut. The shears went *snack*. A long black lock of hair hit the newspapers by my feet.

The Chinese say that our hair and our bodies are given to us from our ancestors, gifts that should not be tampered with. My mother herself had never done this. But after the first few moments I enjoyed myself, pressing the thick black locks through the shears, heavy against my thumb. Emily's hair slipped to the floor around us, rich and beautiful, lying in long graceful arcs over my shoes. She stood perfectly still, staring out the window. The Hudson River flowed behind our reflections, bearing my father's ashes through the night.

When I was finished, the back of her neck gleamed clean and white under a precise shining cap. "You missed your calling," Emily said. "You want me to do yours?"

My hair, browner and scragglier, had never been past my shoulders. I had always kept it short, figuring the ancestors wouldn't be offended by my tampering with a lesser gift. "No," I said. "But you should take a shower. Some of those small bits will probably itch."

"It's already ten o'clock," she said. "We should go to sleep soon anyway." Satisfied, she glanced at the mirror in the foyer. "I look like a completely different person," she said. She left to take her shower. I wrapped up her hair in the newspapers and went into the kitchen. I stood next to the sink for a long time before throwing the bundle away.

The past sees through all attempts at disguise. That night I was awakened by a wrenching scream. I gasped and stiffened, grabbing a handful of blanket.

"*Claudia,*" Emily cried from the other bed. "Claudia, wake up!"

"What is it?"

"I saw Baba." She hadn't called our father Baba in years. "Over there, by the door. Did you see him?"

"No," I said. "I didn't see anything." My bones felt frozen in place. After a moment I opened my eyes. The full moon shone through the window, bathing our room in silver and shadow. I heard my sister sob and then fall silent. I looked carefully at the door, but I noticed nothing.

Then I understood that his ghost would never visit me. I was, one might say, the lucky daughter. But I lay awake until morning, waiting; part of me is waiting still.

DAN CHAON

Fitting Ends

FROM TRIQUARTERLY

THERE IS A STORY about my brother Del that appears in a book
called *More True Tales of the Weird and Supernatural.* The piece on Del
is about three pages long, full of exclamation points and suppos-
edly eerie descriptions. It is based on what the writer calls "true
facts."

The writer spends much of the first few paragraphs setting the
scene, trying to make it sound spooky. "The tiny, isolated village of
Pyramid, Nebraska," is what the author calls the place where I grew
up. I had never thought of it as a village. It wasn't much of anything,
really — it wasn't even on the map, and hadn't been since my
father was a boy, when it was a stop on the Union Pacific railroad
line. Back then, there was a shantytown for the railroad workers, a
dance hall, a general store, a post office. By the time I was growing
up, all that was left was a cluster of mostly boarded-up, rundown
houses. My family — my parents and grandparents and my brother
and I — lived in the only occupied buildings. There was a grain
elevator, which my grandfather had run until he retired and my
father took over. PYRAMID was painted in peeling block letters on
one of the silos.

The man who wrote the story got fixated on that elevator. He
talks of it as "a menacing, hulking structure" and says it is like
"Childe Roland's ancient dark tower, presiding over the barren
fields and empty, sentient houses." He even goes so far as to mention "the soundless flutter of bats flying in and out of the single eyelike window at the top of the elevator" and "the distant, melancholy calls of coyotes from the hills beyond," which are then

drowned out by "the strange echoing moan of a freight train as it passes in the night."

There really are bats, of course; you find them in every country place. Personally, I never heard coyotes, though it is true they were around. I saw one once when I was about twelve. I was staring from my bedroom window late one night and there he was. He had come down from the hills and was crouched in our yard, licking drops of water off the propeller of the sprinkler. As for the trains, they passed through about every half-hour, day and night. If you lived there, you didn't even hear them — or maybe only half-heard them, the way, now that I live in a town, I might vaguely notice the bells of the nearby Catholic church at noon.

But anyway, this is how the writer sets things up. Then he begins to tell about some of the train engineers, how they dreaded passing through this particular stretch. He quotes one man as saying he got goose bumps every time he started to come up on Pyramid. "There was just something about that place," says this man. There were a few bad accidents at the crossing — a carload of drunken teenagers who tried to beat the train, an old guy who had a heart attack as his pickup bumped across the tracks. That sort of thing. Actually, this happens anywhere that has a railroad crossing.

Then came the sightings. An engineer would see "a figure" walking along the tracks in front of the train, just beyond the Pyramid elevator. The engineer would blow his horn, but the person, "the figure," would seem not to notice. The engineer blasted the horn several more times, more and more insistent. But the person kept walking; pretty soon the train's headlights glared onto a tall, muscular boy with shaggy dark hair and a green fatigue jacket. They tried to brake the train, but it was too late. The boy suddenly fell to his knees, and the engineer was certain he'd hit him. But of course when the train was stopped, they could find nothing. "Not a trace," says our author. This happened to three different engineers; three different incidents in a two-year period.

You can imagine the ending, of course: that was how my brother died, a few years after these supposed sightings began. His car had run out of gas a few miles from home, and he was walking back. He was drunk. Who knows why he was walking along the tracks? Who knows why he suddenly kneeled down? Maybe he stumbled, or had to throw up. Maybe he did it on purpose. He was killed instantly.

The whole ghost stuff came out afterward. One of the engineers who'd seen the ghost recognized Del's picture in the paper and came forward or something. I always believed it was made up. It was stupid, I always thought, like a million campfire stories you'd heard or some cheesy program on TV. But the author of *More True Tales of the Weird and Supernatural* found it "spine-tingling." "The strange story of the boy whose ghost appeared — two years before he died!" says a line on the back cover.

This happened when I was fourteen. My early brush with tragedy, I guess you could call it, though by the time I was twenty-one I felt I had recovered. I didn't think the incident had shaped my life in any particular way, and in fact I'd sometimes find myself telling the story, ghost and all, to girls I met at fraternity parties. I'd take a girl up to my room, show her the *More True Tales* book. We'd smoke some marijuana and talk about it, my voice taking on an intensity and heaviness that surprised both of us. From time to time, we'd end up in bed. I remember this one girl, Lindsey, telling me how moved she was by the whole thing. It gave me, she said, a Heathcliff quality; I had turned brooding and mysterious; the wheat fields had turned to moors. "I'm not mysterious," I said, embarrassed, and later, after we'd parted ways, she agreed. "I thought you were different," she said, "deeper." She cornered me one evening when I was talking to another girl and wanted to know if I wasn't a little ashamed, using my dead brother to get laid. She said that she had come to realize that I, like Heathcliff, was just another jerk.

After that I stopped telling the story for a while. There would be months when I wouldn't speak of my brother at all, and even when I was home in Pyramid, I could spend my whole vacation without once mentioning Del's name. My parents never spoke of him, at least not with me.

Of course, this only made him more present than ever. He hovered there as I spoke of college, my future, my life, my father barely listening. When we would argue, my father would stiffen sullenly, and I knew he was thinking of arguments he'd had with Del. I could shout at him, and nothing would happen. He'd stare as I tossed some obscene word casually toward him, and I'd feel it rattle and spin like a coin I'd flipped on the table in front of him. But he wouldn't say anything.

I actually wondered back then why they put up with this sort of thing. It was surprising, even a little unnerving, especially given my father's temper when I was growing up, the old violence-promising glares that once made my bones feel like wax, the ability he formerly had to make me flinch with a gesture or a well-chosen phrase.

Now I was their only surviving child, and I was gone — more thoroughly gone than Del was, in a way. I'd driven off to college in New York, and it was clear I wasn't ever coming back. Even my visits became shorter and shorter — summer trimmed down from three months to less than two weeks over the course of my years at college; at Christmas, I'd stay on campus after finals, wandering the emptying passageways of my residence hall, loitering in the student center, my hands clasped behind my back, staring at the ragged bulletin boards as if they were paintings in a museum. I found excuses to keep from going back. And then, when I got there, finally, I was just another ghost.

About a year before he died, Del saved my life. It was no big deal, I thought. It was summer, trucks were coming to the grain elevator, and my brother and I had gone up to the roof to fix a hole. The elevator was flat on top, and when I was little, I used to imagine that being up there was like being in the turret of a lighthouse. I used to stare out over the expanse of prairie, across the fields and their flotsam of machinery, cattle, men, over the rooftops of houses, along the highways and railroad tracks that trailed off into the horizon. When I was small, this would fill me with wonder. My father would stand there with me, holding my hand, and the wind would ripple our clothes.

I was thinking of this, remembering, when I suddenly started to do a little dance. I didn't know why I did such things: my father said that ever since I started junior high school I'd been like a "-holic" of some sort, addicted to making an ass out of myself. Maybe this was true, because I started to caper around, and Del said, "I'd laugh if you fell, you idiot," stern and condescending, as if I were the juvenile delinquent. I ignored him. With my back turned to him, I began to sing "Ain't No Mountain High Enough" in a deep corny voice like my father's. I'd never been afraid of heights, and I suppose I was careless. Too close to the edge, I slipped, and my brother caught my arm.

I was never able to recall exactly what happened in that instant. I remember being surprised by the sound that came from my throat, a high scream like a rabbit's that seemed to ricochet downward, a stone rattling through a long drainpipe. I looked up and my brother's mouth was wide open, as if he'd made the sound. The tendons on his neck stood out.

I told myself that if I'd been alone, nothing would have happened. I would've just teetered a little, then gained my balance again. But when my brother grabbed me, I lost my equilibrium, and over the edge I went. There were a dozen trucks lined up to have their loads weighed, and all the men down there heard that screech, looked up startled to see me dangling there with two hundred feet between me and the ground. They all watched Del yank me back up to safety.

I was on the ground before it hit me. Harvesters were getting out of their trucks and ambling toward us, and I could see my father pushing his way through the crowd. It was then that my body took heed of what had happened. The solid earth kept opening up underneath me, and Del put his arm around me as I wobbled. Then my father loomed. He got hold of me, clenching my shoulders, shaking me. "My sore neck!" I cried out. "Dad, my neck!" The harvesters' faces jittered, pressing closer; I could see a man in sunglasses with his black, glittering eyes fixed on me.

"Del pushed me," I cried out as my father's gritted teeth came toward my face. Tears slipped suddenly out of my eyes. "Del pushed me, Dad! It wasn't my fault."

My father had good reason to believe this lie, even though he and some twelve or more others had been witness to my singing and careless prancing up there. The possibility still existed that Del might have given me a shove from behind. My father didn't want to believe Del was capable of such a thing. But he knew he was.

Del had only been back home for about three weeks. Prior to that, he'd spent several months in a special program for juvenile delinquents. The main reason for this was that he'd become so belligerent, so violent, that my parents didn't feel they could control him. He'd also, over the course of things, stolen a car.

For much of the time that my brother was in this program, I wore a neck brace. He'd tried to strangle me the night before he was sent away. He claimed he'd seen me smirking at him, though actually

I was only thinking of something funny I'd seen on TV. Del was the furthest thing from my thoughts until he jumped on me. If my father hadn't separated us, Del probably would have choked me to death.

This was one of the things that my father must have thought of. He must have remembered the other times that Del might have killed me: the time when I was twelve and he threw a can of motor oil at my head when my back was turned; the time when I was seven and he pushed me off the tailgate of a moving pickup, where my father had let us sit when he was driving slowly down a dirt road. My father was as used to hearing these horror stories as I was to telling them.

Though he was only three and a half years older than me, Del was much larger. He was much bigger than I'll ever be, and I was just starting to realize that. Six foot three, 220-pound defensive back, my father used to tell people when he spoke of Del. My father used to believe that Del would get a football scholarship to the state university. Never mind that once he started high school he wouldn't even play on the team. Never mind that all he seemed to want to do was vandalize people's property and drink beer and cause problems at home. My father still talked about it like there was some hope.

When my brother got out of his program, he told us that things would be different from now on. He had changed, he said, and he swore that he would make up for the things that he'd done. I gave him a hug. He stood there before us with his hands clasped behind his back, posed like the famous orator whose picture was in the library of our school. We all smiled, the visions of the horrible family fights wavering behind our friendly expressions.

So here was another one, on the night of my almost-death.

Before very long, my brother had started crying. I hadn't seen him actually shed tears in a very long time; he hadn't even cried on the day he was sent away.

"He's a liar," my brother shouted. We had all been fighting and carrying on for almost an hour. I had told my version of the story five or six times, getting better at it with each repetition. I could have almost believed it myself. "You fucking liar," my brother screamed at me. "I wish I had pushed you. I'd never save your ass now." He stared at me suddenly, wild-eyed, like I was a dark shadow that was bending over his bed when he woke at night. Then he sat down at the kitchen table. He put his face in his hands, and his shoulders began to shudder.

Watching him — this giant, broad-shouldered boy, my brother, weeping — I could have almost taken it back. The whole lie, I thought, the words I spoke at first came out of nowhere, sprang to my lips as a shield against my father's red face and bared teeth, his fingernails cutting my shoulder as everyone watched. It was really my father's fault. I could have started crying myself.

But looking back on it, I have to admit that there was something else, too — a heat at the core of my stomach, spreading through my body like a stain. It made my skin throb, my face a mask of innocence and defiance. I sat there looking at him and put my hand to my throat. After years of being on the receiving end, it wasn't in my nature to see Del as someone who could be wronged, as someone to feel pity for. This was something Del could have done, I thought. It was not so unlikely.

At first I thought it would end with my brother leaving, barreling out of the house with the slamming of doors and the circling whine of the fan belt in my father's old beater pickup, the muffler retorting all the way down the long dirt road, into the night. Once, when he was drunk, my brother tried to drive his truck off a cliff on the hill out behind our house. But the embankment wasn't steep enough, and the truck just went bump, bump down the side of the hill, all four wheels staying on the ground until it finally came to rest in the field below. Del pointed a shotgun at my father that night, and my father was so stunned and upset that my mother thought he was having a heart attack. She was running around hysterical, calling police, ambulance, bawling. In the distance, Del went up the hill, down the hill, up, down. You could hear him revving the motor. It felt somehow like one of those slapstick moments in a comedy movie, where everything is falling down at once and all the actors run in and out of doorways. I sat, shivering, curled up on the couch while all this was going on, staring at the television.

But the night after I'd almost fallen, my brother did not try to take off. We all knew that if my parents had to call the police on him again, it would be the end. He would go to a foster home or even back to the juvenile hall, which he said was worse than prison. So instead, he and my father were in a shoving match; there was my mother between them, screaming, "Oh, stop it I can't stand it I can't stand it," turning her deadly, red-eyed stare abruptly upon me; there was my brother crying. But he didn't try to leave. He just sat there, with his face in his hands. "Goddamn all of you," he cried suddenly. "I hate all your guts. I wish I was fucking dead."

My father hit him then, hit him with the flat of his hand alongside the head, and Del tilted in his chair with the force of it. He made a small, high-pitched sound, and I watched as he folded his arms over his ears as my father descended on him, a blow, a pause, a blow, a pause. My father stood over him, breathing hard. A tear fell from Del's nose.

"Don't you ever say that," my father roared. "Don't you dare ever say that." He didn't mean the f-word — he meant wishing you were dead, the threats Del had made in the past. That was the worst thing, my father had told us once, the most terrible thing a person could do. My father's hands fell to his sides. I saw that he was crying also.

After a time, Del lifted his head. He seemed to have calmed — everything seemed to have grown quiet, a dull, wavery throb of static. I saw that he looked at me. I slumped my shoulders, staring down at my fingernails.

"You lie," Del said softly. "You can't even look me in the face." He got up and stumbled a few steps, as if my father would go after him again. But my father just stood there.

"Get out of my sight," he said. "Go on."

I heard Del's tennis shoes thump up the stairs, the slam of our bedroom door. But just as I felt my body start to untense, my father turned to me. He wiped the heel of his hand over his eyes, gazing at me without blinking. After all of Del's previous lies, his denials, his betrayals, you would think they would never believe his side of things again. But I could see a slowly creaking hinge of doubt behind my father's expression. I looked down.

"If I ever find out you're lying to me, boy," my father said.

He didn't ever find out. The day I almost fell was another one of those things we never got around to talking about again. It probably didn't seem very significant to my parents, in the span of events that had happened before and came after. They dwelt on other things.

On what, I never knew. My wife found this unbelievable: "Didn't they say anything after he died?" she asked me, and I had to admit that I didn't remember. They were sad, I told her. I recalled my father crying. But they were country people. I tried to explain this to my wife, good Boston girl that she is, the sort of impossible grief that is like something gnarled and stubborn and underground. I never really believed it myself. For years, I kept expecting things to go back to normal, waiting for whatever was happening to them to finally be over.

My parents actually became quite mellow in the last years of their lives. My mother lost weight, was often ill. Eventually, shortly after her sixtieth birthday, she went deaf. Her hearing slipped away quickly, like a skin she was shedding, and all the tests proved inconclusive. That was the year that my son was born. In January, when my wife discovered that she was pregnant, my parents were in the process of buying a fancy, expensive hearing aid. By the time the baby was four months old, the world was completely soundless for my mother, hearing aid or not.

The problems of my college years had passed away by that time. I was working at a small private college in upstate New York, in alumni relations. My wife and I seldom went back to Nebraska; we couldn't afford the money or the time. But I talked to my parents regularly on the phone, once or twice a month.

We ended up going back that Christmas after Ezra was born. My mother's letters had made it almost impossible to avoid. "It breaks my heart that I can't hear my grandson's voice, now that he is making his little sounds," she had written. "But am getting by O.K. and will begin lip-reading classes in Denver after Xmas. It will be easier for me then." She would get on the phone when I called my father. "I can't hear you talking, but I love you," she'd say.

"We have to work to make her feel involved in things," my father told us as we drove from the airport, where he'd picked us up. "The worst thing is that they start feeling isolated," he told us. "We got little pads so we can write her notes." He looked over at me, strangely academic-looking in the new glasses he had for driving. In the last few years he had begun to change, his voice turning slow and gentle, as if he were watching something out in the distance beyond the window or something sad and mysterious on TV as we talked. His former short temper had vanished, leaving only a soft reproachfulness in its place. But even that was muted. He knew that he couldn't really make me feel guilty. "You know how she is," he said to my wife and me, though of course we did not, either one of us, really know her. "You know how she is. The hardest part is, you know, we don't want her to get depressed."

She looked awful. Every time I had seen her since I graduated from college, this had stunned me. I came in, carrying my sleeping son, and she was sitting at the kitchen table, her spine curved a little bit more than the last time, thinner, so skinny that her muscles seemed to stand out against the bone. Back in New York, I worked with alumni ladies older than her who played tennis, who dressed in trendy clothes, who walked with a casual and still sexy ease. These women wouldn't look like my mother for another twenty years, if ever. I felt my smile pull awkwardly on my face.

"Hello!" I called, but of course she didn't look up. My father flicked on the porch light. "She hates it when you surprise her," he said softly, as if there were still some possibility of her overhearing. My wife looked over at me. Her eyes said that this was going to be another holiday that was like work for her.

My mother lifted her head. Her shrewdness was still intact, at least, and she was ready for us the moment the porch light hit her consciousness. That terrible, monkeyish dullness seemed to lift from her expression as she looked up.

"Well, howdy," she called, in the same jolly, slightly ironic way she always did when she hadn't seen me in a long time. She came over to hug us, then peered down at Ezra, who stirred a little as she pushed back his parka hood to get a better look. "Oh, what an angel," she whispered. "It's about killing me, not being able to see this boy." Then she stared down at Ezra again. How he'd grown, she told us. She thought he looked like me, she said, and I was relieved. Actually, I'd begun to think that Ezra somewhat resembled the pictures I'd seen of Del as a baby. But my mother didn't say that, at least.

I had planned to have a serious talk with them on this trip. Or maybe "planned" is the wrong word — "considered" might be closer, though even that doesn't express the vague, unpleasantly anxious urge that I could feel at the back of my neck. I didn't really know what I wanted to know. And the truth was, these quiet, fragile, distantly tender people bore little resemblance to the mother and father in my mind. It had been ten years since I'd lived at home. Ten years! — which filled the long, snowy evenings with a numbing politeness. My father sat in his easy chair after dinner, watching the news. My wife read. My mother and I did the dishes together, silently, nodding as the plate she had rinsed passed from her hand to mine, to be dried and put away. When a train passed, the little window above the sink vibrated, humming like a piece of cellophane. But she did not notice this.

We did have a talk of sorts that trip, my father and I. It was on the third day after our arrival, a few nights before Christmas Eve. My wife and my mother were both asleep. My father and I sat out on the closed-in porch, drinking beer, watching the snow drift across the yard, watching the wind send fingers of snow slithering along low to the ground. I had drunk more than he had. I saw him glance sharply at me for a second when I came back from the refrigerator a fourth time and popped open the can. But the look faded quickly. Outside, beyond the window, I could see the blurry shape of the elevator through the falling snow, its outlines indistinct, wavering like a mirage.

"Do you remember that time," I said, "when I almost fell off the elevator?"

It came out like that, abrupt, stupid. As I sat there in my father's silence, I realized how impossible it was, how useless to try to patch years of ellipsis into something resembling dialogue. I looked down, and he cleared his throat.

"Sure," he said at last, noncommittal. "Of course I remember."

"I think about that sometimes," I said. Drunk — I felt the alcohol edge into my voice as I spoke. "It seems," I said, "significant." That was the word that came to me. "It seems significant sometimes," I said.

My father considered this for a while. He stiffened formally, as if he were being interviewed. "Well," he said, "I don't know. There were so many things like that. It was all a mess by then, anyway. Nothing could be done. It was too late for anything to be done." He looked down to his own beer, which must have gone warm by that time, and took a small sip. "It should have been taken care of earlier — when you were kids. That's where I think things must have gone wrong. I was too hard on you both. But Del — I was harder on him. He was the oldest. Too much pressure. Expected too much."

He drifted off at that, embarrassed. We sat there, and I could not even imagine what he meant — what specifics he was referring to. What pressure? What expectations? But I didn't push any further.

"But you turned out all right," my father said. "You've done pretty well, haven't you?"

There were no signs in our childhood, no incidents pointing the way to his eventual end. None that I could see, at least, and I thought about it quite a bit after his death. "It should have been taken care of earlier," my father said, but what was "it"? Del seemed to have been happy, at least up until high school.

Maybe things happened when they were alone together. From time to time, I remember Del coming back from helping my father in the shop with his eyes red from crying. Once, I remember our father coming into our room on a Saturday morning and cuffing the top of Del's sleeping head with the back of his hand: he had stepped in dog dirt on the lawn. The dog was Del's responsibility. Del must have been about eight or nine at the time, and I remember him kneeling on our bedroom floor in his pajamas, crying bitterly as he cleaned off my father's boot. When I told that story later on, I was pleased by the ugly, almost fascist overtones it had. I remember recounting it to some college friends — handsome, suburban kids — lording this little bit of squalor from my childhood over them. Child abuse and family violence were enjoying a media vogue at that time, and I found I could mine this memory to good effect. In the version I told, I was the one cleaning the boots.

But the truth was, my father was never abusive in an especially spectacular way. He was more like a simple bully, easily eluded when he was in a short-tempered mood. He used to get so furious when we avoided him. I recall how he used to grab us by the hair on the back of our necks, tilting our heads so we looked into his face. "You don't listen," he would hiss. "I want you to look at me when I talk to you." That was about the worst of it, until Del started getting into trouble. And by that time my father's blows weren't enough. Del would laugh, he would strike back. It was then that my father finally decided to turn him over to the authorities. He had no other choice, he said.

He must have believed it. He wasn't, despite his temper, a bad man, a bad parent. He'd seemed so kindly sometimes, so fatherly — especially with Del. I remember watching them from my window some autumn mornings, watching them wade through the high weeds in the stubble field out behind our house, walking toward the hill with their shotguns pointing at the ground, their steps slow, synchronized. Once I'd gone upstairs and heard them laughing in Del's and my bedroom. I just stood there outside the doorway, watching as my father and Del put a model ship together, sharing the job, their talk easy, happy.

This was what I thought of, that night we were talking. I thought of my own son, the innocent baby I loved so much, and it chilled me to think that things could change so much — that Del's closeness to my father could turn in on itself, transformed into the kind of closeness that thrived on their fights, on the different ways Del could push my father into a rage. That finally my father would feel he had no choices left. We looked at each other, my father and I. "What are you thinking?" I said softly, but he just shook his head.

Del and I had never been close. We had never been like friends, or even like brothers. Yet after that day on the elevator I came to realize that there had been something between us. There had been something that could be taken away.

He stopped talking to me altogether for a while. In the weeks and months that followed my lie, I doubt if we even looked at each other more than two or three times, though we shared the same room.

For a while I slept on the couch. I was afraid to go up to our bedroom. I can remember those first few nights, waiting in the living room for my father to go to bed, the television hissing with laughter. The furniture, the table, the floors, seemed to shudder as I touched them, as if they were just waiting for the right moment to burst apart.

I'd go outside sometimes, though that was really no better. It was the period of late summer when thunderstorms seemed to pass over every night. The wind came up. The shivering tops of trees bent in the flashes of heat lightning.

There was no way out of the situation I'd created. I could see that. Days and weeks stretched out in front of me, more than a month before school started. By that time, I thought, maybe it would all blow over. Maybe it would melt into the whole series of bad things that had happened, another layer of paint that would eventually be covered over by a new one, forgotten.

If he really had pushed me, that was what would have happened. It would have been like the time he tried to choke me, or the time he tried to drive the car off the hill. Once those incidents were over, there was always the possibility that this was the last time. There was always the hope that everything would be better now.

In retrospect, it wouldn't have been so hard to recant. There would have been a big scene, of course. I would have been punished, humiliated. I would have had to endure my brother's triumph, my parents' disgust. But I realize now that it wouldn't have been so bad.

I might have finally told the truth, too, if Del had reacted the way I expected. I imagined that there would be a string of confrontations in the days that followed, that he'd continue to protest with my father. I figured he wouldn't give up.

But he did. After that night, he didn't try to deny it anymore. For a while I even thought that maybe he had begun to believe that he pushed me. He acted like a guilty person, eating his supper in silence, walking noiselessly through the living room, his shoulders hunched like a traveler on a snowy road.

My parents seemed to take this as penitence. They still spoke sternly, but their tone began to be edged by gentleness, a kind of forgiveness. "Did you take out the trash?" they would ask. "Another potato?" — and they would wait for him to quickly nod. He was truly sorry, they thought. Everything was finally going to be O.K. He was shaping up.

At these times I noticed something in his eyes — a kind of sharpness, a subtle shift of the iris. He would lower his head, and the corners of his mouth would move slightly. To me, his face seemed to flicker with hidden, mysterious thoughts.

When I finally began to sleep in our room again, he pretended I wasn't there. I would come in, almost as quiet as he himself had become, to find him sitting at our desk or on his bed, peeling off a sock with such slow concentration that it might have been his skin. It was as if there were an unspoken agreement between us — I no longer existed. He wouldn't look at me, but I could watch him for as long as I wanted. I would pull the covers over myself and just lie there, observing, as he went about doing whatever he was doing as if oblivious. He listened to a tape on his headphones; flipped through a magazine; did sit-ups; sat staring out the window; turned out the light. And all that time his face remained neutral, impassive. Once he even chuckled to himself at a book he was reading, a paperback anthology of *The Far Side* cartoons.

When I was alone in the room, I found myself looking through his things, with an interest I'd never had before. I ran my fingers over his models, the monster-wheeled trucks and B-10 bombers. I flipped through his collection of tapes. I found some literature he'd brought home from the detention center, brochures with titles like *Teens and Alcohol: What You Should Know!* and *Rap Session, Talking About Feelings.* Underneath this stuff I found the essay he'd been working on.

He had to write an essay so that they would let him back into high school. There was a letter from the guidance counselor explaining the school's policy, and then there were several sheets of notebook paper with his handwriting on them. He'd scratched out lots of words, sometimes whole paragraphs. In the margins he'd written little notes to himself: "(sp.)" or "?" or "No." He wrote in scratchy block letters.

His essay told of the Outward Bound program. "I had embarked on a sixty-day rehabilitation program in the form of a wilderness survival course name of Outward Bound," he had written. "THESIS: The wilderness has allowed for me to reach deep inside my inner self and grasp ahold of my morals and values that would set the standard and tell the story of the rest of my life."

I would go into our room when my brother was out and take the essay out of the drawer where he'd hidden it. He was working on it, off and on, all that month; I'd flip it open to discover new additions or deletions — whole paragraphs appearing as if overnight. I never saw him doing it.

The majority of the essay was a narrative, describing their trip. They had hiked almost two hundred miles, he said. "Up by sun and down by moon," he wrote. There were obstacles they had to cross. Once they had to climb down a hundred-foot cliff. "The repelling was very exciting but also scary," he'd written. "This was meant to teach us trust and confidence in ourselves as well as our teammates, they said. Well as I reached the peak of my climb I saw to my despair that the smallest fellow in the group was guiding my safety rope. Now he was no more than one hundred and ten pounds and I was tipping the scales at about two twenty five needless to say I was reluctant."

But they made it. I remember reading this passage several times; it seemed very vivid in my mind. In my imagination, I was in the place of the little guy holding the safety rope. I saw my brother hopping lightly, bit by bit, down the sheer face of the cliff to the ground below, as if he could fly, as if there were no gravity anymore.

"My experience with the Outward Bound program opened my eyes to such values as friendship, trust, responsibility and sharing," Del wrote in his conclusion. "Without the understanding of these I would not exist as I do now but would probably instead be another statistic. With these values I will purely succeed. Without I would surely fail." Next to this he'd written: "Sounds like bullshit (?)."

I don't know that I recognized that distinct ache that I felt on reading this, or understood why his sudden distance, the silent, moody aura he trailed after him in those weeks, should have affected me in such a way. Years later, I would recall that feeling — standing over my son's crib, a dark shape leaning over him as he stirred with dreams — waiting at the window for the headlights of my wife's car to turn into our driveway. That sad, trembly feeling was a species of love — or at least a symptom of it.

I thought of this a long time after the fact. I loved my brother, I thought. Briefly.

None of this lasted. By the time he died, a year later, he'd worked his way back to his normal self, or a slightly modified, moodier version. Just like before, money had begun to disappear from my mother's purse; my parents searched his room for drugs. He and my father had argued that morning about the friends he was hanging around with, about his wanting to take the car every night. Del claimed that he was dating a girl, said he only wanted to see a movie in town. He'd used that one before, often lying ridiculously when he was asked the next day about the plot of the film. I remember him telling my mother that the war film *Apocalypse Now* was set in the future, which I knew was not true from an article I'd read in the paper. I remember making some comment in reference to this as he was getting ready to go out, and he looked at me in that careful, hooded way, reminiscent of the time when he was pretending I didn't exist. "Eat shit and die, Stewart," he murmured, without heat. Unfortunately, I believe that this was the last thing he ever said to me.

Afterward, his friends said that he had seemed like he was in a good mood. They had all been in his car, my father's car, driving up and down the main street in Scottsbluff. They poured a little rum into their cans of Coke, cruising from one end of town to the other, calling out the window at a carful of passing teenage girls, revving the engine at the stoplights. He wasn't that drunk, they said.

I used to imagine that there was a specific moment when he realized that he was going to die. I don't believe he knew it when he left our house, or even at the beginning of his car ride with his friends. If that were true, I have to assume that there would have been a sign, some gesture or expression, something one of us would have noticed. If it was planned, then why on that particular, insignificant day?

Yet I wondered. I used to think of him in his friend Sully's car, listening to his buddies laughing, making dumb jokes, running red lights. It might have been sometime around then, I thought. Time seemed to slow down. He would sense a long, billowing delay in the spaces between words; the laughing faces of the girls in a passing car would seem to pull by forever, their expressions frozen.

Or I thought about his driving home. I could see the heavy, foglike darkness of those country roads, the shadows of weeds springing up when the headlights touched them, I could imagine the halt and sputter of the old pickup as the gas ran out, that moment when you can feel the power lift up out of the machine like a spirit. It's vivid enough in my mind that it's almost as if I were with him as the pickup rolled lifelessly on — slowing, then stopping at last on the shoulder where it would be found the next day, the emergency lights still blinking dimly. He and I stepped out into the thick night air, seeing the shape of the elevator in the distance, above the tall sunflowers and pigweed. And though we knew we were outdoors, it felt like we were inside something. The sky seemed to close down on us like the lid of a box.

No one in my family ever used the word "suicide." When we referred to Del's death, if we referred to it, we spoke of "the accident." To the best of our knowledge, that's what it was.

*

There was a time, right before I left for college, when I woke from a dream to the low wail of a passing train. I could see it when I sat up in bed — through the branches of trees outside my window I could see the boxcars shuffling through flashes of heat lightning, trailing past the elevator and into the distance, rattling, rattling.

And there was another time, my senior year in college, when I saw a kid who looked like Del coming out of a bar, a boy melting into the crowded, carnival atmosphere of this particular strip of saloons and dance clubs where students went on a Saturday night. I followed this person a few blocks before I lost sight of him. All those cheerful, drunken faces seemed to loom as I passed by them, blurring together like an expressionist painting. I leaned against a wall, breathing.

And there was that night when we came to Pyramid with my infant son, the night my father and I stayed up talking. I sat there in the dark long after he'd gone to bed, finishing another beer. I remember looking up to see my mother moving through the kitchen, at first only clearly seeing the billowy whiteness of her nightgown hovering in the dark, a shape floating slowly through the kitchen toward me. I had a moment of fear before I realized it was her. She did not know I was there. She walked slowly, delicately, thinking herself alone in this room at night. I would have had to touch her to let her know that I was there, and that would have probably startled her badly. So I didn't move. I watched as she lit a cigarette and sat down at the kitchen table, her head turned toward the window, where the snow was still falling. She watched it drift down. I heard her breathe smoke, exhaling in a long, thoughtful sigh. She was remembering something, I thought.

It was at these moments that everything seemed clear to me. I felt that I could take all the loose ends of my life and fit them together perfectly, as easily as a writer could write a spooky story, where all the details add up and you know the end even before the last sentence. This would make a good ending, you think at such moments. You'll go on living, of course. But at the same time you recognize, in that brief flash of clarity and closure, you realize that everything is summed up. It's not really worth becoming what there is left for you to become.

PETER HO DAVIES

The Silver Screen

FROM HARVARD REVIEW

FROM THE END of the Second World War until the outbreak of
the insurgency in 1948, the fourteenth Kuala Lumpur branch of
the Malayan Communist Party held its meetings in the Savoy Cinema on Brickfields Street.

The owner of the cinema, Mr. Ming, had joined the party during
the Japanese occupation. In those days he had cycled to work at his
father's rubber plantation on the outskirts of the town. Every
morning he would join the line of workers and schoolchildren in
front of the Japanese sentry at Pudu jail. They would all dismount
at a respectful distance from the sentry, wheel their bicycles to his
post, bow, wheel them on, and remount at an equally respectful
distance beyond. All this under the eyes of the severed heads lined
up along the walls of the jail.

More heads were sure to be added whenever an informer was
standing beside the sentry. Informers were distinguished by the
brown burlap sacks with ragged eyeholes that they wore over their
heads to avoid identification. On mornings when informers were at
the guard post, Mr. Ming bowed and then stood for a moment
before those eyeholes while they appraised him. He felt his scalp
prickle with the stares from the walls of the jail. He used to say he
never believed the war was over until he saw a line of heads on the
wall each covered with a sack. "Someone pulled the sacks off after a
day, but then they could have been anyone's heads," he said. "And
then the British took them down."

Even before he became a communist, Mr. Ming had little respect
for the British. In his eyes their rapid retreat through Malaya and

their ignominious flight from Singapore had tarnished their reputation irreparably. His desire for Malayan independence stemmed as much from a wish for self-rule as from a conviction that the British no longer deserved to govern. "The Japanese, at least," he told his friends, "were famous for their cruelty. All the British are famous for is cricket."

Everyone on the central committee of the fourteenth branch knew Mr. Ming, but like everyone else, he had a code name. Communist code names in the late forties weren't very imaginative. Mr. Chen, the butcher, was known as the Cockerel. Mr. Ho, the rickshaw driver, was the Foot. Mr. Kuk, the fruit seller, was Shorty. In the Chinese community at that time everyone was a communist or a communist sympathizer, and code names were meant more for notoriety than for secrecy. Mr. Ming's code name was the Duke.

This had come about after Ming complained to the artist, Lee, who painted the posters for all his films. He stood outside the cinema one evening watching Lee take down one huge canvas advertising *Stagecoach* and replace it with another for *Fort Apache*. Both starred John Wayne, but the likenesses of him on the two posters bore no resemblance to each other. They both showed a distinctly Asian man in a Stetson, but that wasn't what Mr. Ming was complaining about.

"Ai-yeu," he called up as Lee struggled with the huge canvases. "How are my customers to know that their favorite actor is in both films? You draw a different face each time."

The canvas that Lee was hanging was rolled up like a carpet and stretched across the whole length of the Savoy's façade, nearly twenty feet. He was perched on a long plank running between two rickety bamboo ladders, and he was in no mood for an argument. If he shouted, he was sure he would fall. As it was, he was convinced that Ming's cries from the street would shake the ladders loose and make the plank jump beneath his feet. He clenched his teeth and finished hanging the poster.

On the ground, Mr. Ming was becoming more and more incensed by this silence, which he took for arrogance. "Think you're an artist?" he cried. "Think again! My grandma could paint a better John Wayne."

When he got down, Lee was apologetic. "Sorry, sorry," he said. "I can't help it. I can't paint a face without a model, and I can't paint the same face without the same model. John Wayne is sometimes my father, sometimes my uncle, sometimes the boy who brings me my paints."

This was how Mr. Ming decided that he would be John Wayne. On the pretext of overseeing Lee's work, he became his model. The idea of his own image ten feet high across his cinema was appealing to him. He thought of the great revolutionary paintings of Lenin and Mao and the Man of Steel that he had seen pictures of in communist newspapers.

In time, he found that the affairs of business limited his opportunities for visiting Lee, and he had the young artist sit in on meetings of the communist cell to make sketches for his posters. In this way other members of the party became immortalized. Mr. Chen became the model for Gary Cooper and Humphrey Bogart. Mr. Ho doubled for Charlie Chaplin, a personal favorite. Mr. Kuk, because of his stature, was a natural choice for Audie Murphy, Peter Lorre, and James Cagney. The communists were all secretly interested in the way they were depicted, but of course no one referred openly to the paintings unless to joke, "I was recognized in the street again last night. A young girl asked me for my autograph! I think she'd make a good Lauren Bacall." There was an unwritten law that during meetings Lee would be ignored while the serious business of world communism was conducted. Yet on certain evenings — the night that Lee was sketching his poster of Henry Fonda in *The Grapes of Wrath*, for instance — the communists would argue longer and more passionately, with more sweeping strokes of the hand, their heads held higher and their brows creased deeper.

On the other hand, no one would look up from his food the night that Lee was trying to get a likeness of Sydney Greenstreet. They held their bowls of rice that much closer to their lips and waved their chopsticks before their faces as they talked.

As for Lee, he paid more attention to his sketches than to politics. It wasn't easy capturing the details he needed, and he had to work fast. Sometimes he would find that he had concentrated so hard on his work that he had no idea what had been discussed or even who had spoken. These were hardly ideal working conditions, but he felt pleased now when the Duke came out to watch him hang a new poster and stood silently in the street, nodding with satisfaction.

Lee was rarely addressed by the communists except perhaps to be told where to sit, and never expected to speak himself. The only sounds he was permitted were the quick sighs of his pencil strokes and the occasional scratching of his knife paring a finer point. Some evenings he didn't even wait until the end of the discussion. If he had enough sketches for his poster, he would collect up his pencils and paper and, bowing quickly to the others, leave to catch the last reel of that night's feature. The Savoy was an open-air cinema — four high walls with no roof and a huge canvas screen stretched out against the night sky — and Lee loved to imagine that what he was seeing was the lives of the gods. It was his habit as he watched to leave the sketchbook open on his lap and by the end of the evening he would have covered the page unconsciously with half-formed figures.

He had his own heroes, of course, just like the communists, and for himself he reserved the role of Johnny Weismuller, holding up a small shaving mirror to sketch himself as Tarzan, Lord of the Jungle.

In 1948, when Chin Peng, the chairman of the Malayan Politburo, authorized the first attacks on British plantation owners, the fourteenth branch of the Kuala Lumpur Communist Party went into the jungle along with five thousand other communist fighters. Many, like Chin Peng himself, had fought alongside the British against the Japanese occupying forces three years earlier. Chin Peng, indeed, had been flown to London to march past King George in the victory parade. Mr. Kuk and Mr. Chen had both served with distinction in the war, and Mr. Ho had for a time been a prisoner of the Japanese, but it was Mr. Ming who took the lead in their platoon. The others accepted this in part because Ming had always been the most prosperous among them but also because they based themselves in the jungle near the plantation owned by Ming's father. "Our first Liberated Area," he called it in his opening address to the platoon. The workers from the plantation could be relied upon to turn a blind eye to their movements and also to supply food and medicines as the campaign wore on.

For many months the Duke, Mr. Cooper, Mr. Chaplin, Mr. Murphy, and about twenty young men from the Brickfields area waged a successful campaign against the British and American plantations surrounding the small Ming estate. The Silver Screen Brigade, as they dubbed themselves, was able to harry traffic with impunity and walk at ease into the villages of their immediate area.

Their greatest success in the early days of the emergency — the authorities were forbidden from referring to it as a war for insurance purposes — was an ambush on a British foot patrol. They picked an isolated bend in a forest path and in the ditch to one side planted sharpened stakes. When the patrol came level with their position, they attacked from the other side of the track, driving the British into the ditch. One man was cut down in the first exchange of fire, and several more were badly wounded in the ditch. The Duke was all for charging the British, but Mr. Cooper shook his head slightly. The communist practice was to stay hidden in the jungle and avoid major confrontations. The Duke would have argued, but Mr. Cooper slapped him on the back and cried, "Good shot." In a moment the whole platoon was applauding. All the British heard was a distant cheering.

The dead man, Lance Corporal Burroughs of the Welsh Guards, better known as "Boom-boom" Burroughs, the promising British welterweight — so named for the sound he made as he landed his punches on opponents — lay in the track for two hours before his body could be recovered. His death warranted a front-page story in the *Straits Times* and a small black framed box on the sports pages of the *Daily Telegraph*.

Lee, meanwhile, had lost his job as a poster painter. He had arrived by bicycle at the Savoy one evening with his new canvas draped over his shoulder like a carpet only to find the iron-grille doors padlocked and the foyer dark. He stood in the street for several minutes sniffing the reassuring smell of peanuts and coconut milk from the hawker stall rolled against the back wall. Eventually he slipped around the side of the building and laid his poster gently in the lane. He propped his bicycle against the wall and stood on the saddle to climb over and drop into the shady auditorium. He found the ladders in the usual place under the stairs to Mr. Ming's office and hurried back over the wall again to hang his poster. It was a fine one of the Duke in *The Sands of Iwo Jima*, machine gun in hand, riding on the side of a tank. Lee was especially proud of the flames issuing from the muzzle of the gun, even though he still felt some regret for the Western scene from the previous week's show that he'd had to paint over.

It was only when he was done that he saw the small government notice pasted beside the door to the foyer, and even then he didn't believe it. He had to go back the next night and see the policeman outside. The man stood a little to one side of the main door, looking rather like the guards Lee had seen at the national museum, and every so often stepped forward to wave away people who had come to queue under Lee's poster.

The Savoy Cinema reopened within a couple of weeks and Lee was briefly rehired, but the new owners, two huge bearded Sikhs whom no one could tell apart, dispensed with his services when he began to experiment with cubism. "Sorry, sorry," Lee cried. He claimed his new style was beyond his control. It was a response to the war, he said, but they would hear nothing of it. A new painter — who made every star look like David Niven — was hired.

Lee's family was disgusted with him for losing his job. His father, who ran a machine tool company, had always viewed his son's painting as foolishness, and now it turned out that he could not even make money from it. Once, when his father had asked Lee how he expected to support a family, the young man had said he didn't care about such things. He wanted to be a famous artist. Everything else would follow. "Famous for being dirt poor" was all his father had said.

Lee was his father's second son. As a boy he'd been devoted to his elder brother. They had built and flown kites together, Lee painting the thin rice paper and his brother building the intricate bamboo frames. He felt honored to have any part in the kite building and in his childish way decorated the kites as beautifully as he could, although he knew that they were destined for destruction. His brother would coat the strings with glue and roll them in ground glass, and then he and the older boys would fly them in fights until one string cut through the other, sending the defeated kite sailing out of sight.

When he was younger, Lee had thought himself well suited to the role of younger brother. He felt no jealousy, only pride, when his father praised his brother's skills, and was grateful for his brother's occasional compliments. He had only taken the job at the Savoy as a way of supporting studies in draftsmanship at the technical school

— a skill he thought would earn him a useful place at his brother's side for life. But his brother had died of typhoid a year earlier, so fevered at the end that they had poured ice into the bed with him, and Lee, so used to the life of a second son, found himself unable to assume the new role his father wanted of him. In business dealings he was so timid his father grew exasperated. "You don't strike deals," he told his son one day. "They strike you."

Mr. Lee's business had first blossomed during the Japanese occupation. He'd made a fortune converting cars to run on wood-burning engines when petrol had been rationed. Now once again there was the threat of fuel shortages, and Lee was set to useful work gathering a variety of combustible materials. Banana skins were a favored means of propulsion for his father, as were potato peelings and dung, and the old man delighted in making his son haul the steaming barrels of fuel back and forth across the factory compound. "At least you'll smell famous," he called, watching Lee pause to wrap a handkerchief around his nose and mouth.

It was at this time that Lee remembered the Duke showing him an article in a communist paper proving that all the greatest artists had been communists — it was an inevitable result of dialectical materialism, apparently — and he regretted not joining his former employer in the jungle, although in truth it had never occurred to the communists to invite him.

While one half of the family factory was devoted to propulsion experiments, the business in armor-plating cars boomed. Lee's father would lead weekend expeditions into the local countryside to strip the armor off old Japanese tanks and artillery pieces, and these slabs of steel, some up to three inches thick, were bolted to the Austins and Packards of the plantation owners. Lee was taught how to cut the small slits through which the occupants could return fire, and he was put in charge of painting camouflage. Here at least no one complained about his cubist tendencies, and his khaki period would have been a happy one if not for the constant pressure of commerce. On more than one occasion he was forced to chase after cars, leaving the factory to add one final flourish.

By 1951 the family had outfitted nearly every plantation vehicle in the area, and business was beginning to fall off. However, with the introduction of New Villages in that year, Lee's father saw another wonderful opportunity. Under this British initiative, nearly half a million Chinese rubber tappers and their families were to be resettled in purpose-built villages guarded by British troops. The idea was partly to protect communities living on the jungle fringes and partly to deny the communists access to sympathizers in those villages. This was how Lee came to be entrusted with his father's drilling equipment and an ancient wood-burning Austin Princess. By the businessman's reckoning, 500,000 people meant at least a hundred thousand families, each of whom would need a latrine dug. "At fifty cents a hole, my son, you might as well be drilling for gold," he shouted as he waved Lee off.

Lee hated his job, especially when the village children ran after him laughing and shouting "Mr. Night Soil," but he did come home with many tales. Once he saw Sardin, the famous Dyak tracker whom the British had brought from Borneo. Sardin was famous for the uncanny jungle skills of his people — he was known to have slept under a string of shrunken heads as a child — and for his mouthful of gold teeth. By the time Lee saw him, he had earned nearly enough from the British to have all his own teeth pulled and replaced by gold ones. The whole village crowded around him when he arrived, and whenever he smiled they broke into wild applause.

Lee, of course, sketched the Dyak and his famous smile, but later that evening, looking at his work again, he felt something was missing and drew in the crowd from memory.

Another time Lee saw General Templer himself. A veteran of three wars, the general had begun his career at eighteen in the First World War, gone on to win the DSO in Palestine, and become the youngest general in the British army in World War II. He was Churchill's personal choice for high commissioner during the emergency. The *Straits Times* described him on his appointment as an Olympian figure — quite literally, as it turned out: he had been a hurdler in the 1924 games.

When Lee saw him, the general was confronting a group of Chinese Home Guards who had surrendered their weapons without a fight to the communists. "You're a lot of bastards," Templer barked. "But try this again and you'll find out I can be an even bigger one." Lee, who had learned all his English at the Savoy, understood this kind of language, but he listened politely as the government translator said slowly in Chinese, "His excellency informs you that he knows none of your mothers or fathers were married when you were born." The translator paused to let this sink in. "He does, however, admit that his own mother and father were not married also."

It was shortly after the mission that killed Lance Corporal Burroughs that the Silver Screen platoon heard a car approaching them along a dusty laterite road. They took cover in the tall lalang at the roadside and on a signal from the Duke opened fire when the lone car drew alongside their position. Sparks and bullets flew off the car's armor, but it did not slacken its pace. Incensed, the Duke leapt from his hiding place and began to pursue it. He knelt in the middle of the road and aimed for the car's rear tires, but although he got off six shots in smart order, he missed each time and the car rolled on toward a small hill in the distance.

The Duke turned away, cursing.

"Wait," Mr. Cooper called. "He's stopping."

They all turned to peer at the car on the hillside, which did indeed appear to have pulled up just out of their range. For a full minute they stared hard at the distant car, until someone shouted, "He's not stopping! He can't get over the hill."

And so it proved. Lee sat at the wheel of the Austin with the car in first and the gas pedal flat to the floor, but still the car, with its armor plating, was too heavy for the wood-burning engine. It could only crawl agonizingly slowly up the gentle slope as he watched the communists overtake him in his mirror. Dazed, his ears still ringing from the clamor of ricochets, he was lucky to hear them when they pushed their guns through the slits in the armor and shouted for him to turn off the engine.

It took Lee a moment to realize whose hands he had fallen into. The Duke's hair, previously immaculately oiled and combed into stiff furrows, was shaved to a close stubble, and there was a gauntness to all the men, even Chen, the former butcher. He allowed the relief to show on his face for a moment and then, thinking better of it, threw himself to his knees to beg for his life.

Mr. Cooper had liked Lee ever since the night he had enjoyed, gratis, the favors of a prostitute who thought he really was a film star. Even though the girl in question was known locally as Stupid

Suzie, the event had so impressed him that he was inclined to see Lee in an almost magical light. He could see that the Duke was still furious at his failure to hit the tires of the retreating car. It was a loss of face that he might revenge on Lee, and Mr. Cooper hurriedly pulled him away.

He reminded the Duke that the platoon had recently lost one of their number, an officious young fellow who had been an usher at the Savoy but who'd never looked as imposing with a rifle as he had with a torch. Lee's appearance was an omen, Mr. Cooper said. He would bring them luck. Grudgingly, the Duke said he would give Lee a choice to join them or die.

"What do you say?"

Lee looked up from his knees. "It's better than drilling latrines," he said, and Mr. Cooper laughed and clapped him on the back. He was the first new recruit they'd had in two years. They dubbed him Mr. Weismuller, and someone found him a pencil and paper and they made him propaganda officer, responsible for recording their exploits in sketches. He could have a gun, the Duke said, when he'd proved himself reliable.

Lee soon had a chance to record an early success. The next week their platoon encountered a police patrol on the outskirts of a village and exchanged shots before retreating through the rubber trees. In the camp that evening, Lee drew Mr. Cooper kneeling behind a tree, sighting along his rifle. "A souvenir," Mr. Cooper said when he saw it. "When we win, I'll have it framed and hung in my shop." Lee smiled broadly.

The Duke took a long look at the picture and said that they would attack the village again the next day. Mr. Cooper looked up, surprised. "Don't look so worried," the Duke said. "They won't be expecting it."

He glanced back at the sketch and then at Lee. "Let's hope you can shoot better than you draw," he added, but Lee didn't look up.

When they attacked, they were again met with fire from the village, but this time the Duke ordered them not to fall back. The thin rubber trees offered shadows but scant cover. Mr. Chaplin was shot through the neck before Lee's horrified eyes, and they were dangerously pinned down for some minutes until Mr. Murphy outflanked the defenders. They were local police armed with aging rifles and pistols but not the machine guns of the British. Caught in a crossfire, they were forced to retreat, and for the first time in a month the Duke was able to lead his men into the village. Lee sat to one side, sketching the scene, while the Duke called the villagers to bring out food. The headman, Mr. Pang, came forward and told him that the police would arrest them if they helped terrorists. The Duke had him tied to a rubber tree at the edge of the plantation, paused a moment as if listening, and then hacked both his arms off at the elbow with his *parang*.

"Nothing," the Duke explained to the other villagers, "must come between the fighters and the people." The pencil had broken in Lee's hand, but the Duke lent him a pocket knife and waited patiently while he sharpened it. When he passed it back, Lee hoped the Duke wouldn't notice that his hand was shaking, but the Duke didn't say a word as he snapped the blade away.

Despite temporary successes, morale among the Silver Screen platoon by this time was beginning to fail. The British planters around the Ming plantation and then the authorities began to take notice of the fact that the Chinese-owned plantation went unattacked. The rubber tappers of the Ming estate were among the first to be resettled in New Villages. At first the men of the Silver Screen platoon joked that they would miss the daughters of the village, and then they began to miss the food. For a time they remained in the vicinity of the New Village — Kampong Coldstream, as it was called, after the British troops who guarded it. Sweethearts and other sympathizers within tried to smuggle them food, but the British were vigilant. They found rice in the frame of a boy's bicycle and even in the brassieres of girls going out to the plantation. "The best-tasting rice in the world," Mr. Cooper said ruefully when he told Lee about it.

The platoon began to spend more time hunting through the jungle for food, and their terrorist activity declined, causing dispute among them. The Duke argued that they should attack convoys for food. Mr. Cooper and Mr. Murphy insisted on leading them on long, exhausting foraging missions. Their uniforms, rotted by the damp, fell to rags around them as they gesticulated to one another. Knowing that he was an extra mouth to feed, Lee did not participate in these arguments, but he found himself wishing that they would follow the Duke's lead. The period before an attack, when the men would lie or crouch motionless for hours beside a road, was ideal for his work, and although the violence repulsed him, he couldn't deny that the sketches he had made of the Duke were some of the best he'd ever done. Even the Duke had commented on the improvement. On the odd occasions when Lee thought back to his paintings for the Savoy, he was gripped with embarrassment for their crude appeal.

In the end the men compromised. They spent a long month hunting for food in the jungle, and when that failed they began to attack villages further afield that had yet to be relocated by the British. In the first village, one man clasped his sack of rice to his chest when the Duke tried to pull it from him. He had a pregnant wife to feed, he said. The Duke had him bound and the wife brought out. This was the scene Lee drew: the woman with her belly cut open and the Duke taking the sack of rice from the man's limp hands. For a week afterward they ate well.

At Mr. Cooper's suggestion they tried to plant gardens in the jungle. The Duke watched the men bending over the rows, placing single grains of rice from their meager supplies in the soil with their thumb and first finger. "What are we?" he complained to Lee. "Are we gardeners?" He was looking through Lee's sketchbook, flicking past the scenes of the men at camp but studying the drawings of their fights. "Now that's a picture," he said, jabbing his finger at one, and Lee felt a flush of pride.

The Duke couldn't stop the planting, but he made the men carry their rifles at all times to remind them they were soldiers. They advanced up the rows bent double with their weapons slung across their backs, and the only sound was the occasional cursing when someone's gun slipped and cracked him on the elbow.

They had almost finished when they heard the drone of a British plane overhead. "Come on," the Duke cried. He pummeled the sore shoulders of the soldiers where they sat and dragged them to their feet. They ran bent over from the stiffness of so much planting, but he pushed them before him.

"What are you doing?" Mr. Cooper called. "Don't leave the gardens." He caught the Duke at the edge of the clearing and wrestled him to the ground. For a moment they rolled across the dug earth while the others stooped over them like old men. "Stop!" Mr. Cooper cried when he could free himself. "Listen! It's not a bomber, it's only a propaganda plane." Sure enough, when they listened, they heard only words falling from the sky.

"Comrades," the taped message began, "this is a fellow comrade speaking. I know how you are feeling. You are brave fighters, but you are hungry and tired. You are dirty. You are sick. I know it all. I was all of those things, but now I am well. I eat rice twice a day. I bathe every morning." Lee looked around him and saw the others gazing into the sky, their expressions rapt. "There is hope, comrades. We are all men. We all make mistakes. I made a mistake and put it right. So can you. It's not hard. Just walk to your nearest police station. There is one not far — "

"You idiots," the Duke broke in. "You imbeciles. Do you think those pilots are blind? Do you think they cannot look down into a jungle and see straight lines? There'll be bombers here in an hour."

"Save yourselves, comrades," the plane called. "Save yourselves before it's too late."

No one moved. Their eyes were fixed on the sky over the clearing. Lee turned too and shielded his eyes to look. He could hear the engines of the plane now very clearly, but he could not see it. Suddenly the sky filled with birds.

Not birds, he thought. Paper.

Thousands of sheets of paper were blowing across the treetops and fluttering into the clearing. Men began to rush out from the trees and clutch at them as if they were money. They hopped into the air, catching them in armfuls, stuffing their pockets with them, wadding them up and gripping them in their teeth to free their hands for more. Lee didn't know what they were doing, but he watched the others and did as they did.

"Catch me, comrades, catch me," the plane cried. "I'm falling. Catch me."

The Duke snatched at a sheet, missed, and flailed until he caught one. On it was a photograph of three smiling Chinese in neat outfits of shorts and singlets. They sat at a table and were surrounded by British soldiers. One of the soldiers was pouring tea, another held a bottle of rice wine. The table was covered in food. The Duke could clearly make out dishes of chicken's feet, fishhead curry, clay-pot bean curd, prawns with asparagus, char-siu pork, and

lemon chicken. The camera had been focused on the food rather
than the faces of the three men, but it was still clear that they were
smiling. None of them were eating, but each held out before him a
porcelain cup. At the top of the sheet were printed only two characters: *yam seng,* "Cheers."

"To you, comrades," said the plane. "A toast. To you."

Mr. Cooper was lost in thought. He was remembering the Allied
air drops that he had received in the jungle five years before. He
was remembering the taste of Bourneville chocolate, how the air
seemed filled with its rich, sweet scent as the canisters on their
parachutes wafted down to them. He didn't see the Duke raise his
gun, and he fell to the ground still smiling.

"Now, you dogs," the Duke cried. "We haven't much time. Get
down on your knees and dig."

He made them sift through the earth for the rice they had buried, but the only grains they could find were already germinating
and not fit to eat. Overhead, the voice of the plane receded. It was
chanting a list of rewards paid for communists brought in dead or
alive. The list was still echoing behind them as the Duke led them
away. Any terrorists leading their own comrades out of the jungle
were eligible for bounties of $500 or more per head. For platoon
leaders, the sums mounted dizzyingly into the thousands and tens
of thousands. For Politburo members, bounties of hundreds of
thousands of dollars were rumored. A last gust of wind high above
them carried the voice of the plane back to them once more.
"Think of it, comrades," it said. "Just think of it."

The Duke, in the trees, screamed back, "Forget Chin Peng! What
about me? What reward for the Duke?" And Lee drew him beating
his chest.

Shortly after this the British began sending patrols deeper into the
jungle, and it was one of these that the platoon encountered on
a humid June day in 1952. They were resting in a small clearing,
Lee sketching the men cleaning their weapons, when three British
troopers walked in on them. For a moment no one moved. Instinctively, Lee's pencil began the first stroke that would add the new-
comers to the scene. The troopers were only the advance guard of
their patrol, but despite being outnumbered, they reacted first. Mr.
Murphy was hit in the opening exchange, but the Duke, with Lee's

help, dragged him into the jungle. The Duke was about to return to the fight when the rest of the British entered the clearing and the remaining communists promptly surrendered.

Furious, the Duke watched his men being disarmed, roped together, and then fed. They said little, perhaps aware of their leader's eyes, but they ate eagerly. Lee feared that the Duke would attack the camp, but instead he hoisted Mr. Murphy onto his shoulder. Lee took a last look back at the line of roped men where they lay on the ground, smoking or sleeping, with their hands clasped over their stomachs, and then he was pulled away.

The Duke carried Mr. Murphy for hours even after he lost consciousness, but he died within the day and they buried him between the roots of a banyan tree. Then for almost two weeks the Duke and Lee wandered through the jungle. They hardly spoke to each other. They fought over what little food they could find. The stock of the Duke's rifle rotted in the damp and broke off when he put it to his shoulder. Lee had had to abandon his sketchbook at the camp, and he was reduced to sketching with a stick in the dust of the trail whenever they took a break. Everything he drew looked like food.

Finally, and quite by chance, they were picked up by another communist patrol. They found that they were almost two hundred miles north of their original base. The communists who found them took them to their commander, who fed them and supplied them with maps and food. He refused, however, to allow them to stay with his group. The Duke nodded sagely, but Lee threw himself to his knees before the commander.

"Please," he cried. "I'm a good comrade. Let me join you and be of more use to the party." The commander kicked him in the throat, and Lee couldn't speak for two days.

The Duke told him he'd been a fool but gave him a gun at last — an old carbine that the commander had spared them — and taught him to shoot, thinking it might encourage him.

Lee couldn't understand why the commander wouldn't let them join him. After they left the camp, he stumbled through the jungle in a daze, even though the Duke agreed to carry his pack for him. On the second evening, the Duke made him tea and told him that their mission was to return to their former area and reform their unit. Lee could only wail in disbelief.

"We have lost already. There is no one who will join us now."

The Duke only smiled at him and pulled from his pocket a grubby folded piece of paper. "Have courage," he said gently. It was a British leaflet — by this stage of the war over three billion had been dropped on the jungle — but instead of a photograph, a sketch was printed in the center. It took Lee a moment to recognize it as one of his. The commander of the unit who had encountered them had given the leaflet to the Duke. It listed communist leaders and the rewards for their capture. All the Politburo members were listed, and just below them the name Ming. The bounty was listed as $250,000. The Duke took the leaflet back and brandished it overhead with a flourish. "Fame," he whispered to Lee. "Fame!" he shouted into the jungle. "Who could resist joining me? Who could resist the allure of the Silver Screen platoon? We will be irresistible."

Two days later a train on the Kuala Lumpur–Penang line was flagged down by a ragged figure carrying a gun. Fearing an ambush, although the line had been safe for many months now, the engineer pulled up two hundred yards short of the man. The communist had to shout that he wanted to surrender, and he spun around and flung his gun in a high arc into the jungle. The engineer crept closer with the train and then braked again.

"What's that?" he shouted. "At your feet?"

"He was too heavy," came the reply. "It was the only way to claim the reward."

And Lee held up the severed head of the Duke.

The train took him to a police station in Ioph, where he had to wait for the constable in charge to come back from his rounds. When the man finally did return, he stood for one long moment looking at Lee and his prize. "Savages," he said at last. "I'm surrounded by savages." And he handed over a roll of brown paper. "Wrap that up at once."

Lee went on to record a number of propaganda messages for the sound planes and trucks of the British. He was also instrumental in setting up a theater group of surrendered communists who toured New Villages acting out short plays showing the errors of communism. He did not act in these himself but took the role of producer, with particular responsibility for scene painting. These activities were credited with the surrender of almost four hundred more communists, for which Lee enjoyed a share of the reward with his fellow artists. During this time the British authorities repeatedly warned him against sending any word to his family, but he did pass regular sums of money to his father via policemen he trusted, and for the first time in his life he was truly happy.

JUNOT DÍAZ

Ysrael

FROM STORY

I

WE WERE ON OUR WAY to the colmado for an errand, a beer for my tío, when Rafa stood still and tilted his head, as if listening to a message I couldn't hear, something beamed in from afar. We were close to the colmado; you could hear the music and the gentle clop of the drunken voices. I was nine that summer, but my brother was twelve, and he was the one who wanted to see Ysrael. Rafa looked out toward the mountains and said, We should pay that kid a visit.

II

Mami shipped me and Rafa to the campo every summer. She worked long hours at the chocolate factory and didn't have the time or the energy to look after us during the months school was out. Rafa and I stayed with our tíos in a small wooden house on the edge of Ocoa; rosebushes blazed around the yard like compass points, and the mango trees spread out deep blankets of shade where we could rest and play dominos, but the campo was nothing like our barrio in Santo Domingo. In the campo there was nothing to do, no one to see. You didn't get television or electricity and Rafa, who was older, woke up every morning pissy and dissatisfied. He stood on the patio in his shorts and looked out over the mountains, at the mists that gathered like water, at the brucal trees that blazed like fires on the hogbacks. This, he said, is shit.

Worse than shit, I said.

Yes, he said, and when I get home, I'm going to go crazy — chinga all my girls and then chinga everyone else's. I won't stop dancing, either. I'm going to be like those guys in the record books who dance four or five days straight.

Tío Miguel had chores for us (mostly we chopped wood for the smokehouse and brought water up from the river), but we finished these as easy as we threw off our shirts and had the rest of the day punching us in the face. We caught jaivas in the streams and spent hours walking across the valley to see girls who were never there; we set traps for rats we never caught and toughened up our roosters with pails of cold water. Back home in the capital, Rafa had his own friends, a bunch of tigres who liked to knock down our neighbors and who scrawled *chocha* and *toto* on walls. Back in the capital, he rarely said anything to me except Shut up.

If I was stupid enough to mouth off to him — about the hair that was growing on his back or the time the tip of his pinga had swollen to the size of a lemon — he pounded the hell out of me and then I would run as far as I could. Rafa and I fought so much that our neighbors took to smashing broomsticks over us to break it up, but in the campo it wasn't like that; in the campo we were friends.

The summer I was nine, Rafa shot whole afternoons talking about whatever chica he was getting with — not that the campo girls gave up ass like the girls back in the capital, but he told me that kissing them was pretty much the same. He'd take the campo girls down to the dams to swim and if he was lucky they let him put it in their mouths or in their asses. He'd done Yessica that way for almost a month before her parents heard about it and barred her from leaving the house.

He wore the same outfit when he went to see these girls, a shirt and pants that my father had sent him from the States the Christmas before. I always followed Rafa, trying to convince him to let me tag along.

Go home, he'd say. I'll be back in a few hours.

I'll walk you.

I don't need you to walk me anywhere. Just wait for me.

If I kept on he'd punch me in the shoulder and walk away until what was left of him was the color of his shirt filling in the spaces between the leaves. Something inside of me would sag like a sail. I would yell his name and he'd hurry on, the ferns and branches and flower pods trembling in his wake.

Later, while we were in bed listening to the rats on the zinc roof, he might tell me what he'd done. I'd hear about tetas and chochas and leche and he'd talk without looking over at me. There was a girl he'd gone to see, half Haitian, but he ended up with her mother. Another who believed she wouldn't get pregnant if she drank a Coke afterward. And one who was pregnant and didn't give a damn about anything. His hands were behind his head and his feet were crossed at the ankles. He was handsome and spoke out of the corner of his mouth. I was too young to appreciate his advice, but I listened to him like these things might be useful in the future.

III

Ysrael was a different story. Even on this side of Ocoa people had heard of him, how when he'd been a baby a pig had eaten his face off, skinned it like an orange. He was something to talk about, a name that set the kids to screaming.

I'd seen Ysrael my first time the year before, right after the dams had been finished. I was in town, farting around, when a single-prop plane swept in across the sky. A door opened on the fuselage and a man began to kick out tall bundles that exploded into thousands of leaflets as soon as the wind got to them. At first I thought maybe the paper would expand out behind the plane like smoke and then disappear, but the leaflets came down as slow as butterfly blossoms and the posters were of wrestlers, not politicians, and that was when the children began shouting. Usually the planes only covered Ocoa, but if extras had been printed the nearby towns would also get leaflets, especially if the match or the election was a big one.

I spotted Ysrael in an alley, stooping over a stack of leaflets that had not come undone from its thin cord. He was wearing his mask.

What are you doing? I said, and he answered, What do you think I'm doing?

He picked up the bundle and ran down the alley, away from me. Some of the other boys saw him and wheeled around howling, but he could run.

That's Ysrael! I was told. He's *ugly* and he's got a cousin around

here but we don't like him either. And that face of his would make
you *sick!*

I told my brother later, when I went home, and he sat up from his
bed. Could you see under the mask?

Not really.

That's something we got to check out. I hear it's bad.

The night before we went to look for Ysrael, Rafa couldn't sleep.
He kicked at the mosquito netting, and I could hear the mesh
tearing just a little. My tío was yukking it up with his buddies in the
yard. One of Tío's roosters had won big the day before, and Tío was
thinking of taking it to the capital. People around here don't bet
worth a damn, he was saying. Your average farmer only bets big
when he feels lucky, and how many of them feel lucky?

You're feeling lucky.

You're damn right about that. And that's why I have to find
myself some big spenders.

I wonder how much of Ysrael's face is gone, Rafa said.

He has his eyes.

That's a lot, he assured me. You'd think eyes would be the first
thing a pig would go for. Eyes are soft. And salty.

How do you know that?

I licked one, he said.

Maybe his ears, I answered.

And his nose. Anything that sticks out.

Everyone had a different opinion on the damage. Tío said it
wasn't bad but the father was very sensitive about anyone taunting
his oldest son, which explained the mask. Tía said if we were to look
on his face we would be sad for the rest of our lives. That's why the
poor boy's mother spends her day in church. I had never been sad
more than a few hours, and the thought of that sensation lasting a
lifetime scared the hell out of me. My brother kept pinching my
face during the night, like I was a mango. The cheeks, he said. And
the chin. But the forehead would be a lot harder. The skin's tight.

All right, I said.

The next morning the roosters were screaming. Me and Rafa
collected our shoes from the patio, careful not to step on piles of
cacao pods Tía had set out to dry. He went into the smokehouse
and emerged with his knife and two oranges. He peeled them and
handed me mine. When we heard Tía coughing in the house, we

started on our way. I kept expecting Rafa to send me home, and the longer he went without speaking, the more excited I became. I put my hands over my mouth to keep from laughing. We went slow, grabbing saplings and fence posts to stop from tumbling down the rough brambly slope. Smoke was rising from the fields that had been burned the night before, and the trees that had not exploded or collapsed stood in the black ash like spears. At the bottom of the hill we followed the road that would take us to Ocoa. I was carrying the Coca-Cola empties Tío had hidden in the chicken coop.

We joined two women, our neighbors, who were waiting by the colmado on their way to mass.

I put the bottles on the counter. Chicho folded up yesterday's *El Nacional.* When he put fresh Cokes next to the empties, I said, We want the refund.

Chicho put his elbows on the counter and looked me over. Are you supposed to be doing that?

Yes, I said.

You better be giving this money back to your tío, he said. I stared at the pastelitos and chicharrón he kept under a fly-specked glass. He slapped the coins onto the counter. I'm going to stay out of this, he said. What you do with this money is your own concern. I'm just a businessman.

How much of this do we need? I asked Rafa.

All of it.

Can't we buy something to eat?

Save it for a drink. You'll be real thirsty later.

Maybe we should eat.

Don't be stupid.

How about if I just bought us some gum?

Give me that money, he said.

Okay, I said. I was just asking.

Then stop. Rafa was looking up the road, distracted; I knew that expression better than anyone. He was scheming. Every now and then he glanced over at the two women, who were conversing loudly, their arms crossed over their big chests. When the first auto-bus trundled to a stop and the women got on, Rafa watched their asses bucking under their dresses. The cobrador leaned out from the passenger door and said, Well? And Rafa said, Beat it, baldy.

What are we waiting for? I said. That one had air conditioning.

I want a younger cobrador, Rafa said, still looking down the road. I went to the counter and tapped my finger on the glass case. Chicho handed me a pastelito, and after putting it in my pocket, I slid him a coin. Business is business, Chicho announced, but my brother didn't bother to look. He was flagging down the next autobus.

Get to the back, Rafa said. He framed himself in the main door, his toes out in the air, his hands curled up on the top lip of the door. He stood next to the cobrador, who was a year or two younger than he was. This boy tried to get Rafa to sit down but Rafa shook his head with that not-a-chance grin of his, and before there could be an argument the driver shifted into gear, blasting the radio. "La Chica de mi Escuela" was still on the charts. Can you believe that? the man next to me said.

They play that vaina a hundred times a day. I lowered myself stiffly into my seat but the pastelito had already put a grease stain on my pants. Fuck me, I said, and took out the pastelito and finished it in four bites. Rafa wasn't watching. Each time the autobus stopped he was hopping down and helping people bring on their packages. When a row filled he lowered the swing-down center seat for whoever was next. The cobrador, a thin big-eyed boy, was trying to keep up with him and the driver was too busy with his radio to notice what was happening. Two people paid Rafa — all of which Rafa gave to the cobrador, who was busy making change himself.

You have to watch out for stains like that, the man next to me said. He had big teeth and wore a clean fedora. His arms were ropy with muscles.

These things are too greasy, I said.

Let me help. He spit on his fingers and started to rub at the stain but then he was pinching at the tip of my pinga through the fabric of my shorts. He was smiling. I shoved him against his seat. He looked to see if anybody had seen.

You pato, I said.

The man kept smiling.

You low-down, pinga-sucking pato, I said. The man squeezed my biceps, quietly, hard, the way my friends would sneak me in church. I whimpered.

You should watch your mouth, he said.

I got up and went over to the door. Rafa slapped the roof, and as the driver slowed the cobrador said, You two haven't paid.

Sure we did, Rafa said, pushing me down into the dusty street. I gave you the money for those two people there and I gave you our fare too. His voice was tired, as if he got into these discussions all the time.

No, you didn't.

Fuck you, I did. You got the fares. Why don't you count and see? Don't even try it. The cobrador put his hand on Rafa but Rafa wasn't having it. He yelled up to the driver. Tell your boy to learn how to count.

We crossed the road and went down into a field of guineo; the cobrador was shouting after us and we stayed in the field until we heard the driver say, Forget them.

Rafa took off his shirt and fanned himself and that's when I started to cry.

He watched for a moment. You, he said, are a pussy.

I'm sorry.

What the hell's the matter with you? We didn't do anything wrong.

I'll be okay in a second. I sawed my forearm across my nose.

He took a look around, drawing in the lay of the land. If you can't stop crying, I'll leave you. He headed toward a shack that was rusting in the sun.

I watched him disappear. From the shack you could hear voices, as bright as chrome. Columns of ants had found a pile of meatless chicken bones at my feet and were industriously carting away the crumbling marrow. I could have gone home, which was what I usually did when Rafa acted up, but we were far — eight, nine miles away.

I caught up with him beyond the shack. We walked about a mile; my head felt cold and hollow.

Are you done?

Yes, I said.

Are you always going to be a pussy?

I wouldn't have raised my head if God himself had appeared in the sky and pissed down on us.

Rafa spit. You have to get tougher. Crying all the time. Do you think our papi's crying? Do you think that's what he's been doing the last six years? He turned from me. His left foot was crackling through the weeds, breaking stems.

Rafa stopped a schoolboy in his blue-and-tan uniform, who then pointed us down a road. Rafa spoke to a young mother, whose baby was hacking like a miner. A little farther, she said, and when he smiled she looked the other way. We went too far and a farmer with a machete showed us the easiest loop back. Rafa stopped when he saw Ysrael standing in the center of a field; he was flying a kite and despite the string he seemed almost unconnected to the distant wedge of black that finned back and forth in the sky. Here we go, Rafa said. I was embarrassed. What the hell were we supposed to do?

Stay close, he said. And get ready to run. He passed me his knife, then trotted down toward the field.

IV

The summer before, I pegged Ysrael with a rock, and the way it bounced off his back, I knew I'd clocked a shoulder blade.

You did it! You fucking did it! the other boys yelled.

He'd been running from us and he arched in pain and one of the other boys nearly caught him but he recovered and took off. He's faster than a mongoose, someone said, but in truth he was faster even than that. We laughed and went back to our baseball game and forgot him until he came to town again and then we dropped what we were doing and chased him, howling. Show us your face. Let's see it just once.

V

He was about a foot taller than either of us and looked like he'd been fattened on that supergrain the farmers around Ocoa were giving their stock. Ysrael's sandals were of stiff leather and his clothes were North American. I looked over at Rafa but my brother seemed unperturbed.

Listen up, Rafa said. My hermanito's not feeling too well. Can you show us where a colmado is? I want to get him a drink.

There's a faucet up the road, Ysrael said. His voice was odd and full of spit. His mask was hand-sewn from thin blue cotton fabric and you couldn't help but see the scar tissue that circled his left eye, a red waxy crescent, and the saliva that trickled down his neck.

We're not from around here. We can't drink the water.

Ysrael spooled in his string. The kite wheeled but he righted it with a yank.

Not bad, I said.

We can't drink the water around here. It would kill us. And he's already sick.

I smiled and tried to act sick, which wasn't too difficult. I was covered with dust and I saw Ysrael looking us over.

The water here is probably better than up in the mountains, he said.

Help us out, Rafa said in a low voice.

Ysrael pointed down a path. Just go that way, you'll find it.

Are you sure?

I've lived here all my life.

I could hear the plastic kite flapping in the wind; the string was coming in fast. Rafa huffed and started on his way. We made a long circle and by then Ysrael had his kite in hand — it was no hand-made local job.

We couldn't find it, Rafa said.

How stupid are you?

Where did you get that? I said.

Nueva York, he said. From my father.

No shit! Our father's there too! I shouted.

I looked at Rafa, who, for an instant, frowned. Our father only sent us letters and an occasional shirt or pair of jeans at Christmas.

What the hell are you wearing that mask for, anyway? Rafa asked.

I'm sick, Ysrael said.

It must be real hot.

Not for me.

Don't you take it off?

Not until I get better. I'm going to have an operation soon.

You better watch out for that, Rafa said. Those doctors will kill you faster than the Guardia.

These are American doctors.

Rafa sniggered. You're lying.

I saw them last spring. They want me to go next year.

They're lying to you. They probably just felt sorry.

Do you want me to show you where the colmado is or not?

Sure.

Follow me, he said, wiping the spit on his neck. At the colmado he stood off while Rafa bought me the cola. The owner was playing dominoes with the beer delivery man and didn't bother to look up, though he put a hand in the air for Ysrael. He had that lean look of every colmado owner I'd ever met.

On the way back to the road I left the bottle with Rafa to finish and caught up with Ysrael, who was ahead of us. Are you still into wrestling? I asked.

He turned to me and something rippled under the mask. How did you know that?

I heard, I said. Do they have wrestling in the States?

I hope so.

Are you a wrestler?

I'm a great wrestler. I almost went to fight in the capital.

My brother laughed, swigging on the bottle.

You want to try it, pendejo?

Not right now.

I didn't think so.

I tapped his arm. The planes haven't dropped anything this year. It's still too early. The first Sunday of August is when it starts.

How do you know?

I'm from around here, he said. The mask twitched. I realized he was smiling, and then my brother brought his arm around and smashed the bottle on top of his head. It exploded, the thick bottom spinning away like a crazed eyeglass, and I said, Holy fucking shit. Ysrael stumbled once and slammed into a fence post that had been sunk into the side of the road. Glass crumbled off his mask. He spun toward me, then fell on his stomach. Rafa kicked him in the side. Ysrael seemed not to notice. He had his hands flat in the dirt and was concentrating on pushing himself up. Roll him on his back, my brother said, and we did, pushing like crazy. Rafa took off his mask and threw it spinning into the grass.

His left ear was a nub and you could see the thick-veined slab of his tongue through a hole in his cheek. He had no lips. His head was tipped back and his eyes had gone white and the cords stood out on his neck. He'd been an infant when the pig had come into the house. I jumped back and said, Please, Rafa, let's go! Rafa crouched and using only two of his fingers, turned Ysrael's head from side to side.

VI

We went back to the colmado, where the owner and the delivery man were now arguing, the dominoes chattering under their hands. We kept walking and after one hour, maybe two, we saw an autobus. We boarded and went right to the back. Rafa crossed his arms and watched the fields and roadside shacks scroll past, the dust and smoke and people almost frozen by our speed.

Ysrael will be okay, I said.

Don't bet on it.

They're going to fix him.

A muscle fluttered between his jawbone and his ear. Yunior, he said tiredly. They aren't going to do shit to him.

How do you know?

I know, he said.

I put my feet on the back of the chair in front of me, pushing on an old lady, who turned and glared at me. She was wearing a baseball cap and one of her eyes was milky. The autobus was heading for Ocoa, not for home.

Rafa signaled for a stop. Get ready to run, he whispered.

Okay, I said.

STEPHEN DIXON

Sleep

FROM HARPER'S MAGAZINE

SEVERAL PEOPLE wanted to see him to his car after the burial but
he said, "No, I'd like to walk to it by myself, I don't know why. Do
you mind? And everyone has a ride back? Good. Then thanks for
coming, and I guess I'll be seeing you." He was thinking of sleep
even then, during the short walk. How in maybe an hour, or two to
three, he'll be in bed, under or on top of the covers, phone off the
hook or in some way disconnected, curtains closed. Moments after
she died, or maybe a minute after, but anyway, almost the first thing
he thought once he realized she was dead was "Now I can sleep
better." Or was it "Now I can get some sleep"? Now in the car he
thinks, "What'll be my procedure for today, and one day at a time
after that?" He'll go home, park, pick up the newspaper somewhere
around the carport where it's always delivered, go in the house,
take off his shoes, the tie of course, he won't get the mail, prepare a
scotch on ice with his usual splash of water — a big scotch, so a
couple of splashes: he wants to sleep — sit in his chair in the living
room with the paper and read it while sipping the drink, not let
himself go to pieces, maybe only one section, maybe the whole
paper except the business section. That one he never reads unless it
has something he's interested in continued from the first page.
He'll start with the arts, food, science, and home section, the every-
thing-but-news section, he calls it. It's usually light, uncomplicated,
plenty of photos and reviews and sort of timeless articles, will be
easy to read and maybe even distracting. He won't read the obituary page. It's never in the everything-but section, which may be why
he thinks he'll only read that one. Or maybe he will read it. Hers

will be there, or should, since he placed it yesterday and in plenty of time. "Hello," he said on the phone soon after he got home from the hospital and got the number out of the newspaper, "I'd like to place an obituary for one Wanda Monterra. Would you like me to spell it?" "Eventually, yes," the woman said, "but first let me have yours and how we should bill it." He started rambling on about what he wanted to put in and how he'd like it worded. The woman helped him. "'Loving wife of Courtney Patton,' okay?" "Fine," he said, "but the flowers." "Well, it could be 'in lieu of flowers,' or just 'no flowers,' or something about contributions to charities instead of flowers," and he said, "Come to think of it, none of that. I'd like to keep it short, only the essentials, and not to save money; just that that's how I think an obit should be: who it is, where and what day and time it is, and who survived, I don't know why. Meaning, I don't know why I think an obit should be like this." But when she died, in his arms, in the hospital, she was already dead. Of course she was dead if she'd died, but he means he saw her in the bed looking dead, rushed to her, held her in his arms, first lifted her up from the waist, he means from under her arms till she was sitting up straight from the waist and of course only with his support, and then held her in his arms. She was cold, motionless, lifeless, her eyes were closed, body seemed cold, she had that look he was told in a matter of days to expect, her skin becoming what they also said to expect. He thought, "My darling" — thought this then — "now I can sleep better." Or "Now I can get some sleep." Both sound right but he only thought one of them. And did he say it rather than think it? He doesn't know, and could be he did both. And it wasn't a hard thought or remark, was it? Meaning, not a cold one, a deliberately self-centered thoughtless one, was it? One could even say that at the time he said or thought it he was in some kind of shock. Probably, but probably not.

Meaning, one could say that, but he wasn't.

Now he's home, in the living room in his favorite chair, didn't get the paper, no, got the paper but not the mail. Way he sees it, won't get it for days. Phone disconnected? — forgets but thinks he did, drink in his hand, double scotch with a double splash, unopened newspaper in his lap. It was only yesterday, wasn't it? Knows it was only yesterday, and it wasn't a hard thought or remark, was it? and knows if he knows anything that he wasn't in any kind of shock. He'd taken care of her for months, so was prepared. Well, even then one could still not be, meaning that right up to the last minute and despite every kind of preparation for or against it, one still doesn't know. Meaning . . . well, he knows what. Took care of her for four years or more, five, six, at home, in the hospital, mostly at home but the last year or so each time a little more in the hospital, always by her side when she was home and sometimes in a bed beside hers in the hospital. He could have moved to another room at home. They had two bedrooms and a study that could be turned into one, but he continued to sleep with her. She made such noises at home. Not just snores and groans. He liked to joke about it with her if he thought she was in the right mood for it, though sometimes if he was feeling cross or exhausted because her noises had kept him up the previous night, he joked about it even when he knew her mood was sour or dark, but she never found it funny, no matter how well he thought he'd gauged that her mood was good. "My hibernating Siberian bear — that's what you sounded like last night." "I'm not laughing," she said. Another time: "Really, you slept like a groveling warthog last night, and you rolled over like one too. You thrashed and spit and chomped as if you were eating bark or slop." "Screw you too," she said, "for it should be obvious I can't help it, and you think your blowing and snorting doesn't keep me up?" "Nothing like yours does, because nothing could be louder, and it just kept coming. I felt like leaving the room and sleeping in the guest room or on the couch." "So why didn't you? I only wish I could do that when you wheeze and grunt through half the night. But it'd mean struggling for an hour to get there if I didn't have your help. And if I fell down on the way and you didn't hear me because you were sleeping so soundly, I'd be there till morning." "You're just saying I make noises like that, or if I do, then saying I do it as much as you, to get back at me; but all right, I understand. But it's also that I get anxious every night I go to sleep, thinking I won't get any rest for the next day." "You get plenty; you sleep more than your fill. It's me who's starving for it and needs it much more than you. But as I said, sleep somewhere else if you don't like my moving around in bed and my sounds. And if you do want to sleep with me or just in this bed here, put up with it best you can. But not, which you like to do, wake me by jabbing or stabbing my back or yelling in my ear." "I only do that, and never that hard or loud, to stop you from making those noises; otherwise I'd never get any sleep." Another time: "It seemed like a whole barnyard of animals was sleeping on your side of the bed last night: mooing, whistling, growling, snarling, clicking, snapping, barking, and squalling, besides what seemed like blubbery bubbles popping out of your mouth and nose." "Thank you, oh thank you, but don't give me that crap you couldn't get any sleep again. I got up several times to go potty — I wish I didn't but my stupid body makes me — and you were dead asleep like a baby each time." "I was pretending," he said. "More lies." And he said, "That's what you'd like to believe, and I'm not going to start contradicting you now. Last thing I want, after everything else, is another big argument and you crying away with real fat tears. For the next hour just forget I'm alive." She said something to that but he forgets what. Tonight he'll sleep. Hasn't slept much the last three weeks, but tonight he thinks he will only because he's so tired and what's there now to stop him? Four nights ago she was up all night, coughing, breathing hard, complaining of pain. Took her to the hospital the following morning. Next two nights he slept in the hospital, in a chair in her room or in the visitors' lounge on a chair or couch. They weren't really sleeps. Her noises were very loud when he tried sleeping in her room, and the lounge was cold, and the couch, which was more like a long board with thin plastic cushions on it, was uncomfortable, maybe not so much for sitting but definitely for sleeping on, which might have been what the hospital had in mind when they bought it.

"Do you want to mention surviving parents?" the newspaper obituary person said. "Or even grandparents or children, if there are any?" "Oh yes, her parents," and gave their names. "No grandparents or children, though. We couldn't have any — children, I mean." "I'm sorry," she said, and he said, "Oh, it wasn't a problem for us, and I apologize if I said it in a way to make you feel it was, for we didn't mind no kids. Short as it was, we had a nice life together, thought of each other as soulmates till she got ill. Meaning, we had a nice life together till she got ill, and even after that it was okay, and we were for the most part soulmates till she got very ill. Then we were still pretty good to each other, but as you can imagine, it became very hard on us both." "I'm sorry," she said. Friends wanted to go home with him, and his wife's sister. He forgot to put her name in the obit but she'll understand, if she even sees it, since she should already be on the train home by now and she probably also, like most people, doesn't read newspapers from any city but her own. He said to all of them he wanted to be alone today. He'll sleep, have a drink, have a drink first and then sleep, have two or three drinks, but anyway he'll be all right, so don't worry, he said. Tomorrow too and for the days to come, if they don't mind, till he phones them, if he does, or contacts them in some way. "Oh, do," they said. "A letter maybe," he said. "Whichever way you choose." And he said he would. "You know you can come to our house for dinner any night you want," one friend of theirs said. "Several nights a week even, and for as many weeks as you like. The invitation's open and open-ended." "I know," he said. His in-laws flew in from their city and were flying back soon after the funeral. Nice people. He said goodbye to them at the gravesite and while he was kissing their cheeks he thought, "I'll probably never see them again." It must have been very tough on them the last few days. Of course, what's he saying? And of course for him too.

He sips his drink, opens the paper, starts to pull out the everything-but section, then thinks, "Oh, go to the obits, you know you're curious." Curious? Well, something. He just wants to see, her name, his, together, his right after hers. "Just 'husband,'" he told the newspaper obit woman, "for 'loving' goes without saying, or should. And even if it didn't apply, though in my case it did, it had to have at the start or some part of anybody's marriage, wouldn't you say? And who am I trying to impress with that word anyway?" "That's not why people include it." And he said, "Then why, can you tell me? I've always been interested, or have occasionally, when I've read obituaries, or maybe only one other time but today," and she said, "Lots of reasons, too many to go into, for everyone seems to have his own." A little part of him also wants to see if the obit came out the way he wanted or if the woman didn't instinctively insert a few of those loving and adoring adjectives. No, they're pros, so they wouldn't do that, and they also know the customer pays by the word so might object to anything extra. And then to tear it out. Rather, fold it over in four places and then cut it at the seams carefully. That's what he really wants to do most and maybe even without reading it. For if he doesn't cut it out now he might forget for later and then he won't have it, the paper having gone out with the trash or, if he continues to do some of the same routines he did before she died, the biweekly paper pickup for recycling. And where should he put it after he cuts it out? Little things like that get quickly lost. In the intricately carved Indian wooden box on the fireplace mantel where he already has a pair of cufflinks from when he was a teenager and a gold tie pin from then too with only his three initials on it and some marbles from when he was even younger that his mother found behind her stove twenty years ago when she had it replaced and a couple of his baby teeth, "two of your first three," she said, "though I can't say for sure if either of these is your very first," a metal token from a board game he had when he was around ten, the marriage announcement his in-laws placed in their local paper of his wife and him and her photo, and — who knows? — years from now, two, three, he'll see the obit folded up in the box and look at it as he did the marriage announcement a few days ago, though that one he did intentionally, and remember this day, the funeral, burial, walking from the grave to the car by himself, how he cut the obit out, what gave him the idea to do it — what did? — even him sitting here. So he opens the paper to the obituaries, finds hers, and reads. Everything got in right. The woman was a lot of help. Doesn't say anything about sleep or the need for it. For some reason he thought he put something about it in. He should have, for himself only, no matter how strange it would have seemed to anyone reading it. But why? Well, so years or a year from now when he takes it out of the box and reads it for the first time since today he'll recall his thoughts now about sleep. Not enough reason to risk seeming so senseless, and the newspaper obit woman would never have let him put it in if he'd wanted to and was willing to pay, let's say, even triple the charge. They have standards to maintain that money can't buy. They can't have oddballs and brooders and loonies and practical jokers horsing around or making light of or acting crazy on what should be a solemn page. Most people take the obits quite seriously, and there are many who read them every day, and some where it's the first thing they turn to in the paper. They've told him, at least one or two have, how it makes life for them seem more poignant, or meaningful, or fragile, or something along those lines. Especially

the paid obits that say "surviving parents and grandparents," for
that says something about the deceased's age.
They should have had children. He means he wishes they had
had them, his wife and he. Sure, it would have been sad for a child
to see his or her mother die, but he would have had these kids or at
least one to be with after. He might even be taking care of them this
minute instead of sitting here thinking about them. Making them
lunch, or taking them out for lunch, or lunch home and then going
to the park with them perhaps, places they'd like to go, like the zoo
or merry-go-round or both, and then to someplace in the park for
a snack, or nearby for dinner if it's around that time. Trying to
distract them from their mother's death, is what he's saying, while
at the same time using them to take his mind off it too, rather than
him drinking here alone, paper in his lap, place quiet, shades
down, windows shut, curtains closed, chair he's in lit by a floor lamp
in a room usually flooded at this time with natural daylight. Oh,
best he cut the obit out now, and he tears that page of the paper
out, creases the part around the obit, then thinks, "Too slow, it's
going to tear anyway, or might, paper's so frail," and rips the obit
out, tears off little pieces till the area around it is a square, and puts
it on the side table next to him. No, he might spill his drink on it, or
the next one, or almost certainly the one after that. Or it might be
blown off the table when he just walks past it, or from the little
breeze he makes when he stands, and then get lost under the couch
or something and maybe when he next sees it in a month or two
he'll have, without really looking at it, forgotten what it is, or he'll
remember or read it but it'll be so covered with dust balls and stuff
that he'll just throw it away, though regret that he did later. "Put it
in a safe spot now," he thinks, "and you'll know you have it," and he
gets up and sticks it in the mantel box and then sits again in the
same chair.

So where was he? Children he doesn't have. He'd see to them for
sure. He'd do everything he could for them, try to be both parents,
whatever that means. He would have been such a good father, he's
almost sure of it. He'd probably cry a lot with them; over their
mother, he means. They'd be crying, or intermittently, how could
they not be? and he'd start in too when he saw them that way. He
wouldn't be thinking of sleeping, he doesn't think. Or maybe just
thinking of it but with no immediate plans to carry it out. He'd be

too busy doing other things. He also wouldn't think of cutting out
the obituary. Wouldn't want it around to remind them of their
mother, if they found it. Well, instead he could put it in his wallet,
to take out and look at when he wants, but it'd be in shreds in a
couple of weeks. He's found that newspaper clippings don't last
long there and magazine articles or pieces he's cut out of them do
just a little better.

He did think of sleeping when she died, though. Right after it, he
means. Thought it right after. He held her in his arms. Picked her
up, lifted her from behind. He was facing her, standing up but
leaning over, and put his arms under her and held her back up as
he lifted her toward him. He was standing, or sitting up on the end
of the bed, he forgets which. At the edge of it, he means, and if
there then he would have had to lower the side rail first and he
doesn't remember doing that. The side rail was always up except
when a nurse or aide was changing the bed. So, standing, most
likely. Yes, standing, definitely; it makes sense and it's what he
pictures too. "She's like a rag doll," he thought then, when he was
holding her up. No, he thought that later. No, he thought it then
but told a friend about it at the funeral home that night. "I picked
her up." This was only last night. He can hardly believe it: just last
night. "I picked her up. Lifted her away from the bed. I knew she
was dead. Knew it beforehand, knew it now. She was like a rag doll
in my arms. I know that isn't an original thought or comparison or
whatever it is for what she was but it is what I thought." He didn't
tell this friend that the first thing he thought or said aloud to
himself after he looked at her and thought she was dead was "She's
dead, now I can get some sleep." Or "Now I'll get some sleep." Or "I
can sleep better now" or "Now I can sleep better now that she's
dead" or "I'll be able to." Or was it "Now that she's dead I'm going
to get a lot of sleep"? Or "I'm so tired I'm going to bed right after
the burial and sleep for I don't know how long. A day, I mean a
whole one, or maybe two."

He must have known he wouldn't sleep the night of the day she
died. Wouldn't sleep that night, he means. There were still lots of
things to do and so many things running around in his head, and
where could he sleep, since he wouldn't be home or at least for
sleep till the next day? Then he left the hospital room and went

down the hall. Though first he rested her back on the bed, set her
down with her back back on the bed, just put her back down the
same way she was before he lifted her. He let her down, that's all,
meaning, he put her down, or set her down, and right after that he
kissed her lips. Wanted to do it then before things in her body really
started changing. He was told to expect that too. Of course they
were already changing but weren't yet visible, or to him. Well, to no
one so far, for he was the only one in the room. "Do it now," he told
himself. He definitely remembers saying that, and aloud. "Do it
now, for you're going to do it sometime before you bury her." And
then bent down and kissed her. He didn't press hard with his lips;
he just let them rest on hers for a few seconds. He forgets what hers
felt like, or never recorded the impression — the impression in his
mind, he means — and he also probably closed his eyes — he always did when he kissed; hers had been closed for two days, at least
every time he looked at them — and went outside her room — it
was a private one — shut the door — he didn't want other people
looking in — and went to the nurses' station and said, "I think my
wife died, Wanda Monterra, or Mrs. Patton, you might have her
down as. In fact, I'm almost sure she's dead — I'm positive, really.
She shows all the signs you told me, or some other nurses did, to
look out for — room 823. Please see to her right away." He rushed
back to the room. He doesn't know why he rushed. After all, she
was dead. Maybe because she was alone and he didn't want to leave
her that way; he didn't know why or whom it'd hurt, but something
told him it was wrong. But he thinks he thought then, "Maybe
there'll be a miracle and she'll be alive when I get back, even
beginning to recover. Maybe my kiss did it. That it was all she
needed to pop out of it. What am I thinking of? She's dead, she's
dead, so start getting used to it." He thinks he thought all that but
maybe in different words or with some of the same. A couple of
nurses, doctors, and aides — in other words, several people, maybe
six or seven — barged into the room a minute later, so it took them
about two minutes to come from the time he told the nurse at the
station. They quickly sent him out.

Later, he went to a public pay phone on the floor and called his
wife's parents and a funeral home. First he waited outside her room
for the medical team to come out. A few minutes later two nurses
came out and walked past him and he caught up with them down

the hall and said, "She's dead, my wife, in 823, isn't she?" and the nurse said, "Sorry, I didn't see you. One of the doctors will speak to you when he's through in there. Just stop him." He went back to the door and opened it, wanted to see what they were doing, if they were trying to revive her, if they were only cleaning her up, and an aide standing by the door inside said, "Something you want?" "I'm her husband." And the aide said, "Oh, excuse me. We're not ready yet; soon." A doctor came out about five minutes later, went straight to him, and said, "We thought it would be today, didn't we? We talked about it, you and I, I'm nearly sure I recall that. I knew, at least, it'd be soon: today, tomorrow, or the next day. I think that's what we said, so it's not we're surprised she died today; the medical staff, I'm saying." He asked what he should do now and the doctor said, "You can go in; everyone will leave. Then when you're done you can make your phone calls to people and to the funeral home you have in mind, but because we have some more work to do in here, from one of the phones down the hall. While you're doing that — phoning, I'm saying — your wife will be taken to another place downstairs, so don't be alarmed if you don't see her in here when you return. Though you might see her. Sometimes we don't get things done as fast as we want." He went into the room; the bed had been remade, covers pulled up to her neck and tucked over, her arms evenly by her sides. He lifted her hands and kissed them, said, "Goodbye, my dear." Of course he cried, a little, a lot. In fact, he thinks he broke down; yes, he broke down, so much so that if someone had been there he's sure he would have collapsed or fallen or done something like that into that person's arms. Because no one was there — well, of course someone was, but he knows what he means — he thinks he had to hold on to something to stop him from collapsing: the bed rail or headboard. He tries to picture himself then. He thinks he actually braced his hand against the wall to keep standing, then sat in the chair by her bed and looked at her and left.

He went to the pay phone down the hall and called the funeral home. Then he called her parents in the hotel they were at, hoping they were in. He didn't want to leave a message and have to call again and again. They took it badly. He realizes now he should have called them first and doesn't know why he didn't. There was no rush for the funeral home to send a hearse over for the body. She first had to be examined and there were some documents he had to sign, the doctor had told him, and the hospital was also going to remove a couple of her parts. Her parents had been there that morning and left an hour before she died, telling him they were coming back with their daughter that evening. Their other daughter, he of course means. He hopes he didn't offend or hurt them when he said he'd just got through speaking to the funeral home, which they must have picked up meant he hadn't called them first. Anyway, that's the order he made his calls yesterday, next calling a few friends and coworkers of theirs to tell other friends and coworkers that her funeral will be tomorrow at the Clementz Funeral Home sometime around noon, look for the obituary in the paper for the exact time. He of course first told these people that his wife had died. Then he returned to her room, but the bed was empty and stripped and the linen was in a pile on the floor. He thinks, "Did they remake her bed with fresh linen just for the short time I'd be in the room with her after the doctors and nurses left?" He means, did they remake it only for the time he'd be in there alone? He didn't ask anyone at the hospital if that was so, but if it was it was very considerate of them but probably unnecessary. But it's just linen, probably washed with a ton of other linen in a big vat somewhere in the hospital and not thrown out, so what's the difference? Then he went home, thought of having a scotch but made himself coffee, placed the obit in the paper, said he'd call back in an hour or so with the exact funeral time. Phone rang a number of times but he didn't answer. "Couldn't speak to anyone now," he thought, "just couldn't," and suppose it was someone who wanted a contribution of some sort or was trying to sell him something? A gravesite, for instance. They've called for that, maybe more calls for it than for anything else they're selling. "We don't plan to die," he used to tell them. "We're both very healthy, and besides I don't like these calls coming to my home." Then: "We got two graves that were part of a friend's plot, all we need, so no thank you, and I also have to tell you I don't at all like these calls coming to my home." Changed his clothes, brushed his teeth, thought about shaving but didn't see any reason to. Now he has almost a two-day growth, or is it three? and it doesn't feel itchy, so he'll shave sometime after he wakes up. He's certainly not going to grow a beard. She always wanted him to, or said she thought he might look good in one and only way to find

out was to grow it. Went to the funeral home to choose a casket and
see to some details of the funeral: flowers, officiator — he had
none, so they said they'd get someone for him. She was there by
now, and he waited in the lobby while they worked on her, called
the newspaper with the exact time of the funeral and where the
burial would be, and when the funeral people had her ready he sat
by her casket in the sitting room reserved for her. Some friends and
her family came, sat beside him awhile, tried talking to him but he
wasn't talking. He knew it was just as sad for them, but in different
ways — after all, she was a loved woman and very close to her family
— but nothing he could say could help them and they couldn't
help him. Her mother asked if she could have the casket opened
for a few minutes, and he nodded and left the room. Spent the
night in the sitting room with the casket. Tried sleeping sitting up
on the couch there but only got a half an hour in. He didn't sleep
well, little there was of it. Of course she made no noises. Now that's
a terrible joke. It's not a joke. He means, it wasn't meant as one and
he doesn't know why he said it or what it is. It just came out. Out in
his head, if that's possible. He said it seriously. Said it in his head,
he's saying. He made noises, though. Not while he was sleeping,
he means, though he could have. Things like "Oh, my dear . . . My
darling . . . Oh, my gosh . . ." Not noises really. Just things he said
aloud once everyone was gone. He didn't cry, though. Doesn't
know why. He can't say he did all his crying in the hospital after she
died or over the last two days or three. Memories flooded through
him like crazy in the sitting room. He'd think some of these would
have started his crying, but they didn't. So leave it at that, for who
can explain such things, and why does he think they need explaining anyway? And while he slept, that half an hour, he also saw her
doing things she'd done before she got sick, so maybe he wasn't
even sleeping then. Early next morning — meaning, this morning,
morning of this day, which is still amazing to him; really, still — he
went to a nearby restaurant for coffee and a muffin. Then, back
at the home, he asked one of the funeral directors if they provided toothbrushes and toothpaste. He suspected they did, for the
people who stayed overnight, just as he suspected enough people
stayed the night beside the caskets to warrant the home getting
a large supply of toothbrushes and toothpaste, and he was right.
He wanted his mouth to smell clean. He didn't want to make the
funeral any worse for guests who had to go through what they felt

they had to with him, kissing, hugging, getting their faces close. And he only had the muffin because his stomach was growling and he didn't want to make noises during the service. Then he went back to the sitting room, and after the casket was wheeled into the chapel, spoke a few minutes to the officiator about his wife: where and when she was born, names of her parents and sister, schools she attended and professions she had, facts like that, plus two or three things she used to do to entertain herself: books, classical music, cook — and at eleven or so . . . actually, the funeral was scheduled to start at eleven-fifteen and it did, on the dot. He yawned through a lot of it, at one point during the officiator's long opening remarks found himself falling asleep, but everyone must have known why or could guess.

Now he'll sleep though, for real. He's home, whole thing's over. House is his; paper's his also. He doesn't, he means, have to divide it up every morning as he used to do before she got very sick or read the everything-but section to her when she couldn't sit up in bed, nor from now on think of moving to another room because of the noises she makes. He'll buy half as much food now. Well, he's been doing that for months. "You've got to eat something," he used to say, "you've got to — please, if only for me . . . Well, if you can't, you can't, what can we do?" Won't buy milk because he doesn't drink it; she did, at the end by the spoonful, or tried to, so most of the quarts he bought went to waste. He won't buy lots of things, and he'll throw away lots too. All her clothes; he means he'll give them away. Her catalogues. She had a few hundred of them, and they'll be coming three a day maybe for the next year or two; maybe until he moves. He didn't want to tell the officiator that reading through catalogues was another of her great pleasures; it just wasn't something he wanted said. "In the end they paid off, didn't they?" she said. "For it's much easier ordering by phone than trying to get me to a store." Made sense; he never argued it didn't. If he had any complaint it was she had several boxes of them in the bedroom in addition to all her medical things, so there was little space for him to maneuver around in the dark or anytime wheel her out of the room. A couple of chairs she liked and he didn't — out. Lamp he hated, some things on the walls, and of course all those medical supplies. He won't feed the birds the way she did, filling up feeders every third day and the last three months having him do it, so they'll go too but on their own. He also won't take care of her fruit trees and flower beds. He'll mow the grass only when it's absolutely necessary and water around a little if the grounds look particularly dry, but that's about it. Maybe in time he'll get rid of the house too: sell it. Move into a small apartment. But right now, or soon, sleep. He held her in his arms and said, "Now I can sleep," or one of the others. Held her up, in a sitting position, as he said. He did what he could, took care of her fairly well, did his best, is what he's saying; and that's something — nobody could argue with that, not that anyone would, so why's he bringing it up? He cooked for her, dressed her, changed her bed every other day for months, sponge-bathed her daily, gave her shampoos the hard way, with her head lowered back into a basin, and sat behind her for thirty minutes holding the hair dryer to her hair. "You know," he said, "if you cut your hair to just shoulder length, not that I want you to, it'd probably save me an hour's work a week." Took her out for air in her wheelchair. Took her to places, not just for strolls in the park or on the street — restaurants, coffee shops, public gardens, museums. Tried to make things interesting and normal for her. Got her books from libraries and bookstores, and when she could no longer read, books on tape. Who'll do their income taxes now? That'll be a problem when the time comes around for it, which is a month from now, since he has no head for figures and following written directions and he'd hate spending money on an accountant. Fed her when she had to be fed, made her fresh dishes every day though she ate very little of them, gave her injections, cleaned her up after each bowel movement, did a wash a day at least, sometimes pulled her in her wheelchair up ten steps, twenty, once to a party four flights up but thank goodness some of the guests helped him carry her in the chair downstairs. He did just about everything, he's saying, though he's not boasting, or doesn't think he is. Well, who's to boast to anyway? When he was at work he called her every hour. "How are things?" "Fine." "Feeling all right?" "Good as can be expected." "Anything wrong?" "No, I'm okay." "I shouldn't worry?" "Don't be silly." "You're feeling better then?" "Than what?" "I didn't mean that than, but the other one." "I'm feeling the same." "I'll leave here soon as I can." "Don't hurry for me." "But I want to." "So, good, I like having you home, and it does make things easier." "See ya, sweetheart." "Bye, dear."

Oh, he's going to miss her. He won't be able to sleep. He

shouldn't have cut out the obit. He should have kept the whole page with the date on top and then done something with it, not frame it, of course, then what? He should have gone to a friend's house for the night. How would that have helped? No, he wants to be here alone but he doesn't want to think of her, or as much as he's doing. "Go on, think of her, think of her, why not?" It's the drink. He shouldn't drink anymore today. It'll make him sad, it's making him sad, very sad; so be sad, what of it? Cry, bawl, pound the chair arms with his fists; he should do what he wants or just comes, so long as it isn't destructive. Destructive physically, is what he means. For he doesn't deserve it? The bawling and pounding, he's saying, and who's talking about "deserve"? And he doesn't need a drink. He's tired enough after almost no sleep for three days, and just because of the emotional thing of it he's gone through, to sleep straight for a day without drink. Drink will probably even get him up in a few hours with a stomachache or just to pee. And then keep him up when he wants to sleep. He hasn't had enough to eat. It's okay, the drink feels good, paper on his lap feels good, he's not hungry — it all feels pretty good, in fact; suddenly he doesn't feel so sad. He did, but what's he going to do now? Sleep, what else? Long and hard, then wake up refreshed. It's going to be bad awhile, maybe a month, maybe half a year, maybe more — probably more. Well, that happens and should be expected. What's he mean by that? But start off right. Get to bed, out of your clothes, get under the covers, take the phone off the hook, and just sleep.

He goes into the bedroom. A long yawn — a good sign, the best. Undresses and gets under the covers. The curtains, and he gets up and closes them. Back in bed. "Close your eyes," he thinks. Why did he think that when he was holding her in the hospital, that thing about now he can sleep? There he was, sitting in the chair falling asleep, maybe he did fall asleep for a few minutes but what of it? and when he looked up she looked different. So, something about her look. Wait a minute, he doesn't quite understand. He knew she'd died — that's it. Sensed it, rather — something about the frozenness of her face — and would have been surprised if he'd touched her and found she was alive. Went up to her. Felt her heart, temple, her wrist pulse. Pulled her eyelids back. She was dead, he thought, or maybe just in a deep coma. The deepest of comas, much deeper than the one she'd been in for the last day. The

doctors had talked about a coma so deep it would seem to the
layman's eyes she was dead. Did what they said for him to do if no
doctor or nurse was in the room. Felt around her ankle where the
pulse is. Her foot was cold. Other one, too. For the last half-year
they'd been cold, but now they were very cold. She was dead. No,
there were other things to do, the doctors had said. Put his ear to
her mouth, then to her nostrils. Felt her heart, temple and wrist
pulse again and also her neck's, he'd forgotten to feel her neck's.
She was dead, that's all, he was sure of it, there was nothing about
her that showed any life. The pin, he remembered one of the
doctors saying, and he got it off her side table and pricked the
bottom of her foot. No response. Other foot. Nothing. Several
fingertips. Same thing. That was it. She was lifeless, dead, what else
could she be? "Oh no," he said. Aloud, definitely, remembers it
clearly. And lifted her up and held her to his chest, her chest
against his, her face someplace and same with his, his arms around
her, and he closed his eyes, he thinks, and thought, "Now I can get
to sleep." "Some sleep"? "Sleep better"? "Tonight I can"? "I can
sleep better tonight"? Something like that. Not necessarily one of
those. But how odd. Well, it's inexcusable — excusable, he means.
For he didn't think, "Good, she's dead, now I can sleep." In a way,
though, he felt it, about her being dead. All she'd gone through. It
was good she didn't suffer like some people with her illness do.
Suffer at the end, he means. She just stopped breathing. In a coma
for a day or so and then just went. And he thought something about
his future sleep soon after. Is he a bastard for having thought that?
Of course not. He did his best, as he said. Did what he could for her,
and for years. And just think of his state of mind at that exact time.
The poor dear — she. He could never sleep, never sleep, maybe
never again. That's ridiculous, but he won't sleep well or at all for a
while, that's for sure. The phone rings. Forgot to leave the receiver
off the hook, or he just could have pulled the plug out of the jack. It
rings and rings, and he gets up and goes to it and lifts the receiver.
"Yes?" he says. "My darling, I'm here. Where have you been, why
don't you come see me?" "It's you," he says. "This is wonderful, a
miracle, everything I wanted, you can't believe how great I feel. I'll
be right there wherever you are." She sounds so healthy too. But he
knows he's already asleep.

STUART DYBEK

Paper Lantern

FROM THE NEW YORKER

WE WERE WORKING late on the time machine in the little make-
shift lab upstairs. The moon was stuck like the whorl of a frozen
fingerprint to the skylight. In the back alley, the breaths left behind
by yowling toms converged into a fog slinking out along the streets.
Try as we might, our measurements were repeatedly off. In one
direction, we'd reached the border at which clairvoyants stand
gazing into the future, and in the other we'd gone backward to the
zone where the present turns ghostly with memory and yet resists
quite becoming the past. We'd been advancing and retreating by
smaller and smaller degrees until it had come to seem as if we were
measuring the immeasurable. Of course, what we really needed was
some new vocabulary of measurement. It was time for a break.

Down the broken escalator, out the blue-lit lobby past the shut-
tered newsstand, through the frosty fog, hungry as strays we walk,
still wearing our lab coats, to the Chinese restaurant around the
corner.

It's a restaurant that used to be a Chinese laundry. When customers
would come for their freshly laundered bundles, the cooking —
wafting from the owner's back kitchen through the warm haze of
laundry steam — smelled so good that the customers began asking
if they could buy something to eat as well. And so the restaurant was
born. It was a carryout place at first, but they've since wedged in a
few tables. None of us can read Chinese, so we can't be sure, but
since the proprietors never bothered to change the sign, presum-
ably the Chinese characters still say it's a Chinese laundry. Anyway,

that's how the people in the neighborhood refer to it — the Chinese Laundry, as in "Man, I had a sublime meal at the Chinese Laundry last night." Although they haven't changed the sign, the proprietors have added a large, red-ribbed paper lantern — their only nod to decor — that spreads its opaque glow across the steamy window.

We sit at one of the five Formica tables — our favorite, beside the window — and the waitress immediately brings the menu and tea. Really, in a way, this is the best part: the ruddy glow of the paper lantern like heat on our faces, the tiny enameled teacups warming our hands, the hot tea scalding our hunger, and the surprising, welcoming heft of the menu, hand-printed in Chinese characters, with what must be very approximate explanations in English of some of the dishes, also hand-printed, in the black ink of calligraphers. Each time we come here the menu has grown longer. Once a dish has been offered, it is never deleted, and now the menu is pages and pages long, so long that we'll never read through it all, never live long enough, perhaps, to sample all the food in just this one tucked-away, neighborhood Chinese restaurant. The pages are unnumbered, and we can never remember where we left off reading the last time we were here. Was it the chrysanthemum pot, served traditionally in autumn when the flowers are in full bloom, or the almond jelly with lichees and loquats?

"A poet wrote this menu," Tinker says between sips of tea.

"Yes, but if there's a poet in the house, then why doesn't this place have a real name — something like the Red Lantern — instead of merely being called the Chinese Laundry by default?" the Professor replies, wiping the steam from his glasses with a paper napkin from the dispenser on the table.

"I sort of like the Chinese Laundry, myself. It's got a solid, working-class ring. Red Lantern is a cliché — precious chinoiserie," Tinker argues.

They never agree.

"Say, you two, I thought we were here to devour aesthetics, not debate them."

Here, there's nothing of heaven or earth that can't be consumed, nothing they haven't found a way to turn into a delicacy: pine-nut porridge, cassia-blossom buns, fish-fragrance-sauced pigeon, swallow's-nest soup (a soup indigenous to the shore of the

South China Sea; nests of predigested seaweed from the beaks of swifts, the gelatinous material hardened to form a small, translucent cup). Sea-urchin roe, pickled jellyfish, tripe with ginger and peppercorns, five-fragrance grouper cheeks, cloud ears, spun-sugar apple, ginkgo nuts and golden needles (which are the buds of lilies), purple seaweed, bitter melon . . .

Nothing of heaven and earth that cannot be combined, transmuted; no borders, in a wok, that can't be crossed. It's instructive. One can't help nourishing the imagination as well as the body.

We order, knowing we won't finish all they'll bring, and that no matter how carefully we ponder our choices, we'll be served instead whatever the cook has made today.

After supper, sharing segments of a blood orange and sipping tea, we ceremoniously crack open our fortune cookies and read aloud our fortunes as if consulting the I Ching.

"*Sorrow is born of excessive joy.*"

"Try another."

"*Poverty is the common fate of scholars.*"

"Does that sound like a fortune to you?" Tinker asks.

"I certainly hope not," the Professor says.

"*When a finger points to the moon, the imbecile looks at the finger.*"

"What kind of fortunes are these? These aren't fortune cookies, these are proverb cookies," Tinker says.

"*In the Year of the Rat you will be lucky in love.*"

"Now that's more like it."

"What year is this?"

"The Year of the Dragon, according to the placemat."

"*Fuel alone will not light a fire.*"

"Say, did anyone turn off the Bunsen burner when we left?"

The mention of the lab makes us signal for the check. It's time we headed back. A new theory was brewing there when we left, and now, our enthusiasm rekindled, we return in the snow — it has begun to snow — through thick, crumbling flakes mixed with wafting cinders that would pass for snowflakes except for the way the wind is fanning their edges to sparks. A night of white flakes and streaming orange cinders, strange and beautiful until we turn the corner and stare up at our laboratory.

Flames occupy the top floor of the building. Smoke billows out of the skylight, from which the sooty moon has retreated. On the floor below, through radiant, buckling windows, we can see the mannequins from the dressmaker's showroom. Naked, wigs on fire, they appear to gyrate lewdly before they topple. On the next floor down, in the instrument repair shop, accordions wheeze in the smoke, violins seethe like green kindling, and the saxophones dissolve into a lava of molten brass cascading over a window ledge. While on the ground floor, in the display window, the animals in the taxidermist's shop have begun to hiss and snap as if fire had returned them to life in the wild.

We stare helplessly, still clutching the carryout containers of the food we were unable to finish from the blissfully innocent meal we sat sharing while our apparatus, our theories, our formulas, and years of research — all that people refer to as their "work" — were bursting into flame. Along empty, echoing streets, sirens are screaming like victims.

Already a crowd has gathered.

"Look at that seedy old mother go up," a white kid in dreadlocks says to his girlfriend, who looks like a runaway waif. She answers, "Cool!"

And I remember how, in what now seems another life, I watched fires as a kid — sometimes fires that a gang of us, calling ourselves the Matchheads, had set.

I remember how, later, in another time, if not another life, I once snapped a photograph of a woman I was with as she watched a fire blaze out of control along a river in Chicago. She was still married then. Her husband, whom I'd never met, was in a veteran's hospital — clinically depressed after the war in Vietnam. At least, that's what she told me about him. Thinking back, I sometimes wonder if she even had a husband. She had come to Chicago with me for a fling — her word. I thought at the time that we were just "fooling around" — also her words, words we both used in place of others, like "fucking" or "making love" or "adultery." It was more comfortable, and safer, for me to think of things between us as fooling around, but when I offhandedly mentioned that to her she became furious, and instead of fooling around we spent our weekend in Chicago arguing, and ended up having a terrible time. It was a Sunday afternoon in early autumn, probably in the Year of the Rat, and we were sullenly driving out of the city. Along the north branch of the river, a factory was burning. I pulled over and parked, dug a camera out of my duffle, and we walked to a bridge to watch the fire.

But it's not the fire itself that I remember, even though the blaze ultimately spread across the city sky like a dusk that rose from the earth rather than descended. The fire, as I recall it, is merely a backdrop compressed within the boundaries of the photograph I took of her. She has just looked away from the blaze, toward the camera. Her elbows lean against the peeling gray railing of the bridge. She's wearing the black silk blouse that she bought at a secondhand shop on Clark Street the day before. Looking for clothes from the past in secondhand stores was an obsession of hers — "going junking," she called it. A silver Navajo bracelet has slid up her arm over a black silk sleeve. How thin her wrists appear. There's a ring whose gem I know is a moonstone on the index finger of her left hand, and a tarnished silver band around her thumb. She was left-handed, and it pleased her that I was too, as if we both belonged to the same minority group. Her long hair is a shade of auburn all the more intense for the angle of late-afternoon sunlight. She doesn't look sullen or angry so much as fierce. Although later, studying her face in the photo, I'll come to see that beneath her expression there's a look less recognizable and more desperate: not loneliness, exactly, but *aloneness* — a look I'd seen cross her face more than once but wouldn't have thought to identify if the photo hadn't caught it. Behind her, ominous gray smoke plumes out of a sprawling old brick factory with the soon-to-be scorched white lettering of GUTTMAN & CO. TANNERS visible along the side of the building.

Driving back to Iowa in the dark, I'll think that she's asleep, as exhausted as I am from our strained weekend; then she'll break the miles of silence between us to tell me that disappointing though it was, the trip was worth it if only for the two of us on the bridge, watching the fire together. She loved being part of the excitement, she'll say, loved the spontaneous way we swerved over and parked in order to take advantage of the spectacle — a conflagration the length of a city block, reflected over the greasy water, and a red fireboat, neat as a toy, sirening up the river, spouting white geysers while the flames roared back.

Interstate 80 shoots before us in the length of our racing head-light beams. We're on a stretch between towns, surrounded by flat black fields, and the candlepower of the occasional distant farm-house is insufficient to illuminate the enormous horizon lurking in the dark like the drop-off at the edge of the planet. In the speeding car, her voice sounds disembodied, the voice of a shadow, barely above a whisper, yet it's clear, as if the cover of night and the hypnotic momentum of the road have freed her to reveal secrets. There seemed to be so many secrets about her.

She tells me that as the number of strangers attracted by the fire swelled into a crowd, she could feel a secret current connecting the two of us, like the current that passed between us in bed the first time we made love, when we came at the same moment, as if taken by surprise. It happened only that once.

"Do you remember how, after that, I cried?" she asks.

"Yes."

"You were trying to console me. I know you thought I was feeling terribly guilty, but I was crying because the way we fit together seemed suddenly so familiar, as if there were some old bond be-tween us. I felt flooded with relief, as if I'd been missing you for a long time without quite realizing it, as if you'd returned to me after I thought I'd never see you again. I didn't say any of that, because it sounds like some kind of channeling crap. Anyway, today the same feeling came over me on the bridge, and I was afraid I might start crying again, except this time what would be making me cry was the thought that if we *were* lovers from past lives who had waited life-times for the present to bring us back together, then how sad it was to waste the present the way we did this weekend."

I keep my eyes on the road, not daring to glance at her, or even to answer, for fear of interrupting the intimate, almost compulsive way she seems to be speaking.

"I had this sudden awareness," she continues, "of how the mo-ments of our lives go out of existence before we're conscious of having lived them. It's only a relatively few moments that we get to keep and carry with us for the rest of our lives. Those moments *are* our lives. Or maybe it's more like those moments are the dots and what we call our lives are the lines we draw between them, connect-ing them into imaginary pictures of ourselves. You know? Like those mythical pictures of constellations traced between stars. I remember how, as a kid, I actually expected to be able to look up and see Pegasus spread out against the night, and when I couldn't it seemed like a trick had been played on me, like a fraud. I thought, Hey, if this is all there is to it, then I could reconnect the stars in any shape I wanted. I could create the Ken and Barbie constellations . . . I'm rambling . . ."

"I'm following you, go on."

She moves closer to me.

"I realized we can never predict when those few special moments will occur," she says. "How if we hadn't met, I wouldn't be standing on a bridge watching a fire, and how there are certain people, not that many, who enter one's life with the power to make those moments happen. Maybe that's what falling in love means — the power to create for each other the moments by which we define ourselves. And there you were, right on cue, taking my picture. I had an impulse to open my blouse, to take off my clothes and pose naked for you. I wanted you. I wanted — not to 'fool around.' I wanted to fuck you like there's no tomorrow against the railing of the bridge. I've been thinking about that ever since, this whole drive back."

I turn to look at her, but she says, "No . . . don't look . . . Keep driving . . . Shhh, don't talk . . . I'm sealing your lips."

I can hear the rustle behind me as she raises her skirt, and a faint smack of moistness, and then, kneeling on the seat, she extends her hand and outlines my lips with her slick fingertips.

I can smell her scent; the car seems filled with it. I can feel the heat of her body radiating beside me, before she slides back along the seat until she's braced against the car door. I can hear each slight adjustment of her body, the rustle of fabric against her skin, the elastic sound of her panties rolled past her hips, the faintly wet, possibly imaginary tick her fingertips are making.

"Oh, baby," she sighs.

I've slowed down to fifty-five, and as semis pull into the passing lane and rumble by us, their headlights sweep through the car and I catch glimpses of her as if she'd been imprinted by lightning on my peripheral vision — disheveled, her skirt hiked over her slender legs, the fingers of her left hand disappearing into the V of her rolled-down underpants.

"You can watch, if you promise to keep one eye on the road," she

says, and turns on the radio as if flicking on a nightlight that coats
her bare legs with its viridescence.

What was playing? The volume was so low I barely heard. A violin
from some improperly tuned-in university station, fading in and
out until it disappeared into static — banished, perhaps, to those
phantom frequencies where Bix Beiderbecke still blew on his cor-
net. We were almost to Davenport, on the river, the town where
Beiderbecke was born, and one station or another there always
seemed to be playing his music, as if the syncopated licks of Roaring
Twenties jazz, which had burned Bix up so quickly, still resonated
over the prairie like his ghost.

"You can't cross I-80 between Iowa and Illinois without going
through the Beiderbecke Belt," I had told her when we picked up a
station broadcasting a Bix tribute on our way into Chicago. She had
never heard of Bix until then and wasn't paying him much attention until the DJ quoted a remark by Eddie Condon, an old Chicago guitarist, that "Bix's sound came out like a girl saying yes."
That was only three days ago, and now we are returning, somehow
changed from that couple who set out for a fling.

We cross the Beiderbecke Belt back into Iowa, and as we drive
past the Davenport exits, the nearly deserted highway is illuminated like an empty ballpark by the bluish overhead lights. Her eyes
closed with concentration, she hardly notices as a semi, outlined in
red clearance lights, almost sideswipes us. The car shudders in the
backdraft as the truck pulls away, its horn bellowing.

"One eye on the road," she cautions.

"That wasn't my fault."

We watch its taillights disappear, and then we're alone in the
highway dark again, traveling along my favorite stretch, where in
the summer the fields are planted with sunflowers as well as corn
and you have to be on the alert for pheasants bolting across
the road.

"Baby, take it out," she whispers.

The desire to touch her is growing unbearable, and yet I don't
want to stop — don't want the drive to end.

"I'm waiting for you," she says. "I'm right on the edge just waiting
for you."

We're barely doing forty when we pass what looks like the same
semi, trimmed in red clearance lights, parked along the shoulder.

I'm watching her while trying to keep an eye on the road, so I don't notice the truck pulling back onto the highway behind us or its headlights in the rearview mirror, gaining on us fast, until its high beams flash on, streaming through the car with a near-blinding intensity. I steady the wheel, waiting for the whump of the trailer's vacuum as it hurtles by, but the truck stays right on our rear bumper, its enormous radiator grille looming through the rear window and its headlights reflecting off our mirrors and windshield with a glare that makes us squint. Caught in the high beams, her hair flares like a halo about to burst into flame. She's brushed her skirt down over her legs and looks a little wild.

"What's his problem? Is he stoned on uppers or something?" she shouts over the rumble of his engine, and then he hits his horn, obliterating her voice with a diesel blast.

I stomp on the gas. We're in the right lane, and since he refuses to pass, I signal and pull into the outside lane to let him go by, but he merely switches lanes too, hanging on our tail the entire time. The speedometer jitters over ninety, but he stays right behind us, his high beams pinning us like spotlights, his horn bellowing.

"Is he crazy?" she shouts.

I know what's happening. After he came close to sideswiping us outside Davenport, he must have gone on driving down the empty highway with the image of her illuminated by those bluish lights preying on his mind. Maybe he's divorced and lonely, maybe his wife is cheating on him — something's gone terribly wrong for him, and whatever it is, seeing her exposed like that has revealed his own life as a sorry thing, and that realization has turned to meanness and anger.

There's an exit a mile off, and he sees it too and swings his rig back to the inside lane to try and cut me off, but with the pedal to the floor I beat him to the right-hand lane, and I keep it floored, although I know I can't manage a turnoff at this speed. He knows that too and stays close behind, ignoring my right-turn signal, laying on his horn as if to warn me not to try slowing down for this exit, that there's no way of stopping sixty thousand pounds of tractor-trailer doing over ninety.

But just before we hit the exit I swerve back into the outside lane, and for a moment he pulls even with us, staying on the inside as we race past the exit so as to keep it blocked. That's when I yell to her,

"Hang on!" and pump the brakes, and we screech along the outside lane, fishtailing and burning rubber, while the truck goes barreling by, its air brakes whooshing. The car skids onto the gravel shoulder, kicking up a cloud of dust, smoky in the headlights, but it's never really out of control, and by the time the semi lurches to a stop, I have the car in reverse, veering back to the exit, hoping no one else is speeding toward us down I-80.

It's the Plainview exit, and I gun into a turn, north onto an empty two-lane, racing toward someplace named Long Grove. I keep checking the mirror for his headlights, but the highway behind us stays dark, and finally she says, "Baby, slow down."

The radio is still playing static, and I turn it off.

"Christ!" she says. "At first I thought he was just your everyday flaming asshole, but he was a genuine psychopath."

"A real lunatic, all right," I agree.

"You think he was just waiting there for us in his truck?" she asks. "That's so spooky, especially when you think he's still out there driving west. It makes you wonder how many other guys are out there, driving with their heads full of craziness and rage."

It's a vision of the road at night that I can almost see: men, not necessarily vicious — some just numb or desperately lonely — driving to the whining companionship of country music, their headlights too scattered and isolated for anyone to realize that they're all part of a convoy. We're a part of it too.

"I was thinking, Oh, no, I can't die now, like this," she says. "It would be too sexually frustrating — like death was the ultimate tease."

"You know what I was afraid of," I tell her. "Dying with my trousers open."

She laughs and continues laughing until there's a hysterical edge to it.

"I think that truck driver was jealous of you. He knows you're a lucky guy tonight," she gasps, winded, and kicks off her sandal in order to slide a bare foot along my leg. "Here we are together, still alive."

I bring her foot to my mouth and kiss it, clasping her leg where it's thinnest, as if my hand were an ankle bracelet, then slide my hand beneath her skirt, along her thigh to the edge of her panties, a crease of surprising heat, from which my finger comes away slick.

"I told you," she moans. "A lucky guy."

I turn onto the next country road. It's unmarked, not that it matters. I know that out here, sooner or later, it will cross a gravel road, and when it does I turn onto the gravel, and after a while turn again at the intersection of a dirt road that winds into fields of an increasingly deeper darkness, fragrant with the rich Iowa earth and resonating with insect choirs amassed for one last Sanctus. I'm not even sure what direction we're traveling in any longer, let alone where we're going, but when my high beams catch a big turtle crossing the road I feel we've arrived. The car rolls to a stop on a narrow plank bridge spanning a culvert. The bridge — not much longer than our car — is veiled on either side by overhanging trees, cottonwoods probably, and flanked by cattails as high as the drying stalks of corn in the acres we've been passing. The turtle, his snapper's jaw unmistakable in the lights, looks mossy and ancient, and we watch him complete his trek across the road and disappear into the reeds before I flick off the headlights. Sitting silently in the dark, we listen to the crinkle of the cooling engine, and to the peepers we've disturbed starting up again from beneath the bridge. When we quietly step out of the car, we can hear frogs plopping into the water. "Look at the stars," she whispers.

"If Pegasus was up there," I say, "you'd see him from here."

"Do you have any idea where we are?" she asks.

"Nope. Totally lost. We can find our way back when it's light."

"The back seat of a car at night, on a country road — adultery has a disconcerting way of turning adults back into teenagers."

We make love, then manage to doze off for a while in the back seat, wrapped together in a checkered tablecloth we'd used once on a picnic, which I still had folded in the trunk.

In the pale early light I shoot the rest of the film on the roll: a closeup of her, framed in part by the line of the checkered table-cloth, which she's wearing like a shawl around her bare shoulders, and another, closer still, of her face framed by her tangled auburn hair, and out the open window behind her, velvety cattails blurred in the shallow depth of field. A picture of her posing naked outside the car in sunlight that streams through countless rents in the veil of the cottonwoods. A picture of her kneeling on the muddy planks of the little bridge, her hazel eyes glancing up at the camera, her mouth, still a yard from my body, already shaped as if I've stepped to her across that distance.

What's missing is the shot I never snapped — the one the trucker tried to steal, which drove him over whatever edge he was balanced on, and which perhaps still has him riding highways, searching each passing car from the perch of his cab for that glimpse he won't get again — her hair disheveled, her body braced against the car door, eyes squeezed closed, lips twisted, skirt hiked up, pelvis rising to her hand.

Years after, she called me out of nowhere. "Do you still have those photos of me?" she asked.

"No," I told her, "I burned them."

"Good," she said, sounding pleased — not relieved so much as flattered — "I just suddenly wondered." Then she hung up.

But I lied. I'd kept them all these years, along with a few letters — part of a bundle of personal papers in a manila envelope that I moved with me from place to place. I had them hidden away in the back of a file cabinet in the laboratory, although certainly they had no business being there. Now what I'd told her was true: they were fueling the flames.

Outlined in firelight, the kid in dreadlocks kisses the waif. His hand glides over the back of her fringed jacket of dirty white buckskin and settles on the torn seat of her faded jeans. She stands on tiptoe on the tops of his gym shoes and hooks her fingers through the empty belt loops of his jeans so that their crotches are aligned. When he boosts her closer and grinds against her she says, "Wow!" and giggles. "I felt it move."

"Fires get me horny," he says.

The roof around the skylight implodes, sending a funnel of sparks into the whirl of snow, and the crowd *ahs* collectively as the beakers in the laboratory pop and flare.

Gapers have continued to arrive down side streets, appearing out of the snowfall as if drawn by a great bonfire signaling some secret rite: gangbangers in their jackets engraved with symbols, gorgeous transvestites from Wharf Street, stevedores and young sailors, their fresh tattoos contracting in the cold. The homeless, layered in overcoats, burlap tied around their feet, have abandoned their burning ashcans in order to gather here, just as the shivering, scantily clad hookers have abandoned their neon corners; as the Guatemalan dishwashers have abandoned their scalding suds; as a baker, his face and hair the ghostly white of flour, has abandoned his oven.

Open hydrants gush into the gutters; the street is seamed with deflated hoses, but the firemen stand as if paired off with the hookers — as if for a moment they've become voyeurs like everyone else, transfixed as the brick walls of our lab blaze suddenly lucent, suspended on a cushion of smoke, and the red-hot skeleton of the time machine begins to radiate from the inside out. A rosy light plays off the upturned faces of the crowd like the glow of an enormous red lantern — a paper lantern that once seemed fragile, almost delicate, but now obliterates the very time and space it once illuminated. A paper lantern raging out of control with nothing but itself left to consume.

"*Brrr.*" The Professor shivers, wiping his fogged glasses as if to clear away the opaque gleam reflecting off their lenses.

"Goddamn cold, all right," Tinker mutters, stamping his feet.

For once they agree.

The wind gusts, fanning the bitter chill of night even as it fans the flames, and instinctively we all edge closer to the fire.

DEBORAH GALYAN

The Incredible Appearing Man

FROM MISSOURI REVIEW

"PLUMBER," he says.

His Panama hat is an odd touch, shadowing dark glasses. A blue work shirt and jeans. Cowboy boots, very tooled. But the grin is center stage.

"I didn't call a plumber."

He takes a notebook out of his shirt pocket and looks in it.

"Plumber," he says, "nonetheless."

He smells delicious, like lemongrass and eucalyptus bark, fresh from California. I breathe him in.

"You're not a plumber," I say, looking him dead in the eye. "You don't have any tools."

He leans into the screen door. An amethyst glints in his left earlobe, a dimple in his left cheek.

"Maybe they're in the truck. We could go take a look." He grins again.

"I don't think so," I say.

He inspects the toe of his boot for scuffs. "So," he says. "Are you saying I'm not a plumber?"

I nod carefully.

He looks over his shoulder at an ancient Toyota truck in the drive. I notice the tendons in his shoulders, how they reach up into his neck like gnarled vines. "This is a drawback," he says, his California accent minty, with overtones of diffidence. "This is a serious drawback."

"Yes, it is," I say.

"I'll just have to return at a later time with my credentials." He tips the Panama. "Until then, ma'am."

I let myself watch his walk to the truck, gravel scattering under his boots. He looks improbably young, a gypsy cowboy with shiny black curls bouncing around his hat. Was there a streak of gray or not? His jeans are tight. When he reaches the truck, he looks back at me. One, two, three, I count and shut the door. Three is as long as I can look without looking too long. My hands are shaking. Nothing happened, I tell myself. But my hands are shaking, and there's no denying it.

The Incredible Appearing Man is back.

On Tuesday, Mrs. Burdowski comes to take care of five-month-old Alex while I go to work. She gives him my breast milk out of plastic nursers and complains he ought to be eating cereal by now. She tells Alex I'm depriving him of pabulum. But I like the way she holds him in the crook of one arm so he can always see her face. He adores her weird Polish interpretations of Cole Porter songs and tries to sing along. Because of Mrs. Burdowski, I feel all right about leaving him two days a week so that I can keep teaching at St. Catherine's College for Women. There aren't that many teaching jobs in Cleveland, and I'm anxious to keep this one, at least part-time.

Today I'm teaching Ovid's *The Metamorphoses* to the senior women — something I've never tried before. It somehow ended up on the recommended reading list, a predictable stew of Shakespeare, Whitman, and Frost — with Alice Walker and Toni Morrison tossed in for color. I thought Ovid might be an enjoyable way of introducing them to Greek and Roman literature without dragging them kicking and screaming through Homer or Virgil.

I dismissed *The Metamorphoses* when I first read it in college. The stories seemed embarrassingly stilted, like old episodes of *Love Boat*. Now I see them differently — voluptuous, witty tales of love, sex, and death. Creation and destruction on a Spielbergian scale. Someone in Hollywood should take a look at Ovid.

> Earth, Air, Water heaved and turned in darkness,
> No living creatures knew that land, that sea
> Where heat fell against cold, cold against heat —
> Roughness at war with smooth and wet with drought.
> Things that gave way entered unyielding masses,
> Heaviness fell into things that had no weight.

I wonder if I can explain it to my students. The drama of metamorphoses. How we change. Anthropologists now admit that major advances in certain species thought to have occurred over thousands of years probably happened within the space of a few generations. Why not, when you consider what can happen in the space of a lifetime? How an ideology, inspiring at twenty, turns relentless by forty. By then, for example, you tire of embossing your every deed with its corresponding psychology. *I did it because I was insecure. I did it because I was feeling self-destructive.* Sometimes you want to say, *It just happened.* You want to say, *I don't know.* Maybe, to your grown son or daughter, you will someday say, *I loved your father. Then I didn't. So what?*

How to explain that you grow tired of raking up all those spinners of regret that whirl down year after year? You let a sapling grow once in a while, without pulling it up. You say, *I don't know how it got there. It just grew.*

In class, Ovid bombs. They say he is DWM. Dead, white, and male. They say he is BGS. Before Gloria Steinem. Yet another weary example of phallocentric text.

My black-leather-skirted, Doc Marten–grommeted smart girl is not amused by the story of Apollo and Daphne. She wants to know, what gives Phoebus Apollo the right to stalk Daphne in the woods below Parnassus, turning her into dead wood?

"He chews on her like she's some kind of squirrel," she whines. "It's disgusting."

Nods around the room. My worst student, who probably hasn't read the assignment, agrees. "How can you force us to read this?" She tosses the book on her desk and sulks.

I point out that *The Metamorphoses* is a relatively feminist book for A.D. 8 and that more than half of Ovid's stories feature heroines, which at least is an embryonic form of feminism.

They glower. I don't know how to steer them past this obvious trap. They glare at me like demented raccoons with their kohl-ringed eyes and shaven heads. They want to know, how can I justify the fate of virtuous Io, raped and sentenced to life in the body of a cow by adulterous Jove?

And then there are lines like these, in Gregory's 1958 introduction, to explain:

His many heroines are set before us in dramatic moments of their indecision. Actually they do not meditate; they waver between extremes of right and wrong. They live and act within a world of irrational desires which are as vivid to them as things that happen in a dream. They act in heat and are caught up in disaster.

"We can't accept this," they insist.

"I'm not asking you to," I say, in a small, scared, English teacher voice. "I'm asking you to read it."

I hear an ominous chorus of complaints as the class files out at the end of the hour. I feel like sulking too. Defending Ovid is difficult these days. I understand their moral outrage. But the longer I love, the more I find myself susceptible to irrational desires and instant transformations. A baby, for example, is as irrational and vivid a desire as any heroine could conceive. A baby transforms you, body and soul. The moment you give birth, your mind is instantaneously filled with Styrofoam peanuts. Your past is trash-compacted to make room for all the peanuts. As the baby grows, you add more peanuts, and the little tin can of your past gets more compressed. But it is still there, underneath all the peanuts. The smashed cans of your past never entirely disappear. That is where the Incredible Appearing Man belongs. But he refuses to stay there.

On Wednesday, I'm working out to an exercise video in front of the living room television. Alex rides on my stomach during the abdominals, his fat cheeks jiggling as he bumps up and down. I'm on leg lifts when the truck pulls in. The door slams. It's him, dragging a machine and a short coil of black hose across the lawn. I plop Alex in the playpen with plastic keys to chew and step outside.

"Hello, plumber," I say.

He's crouched in the window well, prying at a window casement with his bare hands. After a moment, he looks around. Mirrored glasses today.

"Radon gas," he says. "No homeowner can ignore it." He waves the black hose at me. "Air sampling is the first step."

I stare at his cheap cotton painter's cap, on which he has scrawled "Radon, Inc." in black marker. He keeps on prying, until I realize he actually might break the window. "Hey," I say. "It opens from the inside." He slides his hands slowly down from the window and stands.

"This is Cleveland," I point out. "We aren't afraid of radon."

He doesn't answer.

"We even smoke out here. Especially in restaurants."

He climbs out of the window well and stands over me. He is six feet three. Black jeans. White T-shirt, taut across his chest. Turquoise in the ear.

"Well," he says. The grin is enchantment. "I guess we have to sample from inside."

The machine is between us in the grass, its black casing mottled with beige mold. The mold is vintage 1950s. I presume the machine is even older. I stare nervously down at it until I suddenly realize what it is.

"So," I say. "You can detect radon with an army surplus Geiger counter?"

He stoops slowly and picks up the black hose.

"You're a stickler for details, ma'am."

"I like to be convinced."

"Of what?" We watch each other. He turns the hose in his hands. I see now that it isn't even part of the machine.

"Authenticity," I say. "I like that in a radon man." I sound tough, but I can't stop myself from looking at the dimple in his cheek, and he notices.

"You don't like spontaneity?" he asks, moving closer.

He smells heady and ozonish, like the punk after lightning strikes bare earth. "You look like someone I used to know," he says, eyeing me behind the shades.

"I don't think so."

"You look a lot like her." He moves with deliberate slowness into the buffer zone midwesterners like to keep between themselves and strangers. He takes my chin in his palm and moves my face from side to side. It's an odd feeling, as if his fingers are wired to some internal circuitry in my brain. I slide my eyes across the street to see if my retired neighbor Caroline is out in her yard pulling weeds and watching this radon man touch my face. Her garage door is open.

He observes me, dreamily. "She had a way of looking disappointed in me, especially when she smiled. Just like you."

"What did you say her name was?"

He doesn't answer but aims the full beam of his grin down upon me. Every time I look, I see my double reflection skittering across his glasses.

"Actually," I say, "we had the house tested for radon when I was pregnant."

"Is that so?" he says, clearly surprised.

"Last year, when I found out I was pregnant," I say redundantly. Alex begins to wail on cue.

"Congratulations. Boy or girl?"

"Boy. Alexander."

"You can't be too safe with a baby in the house." He bites down on the words to hold back something in his voice he doesn't want me to hear. We stand in silence and watch a dingy cloud roll over us and mash out the sun. I can tell that he is stricken as he hoists the machine onto his shoulder and carries it to the truck, the silly black hose dangling at his side.

I wave when he clears the drive. He doesn't wave back.

Then I run to rescue crying Alex, lift him from the playpen and bounce him in my arms. We swing-step over to the front door and look out the screen at the empty driveway. "Look, baby," I say. "The Incredible Appearing Man is gone." Alex swallows his cries and begins, enthusiastically, to hiccup. I hold him close, grateful to be tethered to my life by his birth.

A baby's magic is the power to charm a single day into loops. Each day with Alex is a Mobius strip of devotions to his animal needs. Today, I do everything in a state of grace. I feed him. I change him. I shove great wads of baby laundry into the washing machine. In between, I stand at the window and stare beyond the spot where the Incredible Appearing Man held my chin, down at the scrap of lake just visible from here, my mind bright and empty as a new Kenmore. I wish for what? I don't know. I wash dishes. My secret desires float down the white tile wall behind the sink like barges down a river, long and slow, their contents revealed, the viscous ooze of fossil fuels. The Man and I surface in various states of sexual abandon at the center of each one.

Around five, my blond and temperate husband rides his bike home, half dismounting as he flies along our sloping drive. He drops his satchel in a chair and sits on the sofa with Alex.

"Okay, buddy, this is how you hold the bat." He holds a finger up for Alex to grasp, then swings it. "Strike one," he says. Alex makes a snorting noise, a precursor to a laugh. "Strike two." Mitch looks worried. "Concentrate," he says. Alex squeals with pleasure. I look at him and burst into surprise tears of relief.

"What's wrong?" Mitch says.

"Just tired, I guess."

"Take a nap. I'll take the kid."

The nap stretches into evening. Mitch brings me a plate of frozen tortellini he has prepared with Alex on one hip and gives me a sip of his beer. We eat on the bed while Alex rolls between us on the quilt, working himself into a fuss about his next feeding. Mitch humors him, offering a juicy chunk of cantaloupe to suck.

"Anything happen today?" Mitch asks.

"Nothing happened yet."

Mitch frowns.

I stop chewing.

"What did you say?"

"I mean, nothing happened," I say. "Yet. I mean, with Alex. Alex didn't crawl or learn to read or anything. That's all."

Mitch smiles at me. He takes a sip of beer. "Well," he says sweetly, "keep me informed."

That night in bed, I feel guilty about not telling him about the Man. According to the rules I've made for myself, I should tell him. It's a profoundly familiar, criminal feeling. This isn't the first time I've been in this situation. I don't honestly know if there will ever be a last.

Here is the truth about the Incredible Appearing Man: I met him two weeks before college graduation. He appeared underneath a colossal ginkgo tree on the campus green, handing out flyers for a meditation lecture. I stopped to take one because of his grin. It was rife with the stuff with which a young man's grin should be rife: bravado and sexual innuendo and courage or stupidity, depending on your view. Maybe it also contained cruelty, but I missed that at the time. His hair was black and hung in corkscrew ringlets to his shoulders. His nose was slightly bent. There was something thrillingly unpresbyterian about him. His eyes were yellow with flecks of fire, as if they had been gilded by a Florentine jeweler. I found myself looking in them for too long a time, and without modesty.

I kept the flyer he handed me that day. Finals were nearly over. Everyone was packing up to leave. I went to the guest lecture it advertised in the basement of the Asian Student Center. The teacher, corpulent and robed, kept repeating "Love yourself" between what seemed to me short naps. After a half an hour, he opened his eyes. "Repeat with me," he said, "I love me. I love me. I love me." The Incredible Appearing Man was in the front row with the most devoted students, chanting on pink cushions. Afterward, they presented the teacher with a single rose floating in a crystal bowl. Something went wrong for me that night. Instead of falling in love with myself, I fell in love with the Incredible Appearing Man. I told him so a few days later. We were drinking twig tea from bowls in his rented room. The window was open and the room was rank with the scent of lilacs. Bees came and went through the window while we made love on a mattress on the floor. When I lay on top of him and pressed my face into his warm skin, I realized that the lilac smell was coming from him.

"What's that smell?" I asked shyly. "Soap?"

"I'm not real sure. It happens when I meditate a lot." He stroked my arm and looked apologetic. "It's sort of like stigmata."

He asked for my phone number, but my phone had been disconnected. School was over, and I was planning to leave for home in a day or two. I didn't want to move back in with my parents in South Bend, but I hadn't come up with a job. He stroked my hair. "Please don't go," he said. "We were strangers yesterday. Now we are lovers. It's impossibly erotic, don't you think?"

I spent most of another week on his mattress, going back to the dorm only to bathe and change clothes. On Friday morning, I stepped out of the shower and found the residence hall coordinator standing by my bed.

"Do you realize that this dorm is officially closed and that your key should have been turned in two days ago and that your presence here constitutes illegal entry?"

I adjusted my skimpy institutional towel.

"I'm standing here until you move everything out of this room," she said, slapping her big wooden passkey against her palm. "Pronto."

I drove to his rented room that afternoon, the back of my Gremlin wedged with clothes and dorm room paraphernalia. We made love on the windowsill and on the mattress and up against the wall. I nearly choked on the smell of wild honeysuckle emanating from his skin. We made so much noise that the chemistry post-doc who lived upstairs banged his broom on the floor and cursed. Flakes of plaster floated down and stuck in our hair. We were giggling at him when the Incredible Appearing Man's eyes suddenly welled up with tears.

"Don't go home, Lora," he said. "Come to California with me."

I sat up and looked at him.

"Don't answer yet."

He walked naked out of the room, through the shared kitchen, and up the stairs and apologized to the post-doc, who wouldn't speak to him, and came back with a serving bowl filled with tap water, in which we immersed and tenderly washed each other's hands. "Our destinies are bound together," he said. "With this water, I wash away our separate pasts."

I was a girl from South Bend, Indiana, whose destiny had never been pronounced at all, much less by a naked man with yellow eyes flecked with fire. I said yes. I said yes. I said yes.

We left for California a week later, sold the Gremlin for cash and put our stuff under a canvas in the back of his blue Toyota truck and drove away. I called my parents from a truck stop in Iowa. On the telephone, my father's voice was icy. "Four years of education," he said, "and now you are more ignorant than ever."

I hung up the phone and walked away.

In California, everything came easily to the Incredible Appearing Man. The first day we arrived in Noyo, he rented a cabin from a blond Buddhist monk who worked part-time at a gas station. The monk had moved out of the cabin and into a burned-out redwood tree trunk two miles up a logging road nearby. He rubbed the blond stubble of his shaven head and said, "You can have it for twenty-five dollars a week, unless you think that's too much."

"Is it more like a cabin or more like a house?" the Man asked. "I don't like houses."

"That's cool," the monk said. "You'll love it."

The cabin was filthy with soot from the woodstove. The chinking was all gone, and morning glory vines had worked their way between the logs, blooming inside on sunny days. We ran a heavy utility cord down through the woods about fifty yards to a storage shed on logging company property and stole enough electricity to run my beat-up stereo and a few old lamps. We made love every morning. His body took on the smells of the redwood flora: rhododendron, orchids, and five-finger ferns.

After a few months our money was gone. He carved gray whales and boxes shaped like yin-yang symbols out of fancy hardwoods scavenged from lumberyards and sold them at art fairs up and down the coast. I was a substitute teacher once in a while and a waitress sometimes, looking for a permanent job, which did not exist in that place at that time.

When he made money, I never saw it. If I made some, it went for essentials. We were perpetually behind on the rent. We argued constantly.

When there was nothing to eat, he would admonish me for saying so. "I can't participate in your anxiety. I'm already beyond it," he said frequently. Then he would walk out and disappear into the woods. Sometimes he brought home a bag of rice, borrowed from the monk. When I asked why he wouldn't try to get a job, he said he did not wish to define his life in terms of occupational experiences. So I chopped up a plot in a clearing behind the logging company equipment shed and tried to make a garden, but the eggplants withered and the tomatoes were riddled with fat green worms.

"If you learn to meditate, the garden will thrive on your energy," he said. "I'll teach you."

We sat naked on the cabin floor. He sat across from me and stared into my eyes. "Think nothing," he said. "Be nothing." Then he would vanish. His body was still present, but there was no one home behind his eyes.

When I tried to think nothing, I saw pages and pages of job applications in fine gray print. Lines and lines to be filled in. Education. Experience. Expertise. When those disappeared, I saw Dumbo and the seven dwarves, my notes from Chaucer class, old episodes of *The Dick Van Dyke Show.* At twenty-two, my mind was already a landfill, stuffed to capacity by television and college. There was no emptiness inside me. I could not meditate.

"It just isn't working," I'd say, near tears.

That night when we made love, it was odorless and sad.

After a week of this, he disappeared into the forest each evening to meditate with the tree monk. They spent the month of August building a Zen garden behind the cabin. I lost whole afternoons reading on a blanket in a small clearing while they rolled moss-covered rocks out of the forest and winched them into the bed of the truck. Inexplicably, I agreed to spend two hundred dollars sent by my worried parents on a huge brass gong. Then I broke the strap on one of my sandals shoving the thing into its new pine alcove and realized they were my last pair of shoes. I threw the broken sandal at the gong. It trembled sourly. I sat down on a rock and cried.

"It's a shoe," he said. "Don't you see how silly it is to care that much about a shoe?"

"Why do we have to live like this?" I yelled. "I love you, but I can't take this Zen crap anymore."

"You love me," he said. "Who knows what that means?"

After a while, he wasn't always meditating when he went into the woods. There was a pretty Norwegian woman named Skye who braided chamomile blossoms into her hair and lived in an old shredded camp tent up the logging road, just beyond the monk. She was a dropout from Berkeley who made little poultices out of mud dauber nests and sold them as charms in head shops. She came by all the time and shared her stash with us. About once a month, she and the Man would sit at the kitchen table and drop acid. They would sit there all afternoon and all evening. When they arrived at a certain point in their trip, they would toss back their heads and laugh for hours. They couldn't make eye contact without laughing until they cried.

"What are you laughing at?" I asked one night.

"Who knows?" Skye said, between giggles. "Why does everything have to have a reason?"

And they would laugh on, until three or four in the morning, while I lay on the bed and tried to sleep through the music and their private hysterics.

One day, when I had just been paid for substitute teaching, I bought groceries and set out to surprise him by cooking a real meal. I was making scalloped potatoes when he came in the door, smelling like moss from his hours with the tree monk. He kissed me and asked what I was doing, and when I told him, he smiled. Then he began undoing each of the buttons on my shirt with such tender concentration that I froze, mesmerized into compliance. "Don't move," he whispered. He dashed around the cabin assembling his old Nikon while I stood there, bare-breasted, knife in hand, over a bowl of half-peeled potatoes.

"It's so incredibly quaint, Lora," he said. "It's so you. Here you are, two thousand miles from home. We have to pack in water. We

shit in the woods. But you've found a way to make scalloped potatoes. God, I love you," he said, and snapped the shutter.

"You hate me," I said. "You humiliate me."

He wound the film advance and shot again. "I love you and hate
you equally," he said.

"I hate you," I said, noticing how good it felt to say it.

"Yes, I know," he said. "Our relationship has equilibrium. It's a
form of perfection."

But mostly I loved the Incredible Appearing Man. His thoughts
were like strange fruits dropped from incomprehensible trees. I
turned them over and over. I split their skins and put them to my
tongue, but I was never sure if they were safe to eat. There was
nothing in my background that could have prepared me for him,
yet everything in his had apparently prepared him for me.

He never spoke about his parents. "They're not here," he would
say when I asked for details. He told me only that they were struggling with their materialism and that he recognized it as a legitimate struggle. His father, it turns out, was a vice president at a
textile corporation and his mother a principal at a private school
out east. I learned this much from the tree monk one day, when I
gave him a lift to town. The Man never called them in my presence,
but he must have been in touch, because they sent him money
orders from a New Hampshire address. I found them every once in
a while, folded up in the pockets of his dirty jeans.

My parents worked in a factory. They wanted me to go to college
but not to take anything I learned too seriously. I majored in education for a while and switched to English against their will. I read and
read and tried not to listen to their lectures about my doomed
financial future. I planned to go to graduate school and figure
everything else out later.

Instead, I fell in love with the Incredible Appearing Man. And by
the time the flowers gave out and the cool winds blew in off the
Pacific that first year, I did not immediately recognize myself in the
restroom mirror at the gas station in Noyo, where I had stopped to
drop off the tree monk and fill up the tank and to enjoy the indoor
plumbing. I was someone new and strange, a tall girl with a wild
mop of hair in a pair of worn jeans and a man's shirt, living hand to
mouth in a mostly chopped-down redwood forest. A girl gone back-

ward in time, washing clothes in a tub and putting them up to the
fogged-out sun on a line between two trees. A girl cooking rice on
a cast-iron stove. Someone unlearning herself, unraveling herself
from things taken for granted, while her hair gnarled itself into
mats in the Pacific wind somewhere up above Mendocino. It could
have been all right. It could have been good, if the Incredible
Appearing Man had not been like a black hole in space: I moved
toward him like a captured asteroid in a slow tumble.

It was five-thirty in the morning when I came home on the dawn
after the summer solstice, which also happened to be my birthday,
from a Grateful Dead concert in San Francisco and found him
naked on the bed with Skye, soaked with sweat and smelling like a
eucalyptus grove. They didn't notice me at first, they were so en-
twined, their minds spun off into some vast blue inner space.

And that is why, seventeen years ago, I ended up on a friend's
porch in Mendocino on the Fourth of July, breaking up with the
Man. I was waiting for my ride to Oakland, where I would live the
next four years of my life. I had finally had enough. He insisted
nothing had changed. We argued one last time. Then we just sat
and watched the fireworks sear the edges of muddy clouds somewhere down the coast. I didn't see him again for three years.

When the first episode occurred I was in San Francisco, standing
alone in a friend's kitchen, watching my own wedding reception. I
don't know how he knew. I kept in touch with my friend in Mendocino, but she claimed she hadn't seen the Incredible Appearing
Man in over a year. I had just come up to peel off my pantyhose
when I realized I could see the festivities below from the window
over the sink. On the lawn in black tie and blue jeans, my new
husband, Mitch, laughed at something being sung by a woman in
a Valkyrie helmet. Twenty or so of our closest friends sprawled
around him on the grass with plastic cups of wine and plates of Brie
on their laps. We had been married about forty minutes. The doorbell rang, and I went to answer it. On the stoop was a white cakebox
tied up in string. I looked at the box and then down three long
flights of broken concrete stairs to the street, where the Incredible
Appearing Man stood staring up at me. He was wearing a green
uniform and a matching cap. When he was sure I recognized him,

he blew a solemn kiss and jumped into a green bakery van, double-parked, and drove away before I had time to react. My hands shook as I carried the box inside and untied the string. The cake was iced in marzipan and edged with pale green and lavender morning glories. In the middle, someone had written *Congratulations!* The dot on the exclamation mark had been made into a peace sign. Underneath, in an odd and shaky script, someone had added:

Pure logic is the ruin of the spirit — Saint-Exupéry.

My shock wilted into inexplicable guilt. I felt caught. On the back stoop, I looked to see if anyone was around before I stuffed the cake, box and all, deep into a garbage can. Then I went back to the window and watched Mitch and his best man play guitars. A tidal wave of ambivalence rose up in me and kept on rising. I knew my life was down there, under the willow tree, with a straightforward man to whom I had made all the usual promises. And I knew that part of me was frozen and would never thaw, except under the gaze of the Incredible Appearing Man's golden eyes. I watched, disconsolate, until someone was sent up the stairs to see what had become of me. When I heard my name called up the stairs, I flew back into myself. That was the only time I've experienced true detachment.

The second episode took place in Madison, Wisconsin. We were graduate students, I in comparative literature, Mitch in landscape architecture. I had managed to get a teaching job — a summer session of "Intro to Western Lit" for extra money over break.

On the first day of class, I stood at my desk opposite a wall of windows watching Lake Mendota pitch against the lightning slashing from above. The students shifted in their seats and looked relieved when the department secretary tapped lightly on the door, waving an updated copy of the final enrollment roster and a mimeographed page of faculty announcements.

"Oh," she whispered. "I almost forgot. This came for you."

It was a letter addressed to me, in care of the department, written in the peculiar slanted script of the Incredible Appearing Man. The return address was a student boarding house I vaguely knew on Broom Street. I studied the envelope too intently and too long, and when I looked up, the students were watching me with interest. I shoved the letter in my notebook and cleared my throat and asked them to resume reading sections of Homer aloud.

"Today we're only listening. Listening to our past. It's right here," I said, brightly. "In the room with us."

When class was finally over, I locked myself into the enormous handicapped stall in the women's restroom down the hall and opened the letter. It was written in pale gray ink on a tissue-thin sheaf of paper sealed in a blue airmail envelope, as if his thoughts had flown a vast distance.

Lora,
I was wrong. Now I see I had been completely suspended in your love, as babies are in wombs, and in my consummate satisfaction could not imagine otherwise.

If you need to know, there wasn't anything between Skye and me but a sort of brutish magnetism. Anyway, it had been happening on and off for a while, and so hadn't mattered all along. It was an "aside," as they say in the theater, and I regret it.

I don't expect you to forgive me. But I expect you to be honest with yourself. You married Mitch out of practicality and sadness. Go further in your mind. How long shall we continue this diet of compromise and regret, when we could feast on love?

I will remain on Broom Street until you decide.

"How did it go?" Mitch had asked when he picked me up after class.

"Crummy," I'd said, watching the wipers cut away the rain, only to have it instantly rush down again.

"Why?"

"The students were damp."

"What?"

"They were dull. Unresponsive."

"You said they were damp."

"Maybe I did. Dull and damp."

"That's undergraduates for you," Mitch said.

It was easy to shun him at first — I was angry that he had accused me of marrying Mitch out of practicality and sadness — though I conjured an excuse to drive by the dilapidated house every other day or so. It looked misused and sad with its broken porch furniture and dented garbage cans. There was never any sign of him.

But I was touched by his gesture — the distance he had traveled without hope, waiting in a boarding house on Broom Street. It was the most outrageous act anyone had ever committed on my behalf. For the entire month of June, I moved through my life in a constant state of distraction and arousal.

Then, one hot night in mid-July, Mitch and I were deep in our books when the doorbell rang. It was him, in a Domino's Pizza shirt and cap. He looked uncomfortably thin as he held out the box. "Small cheese and sausage," he said. "Six seventy-five." He took out his change pouch and looked expectantly at Mitch.

"I didn't order a pizza," Mitch said, confused.

"Did you order a pizza, ma'am?" He gazed boldly past Mitch to where I stood nailed to the carpet, three paces back. I shook my head.

"Damn," he said, grinning at Mitch. "It must have been a prank call. Happens all the time."

Mitch looked relieved. "Sorry," he said, and held out the pizza, but the Incredible Appearing Man waved it away.

"It's on me. It's against the policy, but we're so busy tonight no one will notice." He tipped his hat to Mitch and then over Mitch's shoulder to me. "Bye for now," he said.

I scrambled to the window to get another glimpse of him, but he must have sprinted down the block. Mitch was busy with a slice of cheese and sausage and didn't notice how unnerved I was. I couldn't bring myself to eat so much as a bite of the pizza, but I hugged the empty box for a moment before I tossed it in the trash.

Then, on my way to the library one morning in August, I passed up the parking garage and drove instead to the Incredible Appearing Man's boarding house on Broom Street and climbed the stairs to his room. He came to the door with the book he had been reading, open to the page he had been immersed in when I knocked. He looked at me calmly. "Oh," he said. "I didn't expect you. Come in." He wore only a pair of loose green army fatigues. His hair curled damply around his ears and his beard had grown heavy in the night. He looked softer and more real than he had looked in his pizza guise.

The room was a disheartening replica of the one he had lived in when we were first lovers — a stack of books next to a tattered reading chair, a small brown teapot with two cups, and a mattress

on the floor. The walls were painted cheap landlord white, a heart-
less color, colder than snow. There were bits of yellow tape stuck to
them where someone's posters had once hung. It was impossibly
hot. I studied the view below from his grimy window — a dumpster
next to a small plot of crumbling asphalt marked by a sign with
bleeding, hand-painted letters: Residents Private Parking ONLY.

"Do you really work at Domino's?" I asked, looking for his truck
among the rusted foreign-mobiles parked haphazardly beneath.

"God, no," he said. "I drive a cab. Once in a while."

"Deliveries are your vocation, seems to me."

"I have no true vocation," he said. We stood in silence. Sweat ran
down my temples and around my ears into the hollow at the base of
my neck.

"I suppose a man with no vocation can't be expected to own a
window fan."

"The kitchen is down the hall," he said. "I can make us some
iced tea."

As he turned to go, I reached out and placed my hand in the
warm, wet notch between his shoulder blades. I was somewhere up
above myself, floating, letting things happen. "Forget the hospitality," I said. "I came here to make love."

After a week of such meetings in the room on Broom Street, we
began, inexplicably, to laugh, and the longer we laughed, the
longer we could sustain our lovemaking. He gave off bouquets of
wild rose and bergamot, sweet as the Wisconsin prairie. After a
while, I found a way of transforming the guilt of adultery into a sort
of sluiceway, riding it down to the gates of a kind of fierce, unman-
ageable ecstasy.

One late afternoon, bathed in sweat from the sun dead level on
his western windowsill, I awoke at the sound of a Badger Line bus
rounding the corner. I stood up and began to dress, slightly nause-
ated from the smell of wild onions he had begun to manifest.

"Onions?" I asked when he opened his eyes.

"I don't know," he said sleepily. "I suppose I'm hungry."

Fearing nothing, we went around the corner to a small Italian
restaurant and bathed our wet skin in air conditioning. The restaurant was cool and reassuringly empty — too early for dinner, too
late for lunch. After devouring a plate of thick fettuccine, he suddenly put down his fork.

"Come back to California with me," he said.

I looked at him.

"I made a little money," he said, without explanation. "I bought a house in Mendo."

I had a feeling I shouldn't ask how.

"You don't like houses," I said.

"I was thinking of you."

"I can't," I said, "for obvious reasons."

The waiter took our plates. Without plates to look at, we looked nervously at each other.

"I have a life," I said.

"You're not living with the truth, Lora," he said.

"No," I said. "I'm living with a man. He's kind and reasonable. He lets me breathe. I like him."

"You like him," he repeated, then said nothing more, allowing me to absorb my own words. They hung in the chilled air between us until they transmogrified into an argument in his favor.

"I love you," I said, "but I can't live with you. I disappear."

"We disappear into each other," he said. "Yin-yang."

"I don't see it that way."

"Then how do you see it?"

"I see passion on one hand," I said carefully, "and everything else on the other."

"We have the only true marriage," he said. His eyes filled with tears. The waiter looked up from the bar and then discreetly down again, rubbing a wineglass with a large white cloth.

And so we sat, the Incredible Appearing Man and I, who had haunted each other for nearly eight years, right back where we started.

"Don't answer yet," he said, wrapping his hands around a glass of cheap Chianti, feeding it to me and to himself in a furtive communion.

While he finished his wine, I went to the restroom and cried for a few minutes, from terror or guilt or both. I don't know. I would be twenty-nine in a week. I could see the trajectory of my future — a stainless steel arrow soaring straight toward an interesting, reasonable life. I didn't want to see it lose telemetry and plunge. I washed my face and tried to shake off the panic I felt at the prospect of going home to Mitch. He would be cooking dinner now. I would walk in and he would give me a good-natured hug and a cold beer.

"Here's to a long day in the stacks," he would say, trusting and earnest to a fault.

When I returned, the Man had gone. A note on the back of the green paper guest check, which he had left for me to pay, read:

> Meet me at Broom Street on Saturday, no later than six A.M. We will leave early and in haste. Until then, my Beatrice regained.

On Saturday morning, before dawn, I sat on the edge of my bed and watched my husband sleep. In a coat closet by the door, a small blue American Tourister held a few changes of clothes and the contents of my savings account tendered into travelers' checks. In ten minutes, I planned to walk down the street to the mini-mart, where I would climb into a cab I had already called. But for the moment, I sat still and watched. Overnight, Mitch had sprouted a soft reddish beard. He looked — and was — truly innocent. I felt monstrous, doomed by an act I had not yet committed. It had burrowed deeply into my psyche and taken up residence, as if it were a kind of imprint, a map of my fate.

This thought coincided with the arrival of little puffs of magenta clouds on the horizon, like smoke signals spelling out hope. I realized then that I didn't just like Mitch, as I had told the Incredible Appearing Man. I truly loved Mitch, but for a lot of reasons I couldn't bring myself to admit because the Man would have found them utterly contemptible. I loved Mitch because we could go for months without arguing. I loved him because we could argue without making up in bed. I loved him because we could do our laundry on Friday night and call it a date. I loved him because we could fuck matter-of-factly, without olfactory or other manifestations of the Buddha Nature invading our bed. I loved him because it was easy.

And when I allowed myself to accept this, I felt transformed. Out of the range of his golden eyes, I had broken the spell of the Incredible Appearing Man. At six o'clock, I watched the sun break free of the horizon and aim itself straight at me. I kissed my sleeping husband and granted myself reprieve.

A few days later, when I found the courage to drive by the house on Broom Street, I saw the ROOM FOR RENT sign and told myself I would never see him again. I was wrong, of course. A few years later there was the episode in Seattle, where we lived briefly while Mitch worked for a landscaping firm. There was a shameful episode at a college reunion weekend in Indiana, too embarrassing to describe. I finally confessed to Mitch after the episode in Chicago, where we lived for a time before Cleveland. I was shopping at my favorite flower stall at a farmers' market in Old Town. I looked up and there he was, wearing a white vendor's apron, running the stall. I hadn't noticed at first. He was holding the biggest bouquet of dahlias I had ever seen. "I saved this one for you, lady," he said. "You want?" After the market we drove north into the countryside. The bed of his truck was loaded with unsold flowers drooping in buckets. We sat on the gate and kissed and undressed each other in the middle of an abandoned apple orchard. The smell was unbelievable.

At home, I stopped talking to Mitch. I stood over the sink once or twice a day, rearranging daylilies and black-eyed Susans, my market bag permanently slung over one arm. Mitch would come into the kitchen, watch me without a word, shake his head, and go out again.

When it was over, as it always was, I felt I couldn't keep on without offering Mitch an explanation. One night I told him everything. I told him about the cabin and Skye and the smell of honeysuckle and eucalyptus coming from the Appearing Man. I told him about the wedding cake in San Francisco. I told him about the pizza, about Broom Street and Seattle and the Old Town farmers' market. I told him I had no excuse. I told him I was scared, that I had begun to suspect I had willed the Incredible Appearing Man to appear each of the times he had come. I told him I understood that a therapist would say the whole sordid affair was a kind of giant Field Museum of Self-Destructive Behavior, complete with Historical Diorama. I told Mitch that I loved him. I told him I was sorry.

Through all this Mitch sat patiently.

"Will it happen again?" he asked.

"In all honesty," I said, "I don't know."

Mitch got up and went outside. He sat on the front steps of our house in the dark. He sat there all night.

That fall we lived precariously on the outskirts of each other, spending whole evenings without words. We politely waited for each other to finish in the bathroom in the mornings before work, instead of barging in, as was our usual custom. I counted the money I could honestly say was mine and made my plans, expecting that he would ask me to leave. Then one Friday night he walked in whistling. I looked up from my book. There was a bottle of good wine under his arm. He put it on the table with two glasses and set to work on the cork.

"Look," he said. "I refuse to be a jerk about this. You say you love me. Is that true?" He looked directly at me for the first time in weeks.

"Yes," I said.

"Well," he said, "that's good."

"Yes," I said.

He pretended to study the label. "If you can will him to appear, maybe you can will him to disappear."

"Maybe so," I said.

I watched him pour the wine. For months I had waited to be treated with the contempt and sarcasm I felt I deserved. Instead, he offered me forgiveness and a glass brimming with expensive merlot.

"It's your decision."

"I'll give it my best," I said.

And that's where it has stood for seven years, long enough for me to finally believe that I had willed the Incredible Appearing Man to disappear forever. Until now.

On Thursday, Mrs. Burdowski arrives. Seeing that I am running late, she follows me around during my last-minute preparations, flapping her arms. "Go," she says. "Teach these young girls something else besides the sex."

When I walk in my classroom, the students are standing around my desk with pens and notepads. "We are writing a petition to seek removal of Ovid from the recommended reading list," a senior in a laced leather halter and wraparound sunglasses informs me.

"On the grounds that it is offensive to women," says another.

"We ask that you suspend your lectures on Ovid until the curriculum committee has prepared a decision," says my best student. I see, for the first time, a badly executed skull and bones tattoo, which mars her perfect arm just below the shoulder.

I put down my books and sigh. We have had, at this point, only the one brief discussion about Ovid. I have not had a real opportunity to convince them of his merit. I have been distracted and unprepared. I want to reassure them that they are right on one level but that they are missing something they will someday wish they had learned, even if from Ovid.

If nothing else, they should learn about seduction: an impossibly quick and painful magic, a spell one might find oneself bound up in for ten or twenty years, maybe forever. I am thirty-nine. The Incredible Appearing Man is forty-one. Who knows what lies ahead?

Today we would have talked about the ancient newlyweds Deucalion and Pyrrha, whose marriage gift from the gods was a flood that washed away everything in the known world except the boat in which they drifted. Anyone paying more than scant attention could have learned something important about marriage from Ovid:

> It was a world reborn but Deucalion
> Looked out on silent miles of ebbing waters.
> He wept, called to his wife, "Dear sister, friend,
> O last of women, look at loneliness;
> As in our marriage bed our fears, disasters
> Are of one being, one kind, one destiny;
> We are the multitudes that walk the earth
> Between sunrise and sunset of the world,
> And we alone inherit wilderness."

But I look around and see that my students are young and hard as pinioned steel. I see that their hearts have been clear-coated, that they are temporarily encased in their youth and buffed to a glinting shine. I see that they think they have won something and I have lost something, and the thought makes me laugh out loud. They stare at me, appalled.

"Okay, okay," I say. "I respect your position. Let's go on to something you might consider less controversial." They look at me suspiciously for a moment, then slink off to their desks. I ask them to open their anthologies to page thirty-eight, Emily Dickinson. "Who wants to read the first poem aloud?" Hands go up around the room. I offer them my most mysterious smile.

Friday morning, I'm rinsing coffee cups in the sink. Alex is bouncing happily in his swing. I take a moment at the kitchen window to watch a red-capped woodpecker drill at our gnarled sassafras tree. Then I notice a ladder propped against the cherry tree and two boots on the top rung. The boots are attached to legs in jeans. Beyond that, branches.

After a minute, a branch loaded with cherries falls from the tree.

Then another. I stand at the window and laugh. The baby laughs too. I kiss his cheeks, wind up the swing, and head for the back porch.

I stand at the base of the tree and cross my arms. Three more branches bright with cherries fall against my feet. I clear my throat.

"Good morning," he yells down. "Tree trimmer."

He's wearing the Panama and underneath it a blue bandanna, pirate-style, and a sleeveless black T-shirt tucked in tight. His arms are brown and taut with muscle and bone. I stare at the dark stripe of sweat between his shoulder blades as he descends the ladder.

"You don't prune when the fruit is ripe," I say.

"That's not a professional opinion, is it, lady?" His grin is bright and dangerous.

"You're using a hacksaw," I say. "That's not customary."

He steps up close to me, tips the hat, and uses the bandanna to wipe his brow. "No, ma'am," he says. "Not customary at all." He wipes sweat from his forearms in careful swipes. The glasses are impenetrable.

He bends between our legs to pluck a doublet of cherries off a fallen branch, removes the stems, and places one gently to my lips, the other to his own. We split the cherries with our teeth. I take the pit from my mouth and toss it down, and when he reaches for my hand, I see the dark stain of fruit where our fingertips meet.

We kiss and the wind commands the leaves to swim and flash around us like a school of airborne fish. We hold on in the commotion, until our kiss finds its compass, and when it does, the depth of my regret strikes me cold in the heart like the shock of an off-the-dock plunge. We sink to our knees in the soft green grass. He removes his sunglasses and folds and pockets them. I see that his yellow eyes have grown soft and the skin around them creased with care. I see, after all these years, that he is changed into someone capable of real compassion.

The yard is fenced. The neighbors are off at work. We kiss again. I lay my head on the altar of his chest and feel the secret force of blood pound against my cheek. "I have to go," I say. "Alex needs me." But even so, I stay and greet each contour of his body with a gasp of recognition. He reaches for my breasts. My milk comes down hard, and with it, the weight of my heart's true allegiance. Without looking, I know two dark rings have appeared on my shirt. I rise up in fear and crouch over him, one knee on his chest.

"Who are you?" I ask for the first time ever.

"Just someone," he says, "between here and there."

"Are you stuck?"

"Not stuck," he says. "Blessed with the power to move back and forth."

"Between California and Cleveland?"

"Between McDonald's and the Interstate. Between the wide, unfinished pyramids of personal history."

"Here is here and there is there," I say.

"No," he says. "Actually, that's not how it is."

I force myself to get up and walk to the back door and peer in at Alex, slumped over and fast asleep in his rapidly unwinding automatic swing. Then I stride back down the hill and stand over the Incredible Appearing Man, lying quietly in the grass.

"You must go," I say quietly. "I promised you would not come back."

"Promised who?"

"Myself," I say. "I promised myself."

He nods. The air smells singed. Thunder or a detonator blast sucks the air around us toward the lake.

"You love me," he says.

"I love you. So what?"

He blinks at me uncertainly. "We have the only true marriage," he says.

"The only true marriage," I repeat. "Who knows what that means?"

We kiss once more. We kiss until we've kissed in all the rooms in all the houses we will never live in, we kiss past all the arguments we will never finish, past all the betrayals we will never suffer, past the white faces of children we will never make, floating before us like somber ghosts. We kiss past longing. I stand up and look down at the lake.

"It wasn't ordinary," he says.

"No," I say. "It wasn't." Then I turn around and walk into the house.

In the afternoon, while the baby naps, I sit on the back porch and pick cherries off the fallen branches, wash and pit them, letting the dark juice run down my wrists. In the kitchen, I knead pastry dough and sweeten it with confectioner's sugar, cut a generous crust, and ladle a great portion of cherries doused in sugar into it. I lick my fingers and pinch the corners of the dough around the circumference of the pie.

Alex fusses all evening. Mitch and I take turns jiggling him in a zigzag pattern — the only thing that works when his stomach is upset. Dinner is pathetic little trays of microwaved chicken almondine and salty vegetables, served accidentally scorched and eaten fast so that I can nurse Alex once more before bed.

I forget the pie until the smell curls out around the edges of the oven. It emerges puffed and radiant, stained with the juice of cherries pushing out the vents in the pastry.

When the baby finally sleeps, I bring two big slices on plates and forks and glasses of milk on a tray and place them on a coffee table. Mitch is sprawled wearily on the couch with a smattering of papers from his briefcase strewn around on the floor beneath him.

He cannot believe his eyes. "How did you find the time to pick cherries?"

"Alex took a long nap. I felt like doing something different."

"This is otherworldly," he says, rolling a bite of warm cherries around in his mouth as if it were a brilliant Beaujolais.

"Have another piece," I offer. I watch him eat.

The smell of warm cherries haunts the house, though Mrs. Burdowski has cleaned the oven twice in the weeks since I baked the pie. Each time she cleans it, the smell grows inexplicably stronger. She mutters about poltergeists. Most days it seems to have no particular point of origin, but once in a while it seems to waft from me. I am beginning to think we are just going to have to live with it. I know Mitch wonders, but he is too kind to ask. As these things go, it could be worse. Some days, I look out at the lake and think it's rising. Some days I think it's not.

MARY GORDON

Intertextuality

FROM THE RECORDER

MY GRANDMOTHER was serious, hardworking, stiff-backed in her convictions, charitable, capable, thrifty, and severe. I admired rather than liked her, though I always felt it was my failure that I couldn't do both. I was named for her but I believed that I did not take after her. Now, when I trace something in myself to her, it is always a quality I dislike. Most frequently the righteousness that does not shrink from condemnation and that feasts on blame.

And so you can imagine how surprised I was that she came into my mind when I was reading Proust. A passage describing a restaurant in the town of Balbec, modeled on Trouville, a town that existed to arrange seaside holidays for the prosperous and leisurely citizens of the Belle Epoque.

What could be further from my grandmother, who never had a holiday until perhaps she was too old to enjoy it? Her last, her only holiday, happened in the year of her eightieth birthday. One of her sons and his wife invited her to join them in Florida. They would spend two weeks there; she would spend another two, with her sister, who lived in Hialeah.

Just mentioning her sister makes me think of the effective and unsentimental nature of my grandmother's charity. Her sister was eighteen years younger than she, only a year old when my grandmother left her Irish town and crossed the ocean by herself. Twelve years after my grandmother's arrival in New York, having unshackled herself from work as a domestic by making herself a master seamstress, having married a Sicilian against everyone's advice, having borne a child by him and become pregnant with another, my grandmother paid for her mother, four sisters, and two brothers to come across to New York.

When the ship docked my grandmother was in labor, so she couldn't meet it. This meant she couldn't vouch for the new immigrants. So she sent her sister-in-law, whose name was identical to hers. My grandmother was a strapping woman, nearly six feet, with large, fair features. My Sicilian great-aunt was a small dark beauty of five two with the hands and feet of a doll. When my great-grandmother saw my great-aunt pretending to be my grandmother, she refused, the story goes, to set foot off the ship. "If that's what happens to you in America, I'm not putting a foot near the place," she said.

Of course this story must be exaggerated, if not completely untrue. My great-grandmother wouldn't still have been on the ship, she would have had to go through the horrifying ignominy of the many examinations at Ellis Island. But the sense of ignominy was not the kind of thing any of the family would include in their stories. I am used to saying it was because they hadn't the imagination for it. I am used to saying they were a hardheaded, hardhearted, unimaginative lot. But the story of my grandmother that came to me when I was reading Proust makes me think that I have never understood her. Who knows what follows from that failure to understand. What closing off. What punishing exclusions.

My family liked stories that were funny. If a story wasn't funny, there didn't seem to them much point in telling it: life was too hard, and there was too much that was required of them all to do. They would never, for example, have told the story of my grandmother's sister and her children and my grandmother's part in keeping that family intact.

Unlike my grandmother, all of her sisters seemed to have some taste for the feckless. One married a drunk; two married Protestants. My youngest great-aunt had more children than she could afford, although there was nothing to complain of in her husband. He was a good Catholic and had a steady job with the Sanitation. Nevertheless, they couldn't seem to make ends meet. My great-aunt told my grandmother she had no choice but to send her three youngest to an orphanage until things turned around. My grandmother told her sister she'd do nothing of the sort. The children would come to her house to live.

Her sister allowed this to happen, and my grandmother added her sister's three youngest children to her nine. The arrangement went on for two years, until it seemed the time (I don't know what made this clear) for the children to go home.

This wasn't a story told in the family, it was something my mother whispered to me, and it had to be dragged out of her. She had no joy in the telling of it. It was the kind of thing she was ashamed to be taking from where it belonged, that is to say, under wraps.

And they would never have told the story of my grandmother's vacation to Hialeah.

The year was 1959. My father had died two years before, and my mother and I were living with my grandmother in the house the family had been in since 1920. They had come to Long Island from New Jersey, a move made, I can only imagine, in crisis, although the story when it was told never mentioned crisis, or anxiety, or the alarm of forced change.

The family moved from Hoboken to a small town in the southern part of the state called Mount Bethel because there were eight children and my grandfather, a jeweler, couldn't support them in a city. My grandmother had been raised on a farm in Ireland, or that was the story. But I've seen the house she lived in. You couldn't say the family owned a farm — possibly a few acres, possibly a cow, some chickens, possibly a pig. This was the situation she replicated in Mount Bethel, and this situation was the source of the stories about that time. They were stories about animals, the pigs Pat and Patricia, the goats Daisy and Blanche, the chickens, the endless dogs. All these animals seemed to be in a constant state of adventure or turmoil: they were getting sick or getting lost or getting hurt or giving birth, and my grandmother presided over everything, and everything always turned out well.

Then one day the landlord decided he didn't want them there anymore. It was never clear to me exactly how this came about: was it a capricious decision, a vengeful one, had he come to dislike my grandparents, or had they failed to pay the rent? This part of the story was never told. The part they liked to tell (perhaps their favorite story of all, because it contained one of the elements they loved to live by, Punishment) was the story of what happened to the house after the family left. After they'd been gone three months, the house burned down. And they were better off, much better. They'd moved to Long Island, which was farm country then, and very anti-Catholic. A cross had been burned on the rectory lawn. But they were able to buy a house there with just enough land to keep chickens. What happened, they liked to say, proved that God's will was in everything and everything happened for the best.

In 1959, the year that my grandmother took her vacation to Florida, she'd been living in the house for nearly forty years. The house had gone from sheltering nine children to only one, my unmarried aunt, who'd grown to middle age there. Then my mother and I moved in, and there was once again a child for my grandmother to care for: me. I never felt that the house was a good place for a child or that my grandmother was a good person to be taking care of me. I was used to my father, who was playful and imaginative and adoring. My grandmother was busy, and she was a peasant: she didn't believe in childhood as a separate estate requiring special attention, special occupations, to say nothing of diversions. A child did as best she could, living alongside adults, taking what was there, above all doing what she could to be of help, because there was always too much work for everyone.

My grandmother's mark was everywhere in the house. She'd sewed slipcovers for the furniture and crocheted endless afghans and doilies. She'd knitted trivets and braided rugs. She'd laid the linoleum on the kitchen floor and patched the kitchen roof in a bad storm. Every decoration was hers: the pictures of the saints, the pious poems, the planters in the shape of the Madonna's head, the dark iron Celtic cross. Inexplicably: the lamps with scenes that might have come from Watteau or Fragonard, the glass lady's slipper, the tapestry sewing box with the girl in yellow reading by her window in the sun.

The house was my grandmother's and everything in it was hers. Then one day my aunt came up with an idea. The children, all nine of them, would chip in to renovate the house. To modernize it. Walls would be knocked down to create a feeling of space and openness. The back porch, which nobody really used, would be collapsed. The front porch would be added to the living room to make a large room, the side porch would become a downstairs bathroom with room for a washing machine. My grandmother would no longer need to go upstairs to the bathroom or down to the cellar to wash the clothes in the machine with its antiquated wringer. She was getting older, my aunt said: it was time she took things easy for a change.

They planned to do the renovations while my grandmother was in Florida, so that when she came back she would be greeted with this wonderful surprise. They hired a contractor who agreed to do all the work in a month. The house was full of busyness and disarray. And full, for once, of men. We teased my aunt that the electrician was in love with her, the contractor's unmarried brother, the man who installed the washing machine.

Miraculously, everything was done on time. One of my uncles picked my grandmother up at the airport. This had been her first airplane flight. The family — nine brothers and sisters, twenty-one cousins — gathered to celebrate her safe landing and the wonderful surprise that would greet her when she opened the door.

It was a new door that she opened, in a new place. She walked into the house and looked around her in shock and pain. Her kitchen, a lean-to that had been lightly attached to the back of the house, had simply been chopped off, carried away. All the appliances were new, and all the kitchen cabinets. Her dining room was gone, and her carved table, replaced by what was called an "eat-in kitchen" and a "dinette." She walked around the rooms looking dazed. Then she began to cry. She excused herself and walked into her bedroom, which had been left untouched. We all pretended she was tired, and went on with the party as if she hadn't yet arrived. After a while she came out to join us, but she said nothing of what had been done to the house.

What were they all, any of them, feeling? This was the sort of question no one in my family would ask. Feelings were for others: the weak, the idle. We were people who got on with things.

But the new house weakened my grandmother. It turned her old.

Why could none of her children have foreseen this?

Why was I the only one who noticed that she didn't like the new house, that it had not been a good thing for her, it had done her harm?

But perhaps I wasn't the only one who noticed. Perhaps other people noticed as well. I'll never know, because it's not the sort of thing any of us would have talked about.

*

The memory that was brought to life by my reading of Proust happened the summer after the renovation of the house. It must have been a Saturday, because my mother and my aunt, who both worked all week, were home.

My grandmother called us all out to the side steps. She had leaned six green-painted wood-framed screens against the concrete stoop.

"I'm going to make a summer house with them," she said, pointing to me. "It will be yours. It will be for you and your friends."

My alarm was great, and there were, simultaneously, two causes for it. The first and most serious was that I had no idea what was meant by a summer house. I understood that my grandmother, who usually took no time for nor attached any importance to indulgence or endearment, was trying to do something wonderful for me. But I couldn't make a picture of the thing she wanted to do. I saw the six green-painted screens leaning against the concrete, and I couldn't imagine how anything approaching a dwelling could be made of them. And why another house? And where would it be placed?

The second reason for alarm was that I had no friends, and I didn't know whether my grandmother hadn't noticed that. Or whether she had noticed but believed this new thing she would build, this "summer house," would instantly draw people to me, people who once thought of me as having nothing to offer but now would know they had misthought.

In the midst of my alarm, I heard an unthinkable sound. My aunt was laughing at her mother. That low, close-mouthed, entirely mirthless noise that sounded like the slow winter starting of a reluctant car.

"What are you talking about, Ma?" she said. "You can't do that. You're not up to it. And where do you think you'd put it?"

"In the back yard," said my grandmother, with her accustomed force.

"There's no room for it there, we hardly have room for a barbecue. You must be crazy. I never heard you say anything so crazy in your life."

"The boys would help me," my grandmother said. I didn't know whether she meant her sons, her grandsons, or the neighbor children, whom she barely recognized.

"Forget it, Ma," my aunt said. "It's not in the cards."
There was a moment of brittle silence, like a sheet of gray glass
that stretched between them. My mother and I looked at each
other. We were part of the silence, but we knew we were of no
importance in it. We knew that something would happen, and
whatever it was would be important. And we knew that there was
nothing we could do. They'd taken us into the house out of charity.
We were only there because they'd said we could be, and we had no
right to anything.

My grandmother turned her back to all of us. She tucked three
screens under each arm and walked away from us, into the garage,
her back straight, her step unfaltering. She closed the garage door,
passed silently before the three of us, and went into the kitchen to
wash her hands.

The words "summer house" were not mentioned again.

And it's been thirty-five years since I've thought of them. Only
Proust's words brought them back to me, his description of the
dinner in Trouville:

> A few hours later, during dinner, which naturally was served in the
> dining room, the lights would be turned on, even when it was still quite
> light out of doors so that one saw before one's eyes, in the garden,
> among summer houses glimmering in the twilight like pale spectres of
> evening, arbours whose glaucous verdure was pierced by the last rays of
> the setting sun.

I am finishing dinner, alone at my table in the restaurant in
Trouville among women in pink-tinted gauzy dresses languidly lifting ices to their lips, or grapes. Their men are in frockcoats, indo-
lently lighting cigarettes. The champagne is returned, pronounced
"undrinkable." The young waiter reddens, scurries backward, produces the crestfallen maitre d'. Outside the sea laps in the distance,
the shore is phosphorescent, glowworms flicker in the arbor, night
flowers open, scent the air, retreat. Women rise slowly, men take
their arms. No need to hurry, no need, really, to do anything but
make one's way to bed. A dream perhaps of the sun on the ocean,
or a white sail against blue.

And then my grandmother enters in her stern shoes, old lady
shoes, black low-heeled oxfords, a version of which she wears in all

seasons and for all occasions. Her legs are thick in their elastic stockings, the color of milky coffee; she wears them for her varicose veins. Her housedress has a pattern of faded primroses; an apron is pinned to the bodice. Her ring sinks into the fourth finger of her square, mannish hands.

My grandmother doesn't know where to place herself in this company. For them she has only contempt. She is calculating, with a professional's knowledgeable eye, the cost of the gowns, the wastage of good food implied in every half-emptied dish on the exhausted table. She knows that she is saved and they are lost, that she is right and they are wrong, that she is wise and they are foolish.

Or does she? Is she perhaps not judging but yearning? Is she adoring those light, slow-moving people, with their empty hands? Their lovely skins, their high, impractical limbs. Their shoes that could take them nowhere. Perhaps she is not my grandmother, that is to say, not an old woman, but a young girl. Her bones are delicate and long. The skin of her hands is bluish white, transparent. She is hoping that one of them will say, "What a pretty child. Perhaps she'd join us for an ice."

And she will sit with them in a summer house, eating an ice, pistachio, lemon, perhaps in the shape of something, a flower or a bird. They will ask her about herself.

And she will say nothing, because she knows that would spoil everything. She will shake her head, refusing words, lifting the spoon from her dish to her lips, silent. Happy, very happy, thinking perhaps of the word "glaucous," with nothing asked of her and nothing that she needs to do.

DAVID HUDDLE

Past My Future

FROM STORY

A FEW WEEKS after my fourteenth birthday, a friend of my parents, a Mr. Gordon, asked me — quietly and directly — if I would like to have an adventure with him. He posed this question on a sunny afternoon while he and I sat together at the edge of my family's swimming pool, splashing our feet and talking. Mrs. Gordon sat with my mother a few yards away; they were tanning themselves and chatting. I appreciated how perfectly Mr. Gordon pitched his voice as much as if it had been a ring or a bracelet he had brought me. Only I could hear him. Of course I knew that if I wished, I could brush his question aside as more of his teasing. But I knew too that if I let my mother and Mrs. Gordon know what he had just said, he would be in trouble.

I told him yes — a yes just as quiet and direct as his question. There came a pause in our conversation — and our kicking of the swimming pool water — during which he and I regarded each other. I noticed that Mr. Gordon had shaved closely and recently. It pleased me to think that perhaps he had done so for my benefit.

He said, "Well." And I said, "Well?" And he said, "Well, Marcy, I shall be in touch with you."

Thinking about that day and those few minutes of conversation beside the pool, I ask myself if I understood exactly what he had in mind. I wasn't an infant. To be perfectly frank, I *wanted* my adventure with Mr. Gordon to be a sexual one.

Lately I had become ravenous for both experience and information. I'd read a few magazine articles that my parents had given me and parts of the books that they'd hidden away from me. One night, months earlier, when I was supposed to be attending a country-club dance but was instead walking around the golf course for the purpose of smoking cigarettes, I'd incidentally engaged in some very exciting kissing with a boy who had put his hand on my breast.

If he hadn't gotten nervous and laughed about what we were doing — which I took to mean that he was laughing at my breast — that boy could have gone a lot further with me than he did. Had he whispered that he wanted me to take off my clothes, I expect I would have taken them off. It was my first experience with such an intensity; in only a few moments I had reached a point of being vulnerable to the boy. Later in one's carnal education, one learns to stop short of that point or else to move to it as quickly as possible; that night I was intoxicated by what I hadn't ever felt before. The boy was a year ahead of me in school, but the next day, when I reviewed the events in my mind, I understood that he had no more experience than me and probably less knowledge.

I would have tried whatever he knew enough about to ask for. Instead of a request, I got his inane whinny of a laugh.

I was just getting used to my breasts. One seemed to be ahead of the other, which for all I knew made them comical. But I felt certain that even if they were, Mr. Gordon wouldn't laugh. He had always paid a grave attention to me, had brought me presents, had once called me from Singapore to wish me happy birthday. Whereas someone my own age could rather casually humiliate me, Mr. Gordon had for years been offering me a careful regard. So I said, "Yes."

When you go into a room with one other person and lock the door behind you, you are momentarily free of every principle by which people ordinarily speak and act with each other. How you're going to be — what you say and do, what you think and feel — with that person is entirely up to the two of you. You may legislate it as you wish. This is something I learned from spending a number of afternoons in a seventh-floor view-of-the-lake suite in Marsden Towers. Because I was on the track team at school, my parents didn't question me about how I spent my afternoons. I actually had quite a bit of time available to spend with Robert in the suite he had taken for us. Freedom and power came to me in those rooms, which was why I kept wanting to go back there for as long as I did.

There is a wrongness the world would have me feel about what Robert and I did. As if he committed a crime against me beyond even what is considered acceptably criminal. I refuse to feel that wrongness. Robert harmed me no more than I harmed him.

I realize now that my mother worked at being friends with Suzanne Gordon. I realize now that my mother had a crush — of the very civilized and restrained sort — on Robert. Robert was accustomed to being courted by other people. To my mother, he made himself entertaining, as he probably did to anyone who courted him. My mother and Robert had grown up together in Shaker Heights; in the past, whenever they were together, they had enjoyed reviewing the lives of their childhood acquaintances. Robert and my father had a formal regard for each other that was played out in terms my mother and I found amusing. We teased my bookish and decidedly unathletic father about the stilted conversations he and Robert carried on when they were required to chat. Mostly they discussed tennis, which Robert played regularly but didn't keep up with and which my father didn't play but kept up with. My father had no real interest in tennis; it was merely the case that every day of his life he read the *Plain Dealer* very thoroughly.

There was a subtlety to the way my mother and Suzanne Gordon related, a calculated warmth that generated erratic conversations between the two of them. Having thought about her all these years, I have decided that Suzanne was never able to locate herself properly in life, though she was an astute and able person. Sometimes I think I grew up having a crush — of the dry and feeble sort — on Suzanne. I remembered things she said; I liked the idea of her. She had no job; she had no children. Though she volunteered at the hospital and the library, she found no kindred spirits among the other volunteers. Her manner was aloof, her conversation somewhat wry, her frame of reference esoteric. Suzanne spent many hours reading of explorations, expeditions, feats of navigation, and mountain climbing. I suspect that she found almost no one who shared her interests.

The interest she had in Robert, however, she was able to share with my mother. Each knew where the other stood, though I believe that neither ever spoke frankly. As a young child, I had studied the way my mother and Suzanne talked. They sat with their backs straight in their chairs, their ankles crossed, and their hands in their laps, their faces pleasant. Such formal poses perfectly suited Suzanne; I hold vivid memories of her sitting like that in our living room with the light from our bay window catching the reddish highlights of her hair. I could feel the awkwardness of her talk with my mother when they took up certain topics they felt obligated to discuss — such as my father, whom my mother wasn't comfortable discussing and in whom Suzanne had no interest. But when they managed to bring the conversation around to their mutually passionate subject, they became animated, witty, and amused, even slouchy and unladylike in their postures.

"Robert actually laughed at that joke?" my mother might ask, sitting forward in her chair.

Suzanne's laughter would lilt through our house. "Not only did he laugh at that joke, last night he told the same joke to Nick Shelton in this disgusting . . ."

I took these exchanges as the proper way for grown-up women to converse. Out in the future I saw similar conversations awaiting me.

As I imagine most men do, Robert struggled to balance his appetite with his stamina. He was, however, a master of sustaining the illusion of vast possibility within the circumstance of sexual intimacy. He and I did nothing especially strange or hurtful or even, for that matter, adventuresome. I was fourteen. He was forty-one. For a while, that alone was adventure enough for each of us. At first, Robert liked to say that our ages were very nearly the same, the numbers were simply reversed. He seemed to be practicing a joke he might tell people if he and I ever went out together in public: "You know, Marcy and I are the same age, our numbers are merely . . ." I was glad when he stopped saying it.

We did not go out together. Ever.

The project we undertook was informing each other about ourselves. He didn't say so, but I think Robert wished me to teach him how it was to live in my mind and my body. He discerned the questions I wished him to ask me. He knew when to be quiet and let me talk. Or when to let me think through what I had just told him aloud until I came to the next thing I wanted to tell him. He knew when to interrupt me, to get me excited, to make me try to answer four questions at once. Whatever he seemed to want to know about me, I seemed to want to tell.

"Let the commerce commence," Robert liked to say upon entering those rooms at Marsden Towers. I understood him to mean both our talk and our sex. Mostly Robert asked questions, and I answered them. During these conversations, we undressed, we kissed, we nuzzled, we stroked; after a while I understood that we were talking as a way to extend the sex, to stretch it out and make it last. So the talk, for me, became a part of the sex — the commerce. But sometimes the commerce evolved into the silences that we let pass when we were simply breathing with each other in the afternoon sunlight that shone on our bed. Then we concentrated on not talking because the silence had become what would make the sex last.

Though his curiosity about me was his first interest, Robert also wished me to know how it was to be *him*, to live in his mind, his body. Those topics weren't anything I had a natural curiosity about. What I most wanted him to talk about was his wife, but he was reluctant to do so. If I asked him a question about Suzanne, he would answer so carefully that I could almost feel him searching for the most neutral phrasing. Sometimes he would finish up his answer with "Why do you want to know?" Which I hated. I always told him, "Oh, just because . . ." I'm not sure I knew this at the time, but I think I wanted Robert to describe how it was to make love to Suzanne — what little things she might have said, what she liked, even how she might have sighed or whimpered. But of course that was exactly the kind of information Robert wasn't about to give me. And I didn't want him to know I had such a squalid curiosity.

So I asked him questions about "the adult world" — as if it were a scientific topic. I did have a vague curiosity about the concept of being grown up, or perhaps I just had a desire to vent my complaints about grown-ups. Robert listened to me; sometimes he agreed, sometimes he sided with the teacher or the parent I was criticizing. He asked me not to categorize him as "an adult."

One afternoon he told me, "Think of the bodies of human beings as something like cars. We can't see into each other's interiors. Cars see other cars. I'm a station wagon. You're a sports car, but you have your top up so that I can't see who's driving. I just see this little red MG streaking past me on the turnpike. I think to myself, My goodness, I wish I could be like that MG. But the thing about it is, I am exactly like that MG. Except that I just got put behind the wheel of this station wagon — this middle-aged body with a middle-aged male mind under the hood — and I can't get out. I have to keep driving the equipment I've been given. The rules are that I can't give up the controls. But who's driving each one of us is this androgynous blob of a creature, one per car, all exactly the same. The driver of my car is exactly like the driver of your car.

"These creatures have no distinguishable color or shape; they're grayish greenish brown, polymorphous lumps, about the size of an egg. They do not age; they have no gender, no ethnic or racial characteristics. They are neutral creatures — though highly intelligent. And they are impatient with us for having such limited equipment. Mine thinks it's silly of me to worry so much about you getting home on time. But it understands that I am given to worrying. And yours probably wishes you'd keep more of an eye on the clock so as not to take the risk of having your parents quiz you about where you've been. But it understands your inclination to give yourself completely over to what you're doing. If my inner being could talk to your inner being, the two of them would immediately recognize that they're identical. Right away they'd start criticizing us to each other. Mine would say, 'I'll swear, Robert is so damn *middle-aged* sometimes. He just about drives me nuts.' And yours would say, 'I know exactly what you mean. The other day Marcy went shopping with her mother, and you wouldn't believe how she spoke to . . .'"

It was very rare when Robert and I were together that I didn't find myself engaged in whatever we were talking about. I've come to know that he was quite an imaginative man, though when I was with him then, he did not seem remarkable in that way. It was just that he *liked* talking with me so much that he made our conversations interesting. He found ways to do that. And the ways he found had to do with figuring out what I might like to talk about, what would entertain me or interest me or pique my curiosity. He didn't ever condescend; I had a sense of conversing *with* him, as if the two of us were talking our way toward some destination.

Here is something Robert told me he thought a young woman should know: If you think a man might be interested in you but you're not sure, find an occasion to sit close to him. Go with this man to a lecture, say, or a reading, something in an auditorium, and preferably not a movie or a play, both of which can be distracting. Unobtrusively fix yourself not to be touching him but to be very nearly that. If possible, align your upper arm with his upper arm, not touching, of course, but approximately one inch apart. Then it's simple. If he has no interest in you, there will be nothing to notice. If he's interested, you will feel a certain warmth coming from his body. If he's extremely interested, you'll be surprised that his body would so overtly and crudely give him away.

In a man's mind, even when it's clear that he wants a woman to be thinking about him, he would prefer her not to know the extent of his liking her. His body, however, will always reveal how much or how little interest he has. Arranging the appropriate seating is the only difficulty. The man who knows this secret may, even as you are trying to find out about him, easily measure your own interest.

Robert was utterly wrong about what my life was going to be like. Whether or not his little lesson was a useful one I couldn't say. I have had no occasion when it occurred to me to test it.

It ended because of a boy. I shouldn't be ashamed of that, though it always seems to me this was how I betrayed Robert. A boy my own age. I began talking to Robert about this boy. For a while I wasn't thinking about what I might be revealing. I was just telling him about school, and Allen Crandall kept coming up in my conversation. I kept hearing myself say his name. I kept watching Robert when I said it.

That must have been how I realized I liked Allen Crandall. Allen was an athlete and moved through the hallways with a swagger. Allen wasn't afraid to disagree with even the teachers who got mad at you if you disagreed with them. Sometimes I saw Allen looking at me as if he knew something amusing about me, though I knew he didn't. As I talked more and more about Allen to Robert, I began noticing a hardening of Robert's face. So I tried to hush myself up. By that time — or well before it — Robert had discerned my interest in Allen. So he began to question me.

A sadness came into Robert's voice — even into his body — that I hated.

The sadness actually became Robert's oldness. For more than a year, I hadn't paid much attention to his age, but now it seemed evident in everything about him. His face, his clothes, the way he talked and combed his hair and rubbed his temples when he was tired. Even the way he smelled. He had an expensive cologne-deodorant-soap fragrance about him that I had loved from back in my childhood but that now began to bother me. Everything about Robert seemed so inescapably sad. He made me think of my father, alone in the house on Sunday afternoons and listening to one of his classical records turned up loud the way he liked to listen to them.

The commerce had become almost completely conversation — and conversation that neither Robert nor I seemed to enjoy. Quickly after I started talking so much about Allen, the commerce had changed.

"Let the commerce commence!" I called out one afternoon when I burst into the room, feeling exhilarated from my day at school and meaning to make a joke that would cheer us both up. As I came in, Robert was walking toward me in the little foyer. I knew he had in mind to give me one of his sad hugs. I was close enough to him to notice his wince the instant I'd made my joke.

To his credit, Robert managed to stay just far enough ahead of me to know how I felt and what the consequences of my feelings were. One rainy afternoon I walked to the Marsden Towers thinking I just had to make myself tell him I wasn't going to be coming back there anymore. Robert was listening for me. Just as I set my hand to knock, he swung open the door. He was cheerful, teasing, impeccably dressed in a new suit and shirt and brightly striped tie. Usually he took his suit jacket off while he waited for me to arrive, but not today. He wore it buttoned, and for a moment or two he looked as magnificent to me as when I had been a young girl looking up at this grand visitor to our house. When he kissed me on both cheeks and then my forehead, I noticed that his shoes had been freshly polished.

"I'm setting you free, my dear," he said. "Our adventure has reached its conclusion." He had fancy glasses on a tray and champagne for himself and Perrier with a little dish of lemon slices for me. He poured the glasses full, handed me mine, and lifted his to me. "This has been so lovely, Marcy," he said. "I can't begin to tell you."

There was more he planned to say. I wanted to help him say it. I lifted my glass to him too, so that our glasses made the little *tink* that seems so celebratory when you're in the mood for it. Though he opened his mouth to go on, Robert couldn't. Just before he turned to the window, he began swatting the air in front of his eyes. I thought he might be about to sneeze or that he was trying to wave away some insect buzzing at his face. Then, with his back to me, he made a noise. Or I saw how his shoulders moved, and I imagined that he made a noise.

I knew.

"All right, Robert," I said, and I set my glass back down on the tray. "Thank you," I said. I touched the back of his suit jacket. I brushed my hand down his back just a bit. Just enough to feel how much he didn't want me to touch him.

And I knew, then, to leave the room.

As a child, I was sometimes awakened by my parents making love. My room was across the hall from them, and often what woke me was one of them getting up to close the door to their room. Then I could hear only faint noises, their voices more like humming than talking. But even that way, with the door muffling what they said, I could distinguish something different in their tones, a new sound, a quality that I didn't hear them use in their ordinary conversation — like a sound each made especially for the other, as if softly singing.

Sometimes either they forgot about the door being open or else they thought it was too deep into the night for me to be awake. At any rate, they left it open. Then I could listen carefully. I found it very exciting to hear them. I don't know how old I was when I realized what they must be doing. When I was very little, of course, I must have had no idea what they were up to. But I don't remember that. I remember only knowing what the noise meant and wanting to hear every single bit of it.

I've read about children being drawn to the sounds of their parents' lovemaking, but I wasn't ever tempted to go to them or interrupt them. I stayed very quiet, because I wanted them to reach their conclusion. Which was marked by my father's restrained shout — into the pillow I suppose — "Oh, oh! Oh, my darling," he said. I loved that. I loved for him to call out. My father is long dead now, but remembering his voice like that still makes me smile to myself.

As an adult, I have thought about what I heard. I've wondered, for instance, about the extent of my mother's satisfaction. None of the noises I ever heard suggest that she reached orgasm during their intercourse, though the sounds she made do suggest that her intercourse with my father was a pleasure to her. And she always seemed to me someone who was aware of her own sexuality. So what did she do? Masturbate when no one was around? Go without orgasms altogether? In those days there wasn't much sex, I am tempted to say, but of course that would be wrong. Enlightened sex is what there wasn't much of. And I could be wrong about that too. At any rate, I never heard my mother make a noise I could construe as her coming. Publicly, she was a bit of a prude; it's possible she faked *not* having orgasms. I suppose it's improper to wonder very much about your mother coming.

The other part I wonder about is what effect it had on me to eavesdrop on their lovemaking. Did it make me overly interested in sex? Had my parents awakened me and insisted that I listen to them, that would have been sexual abuse. But of course it was very nearly the same experience, my listening to them so carefully from across the hallway. Did it, for instance, make me vulnerable to Robert when he posed his question to me by the poolside? Would I have so readily known what Robert meant if I hadn't had this education, so to speak? Would I have said yes so readily?

Not so long ago, talking with my friend Ute, we came to this topic, our parents' sex lives. I told Ute that I'd often overheard my parents doing it. When I asked her what effect she thought that might have had on me, she said, "I don't know, Marcy. I can tell you that never in all my life did I see or hear any evidence that *my* parents even had sex lives. If you ask me, that was much worse than what you're talking about. I sometimes wonder how I ever got my feet on this planet. At least you know how you got here. At least you know your parents cared about each other enough to do it."

I told Ute I supposed she had a point.

A few afternoons when he thought I would be home by myself, Robert called and attempted to chat with me, politely, about how things were going for me. This was after our last meeting at Marsden Towers, and though I didn't wish them to be, these calls were awkward occasions. Neither of us was able to relax into a conversation.

On an afternoon when Allen Crandall had come home with me, ostensibly to study for an exam, Robert called.

It was spring, near the end of May. Allen and I were exuberant with the end of the school year approaching and with our discovery of each other. We were gossiping about our classmates and mocking them and laughing a great deal while we walked around my house, drinking soda and munching on chips and crackers from the kitchen. I was just then catching on to the way Allen talked, a clipped, half-joking way of saying everything. When the phone rang, I had no doubt about who the caller was. The instant I heard myself say hello — with the fun still in my voice but also a bit of the dread I felt at having to carry on even a short conversation with him — I knew that Robert would know Allen was in the house with me.

There was the slightest bit of a pause. Then Robert's voice came through the receiver: "Hello, Marcy. I hope you're well. I'll call you back another time."

I said, "All right." The line went dead.

And of course Allen asked who it was. Instantly I had to make up something to tell him. "My mom," I said. "She wants me to . . . set out some eggs." I went to the refrigerator, removed a tray of brown eggs, and set them on the counter.

Allen was looking at me with his head tilted when I turned to him. He gave his head a little shake and said, "Speaking of eggs, you think we ought to crack those books?"

I said, "Nah." And I went toward him, meaning to tickle him if I could. I wanted to recover the mood we'd had before the phone rang.

"Weird over here at your house," Allen said, dodging my attack. "Your mom calls and you get sad. You say, 'All right,' hang up the phone, then go to the refrigerator and set out a tray of eggs. Weird, I'd say."

I stopped trying to tickle him. "You haven't seen anything yet, my dear," I said. "My dear" coming out of my mouth made my face turn hot; it was Robert's phrase, not mine. But I was determined not to be undone by Robert's phone call. I began picking up things from throughout the house and setting them in odd places. I carried a magazine from the living room to the kitchen, where I put it in the refrigerator; I plucked down my father's ski hat from the closet and arranged it as the centerpiece of the dining room table; I asked Allen to take off his loafers, which I then ceremoniously carried to the downstairs bathroom and placed in the sink. Allen was kind enough to overlook my desperation in trying to amuse him. He let himself be amused, and soon we'd recovered the old spirit of kidding around.

That was the day I decided I wouldn't ever, under any circumstances, tell Allen about Robert and me. Why *that* day? I suppose because I saw myself taking a great deal of trouble to disguise the fact that my former lover had called me. I realized that even having a former lover, not to mention a man almost three times as old as I was, wasn't something I wanted anybody my age to know. You would think — since I married him — a time would have come when I could tell Allen all about Robert.

Such a time did not ever arrive.

The swimming pool, the commerce, the way we sometimes ordered food sent up to our room and ate it while the commerce went on — it was this intricate and intense part of my life. I wouldn't give it over to Allen. It wasn't so much that I didn't want Allen to have it as that I wanted to hold it entirely to myself — whether from embarrassment or selfishness I have never been able to decide.

I've wondered whether or not Robert had in mind actual intercourse with me. We settled into a rhythm of meeting at the suite he rented at Marsden Towers. Our rhythm had progressed to a point where for at least the last hour I was there, he and I were in bed without our clothes on. Foreplay was what this was; I had read about it. And I appreciated Robert's patience. He seemed in no hurry, seemed to have no *sexual* destination in mind, as if we could simply pass these hours in bed kissing and fondling each other — and of course talking — and that would be fine with him. With his hands and his mouth, he had satisfied me; afterward he was so sweet to me that for a while I had no desire to go any further.

I think Robert wanted no more than that.

But then I wanted all of it. And I didn't want to say I wanted all of it. It seemed so crude of me that I couldn't bear saying it aloud. As a matter of fact, Robert's restraint, his not moving toward penetration, was something I associated with his elegance, his worldly sophistication. So this was a project I set for myself, to move us closer and closer to actual sex without saying that was what I had in mind, to move so gradually Robert would know it had happened only afterward. If my desires were crude, at least I could be subtle in how I went about fulfilling them.

Robert had given me a certain amount of education about my menstrual cycle, so that I was able to calculate the days when I was least likely to get pregnant. Over a couple of weeks, I moved toward fooling around with Robert in bed in positions that were very close to intercourse. When our bodies were like that, I escalated my conversation to an intense and amusing level. Robert was wary of me — I could feel him holding himself away from me. But then, because he liked it, he got used to letting me arrange myself over him that way and to letting me manipulate him with my hand while we carried on this intensely sexual conversation. Truth be told, it was about as exciting a time as I've ever experienced in all of my sexual life. Perhaps that was because I had a conquest in mind, and it was the only time I've ever done such a thing. Robert and I had journeyed through this progressive choreography where I knew all it would take would be only one quick lifting of my hips, a push, and a smooth plunge down.

There came an afternoon when I knew I was going to manage it. The look on his face, the little *O* of his mouth, the stunned knitting of his brow, was priceless. "You're inside me now, aren't you, Robert?" I whispered to him, bending close to his face, squeezing still closer to him, trying to get all the front of my body against him. "You're right in there, aren't you?"

"Pregnant," he mouthed.

"No," I whispered. I couldn't have known I wouldn't get pregnant — and later on Robert would be scrupulous about birth control — but at the moment I was foolishly certain it was a safe time. And what pain I felt was something I seemed to set aside. For that matter, what sexual sensations I felt I knew, I would begin paying attention to very shortly. I wanted only to consider the way the skin around his eyes crinkled in little involuntary tremors. The deepest secret I think I know of men I took from Robert's face in those few seconds.

In the moment when you bring him into yourself, a man is helpless before you. He will take great pains to keep you from knowing that. When he comes, he is vulnerable to all of creation —

which of course frightens him — but when he first goes into you, he is vulnerable only to you — which frightens him most of all. In Robert's face that afternoon, I saw Judith of Bethulia holding up the head of Holofernes and Salome displaying the head of John the Baptist. Though of course I didn't really know what I saw, beyond the little *O* of Robert's mouth and the skin around his eyes. But it wasn't long before Robert and I were past all that. Soon enough we were caught up in the pleasure we had to give each other.

For many months I kept expecting I would see Robert. I knew he was having to maneuver rather carefully to keep from encountering me in the course of socializing with my parents. He did manage that. If he and Suzanne came over to our house, it was at a time when I wouldn't be there. Somehow he kept those occasions to a minimum. When my parents saw the Gordons, it was at a party at someone else's house, a restaurant, or the Gordons' house. My mother was aware that Robert and Suzanne were not at our house nearly as often as they had been in previous years, but it wasn't something she chose to discuss with me. I knew she was keeping it to herself, and I might have been a little irked about that. I do recall a conversation between my parents, in which my mother said, "We don't seem as close to them as we used to be," and my father said, "Oh? I hadn't noticed any change." Since they were talking about something else then, they let the topic of the Gordons drop, which suited me well enough, because my pulse had picked up in a way that made me uncomfortable.

I have always had trouble giving it a name — affair, relationship, arrangement, liaison, I still don't know what to call it. At any rate, in the first months after Robert and I ended whatever it was, I dreaded seeing him. And I thought he might try to see me. When it became apparent that he didn't want to see me, I began wanting to see him.

I wasn't sure why.

I certainly didn't want to *talk* with Robert — because I hadn't liked those telephone conversations we had attempted. So even though talking had been what I most valued about being with him, I knew that I wasn't after any more talk. But now I did want to see him, and not just his face but the whole of him. As if my eyes had to take hold of him.

Maybe more truthfully, what I wanted was for him to look at me and for me then to be able to see what his face would tell me about who I had become. Maybe I thought his face would tell me whether or not I had gone beyond him. For a while I entertained a fantasy that Robert came into our house on one of the afternoons when I was alone. Robert simply walked in. From the living room where I sat, I saw him and wasn't surprised or frightened. He was dressed as he was when I had seen him last, in one of his dark business suits with a white shirt and a bright tie. With his hands in his jacket pockets, he stood in our foyer, looking at me, neither frowning nor smiling. I returned his stare. Then he took his hands from his pockets and made that downward movement, fluttering his fingers, as if he were miming the way leaves would fall from a tree. In our rooms at Marsden Towers, that gesture meant that he wished me to take off my clothes.

By that time — I was sixteen — I knew more about my body and had come to think that how it looked didn't have much to do with who I actually was. It was what it could do that mattered to me. For my school's track team I did hurdles and the high jump. My body's strength and quickness were so important to me that I became irritated when people made so much of how it looked. So in this fantasy, I said, "No, Robert. That isn't possible." My voice had a sternness I had never used with him. I remained sitting. And Robert said nothing then. He merely nodded, looked wistful, turned, and left the house.

When I knew he was gone, I tiptoed quietly to the door, locked it, then stood with my back braced against it.

This moment of my back against the door was extremely satisfying. For a number of months, I found myself moving through this daydream, refining it, taking a peculiar comfort from it.

One evening my parents invited Allen Crandall to join us for dinner at Forlini's, a noisy place that had replaced the bottom floor of one of the city's old department stores. The dining area was so enormous that on a busy night it was like a circus tent. Waiters and waitresses ran, busboys and busgirls ran, even the two hostesses ran and smiled and shouted among the many tables of people as if this were an obstacle course for a clown race. My parents liked Forlini's because the crowd was young and stylish; my father said it was a preview of the people who would be running the city in another ten years. My mother and I liked it for the spectacle, for being able to see so many people all at once, not to mention the zipping back and forth of the waiters and waitresses, who all wore khaki shorts and red T-shirts and who seemed to have been picked for their lively appearances. Allen had never been to Forlini's before; ordinarily he would have concentrated on practicing his conversational skills with my parents, but this evening he seemed nearly overwhelmed by the thick hum of voices, all those bodies, and their laughing, talking, feeding faces. The four of us sat at our table gawking at the people around us.

"Is that Robert? Isn't that Robert and Suzanne?" my mother asked my father. She was sitting up straight in her chair and squinting across the room.

A splash of icewater down my back might have affected me similarly. Shocked as I was, some part of me was oddly angry that my mother had addressed her question only to my father. To her, my acquaintance with Robert was so negligible that it hadn't occurred to her to ask me. That angry part of myself seemed a distinct and dangerous person at the moment. She was a Marcy who wanted to smack the restaurant table hard enough to make the flatware clatter. She was a Marcy who wanted to make a speech to her parents, to Allen, and even to the diners near us: "Is that Robert Gordon? Well, Mother, why don't you ask me? I am the one whose fingertips have touched every square inch of that man's body. I expect I am the one you should ask if the man you're looking at is Robert."

What that Marcy wanted to prove with such a speech seemed just beyond my knowing. As quickly as she had seemed about to burst into the open, she diminished down into my prudent self. I was in fact being so prudent that I couldn't make myself turn directly toward where my mother was straining to see. She must have remembered I could recognize Robert too, because she said, "Right there, Marcy." Then, because she was sitting beside me and I wasn't looking the right way, my mother actually pulled my chin to turn my head in the proper direction.

So I saw him.

My mother held my head turned in Robert's direction, as if she thought she had to keep helping me see him. My eyesight seemed to soar across the room toward him and cast him in a light. So clearly could I see his face that I noticed a ripple of tension pass from his temple down along his jawline. I saw him squint to make out what peculiar thing it was my mother was doing to my head. I saw him half lift one hand toward us, as if to wave or to signal my mother to loosen her hold on me. His other hand he kept at Suzanne's upper arm as they moved toward the steps leading up out of the restaurant.

Red-capped and bandannaed cooks shoved pizzas and casserole dishes into wood-burning ovens while they shouted to each other and to the waiters and waitresses. Robert and Suzanne were far across the cavernous room, which swelled and echoed with the raucous voices of hundreds of people. A woman at a table near us laughed at a very high pitch; she seemed unable to stop herself. Near Robert and Suzanne a man stood up and waved both arms to get the attention of someone. An Edith Piaf song played stridently over the sound system. Even the ceiling lights seemed to flicker.

He was much paler than I had ever seen him, which made me suspect that during the months of our meetings at Marsden Towers he must have used a tanning lamp. I wondered why I hadn't noticed that at the time.

What disturbed me was how Robert's body and Suzanne's body were such a matched set. Robert had dressed down for the evening — in a dark golf shirt and chinos. His thin chest and thick waist were much more visible than when he wore a suit. Suzanne's dress seemed almost designed to accentuate how age had softened her figure. Anyone else looking at the couple leaving the restaurant probably wouldn't have noticed their bodies at all. But I couldn't help it. The two of them were connected by how their bodies were placed in time — I saw that just so clearly, the way I've suddenly realized I was seeing the male and female of a pair of birds. In Robert and Suzanne, this wasn't something I wanted to see. It felt improper, as if I were watching them undress together.

Robert was moving away from me even though he kept his face turned toward me. He appeared almost to be pushing Suzanne to the exit. Though he knew me well enough to know I would never make a scene, he was terrified that I might approach him in front of his wife. He was terrified that I might say hello to him.

I needed him to be so much better than that! A burst of fury came into me — and died almost immediately. But had I been close enough to do so in that single instant, I would have spat upon him.

I've tried to forgive Robert his cowardice of that evening. I don't think I've managed it. What I saw in his pale face staring at me across the room was that with his wife beside him, he couldn't stand to speak to me.

So he ran from a mere child.

Of course he had to turn his face away from me. When Robert did that — when he gave me the back of his thin shoulders to see — I felt released. I felt as if I had just then beaten him at something. I became aware that I had half risen from my chair and my parents and my boyfriend were staring at me. Easing back down into my seat, I turned to them and found three frozen faces. Allen had even paused in chewing his food. Our lives depended on what I was going to do next, I knew that. It took all my strength to smile at Allen and resume eating.

ANNA KEESEY

Bright Winter

FROM GRAND STREET

We believe it to be a case of life and death. It is death to remain connected
with those bodies that speak lightly of, or oppose, the coming of the Lord.
It is life to come out from all human tradition, and stand upon the Word
of God . . . We therefore now say to all who are in any way entangled in the
yoke of bondage, "Come out from among them, and be ye separate, saith
the Lord."
> — *Joshua V. Himes, in the imminent-advent newspaper*
> The Midnight Cry, *August 29, 1844*

Broadhill,
January 12th

John Ephraim,
   If I chose to I could find you and bring you home. I am known in
the several towns where you may be lodged, even as far as Grasstown where the mayor once welcomed my money. Favors are owed
to me up and down this county. I could employ men to go around
the towns and knock on the doors and demand that the landladies
array their boarders on the steps. This would flush you out eventually, no matter how you covered your ears and ignored the noise.
But why should your foolishness disrupt my day's work? Duty and
self-regard forbid me to go snuffing at your footprints. I shall simply
write, and make several copies and distribute them around to those
you may have dealings with. In this way you may receive a letter and
be assured of my feelings in this matter, that is to say, irked, and
faintly amused.
   The horse you rode I will consider leased by the day. I will determine the schedule of repayment when you have come home.
   Your mother is cheerful but weak, and stays abed. She does not

know you've gone. I have said you are traveling with Daniel Kimball to hear the concerts at Braxton. A lie.

your Father

Broadhill,
January 16th

John Ephraim,

Perhaps shame has made you shy. But let me say that if you will see your error and come back, we will forget this episode. It will never color our relations in the future. And your mother need never know.

your Father

January 19th

John Ephraim,

I have had no response from you this week. Twice I sent letters to the Congregation men of Braxton, Lewiston, Rocky Ford, Carlisle, and Grasstown. I have of course bound them to discretion, as reputations are not easily repaired in this county. One letter went along in the pocket of James Spencer, who was traveling to Lewiston. His Marie asks after you, he tells me. I was silent, unwilling to lie — a rude man and a bad neighbor. For this I thank you. The other letters I took myself. I gave them to these church men because who knows where your fellows may gather to worship — I know only that some of them have been expelled from their congregations, and that these ministers may be able to name them. So this is what you want. To leave the world of warm society and sensible character. To shame your family into lies.

Not a man has seen you in any town. I made discreet inquiry, saying my son had passed through recently and asking, had he stopped in to pass the time? No? A heedless young man, too thoughtful, too studious, and thus rude. In this way I dressed your disrespect in the clothes of a common flaw. Again and again, I gave a chuckle that hurt my throat.

But no one had seen you. Once I asked myself if you might be hurt, struck down by robbers on a road. But no. We argued, and you have taken yourself off on your own legs for your own fool's vision. Moreover on my travels a corroborating rumor came to my attention. This was in the hatter's shop in Rocky Ford. The hatter had heard of a gathering, an encampment across the river. People of all kinds were wading the ford with their children, he said, even carrying their babies still in skirts. They've come to play at some absurd game, he said, they're bewitched by preachers with loud voices who rattle chains. And why they chose us, a sensible township, I don't know. Perhaps because they could get space near the river, and so carry water a shorter distance.

I said, Some people will let their fields to any rabble with cash.

You may be among these feverish pilgrims wetting their toes at the ford. Perhaps you wonder if I was tempted to cross and look for you. I was not. My equilibrium is not such that a gadding child can disturb it, and I had business at the bank. My goodbye to the hatter was comfortable. I've known him for years.

Your silence perplexes me, John Ephraim.

your Father

January 24th

John Ephraim,

My hand begins to tire from copying letters. Colleagues at the bank have noticed it shake a bit when I sign my name. They wonder, too, why I send these letters out to Lewiston, Rocky Ford, Carlisle, Grasstown. They may believe I correspond with creditors. Or, perhaps, a woman. They may be saying Josiah Cole has turned from his wife in her illness.

But now I need not copy. I need send only to the minister Gearhart at Rocky Ford, who will find a suitable messenger. I am sure you are there.

For the story of the great blue tent erected at the crook of the river has appeared in the newspapers amid great joking. It's said that wild-eyed unmarried women make up the majority of the congregation, and are given to shouting prayers until they lose strength and must be carried out. Then there are drinkers, crawling babies, servants, and shaking old men who sing. A respectable community, my son! I see that there are many who share your brooding reading of Revelations, many others who have sat in their attics over the last year eschewing decent work and company, totting up numbers from the Bible as though God would speak to us in some heathenish code. There is even a report that your fellows have ordered a hundred bolts of white cloth, that they may sew robes to wear when they ascend. This sewing at least might someday get you respectable employment. We've had tailors in the family before this, and you've already shown you don't mind spending time on your knees. Do you sleep on the ground with strangers, John Ephraim? Pardon my interest. I understand that they are brothers to you, and will live with you when God has annihilated the rest of us in a storm of fire. Well that you should learn their names, I suppose.

I scarcely dare hope that you have sent a letter crossing this, explaining.

your Father

January 25th

John Ephraim,

Let me amend the common saying and tell you that there's no great tomfoolery without some small gain. I had stopped over for supper with Mr. Partle, the new lawyer, and his wife. There was a good roast of pork and a glass of sherry and pleasant talk. The Partle boy is down at college and will begin to learn law in the autumn. Peculiar how many people seem to plan on autumn's actually arriving.

Partle told me of a story he'd heard, that a woman out in Missouri had suckled an elk and raised it as her child. At least, several people had told him it was true. I opined that we were living in a climate of odd gullibility. Of course I did not elaborate. But see how my point was made for me! As I sat with Partle, there was a knock at the door, and on the stoop was a visitor looking for me. I recognized Will Whiting, our hired man years ago when you were a boy. Do you remember him? The one with a face like a shrew, who could not converse with your mother because he was always hiding his teeth.

Will, I said, it's quite a surprise. I thought you were in Indiana with the railroad.

I was, he said, but I've come back with a bad conscience. He took a little parcel from inside his coat. I opened it. Seven dollars in coin.

He said, When I worked for you I stole seven dollars. Now I'm here to settle my accounts. The Lord is coming, he said, and I want to go to meet him free and clear.

And out he goes! Partle and I had a little laugh over him. To think of old Will Whiting taking his soul so seriously. So the advent-

near may have seduced my son, but it has at least given me seven dollars. Partle thought he'd write to all his old hired men anonymously and give them a little shove.

your Father

January 27th

John Ephraim,

Naturally I have had to tell your mother. You may not have considered when you left that she would long for you. Last night she listened to my excuse, and lifted her hand off the blanket.

Enough, now, Josiah, she said. Did he become ill traveling? What is there to tell?

I brought her the newspaper and held the lamp to it. She read slowly.

She said, It's the same as he has been saying these ten months. That God will come to us in the springtime.

They seem very confident, I told her.

So there is no use in planting seeds this year? she asked. Nor in other work?

I told her, No. Nor in repairing the barn or training the foals.

No use to send for a French bonnet?

No use to convert the native. No use to marry.

To marry was ever useless, she said. Oh, your mother smiling.

Then she said, He told us we were in danger. The foolish virgins who keep no oil in their lamps will be shut out from the wedding feast. Ah. This was the danger. Our young man gone.

This is beyond a jest. It is time for you to clear your head and come home.

your Father

February 2nd

John Ephraim,

No answer from you so I will not write.

your Father

February 3rd

John Ephraim,

Gearhart writes that he gives my letters to an old man who claims to belong to your blue congregation. He cannot take them himself, as he is too busy with his own alarmed and talkative flock. But he is not sure this fellow, a troubled drinker of spirits, and full of self-praise, tells him the truth. So I do not know if you read my lines and ignore them, or never receive them at all. Do you reject us utterly? I feel perhaps I

February 4th

I cannot remember what I meant to say, yesterday, so I start again (you see my strict use of paper has not changed). You may be pleased to know that your mother was up today for nearly two hours. I made her a long chair with a few blankets and the pillow from your bed. I brought out another chair and sat with her. It was very warm, and there were birds calling now and then — in February! The skin of her hand is as thin as silk now. I touched it while she slept. So your parents, hopelessly depraved, spent the afternoon. You may think on this.

your Father

February 7th

John Ephraim,

Today I rode to Rocky Ford myself. Some children on the street directed me out to the bank of the river, to a muddy place marked by hooves, where other people had come to look. The river went sliding along, very deep, so the surface spun slowly. There seemed to be no ice at all. Across, in the field, I saw the blue tent snapping in the warm wind above the winter grasses. The teetering skeleton of a fence encircled it, in some places ten feet high. Young boys were hammering boards and raw branches to the uprights. Under the crosspieces, children ran to and fro. One little girl dragged out a basket as big as a wheelbarrow, and began to pull it toward the water. A slender young man came out — my heart leapt, and fell — and took basket and child back inside. I stood until only a few blue triangles and the crackling blue roof were still visible to me. I turned to go.

Behind me a man stood on a tree stump. He was dressed like a farmer, with clumsy chunks of mud on his boots. He spoke down to me in an angry voice, and struck his own leg with his cap. He said, Who are they to build a bloody ark? As full of sin as the rest, and now living like that. A crime. And children with them. He said, They should be whipped.

It took me a long time to ride back to Broadhill, and Marie Spencer, who was looking after your mother, was late for her supper at home.

your Father

February 15th
John Ephraim,
Today I met James Spencer on the street and lifted my hand and smiled, and he went on past as though I'd been a phantom. I was so shaken. No explanation occurred to me at first. I went in at the feed-store and there was talking that hushed as the bell of the door died away. In the silence I bought twenty pounds of oats and had to pat my coat endlessly before I found money in its usual pocket.

Usually when I walk into the bank in the morning there is a flurry of industry at the desks; one can hear quills snap in earnestness. Today there was quiet, and a peering-round over shoulders. I sat in my chair and drew my papers toward me but I could not see. In a moment Satterwhite, James's clerk, came in to explain his absence. Addressing not me but the sleeve of my coat, he said that young Marie Spencer had left home on foot to go to the encampment at Rocky Ford, and had been gone all night before her parents caught up to her. They'd brought her back between them in the wagon and were seen by early risers. She spoke of your son, the clerk told me softly. So you see, John Ephraim, naturally the town has lunged to this repast of gossip. While you dally by the river, they feed on our good name.

At dusk, I walked over to the Spencers' place. I brooded on what could be done to quell the talk, to make the town forget you. It was one of the strange warm evenings we've been having, and I passed through the thin black trees of the woodlot, squinting into the last orange glint of the sun. Over my shoulder I saw that my shadow was as long as a path. Have you noticed, where you are, that though it is warm there are no new leaves?

Kit Spencer did not want to invite me in, I could see. But James motioned at the window. He offered me my usual chair and cup of tea.

When we had drunk, he said, Well, Josiah, she wants to be his wife in Heaven.

I tried to laugh a bit. He did not join me. He looked into the fire and rubbed his pinched nose. His face looked as it did years ago, when the river came up suddenly and drowned the lambs in their pen.

I have been wrong, he said, to trust his interest in her well-being.

Should I have said to him then what I had long hoped, that one day our children might love one another, and unite my family with that of my closest friend? I could not. I was afraid to see the impatient jerk of his face, the disdain. I stirred my tea.

He said, He has convinced her that the world will end and that he knows the day.

I said, It is the mad fervor of youth. It will pass. James, it must pass.

But his face was set against me.

Then we saw young Marie at the door. Come through, my dear, said her father, and she came through the room without looking at me. If you are concerned for her, I will tell you: she looked much as usual, but tired. Her hair was escaping around her face and her red braid was rough and unruly behind. They have shown her that she must remain at home, James says. Twice, though, she has woken up weeping. She believes she will die by fire. For shame, John Ephraim. For shame.

                                                        your Father

                                                   February 24th
Dear John Ephraim,

You may have noticed that I have not written for some time. I had thought of remaining silent and letting curiosity bring you out. But I find there is too much to say to you. It is an empty house, with you gone, and your mother lying quietly abed. I find the space filling up with my thoughts. I build a stingy fire and, when your mother is sleeping, go down and deliberate beside it until it fades. I have been to Sunday services but twice since you went, preferring to worship at home with your mother. I'm not so pleased with this new man Wheelwright. He knows any amount of Scripture, but as for shedding light — he preaches hard on the thinnest verses, with much perspiring and waving of the elbows. In my evenings alone I have turned again to my Bible, and, I must say, have found much censure of your flight. The obvious I need not quote. We both know God's first direction to children, that their days might be long on the land. But do you ever chance to refresh your mind among the Psalms, and read: Rid me and deliver me from the hand of strange children, whose mouth speakest vanity, and their right hand is the hand of falsehood, that our sons may be as green plants grown up in their youth and our daughters may be as cornerstones? And Malachi, who writes that the heart of the children shall turn to the fathers lest the earth be smited with a curse. With these plain instructions and what natural love for us you may still bear, why do you stay away?

To be truthful, I have also been reminded that it is not for a father to provoke his son to anger, and I have sat in reverie, considering it. After a week of such thinking I have decided this. That though your disrespect to your father is a clear sin, though your talk is humbug by his standard, though you have fled your family into a squalid delusion and corrupted the mind of a young girl — though these things be true without doubt in my mind, still I think I may have offended in my own small way. The afternoon before you went, when we spoke hotly near the barn, I implied that your mind was not your own. I saw you step back, brush in hand, from the sorrel who stood stamping and rippling her skin, but I continued, as I felt I must. I did believe it was my duty to decide for you what might enrich or endanger your soul — you were my son, and still young, and living in my house. But when I shook your arm, and called you vain and dramatic, this may have hurt you. I acknowledge it.

Your mother requests that I come to you and ask you back. I cannot see my way to it just now. You must extend your own hand. But may this clear the air between us.

your Father

March 1st

John Ephraim,

For a week I've gone to the bank and concentrated only on that work. My regular hours, my usual dinner in the safety of friends. I've held conversations that never refer to my family. But at my desk I read. In the lectures and letters the papers print, I see that there is discussion of the 18th, 19th, and 20th days of this month, and of whether one must measure time by the time of day in Jerusalem. It is also said that in the encampments the people weave baskets in which they may sit and be whisked to heaven. It is the sneering writers who report this, I admit. I should think it general knowledge that if God wanted to take a man up He would not need to be

provided with handles. I make these jokes to myself at my desk and
then I lift my head and stare out into the street, and my heart
pounds. Since James Spencer has given Marie leave to stay with
your mother (though oh how coldly), I rode today to Rocky Ford.
The earth is hard under the drying decay of leaves; one can
feel the shock of hooves against it. At the side of the road, poor
bleached grasses wave. Some trees bear on their trunks a sleeve of
grime, where ice was pooled only a few weeks past. The sun comes
up strange, I think, with a light that looks very old, sharply yellow,
biting at the eye. And yet nothing grows. Perhaps you have come
out of your tent and seen this. The hatter says the weather is called
a bright winter and, if one accepts the almanac, should precede an
icy wet spring. I think of your tattered, disappointed tent, the rain
thudding on you after the joyless great day.

The streets of Rocky Ford are also odd nowadays. They are dusty,
and cheap newspapers are forever blowing about. The citizenry
look furtive and exhausted. Occasionally I see a strange tight group
of women moving along the walk. They carry baskets and buy flour
and sugar in small supplies. I saw the storekeeper, the old one, sell a
bag of sugar to a woman. He said, Let me sell you the ten pounds,
since the price will be better, and looked at her with his face expec-
tant. She laughed and said, No, sir, I thank you, but I buy sugar for
this week, and next week, and the week after that. Then I'll have no
need to sweeten the food on my table. When she went out, another
woman, who had stood stock still and watched, went flying up to the
old man and scolded him for selling at all to a wretched woman of
the blue tent. The old man's hoarse voice followed me out and was
audible on the street.

Your mother had asked again that I go to see you. I went as far as
the muddy place from which I watched before. Now the wall is high
and sturdy. From where I stood I could see no gate. I did not go
around to the ford to seek you. I am still waiting for you to make
your choice.

your Father

March 2nd
John,

What I did not say yesterday. I heard a conversation that lowered
my spirits. I had gone into the inn between Rocky Ford and Broad-

hill to drink a little wine and some tea. I thought I'd hear the politics, or about a new book to take home to your mother. But the place was crowded with laughing rabble, in for noon dinner. While I sat watching they hooted and slapped each other, and soon one stood up and called in a high, stern voice for all those at his table to be quiet.

Parson, they cried, put down that beer, unseemly fellow!

Their friend shook his finger at them. Look here, you lot of ruined dogs, he said, still in this high voice like a woman's. Here's a prophecy.

The very word prophecy set them howling.

Then he said, I counted the sneezes of my cross-eyed goat and multiplied it by the seeds of a crooked-neck squash, and subtracted the freckles on the neck of my fat little bride! (A roar.)

How long did you count those freckles, sir? said one who wore a red cap.

Two days, said this parson, And carefully. You may be sure I'm in the right.

And what did you learn, brother? sang out another.

Blockhead! he said. The end of the world! Oh, then it was a merry table. One old fellow pushed back from the board and came over near me to rummage among bags on the floor.

The clever herd was clamoring for instruction. When must I be ready for the end? said the red cap.

No need, said the parson. It came and went the day you were born. The world coughed you up and then died.

Why, Parson, said one, soft and sly. That's no prophecy, then. That's history.

The parson looked into his beer and said, It's prophecy in a looking glass.

It's Jesus don't know if he's coming or going, crowed the red cap. Much laughter.

So I been in Hell and never knew the difference, said the sly one.

Here's the richest bit, said the parson. Those as went to Heaven never knew the difference either.

All stopped a minute and drank. The man at the bags stood near me, watching. Suddenly he turned to me and said, That's some bad nonsense, ain't it?

In my surprise I only nodded. He wiped his hands on his pants, and said, This is how you know it's a democracy. When you see fools free to believe in nothing.

And he took up his bags and went out.

While my attention was on him, the table had quieted. The men were at their food. One fellow, who had eyes skewed almost to the sides of his head, said gravely into the silence, I've got a stony soul or two to throw to that boy parson. I can pick them up off the ground, and throw them right to him. Let us see how quick his hands are.

From the table somewhere, Amen.

I confess I was concerned by this. The derision of the newspaper editors has given way to a savage rancor among the people.

Who is this boy parson, John Ephraim?

your Father

March 6th

John Ephraim,

Once I had a little boy, a sturdy gentle fellow, who crouched peering into the nests of grass fowl, and waited for hours at the lairs of small animals, until his knees were locked and painful and I had to work them with my hands. So where is my patient boy in the young man who demands his Lord come now to earth in his own lifetime? I wonder why the brightest young scholar I ever saw hold a slate should abnegate the future?

I have been thinking of you and what you must feel as you wait for the end. It's difficult. If I thought there would be no rough chain of days leading me onward, if I thought that the land I know, weedy, strewn with manure, camped upon by the vengeful obtuse race of man, if I believed it would all soon vanish in one flaming utterance of the holy, I should feel — grief. In your circumstance I could not muster joy. This in case you thought I might perhaps join you under the blue tent.

Marie Spencer has made supper for your mother and has just brought me apples and cheese. I watched her today as she brought water up the hill from the well. One moment she stopped to rest her pail on the ground, and the wind blew and pressed her dress back against her. The cat ran to her, and she picked it up and put it against her shoulder, and took up her pail and walked on. You are giving away forty years of sleep beside this girl. When this fever is off

you, and you come back to look around, what will be left? The door
is closing. The world and its doors. My son a gateless tabernacle. My
wife a room growing darker.

                                                              Father

                                                      March 9th
John,
    I go down the streets now with coat flapping and people stare.
Your mother is worse. She is making preparations. How can you not
come to her?
    I hear her breathing all night. I hear her.

                                                              Father

                                                      March 14th
John Ephraim,
    An ugly scene in Rocky Ford today. I am hardly recovered. I had
gone over to the hatter's to hear the news, over those six miles that
are so familiar now. The fields are densely matted, the shrubs bare
and curling in the heat. Confused birds dart madly before and
behind me as I ride. My winter clothes are heavy and I am wet inside
them.
    The hatter was not there. Business hours, mind you, and a Mon-
day. The door was looped shut with a piece of rope. I could hardly
believe it, but I knew what it meant. This dour and precise little
man, this ready scoffer, had abandoned his life. Strange that I
should not have seen it coming, but I have overlooked before this
what was placed in plain sight. Inside on the floor of the shop, I
could see a man's silk hat. The crown was smashed flat. Beyond
were others, treated likewise. I withdrew from this scene along the
boardwalk, as if from the fatal spill of a runaway wagon. If the hatter
is among you now, I beg you do not tell him the hats are ruined. I
consider him my friend, and hope to see him soon, back in his
shop. I have known him for years, you know.
    But it was more than this. As I came back along the street I saw
two men standing some twenty feet apart from a woman I thought I
knew, looking at her quite rudely. Other people were at their business all along the street, but they moved slow, slower, as though the
spin of the earth were winding down like a clock. It was the woman
who had bought such a small bag of sugar from the grocer a few

weeks ago. She was not as gay, now, turning her shoulder to these men and tucking her chin down. Then — my God! — a stone rang on the iron ground, and skittered along under her skirt. The people listening moved as slowly as lengthening shadows.

I rejoice, said the woman, I rejoice to be persecuted for the sake of the truth.

One rough laugh, a bray, floated down the street. The scene bore no resemblance to civilized life. I hurried into the breach between them, and took off my hat. Gentlemen, I called, look at yourselves.

I might have gone on, but I saw that both victim and perpetrators had faded away. I was left standing alone, while the livid townspeople stumped past me across the baked and splintered storefronts. I still held my hat in my hand. I thought I heard someone breathe, Who does this old beggar think he is?

Were the people this way before you called them lost, John? Was kind company always a deep fraud, and the mild face of the land a harlot mask? The fence you have built has divided us, son from father. You have called us graceless, and we have plucked up that name and wear it.

I went home and sat by your mother; I sit there now as I write. She drinks a little water now and then. I feel severed even from her, by what I cannot describe. I can write only to you, who never respond, and who indeed may never hear me. I am tired now. The world doubles before me.

                                                              Father

                                                        March 16th
John,

I hurry to write because the post bag is leaving and I've detained the man at my desk. I think I will come to you the morning after. If you are willing, come out of there and down to the water to meet me.

                                                              Father

                                                        March 17th
Dear John,

Your great day approaches quickly. I have read that all expectations are now for the night of the 19th. Your mother wishes you well. That is all she will say.

Tonight I read to her from the naturalist's book about northern birds. She fell asleep suddenly, with her body twisted round, and I sat there for a moment with my hand in the book, waiting to see if she would stir. Then suddenly I felt strongly that I must write to you. I thought, this is why the Lord is not coming. Not this year. Not the next. I was sure of it. (But why should I feel so urgent to tell you why the end of the world is not coming, if the end of the world is not coming? I should have plenty of time.) It was this of which I thought, a story you may not know the whole of.

Before your mother and I married, I worked at the bank to earn a home for us. She was waiting. But she had left school and was restless; she spent so much time reading books and seeing lectures that she was full of convictions. These led her to do work through her church down at Braxton. There's a house for the insane there, you know. Faithless, reasonless creatures, calling out like animals. I'd seen them. I was, I confess, against it.

But your mother went to them. She was with another girl; they were both eighteen. She sent me letters. In the mornings she washed their faces and bodies, and fed them by hand. The bedding was always foul and had to be washed nearly every day. Once she wrote me mourning for a white shirtwaist she'd made, that had become so torn, and so dirty with food and refuse, that she'd had to throw it away. But it was as though Providence had ruined her blouse, not people. She did not blame the mad, nor even mention them. In the afternoons, she read Scripture to a huddled group; the men were brought in and seated so they could listen. I remember her writing that Saint Francis had had easy work, preaching to birds. Her audience argued with her, or performed strange sudden dances, or repeated her words a half-measure behind until she could hardly understand her own voice. On the terrible afternoon (she told me when I went down to fetch her) she was reading Psalms — some of the congregation were even asleep in their chairs — and one great sad boy stood up and began singing, and came forward and caught your mother up in his hands. He held her above his head, and she could see the floor turning and the cowering mad women crying. Then he threw her to the ground. Her back was hurt. That is why she has walked so poorly. And perhaps why she is sick now, still a woman in her prime.

I mean just that when I saw your mother sleeping in that twisted way, I think of what she gave, in pain and lost time, in lost work and sickness, to bring God to a place where there was no God. In hope that when she had worked to make earth holy, then God would see his place prepared, and return to us. But John Ephraim! You say God never blinked his distant white eye! That his vision is over-crusted with secret plans, and he will come to earth when it shall suit him, regardless of the extent of goodness, the number of saved. At his whim he will raze our land and purify it for his dwelling — a finer earth will suit him to dwell in, not the one he made long ago, a novice. No. Everything in me rebels at this, a Lord who averts his face from the like of your mother, who wraps his head in a cloak.

For years I have stood at evening on the rise next to Spencer's woodlot and heard every sound and smelled it all, and though the light fades, my eyes are wider and wider open. Then I know a deer has come nosing among the brambles. I do not see her move but feel her there, her wiry fear and unconscious beauty. And by her that landscape is graced. Transformed by that black delicate hoof, the bone shin against which she rubs her face. So the landscape is more graceful for the work we may do, and God sees it. When we have brought all the deer out of the woods to stand in dark-eyed calm, then he will walk among us and feed us from his hand.

You may think I am too selfish an old fellow to speak of such progress. I am sure that I am selfish. But the finer earth must be partly of our making, John. I am sure of this also.

Father

Later. I find I cannot seal this letter without saying it. You have my love. My little boy.

Broadhill,
March 22nd
Dear Reverend Gearhart,

I thank you for your note of March 19th, and the uncollected letter. I am not surprised our letter carrier did not visit you as usual. As you know, it was a difficult morning for many people. I will tell you what I saw, if it will add anything for those who suffered. I went to the camp very early, while it was still night. I won't say I didn't watch the sky as I rode. The stars were weak up there. The nail holes in the tin of my lantern made more light. That night the cold descended — this bright weather has broken all over the state, I hear.

It was a queer pleasure to see the deep frost form in the ditches, and the usual fingers of ice extend from the bank of the river. My horse slipped sharply once at the ford, and I had to get down and walk her. When I arrived at the camp, I looked back across the stream and saw the advancing day as a grayness among the trees. A few people were camped under their wagons, asleep. Beyond them the enclosure looked huge and dark, but above it the tent could be seen, and a little light paled its blue roof. Inside the people were singing. The sound was melodious and brave but very soft. I wondered if some were dozing while others kept the watch, or if all were awake and the gray dawn was striking them, one by one, silent with despair. I stood listening, and my heart was turning inside me.

In the trees across the clearing there was motion. I peered, stopped, blew on my hands, widened my eyes again, but could gather little light. I went over to my horse and put my hands under her blanket to warm them. In retrospect, I believe I saw the ruffians who started the fire. They must have crept up from the south side and there set the brush burning. They must have muffled their lanterns with cloths. If I had seen a glow I might have investigated. But how strange that I should have seen *no* light, that they should have been that stealthy.

The flames came quickly in the vegetation, dry under its frost. Those lying under wagons woke, ran to a small door in the wall, and began pounding upon it. I followed them, and pounded with my frozen hands. The singing separated into individual voices, then ceased. Behind me, my horse reared and tore at her reins. In a few moments the fire drove me back to her. I set her loose. She thumped into the ford, and I followed her, and others were on either side of me, carrying things — a gun, a bag of potatoes. They had abandoned their wagons. The fire was running along the ground, and twigs and branches were jerking and popping as though inspirited. The fence had turned a sweating dark brown, and the uprights were blackening. When the sun came up, that yellow light swallowed the flame, so it appeared simply that the air between us and the enclosure was deforming and wrinkling. I heard shouts and, somewhere, the ringing of an axe on wood. We stood dumbly across the water.

Well, it's as you know. Most came out through the new-cut door and scattered toward us, wailing, through the north-side trees.

Eighteen were burned. A few went into the deep curve of the river and were lost.

My son was not among the living or the dead. Late in the day I walked on the smoldering site of the tent, which had burned and floated away in dark feathers that caught on the trees. I looked under the blankets at the wizened black figures. They had held their hands up at the approach of the fire, and still held them there in postures of fear, or praise. None were my boy. I walked along the river and found nothing. The ice had by then made a deep opaque ruffle along the bank. I suppose we will know little until the next thaw. There are others missing. Mine is not the only one. We may yet have peace of mind.

Thank you for asking after Nell. She continues. This, at least. But I look across a threshold always, into the place where I will live as a man alone. And you will be surprised to know of whom I am thinking, Reverend. It is the letter carrier who fills my mind. Yes, I know I have never met him.

You said he was about my age, perhaps older. I will be fifty soon. He was whiskered, and either drunk or longing to be drunk. But he always put the letters under his coat and touched his forehead respectfully. I can imagine him walking up to John Ephraim in the camp, saying, Here's another, and John opening it with his thin hands, and reading. I do not see his face, of course. To recollect the whole face is hard. I have only the feeling the face gave me. He puts the letters carefully between the leaves of his Bible. My letters make that Bible bristly and awkward to handle.

But if John were never there, or if this old man were a liar? Do you see what I am saying, Gearhart? The man takes the letters back to some room, and opens them with his yellow fingers. But the poor fellow cannot read. What was sent in faith he receives with confusion. Plea, argument, and lament are alike unintelligible to him. He touches the hieroglyphs with his fingers. He puzzles over my words in that high far room, he rubs the page against his sunken cheek and smears the ink. It falls from his hand. Already he has forgotten it. He goes to his window across a floor ankle-deep in letters. He treads on every undeciphered word.

If you have the time, Gearhart, I would like to come and see you. I would like to hear your voice.

                                                    Josiah Cole

JAMAICA KINCAID

In Roseau

FROM THE NEW YORKER

IT WAS PERHAPS inevitable that as soon as I came to know, like the back of my hand, the long walk from my father's house to my school, in the next village, I was to leave it. This walk, all five miles of it one way, five miles of it the other, never ceased to be of some terror for all the children who walked it; we tried never to be alone. We walked in groups always. In any one year, at any one time, there were not more than a dozen of us, more boys than girls; we were not friends — friendships were discouraged. We were never to trust one another. This was like a motto repeated to us by our parents; it was a part of my upbringing, like a rule of good manners: You cannot trust these people, my father would say to me, perhaps the very words that the other children's parents were saying to them, perhaps even at the same time. That "these people" were ourselves, that this insistence on mistrust of others — people who looked very much like us, shared a common history of suffering and humiliation and enslavement and genocide — should be taught to us even as children is no longer a mystery to me. The people we should naturally mistrust were beyond our influence completely, and what we needed to defeat them, to rid ourselves of them, was something far more powerful than mistrust. Mistrust of one another was just one of the many feelings we had for one another, all of them the opposite of love, all of them standing in the place of love. It was as if we were in a joust with one another for a secret prize; any expression of love, then, would not be sincere, for love might give someone else the advantage. We were not friends. We walked together; it was a companionship based on fear, and fear of things we could not see, and when those things were seen we often could not really comprehend the danger, so confusing was much of reality. It was only after we left the immediate confines of our village and were out of the sight of our parents that we drew close to one another.

My father had inherited the ghostly paleness of his own father, the skin that looks as if it were waiting for another skin, a real skin, to come and cover it up; and his eyes were gray, like his own father's eyes; and his hair was red and brown like his father's also, only the texture of his hair, thick and tightly curled, was like his mother's hair. She was a woman from Africa. Where in Africa, no one knew — and what good would it do to find out? — but she was from somewhere in Africa, that place on the map, the one I had seen in school, that is a configuration of shapes and shades of yellow.

I did not tell my father that one day when returning from school alone I saw a spotted monkey sitting in a tree and I threw three stones at it. The monkey caught the third one and threw it back at me and struck me over my left eye, in the hair of my eyebrow, and I bled furiously, as if I would never stop. I somehow knew that the red berries of a certain bush would stop the flow of blood. My father, when he saw my wound, thought that it had come from the hands of a schoolmate — a boy, someone I was so protective of that I would not reveal his identity. It was then that he began to make plans to send me to school in Roseau, to get me away from the bad influences of children who would wound me, whom I protected from his wrath, and who, he was certain, were male. And after this outburst of emotion — which was meant as an expression of his love for me but only made me feel anew the hatred and isolation in which we all lived — his face again became a mask, so hard to read.

And on that road, which I came to know so well, I spent some of the sweetest moments of my life. On a long stretch of it in the late afternoon I could see the reflection of the sun's light on the surface of the seawater, and it always had the quality of an expectation just about to be fulfilled, as if at any moment a small city made of that special light of the sun on the water would arise and from it might flow a joy I had not yet imagined. And I knew a place, just off the side of this road, where the sweetest cashews grew, and the juice from their fruit would cause blisters to form on my lips and my

tongue to feel as if it were caught in a bundle of twine, temporarily
making speech difficult, and I found this — the difficulty of speaking, the possibility that it might be a struggle for me ever to speak
again — delicious. And it was on that road that I first walked directly from one weather system to another: from a cold, heavy rain
into a bright, clear midday heat. And it was on this road that my
half-sister, the girlchild of my father and his wife — the woman who
was not my mother — was traveling on a bicycle to meet a man my
father had forbidden her to see and whom she would marry, when
she had an accident. She fell over a precipice and was left lame and
barren. That is not a happy memory; her suffering, even now, is
very real to me.

Not very long after I came to live with them, when I was a small
girl, my father's wife began to have her own children. She had two,
the first one a boy, the second one a girl. This had two predictable
outcomes: she left me alone, and she valued her son more than she
valued her daughter. That she did not think very much of the
person who was most like her, a daughter, a female, was so normal
that it would only have been noticed if it had been otherwise: to
people like us, despising what was most like ourselves was almost a
law of nature. This fact of my sister's life made me feel overwhelm-
ingly sympathetic to her; she did not like me, she was told by her
mother that I was an enemy of hers, that I was not to be trusted, that
I was like a thief in that house, waiting for the moment when I
could rob them of their inheritance. This was convincing to my
sister, and she distrusted and disliked me; the first words she could
speak that formed an insult were directed toward me. My father's
wife always said to me, in private, when my father was not there, that
I could not be his child, because I did not look like him — and it
was true that I did not have any of his physical characteristics. My
sister, though, did look like him; her hair and eyes were the same
color as his, red and gray; her skin, too, was the same color as his —
ghostly pale. But she did not have his calm or his patience; she
walked like a warrior and could not contain the fury that was inside
her. She did not have his quality of keeping her own counsel; every
thought that came into her mind had to be voiced, so that whenever she saw me, she would let me know immediately what my
presence suggested to her. I never hated her, I only had sympathy
for her; her tragedy was greater than mine; her mother did not love

her, but her mother was alive, and every day she saw her mother
and every day her mother let her know that she was not loved. My
own mother was dead.

And so I had come to know well the world in which I was living. I
knew how to interpret the long silences my father's wife had con-
structed between us. Sometimes these silences were nothing at all,
sometimes they were filled with pure evil; sometimes she meant to
see me dead, sometimes my being alive was of no interest to her.
To observe any human being from infancy, to see this someone come into existence — to see experience collect in the eyes,
around the corners of the mouth, the weighing down of brow, the
thick gathering around the waist, the breasts, the slowing down of
footsteps not in old age but simply with the caution of life — all this
is something wonderful to observe, for such apparently is life itself;
it is an invisible current between the two, observed and observer,
beheld and beholder, and I believe that no life is complete, no life
is really whole, without this invisible current, which is in many ways
a definition of love. No one observed and beheld me; I observed
and beheld myself. The invisible current went out and it came back
to me. I came then to love myself in defiance, from despair, because
there was nothing else; such a love will do, but it will only do; it is
not the best kind, it has the taste of something left out on a shelf
too long that has turned rancid, and when eaten it makes the stomach turn.

When I first saw the thick red fluid of my menstrual blood, I was
not surprised and I was not afraid. I had never heard of it, I had not
been expecting it, I was twelve years old, but its appearance, to my
young mind, to my body and soul, had the force of a destiny fore-
told; it was as if I had always known of it but had never admitted it to
consciousness, had never known how to put it into words. It appeared that first time so thick and red and plentiful that it was
impossible to think of it as an omen or a warning of some kind, a
symbol; it was just its real self, my menstrual flow, and I knew
immediately that its failure to appear, regularly, after a certain in-
terval, could only mean a great deal of trouble for myself. Perhaps I
knew then that the child in me would never be stilled enough
to allow me to have a child of my own. I bought from a baker four
bags — the kind in which flour was shipped — and after removing

the dyed brand markings through a long process of washing and bleaching them in the hot sun, I made four squares from each and used these to catch my blood as it flowed from between my legs. It was around then, too, that the texture of my body and the smell of my body began to change; coarse hairs appeared under my arms and in the space between my legs, where there had been none before, my hips widened, my chest thickened and swelled up, slightly at first, and then there was a deep space between my two breasts; the hair on my head grew long and soft, and the waves in it deepened, my lips spread across my face and thickened into the shape of a heart that had been stepped on. I used then to stare at myself in an old piece of a broken looking glass I had found in some rubbish under my father's house. The sight of my changing self did not frighten me; I only wondered how I would look eventually, and I never doubted that I would like completely whatever stared back at me. And so, too, the smell from my underarms and between my legs changed, and this change pleased me; in those places the smell became pungent, sharp, as if something were in the process of fermenting, slowly; in private then, as now, my hands almost never left those places, and when I was in public, these same hands were always not far from my nose, I so enjoyed the way I smelled.

At the age of fourteen I had exhausted the resources of the tiny school in Massacre, the village between Roseau and Mahaut. I really knew much more than that school could teach me. I could sense from the beginning of my life that I would know things when I needed to know them, and I had known for a long time that I could trust my own instinct about things — that if I was ever in a difficult situation, if I thought about it long enough, a solution would appear to me. I could not know then that there would be limitations to having such a view of life, but in any case my life was already small and limited in its own way.

I also knew by then the history of an array of people I would never meet, and that in itself should not have kept me from knowing of them; it was only that this history of peoples that I would never meet — Romans, Gauls, Saxons, Britons, the British People — had behind it a malicious intent, which was to make me feel humiliated, humbled, small. And once I had identified and accepted this malice directed at me, I became fascinated with this expression of vanity: the perfume of your own name and your own deeds is so intoxicating that it never causes you to feel weary; it is its own inspiration; it is its own renewal; its demise is caused by factors independent of itself. And I learned, too, that no one can truly judge herself, for to describe your own transgressions is to forgive yourself for them; to give voice, to confess your bad deeds, is also at once to forgive yourself, and so silence becomes the only form of self-punishment.

I had never been to Roseau until that day in my fourteenth year when my father took me to the house of a man he knew, Monsieur Labatte, Monsieur Jacques Labatte — Jack, as I came to call him in the bitter, sweet dark of night. He, like my father, was a man of no principles, and this did not surprise or disappoint me — this did not make me like him more, this did not make me like him less. He and my father knew each other through financial arrangements they made with each other. They called each other "friend," and the fragility of the foundation on which this friendship was built would cause sadness only in someone who did not love the world and all the material things in it. And Roseau, even then — when the reality of every situation had to be disguised and called something else, something the opposite of its true self — was not referred to as a city; it was called "the capital," the capital of Dominica. It, too, had a fragile foundation, and from time to time was destroyed by forces of nature, by a hurricane or by water coming from the sky as if suddenly the sea were above and the heavens below. And again, Roseau could not be called a city, because it could not embody such a noble inspiration, it was not really a center of commerce and culture, of exchange of ideas among people, not a place of intrigue, a place in which plots are hatched and the destinies of many are determined. It was an outpost, a way station for people for whom things had gone wrong, either because of their own actions or through no fault of their own; and there were then so many places like Roseau, outposts of despair; for conqueror and conquered alike these places were the capitals of nothing but despair; this did not surprise the ones forcibly brought to live in such a place; it only surprised the ones who chose it as the place to spend the rest of their lives.

But even so, in this place there was some beauty, unexpected and therefore thrilling: it could be seen in the way the houses were all closely pressed together, jammed up, small and crooked, as if ill-built on purpose, painted in the harsh hues of red, blue, green, or yellow, or sometimes not painted at all, and the bare wood thus exposed to the elements turned a bright gray; and in this sort of house lived people whose skins glistened with exhaustion and whose faces were sad even when they had a reason to be happy, people for whom history had been a big, dark room, and this had made them hate silence. Sometimes there was a gentle wind and sometimes the stillness of the trees, and sometimes the sun setting and sometimes the dawn opening up, and there was the sweet, sickening smell of the white lily that bloomed only at night, and the sweet, sickening smell of something dead, animal, rotting. And this beauty, when I first saw it — I saw it in parts, not all at once — made me glad to be alive, and I could not explain it, this feeling of happiness, gladness, at the sight of the new and the strange, the unfamiliar; and then, long, long after, when all these things had become a part of me, a part of my everyday life, this feeling of happiness was no longer possible. But I would yearn for it — to feel new again, to feel the irritation of the new again, to feel within myself a fountain of joy springing up from this irritation. I long now to feel fresh again, to feel I will never die, but that is not possible. I can only long for it; I can never be that way again.

After my father removed me from his house and from the presence of his wife, I came to understand that he knew it was necessary to do so. I never knew what he noticed about me, I never knew what he wanted of me or from me; at the time it seemed to have a purpose, this removing me to Roseau. He wanted me to continue to go to school and someday to become a schoolteacher; he wanted to say that his daughter was a teacher in a school. That I might have had aspirations of my own would not have occurred to him, and if I had any aspirations of my own I did not know of them. How the atmosphere in his own house felt to him, I did not know. What he saw in my face, he never told me. But he took me to this house of a man he knew in business and left me in the care of this man and his wife. I was a boarder but I paid my own way. In exchange for my room and board I performed some household tasks. I did not object, I could not object, I did not want to object; I did not know then how to object openly. I met Monsieur and Madame in the afternoon, a hot afternoon; I met her first, alone; he was in a room by himself, in another part of their house, in a room where he kept money, which he liked to count over and over again; it was not all the money he had.

When I first met Madame Labatte, she was standing in the doorway of her nice house, with its nice clean yard full of flowers and piles of stones neatly arranged; to her left and to her right were two large clumps of plumbago with blue blooms that were still in the hot air. She wore a white dress made of a coarse cloth, and it was decorated with embroidery of flowers and leaves; I noticed this because it was a dress people in Mahaut would only have worn to church on Sundays. Her dress was not worn out and it was clean; it was not stylishly cut; it was loose, fitting her badly, as if her body were no longer of any interest to her. My father spoke to her, she spoke to my father, she spoke to me; she looked at me, I looked at her, but it was not to size each other up. I did not know what she thought she saw in my eyes, but I can say now that I had an instinctive feeling of sympathy for her; I did not know why sympathy, why not the opposite of that, but sympathy was what I felt all the same. It might have been because she looked like someone who had got something she had so very much wanted.

She had very much wanted to marry Monsieur Labatte — I was told that by the woman who came each day to wash their clothes. To want desperately to marry men, I have come to see, is not a mistake women make; it is only that, well, what else is left for them to do? I was never told why she wanted to marry him, but I made a guess: he had a strong body, she was drawn to his strong body, his strong hands, his strong mouth; it was a big wide mouth and it must have covered hers up whenever he kissed her; it swallowed mine up whenever he kissed me. She was not a frail woman when they first met; she only became frail afterward. He wore her out. When they first met, he would not marry her, he would not marry any woman then. They would bear him children, and if the children were boys, these boys were given his full name, but he never married the mothers. Madame Labatte found a way; she fed him food she had cooked in a sauce made with her own menstrual blood, and it bound him to her, and they were married. In time, this spell wore off and could not be made to work again. He turned on her — not in anger, for he never became aware of the trap that had been set for him; he turned on her with the strength of that weapon he carried between his legs, and he wore her out.

Her hair was gray, and this was not from age; like so much about

her, it had just lost its vitality, it lay on her head without any real life
to it; her hands hung at her side, slack; she had been beautiful
when she was young, the way all people are; but on her face then,
when I met her, was the defeated person she had become. Defeat is
not beautiful; it is not ugly, but it is not beautiful either. I was young
then, I did not know; when I looked at her and felt sympathy, I also
felt revulsion. I felt: this must never happen to me. I meant that I
would not allow the passage of time or the full weight of desire to
make a pawn of me. I was so young, and felt my convictions power-
fully; I felt strong and I felt I would always be so. And at that
moment the clothes I was wearing became too small, my bosoms
grew out and pressed against my blouse; my hair touched my shoulders in a caress that caused me to shiver inside; my legs were hot
and between them was a moisture, a sweet smelly stickiness. I was
alive, and I could tell that standing before me was a woman who was
not; it was almost as if I sensed a danger and quickly made a defense
for myself; in seeing the thing I might be, I too early became its
opposite.

This woman liked me, and her husband liked me. It pleased her
that he liked me. By the time he emerged from the room where he
kept his money to greet my father and me, Madame Labatte had
already told me to make myself at home, to regard her as if she were
my own mother, to feel safe whenever she was near. She could not
know what such words meant to me — what it meant to hear a
woman say them to me. Of course I did not believe her, I did not
fool myself, but I knew that when she was saying those things to me
she really meant to say them. I liked her so very much, her the
shadow of her former self, so grateful for my presence because she
was no longer alone with her prize and her defeat. He did not speak
to me right away; he did not care that it was me and not someone
else my father had asked him to accommodate. He liked the quiet
greed in my father, and my father liked the simple greed in him.
They were a match; the one could betray the other at any time,
perhaps at that moment they had already done so. Monsieur Labatte was already a rich man, richer than my father. He had better
connections; he had not wasted his time marrying for love, marrying a poor Caribe woman — my mother.

I occupied a room that was attached to the kitchen; the kitchen was
not a part of the house itself. I was enjoying the absence of the

constant threat posed to me by my father's wife, even as I could feel the burden of my life — the short past, the unknown future. I could write letters to my father, letters that contained simple truths: the days seem shorter in Roseau than the days in Mahaut; the nights seem hotter in Roseau than the nights in Mahaut; Madame Labatte is so very kind to me, she saves, as a special treat for me, a part of the fish that I love; the part of the fish that I love is the head — and this was something my father would not have known, something I had no reason to believe he wished to know. I sent him these letters without fear. I never received a direct reply, but he sent word to me through the letters he wrote to Monsieur Labatte; he always hoped I was getting along in a good way and he wished me well.

My friendship — for it was that — with Madame Labatte continued to grow. She was always alone, and that was true even when she was with others; she was so alone. She thought that she made me sit with her as she sat on the veranda and sewed or just looked out blankly at the scene in front of her, but I wanted to sit with her. I was enjoying this new experience, the experience of a silence full of expectation and desire; she wanted something from me, I could tell that, and I longed for the moment to come, the moment when I would know just what it was she wanted from me. It never crossed my mind that I would refuse her.

One day, without any preparation, she gave me a beautiful dress that she no longer wore. It still fit her, but she no longer wore it. As I was trying on the dress I could hear her thoughts: she was thinking of her youth, of the person she was when she first wore the dress she had just given me, and of the things she had wanted, the things she had not received, the emptiness of her whole life. All this filled the air in the room we were in; the bed in which she slept with her husband was in this room. My own thoughts answered hers: "You were foolish, you should not have let all these things happen to you, it is your own fault." I was without mercy in my judgment, and my merciless thoughts, my condemnations, filled my head with a slow roar until I thought I would faint, and then this thought came upon me, slowly saving me from doing so: she wants to make a gift of me to her husband; she wants to give me to him; she hopes I do not mind.

I was standing in this room before her — my clothes coming off, my clothes going on, naked, clothed — but the vulnerability I felt was not of the body; it was of the spirit, of the soul. To communicate so intimately with someone, to speak silently to someone and yet to be understood more clearly than if you had shouted at the top of your voice, was something I did not experience with anyone ever again in my life. I took the dress from her. I did not wear it; I would never wear it; I only took it and kept it for a while.

The inevitable is no less a shock because it is inevitable. I was sitting, late one day, in a small shaded area behind the house where some flowers were planted, but this place could not be called a garden, for not much care was applied to it; the sun had not yet set completely, it was just that moment when the creatures of the day are quiet but the creatures of the night have not quite found their voice. It was that time of day when all that you have lost is heaviest in your mind: your mother, if you have lost her; your home, if you have lost it; the voices of people who might have loved you but did not; the places in which something good, something you cannot forget, happened to you. I did not wear undergarments anymore — I found them uncomfortable — and as I sat there I touched various parts of my body, sometimes absentmindedly, sometimes with a purpose in mind. I was running the fingers of my left hand through the small thick patch of hair between my legs and thinking of my life as I had lived it so far, fifteen years of it now, and I saw that Monsieur Labatte was standing not far off, looking at me. He did not move away in embarrassment, and I, too, did not run away in embarrassment. We held each other's gaze. I removed my fingers from between my legs and brought them up to my face; I wanted to smell myself. It was the end of the day, and my odor was quite powerful. This scene of me placing my hands between my legs and then enjoying the smell of myself and Monsieur Labatte watching me lasted until the usual sudden falling of the dark, and so when he came closer to me and asked me to remove my clothes, I said, quite sure of myself, knowing what it was I wanted, that it was too dark, and I could not see.

He took me to the room in which he counted his money, the money that was only some of the money that he had. It was a dark room, and so he kept a small lamp always lighted in it. I took off my clothes, and he took off his clothes also. He was the first man I had ever seen unclothed, and this surprised me: the body of a man is not what makes him desirable; it is what his body might make you feel when it touches you that is the thrill, anticipating what his body will make you feel. And then the reality was better than the anticipation, and the world had a wholeness to it, a wholeness with a current of pure pleasure running through it. But when I first saw him, saw his hands hanging at his sides — not yet caressing my hair, not yet inside me, not yet bringing the small risings that were my breasts toward his mouth, not yet opening my mouth wider to place his tongue even deeper in my mouth — and I saw the limp folds of the flesh on his stomach, the hardening flesh between his legs, I was surprised at how unbeautiful he was all by himself, just standing there, and it was anticipation that kept me enthralled. And the force of him inside me, inevitable as it was, again came as a shock, a long sharp line of pain that then washed over me with the broadness of a wave, and then another wave; and in response to each I made a cry that was the same cry, a cry of sadness — for without making of it something it really was not, I was not the same person that I had been before.

He was not a man of love, and I did not need him to be. When he was through with me and I with him, he lay on top of me, breathing indifferently; his mind was on other things. I could see that on a small shelf behind his back he had lined up many coins, turned heads up; they all bore the face of a king.

In the room where I slept, the room with the dirt floor, I poured water into a small tin basin and washed off the thin crust of blood that had dried down the inside of my legs. I knew why it was there; I knew what had just happened to me. I wanted to see what I looked like but I could not, I did not have a looking glass of my own. I felt myself, and my skin felt smooth, as though it had just been oiled and freshly polished. The place between my legs ached, my breasts ached, my lips ached, my wrists ached; when he had not wanted me to touch him, he had placed his own large hands over my wrists and kept them pinned to the floor; when my cries had distracted him he had clamped my lips shut with his own mouth; and it was through all the parts of my body that ached that I relived the deep pleasure I had just experienced. When I awoke the next morning, I did not feel that I had slept at all; I felt as if I had only lost consciousness, and I picked up where I had left off in my ache of pleasure.

It had rained during the night, and in the morning it did not stop, and in the evening after the morning it did not stop; the rain did not stop for many, many days. It fell with such force and for such a long time that it appeared it would change the face and the destiny of the world, the world of outpost Roseau, and that after it stopped, nothing would be the same; not the ground itself that we walked on, not even the outcome of a quarrel. But that was not so; after the rain stopped, the waters formed streams, the streams ran into rivers, the rivers ran into the sea; the ground retained its shape. I was the one who was in a state of upheaval. I would not remain the same, even I could see that. The respectable, the predictable — such roles were not to be my own destiny.

During the days and nights that the rain fell, I could not keep to my routine: make my own breakfast, perform some household tasks in the main house, where Madame and Monsieur lived, walk to my school, where all the students were female, and shun their childish company, return home, run errands for Madame, and, returning home again to perform more household chores, wash my own clothes and generally take care of my own self and my things. I could not attend to any of that; the rain made it impossible.

I was standing in the middle of a smaller version of the larger deluge; it was coming through the roof of my small house, which was made of tin. I had the same sensations, and I was not used to them yet, but the rain was familiar. A knock at the door, a command; the door shook open. She came to rescue me: she knew how I must be suffering in the wet, she had been in the kitchen and from there she could hear my suffering, my suffering caused by this unexpected deluge, this unconscionable downpour; to be alone in it would be the cause of much suffering for me; she could already hear me suffering so. But I was not making a sound of complaint, only the soft sighs of satisfaction remembered. She took me into the house and she made me coffee. It was hot and strong, with fresh milk he had brought that morning from some cows he kept not far from the house. He was not in the house now; he had come and he had gone away. I spent the days with her; I spent the nights with him.

It was not an arrangement made with words, it could not be made with words. On that day she showed me how to make him a cup of coffee; he liked to drink coffee with so strong a flavor that it overwhelmed anything that anyone wanted to put in it. She said this: "The taste is so strong you can put anything in it, he would never know." When we were alone we spoke to each other in

French patois, the language of the captive, the illegitimate; we never spoke of what we were doing and we never spoke for long; we spoke of the things in front of us and then we were silent. A silence had preceded the instructions about how to make coffee, and a silence followed it. I did not say to her, I do not want to make him coffee, I shall never make him coffee, I do not need to know how to make this man coffee, no man shall ever drink coffee from my hands made in that way! I did not say this. She washed my hair and rinsed it with a tea she had made from nettles, she combed it lovingly, admiring its liveliness (for my hair then looked like a nest of snakes, all about to strike), she applied oil she had rendered from castor beans to my scalp, she plaited it into two braids, just the way I always wore it; she then bathed me and gave me another dress that she used to wear when she was a young woman. The dress fit me perfectly, and I felt most uncomfortable in it; I could not wait to remove it and put on my own clothes again.

We sat on two chairs, not facing each other, speaking without words, exchanging thoughts. She told me of her life, of the time she first went swimming: it was a Sunday, she had been to church, and she went swimming and almost drowned, and never did it again; to this day, many years after (it had happened when she was a girl), she never goes into the water of the sea, she only looks at it; and to my silent question, if when she looks at the sea, she regrets that she is not now part of its everlastingness, she did not answer, she could not answer. So much sadness had overwhelmed her life; the moment she met her Monsieur Labatte — she called him Monsieur Labatte then, she called him Monsieur Labatte later, she calls him "him" now — she wanted him to possess her. She cannot remember the color of the day; he did not notice her, and he did not wish to possess her; his arms were powerful; his lips were powerful; he walked with a purpose, even when he was going nowhere. She bound him to her with a spell; she wanted to graft herself onto him. She wanted only to have him, but he would not be had, he would not be contained, and to want what you will never have, to know too late that you will never have it, is the beginning of a life overwhelmed with sadness. She wanted a child, but her womb was like a sieve — it would not contain a child then, and it would not contain anything now; it lay shriveled inside her, and perhaps her face mirrored it, shriveled, dried, like a fruit that has lost all its juice.

Did I value my youth? Did I treasure the newness that was me,
sitting next to her in a chair? I did not, how could I; in my column
of losses, youth had not yet been entered; in my loss column was my
mother. Love was not yet in my loss column: I had not yet been
loved, and I could not tell if the way she had combed my hair was an
expression of love. I could not tell if the way she had gently bathed
me — passing the piece of cloth over my breasts, between the front
and back of my legs, down my thighs, down my calves — was love; I
could not tell if wanting me dry when I was wet, if wanting me fed
when I was hungry, was love. I had not had love yet, it was not in my
column of gain, so it could not be in my column of loss.

The rain fell, and we no longer heard it; we would only hear its
absence. My days were full of silence, yet crowded with words; my
nights were full of sighs, soft and loud with agony and pleasure. I
would call out his name, Jack, sometimes like an epithet, sometimes
like a prayer. We were never the three of us together; she saw him in
one room, I saw him in another. He never spoke to me. He was
behaving in a way he knew well, and I was following a feeling I had,
I was acting from instinct, and the feeling I had, the instinct, was
new to me. She heard us, though she never let me know that she
did; she could hear us.

She had wanted a child, I could hear her say that. I was not a
child, I could no longer be a child; she could hear me say that. But
again she wanted something from me: she wanted a child I might
have, and I did not let her know that I heard that, or that this vision
she had — of a child inside me, eventually in her arms — would
hang in the air like a ghost, for my eyes only, but I would never see
it. It would go away and come back, this ghost of me with a child
inside me; I turned my back to it, my ears grew deaf to it, my heart
would not beat. She was stitching me a garment from beautiful old
clothes she had kept from the different times in her life — the
happy times, the sad times; it was a shroud made of memories, and
how she wished to weave me into its seams, its many seams, how
hard she tried! But with each click of the thimble striking the
needle, I made an escape. Her frustration and my satisfaction were
palpable.

It was not possible for me to become a schoolgirl again, only I
did not know this right away. The climate remained the same; the

weather changed. Monsieur went away, and I did not see the counting room for a while. In each corner and along the sides of the
floor he had small mountains of farthings; on a table he had piled
other coins — shillings and florins; he had so many coins all over
the room, in stacks, that when the lamp was lit, they made the room
brighter. Sometimes, in the night, I would awake to find him counting his money, over and over, as if he did not know how much he
really had, or as if counting would make a difference. He never
offered any of it to me; he knew I did not want it. The room was not
cold or warm or suffocating, but it was not ideal. I did not want to
spend the rest of my life in it; I did not want to spend the rest of my
life with the person who owned such a room.

He was not at home, and my nights then were spent in my room
off the kitchen. My days were spent in a schoolhouse. This life of
mine in the school had never offered me the satisfaction I was told
it would; it only filled me with questions that were not answered;
it only filled me with anger. I could not like what it would lead to: a
humiliation so permanent that it replaced your own skin. And your
own name, whatever it might be, was not the gateway to who you really were, and you could not ever say to yourself, "My name is Xuela
Claudette Desvarieux." This was my mother's name, and I cannot
say it was her real name, for in a life like hers or mine what is a real
name? My own name is her name, Xuela Claudette, but in the place
of the Desvarieux is Richardson, which is my father's name; but who
are these people Claudette, Desvarieux, and Richardson? To look
into it can only fill you with despair. For the name of any one
person is at once their history recapitulated and abbreviated, and
on declaring it that person holds himself high or low, and the
person hearing it holds the declarer high or low. My mother was
placed outside the gates of a convent when she was perhaps a day
old, by a woman believed to be her own mother; she was wrapped in
pieces of clean old cloth, and the name Xuela was written on these
pieces of cloth; it was written in ink, the color of which was indigo,
in a dye rendered from a plant. She was not discovered because she
had been crying (even as a just-born baby she did not draw attention to herself); she was found by a nun who was on her way to
wreak more havoc in the lives of a vanishing people, and her name
was Claudette Desvarieux. She named my mother after herself, and
how the name Xuela survived I do not know, but my father gave it

to me when she died, just after I was born. He loved her, and I do not know how much of the person that he was then, sentimental and tender, survived in him.

This moment of my life was an idyll of peace and contentment, of innocent young womanhood during the day, which was spent in a large room with other young women, all of them the product of legitimate unions, for this school, founded by missionary followers of John Wesley, did not admit children born outside of marriages. This, apart from everything else, kept the school very small, because most children in Roseau were born outside of a marriage. So I spent the day surrounded by the eventually defeated, the eventually bitter, by the dull hum of the voices of these girls, whose bodies, already a source of anxiety and shame, were draped in a blue sack made from coarse cotton: a uniform. And then my nights of silences and sighs, all an idyll: its end I could see, and I did not know how or when this end would come, but I could see it all the same. This thought did not fill me with dread.

I became very sick. I was with child, but I did not know it; I had no experience with the symptoms of such a state and so did not immediately know what was happening to me. It was Madame Labatte who told me what was the matter with me. I had just vomited everything I had eaten and I felt that I would die, and so I called out her name. "Lise!" I said, not "Madame Labatte"; she had put me on her bed to lie down; she was lying next to me, holding me in her arms. She said I was with child. She said it in English. Her voice had tenderness in it and sympathy, and she said it again and again, that I was having a child, and then she sounded quite happy, smoothing down the hair on my head, rubbing my cheek with the back of her hand, as if I were a baby too, in a state of irritation which I could not articulate, and her touch would prove soothing to me.

Her words, though, struck a terror in me. At first I did not believe her, and then I believed her completely and instantly felt that if there was a child in me, I would expel it through the sheer force of my will. I willed it out of me, day after day I did this, but it did not come out. From deep in her underarms I could smell a perfume, which was made from the juice of a flower, and this smell would fill up the room, fill up my nostrils, would go down into my stomach and come out through my mouth in waves of vomiting, the taste of it slowly strangling me. I believed then that I would die, and perhaps because I no longer had a future I began to want one very much. But what such a thing could be then for me, I did not know; for I was standing in a black hole, and the other alternative was another black hole, and this other black hole was one I did not know. I chose the one I did not know.

One day I was alone, still lying in Lise's bed, and she had left me alone. I got up and walked into Monsieur Labatte's counting room, and reaching into a small crocus bag that had in it only shillings, I removed one handful of these coins. I walked to the house of a woman who is dead now, and when she opened her door to me I placed my handful of shillings in her hands and looked in her face. I did not say a word. I did not know her real name; she was called Sange-Sange, but that was not her real name. She gave me a cup full of a thick black syrup to drink and then led me to a small hole in the dirt floor where I could lie down. For four days I stayed there, my body a volcano of pain, and nothing happened, and then, for four days after that, blood flowed from between my legs slowly and steadily like an eternal spring. And then it stopped. The pain was like nothing I had ever imagined before; it was as if it defined pain itself, and all other pain became only a reference to it, an imitation of it, an aspiration to it. I was a new person then. I knew things I had not known before, I knew things that you could only know if you had been through what I had just been through. I had carried my own life in my own hands.

WILLIAM HENRY LEWIS

Shades

FROM PLOUGHSHARES

I WAS FOURTEEN that summer. August brought heat I had never known, and during the dreamlike drought of those days, I saw my father for the first time in my life. The tulip poplars had faded to yellow before September came. There was no rain for weeks, and the people's faces along Eleventh Street wore a longing for something cool and wet, something distant, like the promise of a balmy October. Talk of weather was of the heat and the dry taste in their mouths. And they were frustrated, having to notice something other than the weather in their daily pleasantries. Sometimes, in the haven of afternoon porch shade or in the still and cooler places of late night, they drank and laughed, content because they had managed to make it through the day.

What I noticed was the way the skin of my neighbors glistened as they toiled in their back yards, trying to save their gardens or working a few more miles into their cars. My own skin surprised me each morning in the mirror, becoming darker and darker, my hair lightening, dispelling my assumption that it had always been a curly black — the whole of me a new and stranger blend of browns from day after day of basketball on asphalt courts or racing the other boys down the street after the Icee truck each afternoon.

I came to believe that it was the heat that made things happen. It was a summer of empty sidewalks, people I knew drifting in and out of the alleyways where trees gave more shade, the dirt there cooler to walk on than any paved surface. Strangers, appearing lost, would walk through the neighborhood, the dust and sun's glare making that place look like somewhere else they were trying to go. Sitting on our porch, I watched people I'd never seen before walk by, seemingly drawn to those rippling pools of heat glistening above the asphalt, as if something must be happening just beyond where that warmth quivered down the street. And at night I'd look out from the porch of our house, a few blocks off Eleventh, and scan the neighborhood, wanting to see some change, something besides the nearby rumble of freight trains and the monotony of heat, something refreshing and new. In heat like that, everyone sat on their porches, looking out into the night and hoping for something better to come up with the sun.

It was during such a summer, my mother told me, that my father got home from the third shift at the bottling plant, waked her with his naked body already on top of her, entered her before she was able to say no, sweat on her through moments of whiskey breath and indolent thrusting, came without saying a word, and walked back out of our house forever. He never uttered a word, she said, for it was not his way to speak much when it was hot.

My mother told me he left with the rumble of the trains. She was a wise woman and spoke almost as beautifully as she sang. She spoke to me with a smooth, distant voice, as if it were the story of someone else, and it was strange to me that she might have wanted to cry at something like that but didn't, as if there were no need anymore.

She said she lay still after he left, certain only of his sweat, the workshirt he left behind, and her body calming itself from the silent insistence of his thrusts. She lay still for at least an hour, aware of two things: feeling the semen her body wouldn't hold slowly leaving her and dripping onto the sheets, and knowing that some part of what her body did hold would fight and form itself into what became me nine months later.

I was ten years old when she told me this. After she sat me down and said, *This is how you came to me,* I knew that I would never feel like I was ten for the rest of that year. She told me what it was to love someone, what it was to make love to someone, and what it took to make someone. *Sometimes,* she said, *all three don't happen at once.* When she said that, I didn't quite know what it meant, but I felt her need to tell me. She seemed determined not to hold it from me. It seemed as if somehow she was pushing me ahead of my growing. And I felt uncomfortable with it, the way secondhand shoes are at first comfortless. Soon the pain wasn't greater, just hard to wear.

After that, she filled my home life with lessons, stories, and observations that had a tone of insistence in them, each one told in a way that dared me to let it drift from my mind. By the end of my eleventh year, I learned of her sister Alva, who cut off two of her husband's fingers, one for each of his mistresses. At twelve, I had no misunderstanding of why, someday soon, for nothing more than a few dollars, I might be stabbed by one of the same boys that I played basketball with at the rec center. At thirteen, I came to know that my cousin Dexter hadn't become sick and been hospitalized in St. Louis but had gotten a young white girl pregnant and was rumored to be someone's yardman in Hyde Park. And when I was fourteen, through the tree-withering heat of August, during the Watertown Blues Festival, in throngs of sweaty, wide-smiling people, my mother pointed out to me my father.

For the annual festival, they closed off Eleventh Street from the downtown square all the way up to where the freight railway cuts through the city, where our neighborhood ends and the land rises up to the surrounding hills, dotted with houses the wealthy built to avoid flooding and neighbors with low incomes. Amidst the summer heat was the sizzle of barbecue at every corner, steamy blues from performance stages erected in the many empty lots up and down the street, and, of course, the scores of people, crammed together, wearing the lightest clothing they could without looking loose. By early evening the street would be completely filled with people and the blues would have dominion over the crowd.

The sad, slow blues songs my mother loved the most. The Watertown Festival was her favorite social event of the year. She had a tight-skinned sort of pride through most days of the year, countered by the softer, bare-shouldered self of the blues festival, where she wore yellow or fiery orange outfits and deep brownish red lipstick against the chestnut shine of her cheeks. More men took the time to risk getting to know her, and every year it was a different man; the summer suitors from past years learned quickly that although she wore that lipstick and although an orange skirt never looked better on another pair of hips, never again would she have a man leave his workshirt hanging on her bedpost. With that kind of poise, she swayed through the crowds of people, smiling at many, hugging some, and stopping at times to dance with no one in particular.

When I was younger than fourteen, I had no choice but to go.

Early in the afternoon, she'd make me shower and put on a fresh cotton shirt. *You need to hear the blues, boy, a body needs something to tell itself what's good and what's not.* At fourteen, my mother approached me differently. She simply came out to the yard where I was watering her garden and said, *You going?* and waited for me to turn to her and say yes. I didn't know if I liked the blues or not.

We started at the top of Eleventh Street and worked our way downtown over the few hours of the festival. We passed neighbors and friends from church, my mother's boss from Mills Dry Goods, and Reverend Riggins, who was drinking beer from a paper cup instead of a can. Midway down Eleventh, in front of Macky's Mellow Tone Grill, I bumped into my cousin Wilbert, who had sneaked a tallboy of Miller High Life from a cooler somewhere up the street. A zydeco band was warming up for Etta James. We stood as still as we could in the intense heat and shared sips of that beer while we watched my mother, with her own beer, swaying with a man twice her age to the zip and smack of the washboard.

Etta James had already captured the crowd when Wilbert brought back a large plate of ribs and another beer. My mother came over to share our ribs, and Wilbert was silent after deftly dropping the can of beer behind his back. I stood there listening, taking in the heat, the music, the hint of beer on my mother's breath. The crowd had a pulse to it, still moving up and down the street but stopping to hear the growl of Etta James's voice. The sense of closeness was almost too much. My mother was swaying back and forth on her heels, giving a little dip to her pelvis every so often and mouthing the words to the songs. At any given moment, one or two men would be looking at her, seemingly oblivious and lost in the music.

But she too must have felt the closeness of the people. She was looking away from the stage, focusing on a commotion of laughter in front of Macky's, where voices were hooting above the music. She took hold of my shoulders and turned me toward the front of Macky's. In a circle of loud men, all holding beer, all howling in laughter — some shirtless and others in work clothes — stood a large man in a worn gray suit, tugging his tie jokingly like a noose, pushing the men into new waves of laughter each moment. His hair was nappy like he had just risen from bed. But he smiled as if that were never his main concern anyway, and he held a presence in that circle of people which made me think he had worn that suit for just such an appearance. My mother held my shoulders tightly for a moment, not tense or angry or anxious, just firm, and then let go. "There's your father," she said, and turned away, drifting back into the music and dancing people. Watching her glide toward the stage, I felt obligated not to follow her. When I could see her no longer, I looked back to the circle of men and the man that my mother had pointed out. From the way he was laughing, he looked like a man who didn't care who he might have bothered with his noise. Certainly his friends didn't seem to mind. Their group commanded a large space of sidewalk in front of the bar. People made looping detours into the crowd instead of walking straight through that wide-open circle of drunken activity. The men stamped their feet, hit each other in the arms, and howled as if this afternoon were their own party. I turned to tell Wilbert, but he had gone. I watched the man who was my father slapping his friends' hands, bent over in laughter, sweat soaking his shirt under that suit.

He was a very passionate-looking man, large with his laugh, expressively confident in his gestures, and as I watched him, I was thinking of that night fourteen years ago and the lazy thrust of his which my mother told me had no passion in it at all. I wondered where he must have been all those years and realized how shocked I was to see the real man to fill the image my mother had made. She had made him up for me, but never whole, never fully able to grasp. I was thinking of his silence, the voice I'd never heard. And wanting nothing else at that moment but to be closer, I walked toward that circle of men. I walked as if I were headed into Macky's Mellow Tone, and they stopped laughing as I split their gathering. The smell of liquor, cheap cologne, and musky sweat hit my nostrils, and I was immediately aware not only that I had no reason for going or chance of getting into Macky's, but that I was also passing through a circle of strangers. I stopped a few feet from the entrance and focused on the quilted fake leather covering the door's surface. It was red faded fabric, and I looked at that for what seemed a long time, because I was afraid to turn back into laughter. The men had started talking again, slowly working themselves back into their own good time. But they weren't laughing at me. I turned to face them, and they seemed to have forgotten that I was there.

I looked up at my father, who was turned slightly away from me.

His mouth was open and primed to laugh, but no sound was coming out. His teeth were large, and I could see where sometime before he had lost two of them. Watching him from the street, I had only seen his mouth move and had to imagine what he was saying. Now, so close to him, close enough to smell him, to touch him, I could hear nothing. But I could feel the closeness of the crowd, those unfamiliar men, my father. Then he looked down at me. His mouth closed, and suddenly he wasn't grinning. He reached out his hand, and I straightened up as my mother might have told me to do. I arced my hand out to slide across his palm, but he pulled his hand back, smiling — a jokester, like he was too slick for my eagerness.

He reached in his suit jacket and pulled out a pair of sunglasses. Watertown is a small town, and when he put those glasses on, he looked like he had come from somewhere else. I know I hadn't seen him before that day. I wondered when in the past few days he must have drifted into town. On what wave of early morning heat had he arrived?

I looked at myself in the reflection of the mirrored lenses and thought, *So this is me.*

"Them's slick basketball sneakers you got," he said. "You a bad brother on the court?"

I could only see the edge of one eye behind those glasses, but I decided that he was interested.

"Yeah, I am! I'm gonna be like George Gervin, you just watch." And I was sure we'd go inside Macky's and talk after that. We'd talk about basketball, and then he'd ask me if I was doing well in school, and I'd say not too hot, and he'd get on me about that as if he'd always been keeping tabs on me. Then we would toast to something big, something we could share in the loving of it, like Bill Russell's finger-roll lay-up or the pulled pork sandwich at Round Belly Ribs or the fact that I had grown two inches that year, even though he wouldn't have known that. We might pause for a moment, both of us quiet, both of us knowing what that silence was about, and he'd look real serious and anxious at the same time, a man like him having too hard a face to explain anything that had happened or hadn't happened. But he'd be trying. He'd say, *Hey, brother, cut me the slack, you know how it goes . . .* and I might say, *It's cool,* or I might say nothing at all but know that sometime later on we would spend hours shooting hoop together up at the rec center, and when I'd beaten him two out of three at twenty-one, he'd hug me like he'd always known what it was like to love me.

My father took off his sunglasses and looked down at me for a long silent moment. He was a large man with a square jaw and a wide, shiny forehead, but his skin looked soft — a gentle, light brown. My mother must have believed in his eyes. They were gray-blue, calm and yet fierce, like the eyes of kinfolk down in Baton Rouge. His mouth was slightly open; he was going to speak, and I noticed that his teeth were yellow when I saw him face to face. He wouldn't stop smiling. A thought struck me right then that he might not know who I was.

One of his friends grabbed at his jacket. "Let's roll, bro, Tyree's leavin'!"

He jerked free and threw his friend a look that made me stiffen.

The man read his face and then laughed nervously. "Be cool, nigger, break bad someplace else. We got ladies waitin'."

"I'm cool, brother. I'm cool . . ." My father looked back at me. In the mix of the music and the crowd, which I'd almost forgotten about, I could barely hear him. "I'm cold solid." He crouched down, wiped his sunglasses on a shirttail, and put them in my pocket. His crouch was close. Close enough for me to smell the liquor on his breath. Enough for him to hug me. Close enough for me to know that he wouldn't. But I didn't turn away. I told myself that I didn't care that he was not perfect.

He rose without saying anything else, turned from me, and walked to the corner of Eleventh Street and the alleyway where his friends were waiting. They were insistent on him hurrying, and once they were sure that he was going to join them, they turned down the alley. I didn't cry, although I wouldn't have been embarrassed if I had. I watched them leave, and the only thing I felt was a wish that my father, on this one day, had never known those men. He started to follow them, but before he left, he stopped to look over the scene there on Eleventh Street. He looked way up the street, to where the crowd thinned out, and then beyond that, maybe to where the city was split by the train tracks, running on a loose curve around our neighborhood to the river; or maybe not as far as that, just a few blocks before the tracks and two streets off Eleventh, where, sometime earlier than fourteen years ago, he might have heard the train's early morning rumble when he stepped from our back porch.

WILLIAM LYCHACK

A Stand of Fables

FROM QUARTERLY WEST

I. Miss Oliana and Her Wish Come to Life

Once upon a time there lived a beautiful young schoolteacher in a
fishing village by the sea, and all the children adored her. She
would enter the class like a source of light, smile her good morning,
and begin their arithmetic. "Hop, hop!" she'd call to them if they
dallied. And they rarely dallied.

In the afternoons, as the students scratched their tablets full of
compositions, Miss Oliana would stand beside the windows and
gaze out over the glittering bay and sea below. It was a grand view,
wide with light, and she'd watch the clouds and the shadows of the
clouds run in toward the land. She'd watch the fishermen row
home, their boats riding deep with fish, and the gulls slow-wheeling
overhead.

The years all passed like this, and Miss Oliana found herself
teaching the children of her former students. Then she found herself teaching their children's children. Yet never did she despair of
these passing years, or the fact that she'd never married or had her
own children.

No, if Miss Oliana felt any thorn of regret, it had something to do
with those lengthening stares over the water during the quiet, sun-
lanced afternoons. And as the children read their compositions
from the front of the class, she would feel herself drift back beyond
the bay to the hammered-looking sea, to the dull draw of the horizon and the spikes of sunlight.

And the children, so eager to please, would patiently wait for her response, which would be something quick, something that could apply to any child or any essay. And Miss Oliana would scold herself for neglecting these children. She would sit up straight, redouble her attention, and hear not the words this time but the song beneath the words, the small voice so like those before and those to come that they sounded eternal: all that had been being all that would be being all that was. And she would weep.

And the child at the front of the class would stop, mid-sentence.

And Miss Oliana would touch her eyes, clear her throat, say, "Continue, please. It's lovely, is all."

And they'd continue, for no one in the village could conceive of a thing contrary to her.

More years passed the same, and more men went to sea. Women cured endless piles of fish, and more men drowned and washed ashore as their widows mourned the seasons which beat relentless and rocking as waves. Storms brought down buildings. Long wars ravaged the inland. Kings gave way to presidents, horses to trucks, boats to planes, letters to telephones, and still nothing changed in the village. The next generations all passed under the watchful eye of the village schoolteacher, Miss Oliana.

As she grew ever more ancient, she also grew more restless for the horizon, of which she never tired. She had never heard of so long a life as her own and wondered if something was preventing her passing. In her darker moments she actually suspected the reality of her life: a melody's end is not its goal, but if a melody never finds its end, is it a melody? She worried and she wondered and through the fall and winter these moods persisted as she stared out on the afternoon sea, the children filling notebook after notebook behind her.

What she hoped would pass did not pass. If anything, her restlessness grew stronger and more uncomfortable, until she could resist it no longer. She felt pulled almost bodily toward the thin draw of the horizon, and she began to rise each morning before dawn and swim into the bay.

She also began to set her small household in order. She labeled each object — teakettle, mantel clock, lamp — with the name of its heir, signed her bank account to the school, and took her secret last farewells of everyone in the village, though none suspected the old woman's designs. She would go unnoticed on the day of the village festival, and soberly she prepared to take leave of the small village and house.

On the night before the festival, Miss Oliana laid out her clothes for the morning and slept lightly through the long trains rumbling heavy into town with circus animals and carnival rides and steam-driven calliopes. The men who raised the tents and slaughtered the calves by torchlight were never known for their quiet, reflective ways. They were loud and boisterous and half drunk with their work and travel and the clean night air and the pretty country women, among other spirits.

But Miss Oliana must have slept, for she woke with the grainy light of morning and went to the shoreline and stowed her towel and clothes on the beach. She looked back at the sleeping gray hills of the village as she greased her body with a thick, herb-scented tallow which would keep her warm. Then she waded out into the long cold water toward the rising sun, and a swell came to lift her off her feet, away from the village.

II. Men and Horses, Hoops and Garters

She'd washed in from the sea long ago, a little orphan girl rowed ashore by a forgotten fisherman who'd found her tangled in his net. The village took her and raised her as one of their own. They didn't tell her how she had come from the sea, her hair all tangles of seaweed and tiny crustaceans and shells.

As the years passed they saw the steady glow of miracle around her, a glow that would outlive its memory and its reason and would endear her to the children she came to teach at the village school. She taught for years and years and it took the strange, recurring event of her swims out to sea for the villagers to show their appreciation. The town elder-fathers proposed and organized the special gala in her honor, to be held on the famous summer-circle festival.

It was the custom of the village that each summer it play host to a grand festival for the entire country. The festival not only proved an economic godsend to the village and its merchants and craftspeople but also brought citizens and entertainers from all across the land to the village.

Word went out. The public relations people of the president of the country had decided that he would confer the special National Treasure Medal upon her. Invitations were mailed to all corners of the country. A truly lavish and splendid affair was planned. Master chefs from the city were commissioned; the national hybridizers worked feverishly to create a new bouquet in her name; the pigs were penned beneath apple and pear trees to sweeten them for the slaughter; hot-air balloons were sewn into the shapes of books and inkwells and apples; fireworks were sent from China; and even the gypsy harlequin troupe agreed to attend. As a special gesture, the town committed taxes to break ground on a new school in her name. And, miracle of miracles, the entire affair was kept so hush-hush that Miss Oliana never even suspected such a gala production, let alone in her honor.

The summer preparations moved perfectly, as they invariably do when one is performing the right deed. And the day soon came to be, but when the people went to carry the guest of honor to the fairgrounds and to the silently awaiting crowds, Miss Oliana did not answer her door.

The door was unlocked, and someone entered the house to find the place tidy and empty. News spread fast, and if you had been above the crowd you'd've seen the whispers sweep over the people, the inner life of rumor. The president stood at the podium and talked to the people without a script, called for a search of the shoreline, lent his leadership. The people all went to the shore, and the ones who had gone into her house had found their names on the objects — teakettle, mantel clock, lamp — and they had taken the things in their arms and cradled them down to the beach, where they assembled sadly with the others.

The search parties were formed, men in boats, women along the shore; circus bears combed the woods for the old woman. And the antiques began to warm in the hands of those who held them. The pitcher cleared its throat and pursed its lips, as if to speak. The chair stretched its stiff, straight back. The clock took its hands down from its face. And so totally overcome with fright and awe were the townsfolk that they never noticed the young man rowing in to shore with a boat full of tiny silver fishes. The boat tipped on its keel when the waves nudged him onto the beach, and the tiny fish spilled to the sand with the tinkling sounds of bright silver coins.

III. Sixty Silver Wishes

Anywhere you find timeless fishing villages along the sea, you'll find the same unlucky fisherman who lives there alone in his miserable little hovel close to the sea. He is a fixture of these towns, a battered old bird against whom all others can take measure and say, "But not for the grace of God . . ."

And he rows home each dusk with his leaking boat empty of all but a tangled net and the scrap fish which he cleans and cooks for dinner. The village has stopped admiring the decrepit persistence of his folly, has run dry of pity for him, and has developed a taste for ridicule: a grunting old visage he is, of few words and no friends, whom children are warned against going near, and around whom stories are wrapped.

Aside from the dark tall tales that grow around these men like mice from rags or flies from meat, no one truly knows any longer where they come from or where they go. And so it was in this certain fishing village by the sea that was known through the country for its grand summer-circle festival fairs.

He lived in a miserable hovel close to the sea all alone, and ever since his wife and daughter had died many years ago, he went out to sea every day, regardless of weather or events or anything. He went to the sea every day and fished and fished, and on the day of the fireworks and the circus tents his net felt heavy and full when he tried to haul it aboard, so heavy that he nearly lost his balance and fell into the water himself. He drew the net to the side of the boat and saw a young woman in his net. She had long brown hair twisted up with seaweed and shells, and he could tell she was quite beautiful except her mouth and eyes had been swollen with the stings of jellyfish. Her arms and legs were coated with bright fish scales and she glittered in the low sunlight.

She smiled up to him and he pulled her into the boat and she said, "You have to put me back." She had a smooth and sweet voice and he could only stare at her, rub his eyes, look away.

"Return me," she said. "Throw me back."

"How could I ever?" asked the man, looking at her in his nets.

"Dear fisherman," said she with a sigh. She explained she had no storybook magic for him, nothing to give back, no wishes or favors to grant. "Just throw me away," she said.

She sat up in the bow and began to let herself over the edge of his boat, and for the first time in many years the man saw his life not as it could be but as it was, and his heart sank to the bottom of the sea, where his nets never touched or stirred, and he didn't want to let her go. He said, "Please wait."

She waited a moment and smiled and curled herself over the side of his boat. When the man pulled his net back in, he could hardly lift it aboard. He spilled the tiny fish into the bow of the boat and rowed to shore, feeling stronger by the stroke.

He rowed toward shore and heard the sad accordions and the mournful clinks of the elephants shifting their chained feet. The people, more than had ever assembled on the beach before, stood holding objects in their arms like magic gifts to the sea. Kettle, clock, comb, and shoe. Lamp, spoon, and cup.

And when the man landed, his boat tipped and all of his fish spread bright over the sand like coins of silver.

He stepped out of the boat and stood and waited on the shore with all the others who longed dimly for the child girl to wash in from the sea, each wave and gull charged with miracles galore, the world within reach of delight.

JOYCE CAROL OATES

Ghost Girls

FROM AMERICAN SHORT FICTION

THIS STORY I want to tell took place in upstate New York, in the Chautauqua Mountains, in August 1972.

It was a time when Momma had to take us — her and me — into hiding. The first time I saw what isn't there to be seen.

Arrangements had been made for Daddy's friend Vaughn Brownlee he'd known in Vietnam to fly us from Marsena where we'd been living to Wolf's Head Lake in the Chautauqua Mountains where we'd stay at somebody's camp. How long? Momma wanted to know, and Brownlee shrugged saying, As long as required.

I was five years old and sharp for my age, Smart-Ass they called me but I didn't know if Momma and me had to go into hiding because Daddy had enemies who wanted to hurt us or if it was Daddy himself who was the danger.

Some things you know without asking. Other things, you can't ask. And you never know.

That airstrip at Marsena! — just a single unpainted hangar outside town, rusty tin-corrugated roof and rotted windsock slapping listless in the breeze, a single dirt runway between cornfields you'd swear wouldn't be long enough for even the smallest plane to rise from. On the far side of one of the cornfields, out of sight from the airport, was the Chautauqua River, narrow as a creek above Marsena, rocky whitewater rapids. There were airports Daddy used in those years at Mt. Ephraim, Tintern Falls, South Lebanon and each one of them is clear in my memory but Marsena is the most vivid because of what happened afterward. Also, the biggest plane you could rent at Marsena was an ex–Air Force trainer with a cano-

pied open cockpit, a two-seater that flew at an altitude of twelve
thousand feet, higher than any of the other planes, that was
Daddy's favorite. It was a Vultee basic trainer — VULTEE in fading
black letters on the fuselage — Daddy said of another era, World
War II, not his war but his own father's now gone. That past spring
he'd taken Momma up in the Vultee and they flew to Lake Ontario
and back, gone for almost an hour and I kept having to go to the
bathroom to pee in the concrete-stinking stall where the hard dry
shells of beetles lay underfoot, at last returning to the airport and
buzzing the hangar so Gus Speer the owner ran out shaking his fist,
and the others hanging around watching and drinking beer on a
Sunday afternoon and Daddy in the Vultee was circling the field,
landing in a deafening blurred roar like a dream you can't wake
from, Fucking-O perfect landing they said. And taxiing back to the
hangar, and the sun glaring like knife blades off the wings. And the
terrible wind of the twin propellers dying. And Momma emerged
from the cockpit shaken and white-faced and not so pretty, dazed
pulling off her helmet and goggles and trying to smile squinting at
me and the others, and climbing down half falling into Daddy's
arms, groping as if she couldn't see him clearly, nor the ground
which must have seemed strange to her, so solid, but still Momma
was smiling, her happy smile, her mouth bright red like something shiny pressed into soft white bread dough. And there was the
promise Daddy would take me up in the Vultee some Sunday afternoon too.

One of these days, Birdie, Daddy would say. Smiling the way he
did. Like there was some secret understanding between him and
me, even Momma couldn't guess.

Birdie wasn't my name! — my name is Ingrid.

Momma pulled me by the hand murmuring under her breath
Oh God, oh Jesus, and there was Brownlee waiting for us on the
other side of the hangar, with a look of a man who isn't happy with
waiting. His big sunburnt face like a red cabbage, and his mouth
working — he was always chewing something, a big wad of gum, or
a plug of tobacco. Brownlee was heavier than Daddy in those days,
in his flying clothes a sky-blue nylon zip-up jacket and oil-spotted
khakis, brown helmet and goggles that made him look like a big
beetle on its hind legs. Brownlee waved at us and Momma pulled
me along. The plane he'd be flying was one of the small ones, a

two-seater Cessna silvery yellow across the wings, with fading black trim. One propeller. Seeing it, hearing the motor, I pulled back on Momma's arm and she didn't like that. She was half carrying half pushing me. "Honey, stop crying!" she said. "Crying never did anybody any goddamned good."

I didn't know I'd been crying. Momma's eyes were wet too. Shining like tarnished coppery pennies.

I knew not to cross Momma in certain of her moods. However scared I was. Just let myself go limp, a rag doll, boneless.

Brownlee stared at Momma like it hurt him to see her, the way men stared at Momma in those days. Saying, "O.K., Chloe, let's go. We need to land up there before dark."

Brownlee and Daddy had been navy pilots in the war, airman first class they called each other, saluting, sneering like kids. Like the words tasted bad in their mouths. But the war was over for them now. That's some of the trouble, Momma said.

Brownlee helped Momma into the Cessna stooping beneath the wing, then I climbed inside onto her lap. It was unlawful for Brownlee to take us like this, no belt for me, the space cramped smaller than a motorcycle sidecar. But Gus Speer who owned the airport was a friend of Daddy's and Brownlee's and no friend of the law.

Brownlee shut Momma's door. She latched it from the inside. We watched as Brownlee spat into the dirt and hitched up his khaki trousers slung low on his hips and went to start the propeller, that way of squinting that was Daddy's way too, starting a propeller by hand. Slow at first like a ceiling fan you can follow the turning of the blade with your eyes then faster and faster until you can't make out the blade any longer only the blurred circular motion it would hurt you to set your hand inside.

"Now sit still, Ingrid," Momma said. "And be brave, O.K.?"

Brownlee spat out the rest of what was in his mouth and climbed into the cockpit behind us with a grunt. The plane creaked beneath his weight. Momma was holding me tight murmuring under her breath Oh God, oh Jesus, her quick warm breath, her beery-sour breath in my face. She'd been drinking beer in the car, her and the man who'd driven us to the airport whose name I didn't know, a six-pack she'd taken from the refrigerator on our way out the door. No time for Momma to throw together more than a few things of ours in her zebra-stripe tote bag. We'd only been living in the farmhouse off a dirt road outside Marsena for about two weeks, there were other people living there too and trouble of some kind and Daddy drove away in the night and next day men came by to ask about him, yesterday morning two Eden County sheriff's deputies. The first thing you hear when a police car turns up the drive is radio voices, ratchety and loud. Looking for Lucas Boone, they said. The German shepherd was barking like crazy straining at his leash, neck hairs bristling and ears laid back and one of the deputies had his pistol drawn ready to fire but Happy was tied to a clothesline post and Momma was screaming, Don't shoot him please! — he's no harm to you! and the deputy didn't shoot Happy.

Brownlee was asking Momma was she belted in? O.K.?

Momma said, "O.K." Hugging me tight.

Brownlee started the Cessna in motion, taxiing out the runway. Slow at first. The wheels bumping. Gus Speer in his overalls lifted a hand as we passed, a worried look on his face. We passed the row of parked planes, the Vultee at the end. The sun was beginning to set like fire melting into the sky atop the cliff above the river. Momma whispered to me gripping me tight saying it was a short flight, we'd be there before we knew it, just stay still. I understood that if there was any danger Momma would be holding me like that, Momma would never give me up. Daddy had said these little shithead civilian planes were the dangerous ones not the bomber jets he'd flown in Nam but I was thinking even if we crashed and died I would be safe in Momma's arms.

The plane was rushing along the runway and the wheels began to skip. With Brownlee behind us it was like no one was the pilot, no one in control just Momma and me staring past the plane's nose and the spinning blades. There was a sickening lurch into the air, straight into the wind. The hard-packed dirt rushing beneath like a torrent. Weeds coated with dust, and a stack of scrap lumber and corrugated tin in a field, and beyond the cornstalks in almost uniform rows dun-colored and bleached in the heat of August looking like paper cutouts. We were in the air now, and banking right. Headed north where the sky was dense with clouds. We saw telephone poles and wires above the highway, and the asphalt highway too, and a lone pickup truck moving on it, everything falling suddenly away as if sucked down. And now the Chautauqua River was visible, the color of tin, rippling red streaks from the sunset, a

long snaky stretch of it out of sight. The plane was shuddering so in
the wind, the engine was so loud, you would think it would break
into pieces, it would never hold.

"Here we go," Momma said, raising her voice so I could hear her
over the propeller, "— we're having *fun*, aren't we?"

*She knows I love her, I'm crazy about her doesn't she. It's just a hard time
right now.*
　　Of course she knows, Luke.
　　And you too?
Momma's voice dipped so I almost couldn't hear lying still not
breathing my eyes shut tight so I was seeing flashes of light like
fireflies against my eyelids. *That's what I've been saying, darling. Me
too.*
　　*Because I wouldn't want any further misunderstanding. Not at this
crucial time.*
　　Luke, no! There's no misunderstanding on my part.
　　*That's how people get hurt. They cause their own sorrow. If things get
confused.*
　　That can't happen with us, we've been together too long. You know that.
　　I know it, and I want you to know it too. And her.
　　Ingrid's too young to understand, darling.
　　Well, you explain to her, then. You're her mother for Christ's sake.

North of Marsena, in the mountains, everything was changed. The
wind was stronger and Brownlee seemed to be having trouble keeping on course. I'd been asleep on Momma's lap, the wind was so
loud shaking the plane, voices shouting past, I couldn't stay awake.
My drooling mouth against Momma's soft breast so finally it hurt
her and she woke me up.

Outside the sky was darkening in the direction we were headed.
Clouds roiling up at the horizon thick with storms, heat lightning
flashing in the distance like eyes blinking. Below were thick ex-
panses of woods, foothills and mountains and curving streams and
pockets of low-lying clouds. The sun was just a narrow funnel of
rapidly diminishing pale red light and it scared and excited me
seeing it from such a height like we were above the sun, we could
see it sinking over. *The edge of the world that's always there whether you
see it or not or know of it or not. So close you could be sucked over easy
as sleep.*

Momma pointed out Wolf's Head Lake, or what she thought was the lake, below us. The valley was a deep ditch of shadow smudged with mist. A mirrorlike patch of water inside. We were starting to descend, not smoothly but in lurches, like going down steps in the dark. I wasn't afraid, with Momma holding me so tight. I stared at the light skimming the mountaintops, the pines beginning to become distinct, individual. And there was a road! — curving alongside one of the mountains, suddenly visible. And another road, crossing a strip of water. Narrow lakes like fingers, so many of them, and closer in farmland and pastures in neat rectangles, I could see cattle grazing, the tin-glaring roof of a barn, a truck moving along a highway. We were coming in to land — where? A narrow airstrip ahead. The plane's shadow wasn't visible skimming the ground below, the sun was too far gone.

Momma said worried in my ear, "Hold on, darling. It might be a little —" but already the runway was coming up fast, our little plane swerved in a gust of wind and Brownlee cursed behind us and there was a split second when he might've raised the nose and risen again to circle for another try but instead he brought us down clumsily hitting the ground so Momma and I screamed and the plane went bouncing and skipping and finally rolled dazed along the runway the right wing tilted almost skimming the ground. We came to a skidding stop at the end of the runway, a field beyond, as the first fat hissing raindrops began to fall.

Momma was half sobbing screaming at Brownlee, "You asshole! All of you! You want to kill us don't you!"

A woman friend of Brownlee's named Maude was waiting for us at the airport and by the time we drove out to Wolf's Head Lake to the hunting camp it was dark and raining hard. The mountain road curved, the car's yellow headlights flew ahead. Where we'd all be staying wasn't a house exactly, they called it a lodge, single story with missing shingles and a crumbling stone chimney and a rotted porch across the width of the front. Wild bushes pushing up close. Scrap lumber, an old auto chassis in the yard. Inside it smelled of kerosene. There were few pieces of furniture — a battered sofa, some chairs — and no carpet on the loose-fitting floorboards. Above the fireplace stuffed with debris was a deer's handsome mounted head and antlers. From Daddy I knew to count the points: there were ten. I stood staring at the deer on the wall seeing his fur was faded to the color of sand and mangy with time, his dark glassy eyes were coated with dust.

Brownlee said, like he was playing Daddy, in that way Daddy would with me, "He can't see you, Birdie: he's blind."

I said, "I know that."

Brownlee said, smiling, and winking at Momma and the woman named Maude, "I mean he's blinder than blind, poor fucker. His eyes are glass."

Momma said, "Did you shoot him, Vaughn? — he's your trophy?"

"Hell, no. I'm not a hunter. I don't give shit about hunting animals."

Brownlee said this and there was a silence and the woman named Maude laughed like she was clearing her throat, and Momma said nothing just took my hand and pulled me along into one of the back rooms where we'd be sleeping. When she switched on the light the first thing we saw was something dead on the floor beneath a window. "Jesus!" Momma said. She thought it was a bat, kept me from getting too close. I stared seeing two long columns of black ants leading to it from the wall.

Not death only but what follows, you don't want to know.

The things I saw in Nam, Daddy said, *oh sweet fucking Christ you don't want to know.*

Momma was breathing hard. Ran her hands through her hair in that way of hers, angry, but like she's about to cry too. Instead lighting a cigarette from out of her tote bag. She laughed, her eyes shining so you'd swear she was happy. "What the hell, honey, right? We're alive, and we're here."

"Is Daddy going to be with us?"

Momma was stamping the ants to death. Both feet. These tinsel-looking flat sandals, and her feet delicate, narrow, bluish pale, red polish on the toenails chipped. Momma was wearing her white rayon slacks fitted close to her body, her shiny white plastic belt that made her waist so tiny, red jersey top that pulled across her breasts. A thin gold chain with a green cross on it Daddy said was jade, bought in Saigon. Momma was so young, only twenty-three. She was just a girl, wasn't she. And so beautiful, it hurt you to look but you had to look. Silky white-blond hair, her brown eyes set deep, her mouth that seemed always pouting, even when she smiled. Momma was smoking her cigarette at the same time pushing the dead thing away with her foot, toward the door, the door was open and in the front room Brownlee and the woman named Maude were talking. Sometimes when Momma spoke up her voice was so loud and laughing-angry you'd be surprised, and it was like that now.

"Say, Vaughn — Airman First Class Brownlee — get your ass in here, will you? There's something nasty scaring my little girl I want taken care of *now.*"

I was disappointed, Wolf's Head Lake wasn't close by the damn old "lodge" at all. A mile away, at least, down a bumpy dirt lane. You couldn't hear any waves, and you couldn't smell any water. Outside everywhere you looked, no moon, no stars and nothing but pitch-black night.

Maude had brought some food in grocery bags that ripped and spilled on the counter and she and Momma made supper finally though it took a long while, always it seemed to take a long while to make meals in those days because people got interrupted, there was drinking to be done, cigarettes lit and relit, pots and pans missing or nonexistent and often there was a problem locating cutlery — what was called "silverware." And there were arguments, discussions. But finally a meal would be prepared like this late-night supper which was hamburger patties grilled in the fireplace, big doughy-soft buns the size of a man's hand, and catsup, and relish sugary-tasting as candy, and Frito-Lay potato chips the kind that came in the cardboard box and smelled of the cardboard — we were all starving, especially Brownlee who as he ate blinked like his eyes were welling tears. And there was beer for them, just water for me Momma wasn't too happy about — rust-streaked trickling out of the kitchen faucet.

It started then, my way of eating. If it's ground meat like hamburger pink or runny-red in the center I'll eat just the edges shutting my eyes, if it's muscle-meat like steak or cutlets where you can see the texture of the flesh I can't eat it at all unless I'm drunk or stoned and somebody can talk me out of seeing what it is.

It was around midnight when we were eating and headlights flashed up the drive and I ran to see if it was Daddy but it wasn't — two men I'd never seen before, one of them with spidery tattoos up and down his arms. They'd brought more six-packs of beer, and a bottle of Four Roses, and a little plastic baggie of what Momma

called "dope" — which she said scared her for the weird thoughts it
made her think but she couldn't say no to trying it most of the time.
Later on they played cards, Momma and Maude and Brownlee who
got happy and loud when he drank and the man with the tattooed
arms whose name was Skaggs and the other man, a little younger,
with a mustache, moist yellowish dark eyes like Happy's eyes, whose
name was McCarry. McCarry's hair was greased back in quills and
his skin was pimply but he was sweet-boy-looking sitting close beside
Momma offering to help her with her cards but Momma laughed
saying no thanks, friend, she didn't need anybody's help she'd
been playing gin rummy since the age of ten.

"And winning my fair share too."

"*That*, Miz Boone, I don't doubt."

It was one of those times that any minute Daddy would drive up
and come through the door except he didn't and I started to cry
and Momma said I was tired and it's time for bed and I said no I
didn't want to go to bed not in that nasty bed I was scared I said and
everybody was looking at me holding their cards, Momma's voice
was soft and pleading and guilty-sounding stroking my face she said
was feverish, my skin was sunburnt, my hair all tangles and I kicked
at her and she grabbed my ankles to stop me and a little table fell
over with some empty beer cans on it and a Styrofoam cup used as
an ashtray and Maude helped Momma and I squirmed away from
them but Momma caught me harder, carried me into our room, I
went limp and boneless and too tired to cry or protest, Momma
shined a flashlight into the corners of the room and under the bed
to see there wasn't anything waiting to hurt me, Momma pulled off
my T-shirt and slacks and laid me atop the lumpy bed that creaked
and pulled a spread over me, it was a thin chenille spread with a
smell of damp and mildew, a familiar smell like the smell of Black
Flag insecticide that was an undercurrent in the air, you could
never escape. Momma said, "Things are going to be O.K., Ingrid,"
kissing me on the cheek, her kiss tasting of beer and cigarette
smoke, "— we'll make it up to you, honey, we promise." I grabbed
her hair to pull her down next to me but she slapped my hand away
and then she was gone back out to the card game and I'd wake up
hearing low murmurous voices like water rushing past, the noise of
the water churning white and frothy below the dam at Marsena,
Daddy lifting me on his shoulder to see it better, except Daddy
wasn't here, I was somewhere hearing men's voices I didn't know,

now and then they'd laugh loud, and women's voices too, that
rising-wailing sound of women's voices late at night. *Oh you bastard! You goddamned motherfucker-bastard!* — a woman's voice loud in
teasing.

Waking then when Momma came tiptoeing into the room carrying her sandals. Trying to be quiet but colliding with a chair and
cursing under her breath and climbing onto the bed and the
springs creaking beneath her and she was too exhausted even to
draw the cover partway over her, just fell asleep. A wet gurgling click
in her throat. "Momma," I whispered. "Momma, I hate you." She
didn't hear, she was starting to snore, not like Daddy snored but
softer and discontinuous like asking questions? each little breathy
snore a question? and I smelled Momma's special smell when she
was tired and hadn't washed in a while, I tried to nudge into her
arms so she might hold me like she used to all the time when I was
little, "Momma, I love you," I said. Big Mommy Cat she'd call herself and I was Baby Kitten and we'd nap together during the day
sometimes, sometimes in the back seat of the car if Daddy was late
getting back but Momma was deep asleep now and didn't give a
damn about me. I was wide awake. Those shrill insect noises outside
in the night like tiny chainsaws and there were goddamned mosquitoes in the room that'd come through the broken screen drawn by
the smell of our blood. Bites on my face that swelled and itched, I
scratched at them hard and mean to spite Momma, it was Momma's
fault I was so bit up, in the morning she'd be sorry.

Now this happened. I'd been hearing these voices thinking it was
Maude and somebody else, but after a while I decided it was not, it
was girls' voices, *little girls somewhere outside.* I climbed down from the
bed where Momma was sleeping so hard and I went to the window
to look out and the sky surprised me, it was lighter than the trees, a
hard-glaring blue like ink. The insects were singing like crazy but
over on top of them were these girls' voices, " — *eena?*" one of them
was saying, " — *eena?*" like it was part of a name. I couldn't make out
any words, I pressed my face against the dirty screen and at first
I couldn't see anybody but then I saw them, I'd been looking at
them not recognizing what it was, these figures toward the front of
the lodge by the porch. The girls were a little older than me I
estimated, and they were sisters. I knew that. They were sisters
crouched and hiding, the taller one hugging the other who was
crying trying to make her hush, " — *eena? — eena?*" I wondered if

they'd just crawled out from under the porch? or were they about to crawl under the porch? Was somebody after them, was that why they were so scared? Out there in the dark, in the dripping bushes. If they were Maude's children where'd they been earlier, why hadn't they eaten with us, I wanted to wake Momma to ask but didn't dare, I knew that kind of hard panting sleep of Momma's, skin clammy with sweat.

The girls made me feel sad. And scared something was going to happen that couldn't be stopped.

How long I listened to them not hearing any actual words but only their voices, I don't know. Pressing my face against the screen until finally the voices went away, the little girls were gone without my noticing and there were just the night insects like before, crazy and loud. And Momma's breathless little pants and snores in the bed behind me.

"Momma? — hey!"

It was early morning. I tried to wake Momma but she groaned and shoved me away. She was still sleeping hard, her mouth open, eyelids fluttering and twitching like she was arguing with someone in a dream. I laughed seeing Momma's face swollen with mosquito bites, her upper lip was swollen twice its normal size. Her red jersey top was pulled off one shoulder and her bra strap, which was white, but a kind of yellow-white, was twisted. Momma'd kicked the chenille cover onto the floor, I saw her white rayon slacks were stained, she wasn't going to like that. I touched her in stealth like I'd do sometimes when she didn't know, when she was flat on her back asleep I'd touch her stomach, that's where I'd come from Momma had told me, I'd stare and stare wondering was it so, how could I be so little, wouldn't I suffocate, it scared me to think of it and so I did not think of it except at such times and even then I didn't think of it, I said, "Momma damn you!" — gave up trying to wake her and went into the front room barefoot quiet as I could hoping nobody would see me, I hoped Skaggs and McCarry were gone, the room was empty except for the buck's head above the mantel, those glassy-dusty eyes watching me.

Always, there's been somebody watching me. Holding me in His vision, so I can't escape even if I wished to escape.

This was a room like so many rooms where there'd been a party and the smells of such a room in the morning, the stale smoke, the beer spillage, potato chips — these were smells I knew. Scattered over the table they'd been using which was a wooden table with scars and burns in it were beer cans and bottles and Styrofoam cups and ashes and butts, a flattened Frito-Lay box, playing cards. I always liked playing cards, watching Daddy and Momma and their friends at their games, the cards were precious things because adults handled them with such importance, you didn't ever interrupt them at a serious moment, especially you didn't interrupt any man. There was the queen of hearts on the floor I picked up to look at, also the ace of clubs, the cards were sticky and the reverse side disappointing — no picture just a design of black and mustard yellow stripes.

Outside in the puddled-dirt drive Maude's car was the only car I was glad to see, Skaggs and McCarry were gone. There'd been times when people who showed up late at night were not gone in the morning nor would be gone for days, a friend of Daddy's once only a few months ago before Marsena in a back bedroom shouting and crying and Daddy had to watch over him, try to talk to him Momma said, he'd had a shotgun with him and some grievance to make right and Daddy and Brownlee had finally talked him out of it but it was a long time before he went away.

I went outside. Barefoot onto the splintery porch. Some of the planks too were rotted, you had to be careful where you walked.

I was shivering looking to where the little girls had been hiding — but I couldn't see anything. Tall grasses gone to seed, a straggly bush speckled with aphids. Momma wouldn't like me going barefoot out here, but I crawled under the railing and jumped down to the ground and it was strange how still my mind got, and how empty like I was waiting for something to fill it. "Hey? Are you here? Where are you? — I saw you," I said, like calling out but not raising my voice much, too scared to raise my voice. I squatted down to look under the porch but couldn't see much — it was a nasty dark cobwebby place, smelling of damp. That was when I started shivering hard and jumped up and backed away.

Walked around the yard, in the high grass that was wet from the night, and some of it sharp against my feet, and cold. My eyes swung up seeing how clear the sky was this morning, no clouds, everything washed clean, a sharp whitish light so you couldn't tell where the sun was, and everywhere, excited, calling out to one another, were birds in the pine trees.

There was an old rotted doghouse or rabbit hutch I looked into behind the lodge but nobody was there, nor any sign of anybody.

When Momma was up finally and her face mottled and swollen with mosquito bites, her lip still swollen so she looked like somebody'd punched her with his fist, I told her about the little girls, I was talking fast and excited and Momma said, squinting at me like the morning light was hurtful to her eyes, "Honey, you were just dreaming, there aren't any other children here. Only you." I said, "Yes there are, Momma. I heard them, and I saw them." Momma went out into the kitchen where she tried to get the gas stove to light up so she could make coffee and I followed her repeating what I'd said, the girls were here somewhere hiding I said, but Momma didn't pay too much attention to me. She was cursing under her breath looking for something then she found a box of wooden matches and with a shaky hand tried to light one, scraping it against a stove burner but the match must've been damp, the stick broke in her hand, she let the pieces fall to the floor and went to get her silver lighter Daddy'd given her out of her tote bag and that did work, a bluish flame flaring up at one of the burners with a hissing noise. I repeated what I said about the little girls I'd seen them right outside by the front porch and they were sisters and they were crying because somebody was after them, it wasn't any goddamn dream I told Momma it was *not*. Bringing my bare heels down hard on the worn-out linoleum floor so the floorboards wobbled. Not minding how I was hurting myself till Momma slapped at me to quiet me.

I was like the gas burner flaring up, the blue flame going to orange if the gas's turned too high.

The others came in, Maude and Brownlee, and after a while we ate breakfast, some stale sweet rolls out of a package, and some mealy bananas, and the adults had coffee and smoked their cigarettes and I was telling them about the little girls I knew were somewhere at the camp, Momma kept trying to shush me but I wouldn't be shushed and there came a look into Maude's face and her eyes moved onto me for the first time like she hadn't seen me before. "What little girls are you talking about, Ingrid?" she asked. I

said I didn't know their names, how would I know their names. I'd
seen them in the middle of the night when everybody was asleep,
out by the front porch they'd been, hiding in the grass, and crying.
They were scared of something, I said. Like somebody was after
them.

"What's this?" Maude asked, looking from me to Momma and
back again. "When was this?"

Maude was older than Momma by five or six years, heavier, with
streaked brown hair tied up in a kerchief, eyebrows plucked thin
and arching like she was in perpetual surprise, and her bloodshot
eyes too she was always widening to show surprise or interest or
mockery. She was good-looking I guess but I didn't like her and for
sure I knew she didn't like me. Earlier that morning I'd heard her
and Brownlee curse each other because Brownlee was flying back
to Marsena instead of staying with her the way she wanted. Now she
was staring at me asking what did the little girls look like? and I tried
to say but there weren't the right words, I was getting excited and
picking at my mosquito bites and Momma took both my hands to
calm me saying, "Ingrid, that's enough. Jesus, you had one of your
dreams, that's all." But Maude was exhaling smoke in that slow
watchful way of grown women, and she was looking at Brownlee,
and Brownlee who hadn't been listening said, "What?" like he was
pissed and Maude said, "Vaughn, she's talking about Earl Meltzer's
little girls — that's who she's talking about. My God." Brownlee
said, "She isn't talking about anything, she's just a kid making
things up," and Maude said, shaking her head, her voice quick and
scared, "She's talking about Earl Meltzer's little girls, there's nobody else she's talking about."

Now Momma set her coffee cup down. "Who's Earl Meltzer? —
what is this?"

Brownlee was telling Maude, "She couldn't know about them, it
was two-three years ago at least. So drop it. You're wasted from last
night." But Maude was making these soft sighing scared-sounding
noises to herself, fluttering her eyes, "Oh God, oh Jesus. She's seen
them. Those poor little girls," and Momma said, "Maude? Vaughn?
What the hell is this?" and Brownlee was telling Maude, "Look,
somebody must've told her, that's all. She had a dream, that's all."
Momma said, "Tell her what, for Christ's sake?" Momma's eyes were
sore-looking and her lip so swollen she hadn't even tried to put

on lipstick like she always did, her skin looked dry as ashes in the morning light. Maude said, "Meltzer's little girls Cheryl and Doreen — *I* knew them! Meltzer and Lena his wife weren't living together, Lena was living with this other guy in Watertown, and one night Meltzer went with a gun to get the girls from Lena's mother where they were staying, and he brought them out to the camp here, and —" and Brownlee cut her off saying, "Maude, shut the fuck up, you'll scare the kid," and Maude said, "*You* shut the fuck up, God damn you — you were a buddy of Meltzer's weren't you — thank God the prick put a bullet through his own brains too —"

Brownlee brought his hand, his opened hand not his fist around and hit the side of Maude's face, she screamed spilling hot coffee, and Momma screamed, and already I was running, out of the kitchen and through the back door where the screen was rusted and torn and I forgot I was barefoot running in the high grass around the side of the lodge, I wasn't crying because it wasn't me he'd hit, but I was scared, I crawled under the porch near by where the girls had been and jays were screaming at me out of the pine trees and I pushed my way head-on through a rotted lattice covered in poison ivy and cobwebs till I was inside in this dark place smelling of something sharp crawling on my hands and knees and stones were stabbing me, pieces of glass, I was panting like a dog crawling halfway under the porch hearing how back in the kitchen they were still arguing.

Then it was quiet. It was still. Under the porch where the sun came through cracks in the floorboards in cobwebbed rays and there was this smell so sharp my nostrils pinched like something had died there, and old soft decayed leaves sticking to my skin, gnats buzzing in my face. And a mosquito whining, close by my ear. I knew to make myself as small as I could hugging my knees to my chest, hunched over so nobody could see if they came looking peering through the lattice. My right knee stung where it was bleeding but I wasn't crying. My hands were bleeding too, but I paid them no mind. Momma's footsteps came quick overhead, I knew they were Momma's, so light and fast and then she was on the porch calling, "Ingrid? Honey, where are you?"

I waited like I knew to wait. I was used to hiding and sometimes I'd hidden nobody had even known I was gone, that was the safest kind of hiding and a principle to take to heart all your life.

So Momma didn't know where I was and she came down the porch steps talking to herself, muttering and cursing and I could see her legs, her legs in the white slacks, not clear but like I was seeing them through greenish water. Momma calling my name in that tight-scared way of hers so I knew if I revealed myself she'd be angry so I stayed where I was not making a sound.

I saw them then. At the farthest corner where it was darkest. The sisters crouched together in each other's arms. I saw their faces that were pale but smeared with something — dirt? blood? and I saw they were crying and they saw me, for a long time we looked at each other. "I'm an alive girl," I whispered. "I'm an alive girl not like you."

ANGELA PATRINOS

Sculpture 1

FROM THE NEW YORKER

AT THE BEGINNING of September, I went to the Artemis Academy of Figurative Art looking for work. There I was told a female model was needed for Sculpture 1. The pay wasn't as much as I had hoped, but I filled out the form with my name, Martha Gilmeister, my Social Security number, and the rest of it. This was a year ago; I was twenty-two. I'd been in New York City for nine months. The week before, I'd been working as a go-go dancer but not naked — not even partially. I felt I'd be O.K., though, as a nude model because I was used to standing on platforms and being looked at.

And so, on Monday morning, on the third floor of the academy, I walked from the dressing room toward the sculpture studio wearing a new but cheap navy-blue robe, unprepared for the fear that was rising inside me. Garbage pails full of wet gray clay stood outside the studio door. Inside, bricks of fresh clay wrapped in plastic lay in opened cardboard boxes. The floor was chalky with dried clay. Metal and wood sculpture stands were being wheeled around by students, many of whom were my age, but the fact that they were in school made them seem younger to me. On top of the stands, nailed to boards, were wire armatures, three feet tall, ready to be bent into pose.

I sat on a stool and faced a wall of windows, which faced some windows of another building across the way, where a couple of people moved about in an office. Leaning against a windowsill next to his armature and stand was an Indian man in his middle forties. He had a container of coffee in one hand and a half-eaten Danish in the other. I'd seen him that very morning, walking from the subway, his head bent under a broken-jointed umbrella, the material flapping as he walked. He wore purple-and-black running shoes with shards of neon-green reflectors on the heels. It was the reflectors that reminded me I'd seen him earlier — it had surprised me how they shone even on this gray, wet day. He was wearing a maroon sweater over an oxford shirt and had a high, compact belly.

The instructor came in and began yanking open the skinny locker doors that lined one wall. "It's not here," he said. "Nothing's ever where it's supposed to be, because the right hand of this school is the left's biggest mystery." Creases ran from his nose to the corners of his mouth; his brow was knotted, but no laugh lines marked the skin around his eyes. He told me his name, Dewey Boxwell, and I laughed, mostly from nerves. No one else laughed: they knew his name and knew that he was an established sculptor.

Boxwell found what he was looking for in the last locker, a human skeleton, and hooked it onto a stand. The skeleton was so small that I thought it had been removed from a museum exhibit on evolution. Boxwell told me to get up on the platform, which was in the center of the room. The platform was two and a half feet high and had an outsized lazy Susan in the middle, so the model could be rotated periodically. I knew I would get a break every twenty minutes, but what did twenty minutes feel like? I didn't know.

As I untied my robe, the young students turned to their armatures and Boxwell blew his nose. But the Indian watched. The robe slipped out of my hands and I lowered myself to pick it up, bending at the knees so as not to stick out my behind. My nipples brushed my thighs, one knee made a clicking noise. I thought of home — Milwaukee! Lawn Avenue! My heart ticked rapidly. The robe was retrieved, and I stepped onto the platform. Single lines of sweat ran from my armpits down my thick torso.

As a teenager I'd worn a bracelet popular with the girls at Pershing High: a thin gold chain studded with diamond chips. The first morning after I got one, I put it on and felt dainty, but by the last class of the day the smallness of it made me feel looming and slablike, and the recollection of the way my voice had sounded begging my parents to buy it pained me. I gave it away to a girl who thought I was doing it to be her friend.

I moved through the school hallways supporting my books on wide hips; my straight dark hair was pulled back in a ponytail, which I used hair spray on. I had a thin nose and a thin mouth set into a heavy, fleshy face. There were small scars under my eyebrows: during my second sophomore year (I'd flunked the first), I'd used a depilatory instead of tweezers and blistered the area so badly that it looked as though I'd whacked myself with a hot curling iron.

After I was finally permitted to graduate, I got a full-time job at the Milwaukee County Zoo, where I sat in a booth giving parking passes to hands sticking out of car windows. For four years I worked at the zoo and lived at home. Sometimes, when I was in the primate house on my lunch break, the gorilla would lift a black hairy arm and pound with his fist on the thick Plexiglas in weighted slow motion. Then he'd pause, rest his human fist on the concrete floor, and decide if the glass needed pounding once more. Do it again, I thought.

One summer evening, a party was held near the flamingo pond. I sold a parking pass to one of the guests. He had a New York license plate. On his way out, sitting behind the wheel of his car with his tie untied, he asked if he could call me. He said he'd be in town a few more days. Enough times I'd sat in the easy chair in front of the TV, saying to the girl on the screen, "Don't do it! Don't do it!" — knowing that she would and savoring the mistakes she was about to make.

This man, Ray, smiled both times he saw me in my ill-fitting bra, with the back riding up. Two weeks later, I moved to New York. Ray hadn't encouraged me — he didn't know I was there until after I had moved. My parents were surprised but probably relieved; there were houses in my neighborhood where thirty-five-year-old "kids" still lived with their mothers and fathers.

Ray and I went out a few times, but then he became too busy to see me. That was O.K. There wasn't room in the city for what had begun in another place. At first the speed of the subways scared me, and for a week I walked and walked, stopping to rest in the nearest park, drinking a soda or a can of beer from a paper bag. I found a two-room apartment in Alphabet City, which I shared with a girl who was a student at NYU, and I looked for a job. I failed as a temp, was fired as a waitress, and then got the idea to try go-go dancing, because Ray had once taken me to a place in Chelsea that had dancers. My roommate thought it would be a cool job.

For three months, at nine o'clock in the evening, I folded my net stockings, hot pants, and halter top neatly into a knapsack, put my lace-up boots in a shopping bag, and walked to the subway, token in hand so I wouldn't have to struggle to get it out of my tight jeans pocket. Each night the bouncer would look at me as though he'd never seen me before and then, without expression, say, "Marty."

My hips were agile but I was not a good dancer. Sometimes I would just stop moving and look around at all the activity in the place. I became aware that I was making less in tips than the other girls, so one night I stood in front of the clock on the microwave in my apartment until nine o'clock came and went, and again I was out of a job.

That first day at the academy it took only ten minutes for my curiosity to eclipse my fear. When that wore out, an interesting boredom took over, and when the boredom became ordinary I rested my eyes on the man from India. I felt it was lucky that there was such an ugly face to look at. Because of this, I liked him more than I had at first.

His cheeks were brown, with yellow highlights and an underlying blush. Near his eyes and nose, the skin was darker and ashy. His hairline receded almost to the top of his head; the hair in back was shiny and black and trimmed neatly down to his neck, where there was a roll of skin the width of a finger. His upper teeth pushed out too far over the lower, and this appeared to make it difficult for him to put his lips together.

He stood a couple of inches away from his armature while he worked, pinching off pieces of clay from the lump on his stand and pushing them into the wire. "Get into the habit right now of standing back so you can see what the hell you're doing," Boxwell told him. The Indian took three steps back and knocked into the skeleton, which clacked against its stand.

During the one-hour lunch break, I rested on a torn vinyl couch in the hall, near a pay phone and the elevator. I wished I had a magazine. The elevator was broken, and from behind the closed doors I could hear the clanking of attempted repairs. Just before the afternoon session was to begin, the Indian man came up to me and held out a brown paper bag heavy with food smells.

"I could not eat it all," he said.

"No, thanks," I said.

"Take it," he said.

"No, thank you," I said.

He stood there looking at me with his sea-horsy face.

"I'm not hungry," I said.

He put the bag next to me on the couch and walked into the studio. I waited and then set the bag down inside a trash can and placed an old newspaper over it. I paused — I'd been taught not to waste. I reached back into the trash can for the bag. One of the other models, who'd been passing, stopped and looked at me.

"Did that Indian guy just try to give you his leftovers?" she asked.

"Uh, yeah," I said. "I mean, I guess."

"He tried to give me some the other day. I threw it out. Just wait — he'll ask you out for coffee next."

The sun came out in the afternoon, and by four o'clock it was glaring off the windows of the building across the way. At four-thirty, class was over and I put my robe on and left the studio. The passage of the day felt miraculous — miraculous, I mean, in the true sense. In the bathroom, I changed into my jeans and shirt and noticed that my hands were shaking. I had the feeling that my childhood had suddenly and disproportionately grown further away, yet this new distance between it and me made me more of a child instead of less. Hours of nakedness had done that.

When I got home, I found the bag of food in my knapsack. It turned out the food wasn't leftovers — it was a full and untouched container of rice, vegetables, and chicken. Heated up, it was good.

By the beginning of my third week at the academy, the job had become pedestrian: students needed to see the human figure and I was, for now, that figure. I urged the hours along by taking note of the forming sculptures around the room. The young students seemed to know what they were doing, but the Indian man — whom I had begun to refer to in my mind as Gandhi — clearly did not.

"Proportions," Boxwell told Gandhi one Monday, "aren't your only problem. Your forms look flat and dried out. Only cadavers are flat and dried out." He exhaled loudly, preparing for the chore of instruction. "Crouch down below the platform," he said, "so you can view the model from an oblique angle. So you can see how dynamic the form is."

Gandhi approached the platform. "Do not worry," he said to me, moving closer and then stooping below me.

I myself had observed from such an angle the dynamic forms passing to and from Lake Michigan as I lay on the beach back home: testicles like fetal pigs squeezed into nylon, and monumental female behinds. Now I looked down past the swells and knobs of my body at Gandhi. The smell of my sweat mixed with the scent of my antiperspirant. I prayed that he could not make out the details of my genitalia, but if he could I hoped the sight would in some way hurt him, like a jellyfish dragging along someone's unlucky face.

The brown of his pupils seemed to bleed into the whites, which weren't really white but a yellow-pink. There was a tiny black mole on his right lower eyelid.

He was standing on Eighth Avenue, near the steps of the academy. "I'm sorry for saying to you 'Don't worry' in the class," he said. "I did not want to draw attention, but you seemed tense. You are brave. I don't think I could do it — stand there — and my point is, for this I admire you."

I rolled my eyes. "A lot of people do this," I said.

"Yes, but they are stupid people. I am Fazal Abdul Malik. Would you like to get a coffee?"

I was embarrassed for myself. I hadn't realized how much I longed for company.

"I am not artist," he told me as we sat at the counter of Nick's Coffee Shop, "but ever since I went to Italy I want to try and make sculptures. I will try to make a good one of you, don't worry."

I said I didn't care if he made a good one or not. He dismissed this with a wave of his hand.

"The academy must have been hard to get into," I said.

"The school takes anyone who does not need scholarship," he said. "They have money troubles. Everyone knows this."

I didn't know this. "It doesn't embarrass you?" I asked.

"I am there to make sculpture. The problem with school is not my problem. Are you married?"

I laughed. No one had asked me this before. "Yeah, right," I said, and to make sure he didn't misunderstand me, I shook my head.

"I have a wife in Pakistan," he said.

"Here I was thinking you were from India," I told him. "I was thinking of you as Gandhi."

"Gandhi! I am glad to not be!" He let out a high-pitched laugh, and I felt people turn to look at us.

"What's your wife like?" I asked.

"I don't know," he said.

"You don't know?"

"My point is, I know, but what to say? I'm afraid of her. I think she will shoot me when she sees me. I think she has already killed me five times." He laughed.

I didn't know what he meant so I just smiled. Then he asked, "You know the Michelangelo *David*?"

"I've seen postcards," I said. And what else, I thought. "And those little plaster imitations or whatever."

"It is not the same. This is very beautiful sculpture. Are you student?"

"No."

"What university did you come from, then?"

"I didn't go to college."

I was too close to my failures to boast about my past, but I could not stop myself from adding, "I hardly made it through high school. I even flunked a grade. Tenth." In case he didn't know what "flunked" meant, I said, "They made me do it over again."

He frowned and sipped his coffee, one pinkie lifted. I looked around at the other people in the place, wondering how this conversation was going to end. Then he said, "I have fat belly, but my legs they are skinny. Also, I have short neck. Have you noticed these things?"

"I guess," I said.

"Do you like?"

I thought I was misunderstanding him. "Do I *like*?"

"Do you" — he made an emphatic sweeping gesture along his body — "*like*?"

He took a photograph out of his wallet. It was of him without a shirt. His belly was a milky ash-brown. He was standing next to a woman.

"My wife is pregnant here, but see — she does not look it. What I tell people when I show them this picture is 'Guess which one is pregnant.'" He feigned seriousness and then laughed.

The woman in the photo had short black hair and chipped teeth. She had a hard, unforgiving face that didn't match her soft body. He put the photo away and looked at me. He pointed to the mole on his right lower eyelid.

"My mother had one also, but she used to draw over it with kohl. Now my daughter has one. Do you have children?"

I said I had none.

"Not anywhere?"

"Not that I know of."

"Ah, I was thinking" — he pressed his fingertips to his forehead — "I was thinking somewhere in my head that you were like a man — for just a small moment I was thinking that maybe you could have children you don't know about." He shook his head. "Sometimes I don't think right. But it's not because I see you as man. How could I? There you stand at the school."

By this point, I'd stopped listening to him. I was thinking how strange it was that he should show me a picture of himself without a shirt. Maybe he felt it was fair, because he'd seen me naked. But it wasn't as though I'd chosen what he had seen, and this made me want to make a selection, have a choice. It would have to be something personal — something I could tell him. I could tell him about Ray, but that didn't seem very personal. I could tell him about the go-go bar and how I'd gotten less in tips than the other dancers, but that still kind of bothered me.

"Sometimes I don't remember if I dreamed something or if it really happened," I said. I'd heard a woman tell this to a man on the subway the other day.

"This never happens to me," he answered. "Sometimes they are very, very good and so it's impossible to take for real. Or they are very bad and so, same story. When you are awake, things are more . . . *even.*"

Yes, I wanted to say, you're right, but I'd noticed that at the word "even" he had glanced at my chest, which is large and a bit lopsided. I told myself he already knew what I looked like, so what harm was a glance at my breasts, now that they were covered. I wanted to leave. I dug into my knapsack for money to pay for my coffee.

He reached over and pulled my hand out. A dollar bill drifted to the floor. "Do not offend me," he said, "by taking out this money."

On the train I could still feel the pressure on my wrist from his grasp.

By October I was modeling at the academy four days a week, not just for Sculpture 1 but also for painting, life drawing, and something called écorché. In sculpture class, I noticed that Boxwell continually had words for Fazal that were more nasty than constructive. Sometimes I was grateful for the meanness, because it distracted me from the numbness and the pain in my legs, which was nearly unbearable at times. I saw the frustration and anger in Fazal's face when Boxwell spoke to him. Then I noticed the slight smiles some of the other students comforted themselves with, and I felt blood flow back into my fatigued, dense flesh.

Since the conversation we'd had over coffee, he and I had not spoken, but one Friday, at quarter to five, he was standing outside again. His posture was tight, and he shifted back and forth. When he saw me acknowledge him, he smiled as if we were dear friends, which annoyed me. But in his smile was eagerness, awe, and relief. The eagerness and awe were so real that they made me uncomfortable, and although the relief was somehow fake, this was what made me walk with him to a bar on Hudson Street.

Sitting at the bar, Fazal was quiet. I didn't want to talk about his failures at the academy, so I came up with something I thought was safe. "Talk in your language," I said.

For a moment he was silent. Then words came, and it seemed they could not stop. This isn't a real language, I thought, though I knew it was. What if my life depended on learning it? I could feel panic: I'd never be able to learn, even to save my life! As he continued, I started to pick up similar sounds and the pauses they were joined to and thought maybe I would be able to save myself. I was so lost in this make-believe test that I didn't notice at first that tears were forming in his eyes. They spilled onto his cheeks and tracked along the sides of his nose and finally curved into his upper lip.

Since moving to New York, I had seen many things: a man defecating in the park, a woman with bright-red lipstick and no teeth, a crouching boy using the reflection in a hubcap to find a vein in his neck for a needle. But the sight of this man crying stung me. I stared at his shining face. I must have sensed that he was not asking for comfort and that to give it would be, in spite of his suffering, unnecessary. Or superfluous — I don't know. I didn't comfort him, though.

Fazal removed the damp napkin from under his glass of beer and blotted his eyes and wiped his mouth with it. He told me that he spent all his time at the academy — sometimes he even stayed overnight — and no one there had asked about his language before. The only time he spoke Punjabi was with a shop owner from whom he bought special groceries a few times a month. This man was from India. But even if they had been from the same place, Fazal would not have been friends with him. "You can tell if they are of the like mind," he said, "or if they are only taxi driver."

He turned and looked me in the face. "And now you want to hear it but you do not know what I say. Martha, often I am thinking of you. Do you know why?"

With dread I thought, He's going to tell me he's in love with me. In my mind I heard myself telling somebody, "This old Pakistani guy, he thinks he's in love with me."

But he said, "You are the only naked woman in my life."

I said that the lives of students at the academy were filled with naked women.

"Yes, but they are only picky nudes," he said, "and they act stuck up."

When I got home that night I said to my roommate, "This Indian guy, he thinks he's in love with me."

Of course I didn't believe it — that is, he hadn't said this, he hadn't even meant it. He had meant what he said.

The next Monday, Boxwell told Fazal that the head on his sculpture was too big and the hands and feet looked like stiff little flippers. "And those legs," he continued. "I don't know what they are, but they're not" — he jabbed at the clay — "*legs.*"

Boxwell walked away, and Fazal pulled a large strip of clay off his sculpture and mashed it into the lump on the stand.

He was waiting for me outside at the end of the day. "I take 9 train," he said.

He lived at a hostel on Amsterdam Avenue. A printed fabric smelling of sausage covered the single bed, which served also as a couch. At a dresser, Fazal stood and unscrewed the lid of a tiny

bottle and dabbed some scented oil on his neck. Above the dresser
was a large poster of Michelangelo's *David*.

To stall for time, I asked how he met his wife.

"Why do you want to hear?" he said.

"Just because."

He sighed. "My sister said, when I was thirty-seven, 'I know someone for you to marry.' My sister had a friend who had a sister. One
day my sister, the woman, and I went walking. Sometimes my sister
left me and this woman alone. And then, later, I went alone with my
sister. 'Do you like each other?' she asked me. 'Yes,' I said, 'is O.K.'
She was already thirty when we met and so it was past time for her to
marry. But we both inside were thinking we could have done better.
It is hard to get rid of that thought."

He looked at the poster for a moment and then continued.
"Martha, it is bad to always expect pain, but pleasure it is good to be
prepared for, right?" He removed a condom from the top drawer
and turned to me. "It will be nice for you," he said. "First I will use
my tongue."

He swooped down on me and pressed his lips on mine while
reaching for the zipper on my jeans. My underwear was damp,
which made no sense, because I wasn't attracted to him in that way.
Maybe it was my body's way of telling me that it had stood around
naked long enough without being touched. I grabbed Fazal's hands
with my own and pressed his fingers together as hard as I could,
squeezing them into clumps. When I let go, his knuckles were
white. He sank into the couch as if I'd given him an injection.

"Forgive me for being too quick," he said. "It is just that I feel
things must happen now if they are to happen at all."

That was the feeling I'd had in Milwaukee — the one that made
me leave town. "I understand," I said.

"I understand," though, was the wrong thing to say. He tried to
kiss me again and I had to put my hand over his face and push it
away. I could feel his reaching tongue on my palm. "I'm going to
leave," I threatened.

"Martha, don't leave. What else do you want to know? I will tell
you anything."

I remembered that he had a daughter, so I asked about her.

"The last time I saw her was one year ago, at my mother's funeral.
She kept running from me when I wanted to hold her. It is good for

young girls to be afraid of strangers, so I should be happy for this, right?"

I said nothing.

"O.K., enough," he said. "Tell me what you think about the Michelangelo. For me, it is my favorite work of art."

I looked at the poster. "I don't like how its head doesn't match the body," I said. "It looks weird. Personally, I would have made the statue life-size. So people could relate to it more." I just added that — I hadn't considered it at all.

Abruptly, Fazal stood and turned his back to me. "If it were life-size," he said, "there would be no genius." He didn't even glance at me. It was hard to believe that minutes ago he'd wanted to have sex. Well, this is the end of this, I thought.

The following afternoon, Fazal tore the head off his sculpture and then removed a leg.

Boxwell, who was standing right there, said, "What are you doing?"

"I am starting again."

"It's too late for that. Put what you've taken off back on and do what you can with it."

Fazal did as he was told. It looked like a car accident. Then he left the studio.

After his exit, the dean of the academy ushered in a group of men in dark, double-breasted suits and shiny shoes and women with flat-link gold necklaces. There was to be a cocktail party for potential benefactors that evening at the school; the catering company had been setting up in the lobby that morning. I'd had no idea, though, that these people would be brought into the studio while I was on the platform.

When Boxwell noticed the group, he stepped in front of Fazal's sculpture and threw a large sheet of clay-splattered plastic over it. But the people were not really looking at Fazal's sculpture or at anyone's sculpture. They weren't looking at Boxwell or at the students. They were trying to look at these things until finally they gave in and looked at me.

Fazal returned and pushed past the group. He stood next to the skeleton and spoke. "It is inappropriate for these strangers to come in while the model is posing. There is nothing decent about this

school. The instructor is hiding my sculpture while I am in toilet."
He walked over to his sculpture, took the plastic off, and began to
work, pinching and pushing the clay, his face inches away from it.

The dean ushered the group out with Boxwell following. "We
have a few students who don't belong here," Boxwell was saying. It
was not time for my break, but I stepped off the platform and put
my robe on.

"Go back up," Fazal told me. "The class is almost over for today
and I have work."

"That's not her problem, man," one of the students said.

I took my robe off and went back up.

Again, he was waiting for me outside. Tiny flakes of snow, visible
only against dark buildings, fell. "I have been awake since yesterday," he told me. "Will you come to my room?" His hands were
pressed together.

My roommate subscribed to a number of thin, dull magazines,
which I rarely looked at. But one evening I picked one up and
turned to the ads in the back. "Teach English in Tashkent, Uzbekistan, No Experience Necessary," one said. I showed it to my roommate, laughing. She didn't know why I thought it was so funny.
Neither did I — something about teaching a whole language and
not needing to know how to do it. I sent for the information, and a
couple of weeks later some pamphlets and an application form
arrived. This was after Fazal had returned to Pakistan and I knew I
was going to lose my job at the academy. There were rumors that
the school might close down.

Tashkent is the capital of Uzbekistan, a country in Central Asia
in what used to be the Soviet Union. I had to come here to be able
to say that. That is, know it by heart. It's a lethargic city made up
of ugly modern buildings. But the buildings are not tall — there is
plenty of open, dusty space for the sun to spill onto. A few mosques
remain. I walked by one of them yesterday in the afternoon, and
inside, where it was cool and dark, four mullahs were playing Ping-
Pong.

You can't get a beer. The non-Americans I've met are infatuated
with American English. Twice I've been told that I resemble Julia
Roberts, and I have to remind myself that this comment isn't coming from stupid people. After all, every Pakistani I've met reminds
me of Fazal, simply because of the accent.

Below Uzbekistan is Afghanistan and below that is Pakistan. I should say "south," but I do think of Pakistan as being under where I am, and I think of Fazal looking up at me from that oblique angle. I look down at his receding hairline.

I went with him on that day when he asked — it was the last time I saw him. We didn't sit down when we got to his room. He only wanted to change his clothes, he said, and then he'd take me out to dinner. It was early, only five-thirty. I knew we wouldn't make it to dinner.

"I am sorry," he said, "for reacting the way I did to your opinion about —" He flicked his hand over his shoulder toward the Michelangelo poster behind him. "I know you are only ignorant about the art. Last night I sat here looking at —" Again, the gesture. "Maybe you were right, maybe it was cruel to make him so big. He is nothing but joke now. Oh, Martha, I have dread to go back home. I have failed. But I would like you to talk to me. Tell me something — I am begging you."

"Don't beg me," I said.

"I am not attractive when I beg? O.K., I will stop. Otherwise you will not lie down on the bed with me, right?"

He removed the cushions from the couch and we lay down. Almost immediately he began to snore; I remembered he hadn't slept in two days. I was hurt. I was relieved. I wasn't tired, though, and so I got up and quietly let myself out.

SUSAN PERABO

Some Say the World

FROM TRIQUARTERLY

THERE IS FIRE in my heart. I do what I can.

I sleep deep sleep. I sit in my bedroom window, bare feet on the roof, and scratch dry sticks across the slate. In the two months I've been living here, though, I've spent most of my time playing board games with Mr. Arnette, my mother's new husband. He seems to have an unending supply of them in his basement from when his kids lived at home. My mother isn't around very often. She works at the makeup counter at Neiman Marcus, although she really hasn't needed to since she and Mr. Arnette were married. Mr. Arnette retired a few years ago, at forty, when he sold the windshield safety-glass company he had started right out of high school for what my mother described as "a fancy sum, for something that still shatters." It was right after that that she met and married him. But she works anyway, only now she calls it a hobby.

It's early March; more important, Monday night, the night my mother pretends to be in class at community college. This semester it's poetry, but she's run the gamut. Two summers ago she thought she had me convinced she'd taken up driving.

When she comes in the door a little after nine, she sets her clearly untouched poetry book on the end table next to where I am on the couch.

"How was it?" Mr. Arnette asks, smacking his gum and not looking up from the board.

"Oh my," my mother said. "You wouldn't believe the things those people wrote then."

"Who'd you do tonight?" I ask her. It is a game that I have worked

up. Sometimes I suspect that Mr. Arnette is playing it as well, but
other times I think he's just being duped by her. You can never tell
with Mr. Arnette. Sometimes I imagine he has a secret life, although
he rarely leaves the house. He seems the type of guy who might
have boxes of knickknacks buried all over the world for no reason.

"What's that?" my mother asks, separating the lashes over one
eye, which have been caked with sweat-soaked mascara.

"Who'd you do tonight?" I put a cigarette in my mouth, wait for
one of them to light it.

"Oh, Browning," my mother says.

"Which one?" Mr. Arnette asks. He looks up at me, not her, then
takes the lighter from his shirt pocket and snaps on the flame in
front of my face, so close I could reach out and swallow it.

"Which *one?*" she asks.

"Which Browning," Mr. Arnette says. The lighter disappears back
into his shirt.

My mother misses a beat, then says, "All of them."

She hovers over the Parcheesi board, feigning interest in the
game, and her mink stole knocks one of my pieces to the floor. Mr.
Arnette makes a disgusted sigh, although it was he, I know, who
bought her the thing. She likes to wear it to work, along with a lot of
expensive jewelry. She does not work *for* her customers, she recently explained to me, she works *with* them.

She pats my head. "About your bedtime," she says, as if I am
twelve and have to get up early to catch the school bus, not eighteen and drugged beyond understanding anything much more
difficult than Parcheesi and knowing that my mother, at forty, is
sneaking around in motel rooms.

My parents were divorced when I was five. I have not seen my father
since then, but even so I've been able to keep track of his moods. If
my mother is irritable on Monday nights, I know that my father is
considering calling everything off. If she is sad, I know that he has
asked for her back. If she is her usual perky self, like tonight, I know
that things have gone as planned. They have met every Monday in
the same motel since I was in the sixth grade and playing with
lighters under my covers after bedtime. I used to find motel re-
ceipts, not even torn or wadded up but just lying in the kitchen
wastebasket next to orange peels and soggy cigarettes, with "Mr.

and Mrs." and then my father's name following. Still, my mother, through eight years and two more husbands, has never spoken of it to me and acts as if I could not possibly have figured it out. Thus over the years I have been forced to make up my own story of them: passionate but incompatible, my father a dashing and successful salesman, only through town once a week, only able (willing?) to give my mother three hours. Other times I think it is she who insists on being home each Monday by nine, she who likes doling herself out on her terms, only in small doses. I imagine that they do not talk, that their clothes are strewn around the room before there is time to say anything and back on by the time they catch their breath. It is easier for me to think of it this way, because I can't imagine what they might possibly say to each other.

At Neiman Marcus, where my mother works, they found me in a dressing room last winter with a can of lighter fluid and my pockets stuffed with old underwear and dishtowels. This incident was especially distressing because everyone finally thought that after nearly eight years I had been cured, that the fire was gone, that I was no longer a threat to society. The police led me out of the store hand-cuffed, first through women's lingerie and then smack past the makeup counter, where my mother was halfway pretending not to know me, or to know me just well enough to be interested in what was taking place. They put me away for almost a year for that one, my third time in the hospital since the first fire. The length of my stay was caused by pure frustration, I'm convinced, on the part of my doctors. The "we'll teach her" philosophy of psychology. Two months ago they let me out again, into a different world, where my mother is married yet again and I spend my days spitting on dice with her husband and asking politely for matches to light my ciga-rettes. Either the doctors think I am cured or they have given in, the way I have, the way I did when I was only eleven, when I realized that fire was like blood, water, shelter. Essential.

The thing about fire is this: it is yours for one glorious moment. You bear it, you raise it. The first time, in the record store down-town, I stood over the bathroom trash can, thinking I would not let it grow, that I would love it only to a point and then kill it. That is the trick with fire. For that thirty seconds, you have a choice: spit on it, step on it, douse it with a can of Coke. But wait one moment too long, get caught up in its beauty, and it has grown beyond your control. And it is that moment that I live for. The relinquishing. The power passes from you to it. The world opens up, and you with it. I cried in the record store when the flame rose above my head: not from fear, but from ecstasy.

I sleep sixteen hours a day, more if it's rainy. Another rationale: enough Xanax and I will be too tired to start fires. I am in bed by ten and don't get up till nearly noon. Usually I take a nap before dinner. The rest of the time is game time. It's a murky haze, more often than not. Me forgetting which color I am, what the rules are. Sometimes Mr. Arnette corrects me; other times he lets it go and it is three turns later by the time I realize I have moved my piece the wrong way on a one-way board.

We are on a Parcheesi kick now. Seven or eight games a day. We don't talk much. Mostly we just talk about the game, about the pieces as if they are real people, with spouses and children waiting in some tiny house for them to return from their endless road trips. "In a slump. You're due," Mr. Arnette will say to his men. Sometimes he whispers to the dice. I suspect this is all to entertain me, because he is always checking my reaction. Usually I smile.

Twice a week Mr. Arnette drives me across town to see my psychiatrist. He reads magazines in the waiting room while I explain to the doctor that I am fine except for the fact that I take so much Xanax I feel my brain has been rewired for a task other than real life. The doctor always nods at this, raising his eyebrows as if I have given him some new information that he will get right on, and then tells me the medication will eventually remedy any "discomfort" I might be feeling. I am used to this, and have learned not to greet with great surprise the fact that no one is going to help me in any way whatsoever.

It's Friday, and on the way home from the doctor's we drive by a Lions Club carnival that has set up in a park near Mr. Arnette's house. It is twilight, and my mother will be waiting for us at home, but for some reason Mr. Arnette follows the waving arms of a fat clown and pulls into the carnival parking lot.

"What do you say?" he says. He takes a piece of gum from his pocket and puts it in his mouth.

I look out the window at the carnival. I don't get out much.

Grocery stores are monumental at this point, and the sight of all these people milling around, the rides, the games, frightens me. A Ferris wheel directly in front of me is spinning around and around, and it makes me dizzy just watching it.

"I'm kinda tired," I say.

Mr. Arnette chews louder, manipulates the gum into actually sounding frustrated.

"I think it'd be good for you," he says. He has never said such a thing before, but instead of causing me to feel loved and comforted, it makes me nauseous. I've been told everything from shock treatments to making lanyards would be "good for me," and in practically this same tone.

I feel like crying, and know if I do that he will panic and take me home. But I don't have the time. He is out of the car before I can well up any tears, and I continue to sit, my seatbelt still on, staring out the window into the gray sky. Mr. Arnette stands in front of the fender, gesturing for me to join him.

The last time I was at a carnival was the Freshman Fair at my high school, five thousand years ago. I went on a Saturday night with a boy named Dave who took pictures for the school paper. He held my hand as we walked through the crowds of people and he was sweaty — greasy, almost. He stuck his tongue in my ear in the Haunted House ride and I barely noticed because they had a burning effigy of our rival school's mascot on the wall. The fire licked along the walls and I realized with absolute glee that they had set up one hell of a fire hazard.

Mr. Arnette gets back into the car with a sigh but does not drive away.

"You need to get out more," he says, and I wonder what has changed, wonder if he had a fight with my mother, or sex with my mother, or some other unlikely thing.

"Used to take the kids here," he says, spinning the keys around his finger. I don't even know his kids' names. They call occasionally, but he speaks so rarely when he's on the phone with them that I can't pick up very much information. I imagine them jabbering away somewhere about work and weather and the price of ground round while he sits on the kitchen stool, picking his fingernails and nodding into the phone.

"I'm not exactly a kid," I say.

"You don't like carnivals?"

"I just don't feel like it."

"If she doesn't feel like it, then she doesn't feel like it," he says, as if there is someone else in the car, another part of him, maybe, who he is arguing with.

We continue our drive home in silence. When we stop at a red light, he says, "Why do you take all that shit if it makes you feel so bad?"

I laugh at him. It is a question so logical that it pegs him for a fool, and I can't believe I'm really sitting here with him.

"It's not quite that simple," I say.

He shrugs, gives it up, continues the drive home. He is not a fighter, not a radical. Once I came upon him in my bedroom, looking through a photo album of people he had never met. I stood in the doorway and watched him for nearly ten minutes as he smiled slightly, turning the pages, and I imagined him making up lives for the people in my life. He is that way. Content not to get the whole picture.

I'm standing in the bathroom, trying to stir up enough nerve just to dump them, the whole bottle. My mother taps lightly on the door. I spend more than two minutes in the bathroom and she gets edgy.

"Honey?"

"Just a second," I say. I'm holding them in my hand, all of them. There must be a million of them, at least, enough to confuse me until I hit menopause.

"Are you sick?"

I close my hand around the pills and open the door just far enough for her to get her foot in it.

"Mother," I say. "I'm fine. I'm just putting on a little makeup."

This gets her, physically sends her back a step. She wants to believe it so much that I can see her talking herself into it.

"But it's almost time for bed," she says.

"Just to see how it looks," I say, giving her a big smile through the crack and inching the door closed again. I hear Mr. Arnette's heavy footsteps come tromping up the stairs.

"What's the fuss?" he asks.

"She's putting on makeup," my mother says in a stage whisper. "Maybe she's trying to look cute for you."

That takes care of my clenched hand. It opens of its own accord at my mother's words, and the pills sink to the bottom of the toilet, falling to pieces as they go.

"I think she's really just feeling up to it, starting to feel better," I hear my mother say. It is a new tone for her, and this time it's really a whisper, really some sentiment she doesn't want me to hear. I put my ear against the door. "I'd do anything to make her happy," she says. It makes my chest hurt, she believes it so much.

Sunday has come and my eyes can't stay open wide enough. I feel as if I have gotten glasses and a hearing aid over the weekend; colors are brighter and words sharper. No echoes. Words stop when mouths stop. My mother looks at me suspiciously when she comes into the kitchen early in the morning and finds me cooking bacon.

"What's gotten into you?" she asks, pleasantly enough but with a flicker of panic in her face. Me around the oven means bad news for her. But the heat rising from the burners is only making me warm, and the smell of the bacon is so good that I can't think of much else.

"Just feeling awake," I say.

She smiles, nods, then studies me.

"I'm fine," I tell her.

Mr. Arnette drags into the kitchen, his hair mussed and his robe worn. I have never seen him in the morning.

"Well, look who's up," he says. He winks at me.

"Why don't I finish up and you two go in and start a game," my mother says brightly. Mr. Arnette sits down at the table and opens the newspaper.

"I don't feel like it," I say. "Why don't we do something today?"

"We have to go to a party later," my mother says, glancing at Mr. Arnette for support. "I don't think you'd have very much fun there."

I set a plate of eggs and bacon in front of Mr. Arnette.

"Where's mine?" my mother asks.

"You hate eggs," I say.

"We don't *have* to go to the party," Mr. Arnette says.

My mother frowns, looks from him to me.

"Well, I do," she says. "And I think it would be right for you to come with me. She can take care of herself."

I see my mother now, like she has been stripped down out of her clothes and her skin and even her bones. Her soul is steamed over and dripping fat droplets.

"You all go on," I say. "I don't mind."

I spend the day with my father. I sit out on the porch with the old photo album. The pictures make sense now, fit into an order I have never seen before. My father as a young man raises a tennis racket over his head. He is swinging at something: a butterfly or a bug, though, not a ball. In another he stares away into the distance while my mother pulls his arm, trying to get him to look at the camera. They are so clear now, my father and his bird nose. In one picture he holds me on his lap. I am crying, screaming, and my father is looking at me, perplexed. He is barely twenty, I know, and cannot believe that I am his.

My mother and Mr. Arnette do not come home until late. I've lost track of time, still sitting with the photo album when the headlights swim into the driveway. They get out of the car and my mother takes Mr. Arnette's hand, swings it wildly around.

"Oh, darling!" my mother exclaims. I am not sure if it is to me or Mr. Arnette.

They are both drunk. My mother stumbles going through the door and Mr. Arnette catches her, leads her inside. Then he comes back out, grunts, and sits down on the porch step.

"What have you been doing all night?" he asks.

"Looking through this," I say, holding up the album.

He is quiet for a moment. Then he says, "You ever see your father?" He says it almost as an afterthought, but to something that wasn't said. He says it like we've been on the porch together all night, discussing my father for hours like he was really one of the family.

"Just in here," I say.

"Think he's still a good-looking guy?"

"Dashing, I imagine," I say.

He snorts out a laugh.

"Why'd you marry her?" I hear myself ask.

He leans back, rests his head on the wood inches from my feet.

"Company," he says. He yawns. And I can see him now, too. Safety glass that still shatters. He begins to snore.

"Mr. Arnette?" I say. I reach down and just barely touch the top of his head. He doesn't move.

I go into the house and up the stairs. Their bedroom door is closed, and I imagine my mother is in about the same shape as he is but that they will sleep it off in different places, with dreams of different people's arms.

When I open my door, my mother is standing in my room, the empty bottle of Xanax in one hand, the other hand palm up, as if she were questioning someone even before I arrived.

"Wait a minute," I say. "Just wait."

"I knew it," she says. "I knew there was something wrong."

"Nothing's wrong," I say. "What are you doing in my room? You scared me, standing there like that."

Her mouth opens. "I scared you?"

"I don't think I need those anymore," I say.

"Forgive me if I find it difficult to trust your judgment," she says.

I want a cigarette bad. I had to go all night without them, and I go to the dresser for my pack.

"A light," I say. "Do you have a light?"

"Not on your life," she says.

"I'm fine," I say. I accidentally break the cigarette between my fingers and reach for another one.

She sits down on the bed. "You hurt people," she says quietly. "Not just me. You think you take those pills because I don't want you to hurt me?"

"I never hurt anybody," I say.

"You are so lucky," she says. "You could have killed both of us five times over. In the dressing room, did you ever think about the woman in the next one?"

"I wasn't trying to hurt anybody," I say. "You don't understand."

"You're right about that," she says. She sets the empty bottle on the bed and stands up. "I'm sorry," she says. "I can only live with this for so long."

She leaves. I hear her bedroom door close. The house is silent. Below me, Mr. Arnette sleeps on the porch.

I sit down on the bed. I am crazy, all right. I have always been crazy. I see my mother standing on the front porch as I get out of my first police car, only fourteen, braces squeezing my teeth. She stares at me in disbelief when the police tell her that I have caused over a thousand dollars in damage at the record store, a thousand dollars with only one match. It is then that she begins to look at me like a stranger.

It's Monday again, and she is in her bedroom preparing. Mr. Arnette sits in the rocking chair watching a basketball game. I am on the couch. Cheers from the crowd.

"She wants you to go back into the hospital," he says. He doesn't look at me. He moves his glasses from hand to hand.

"I know," I say. "It's O.K. It's not so bad there."

"Anybody play Parcheesi?"

A man on the court has lost his contact lens. Players are on their knees, hunting.

"Cards mostly," I say. "Lots of jigsaw puzzles."

He nods. "You take those drugs today?"

"No," I say. "Soon enough. It's funny, being able to see so well. But not great so much."

My mother comes into the room and picks up her purse. "Have a good game," she says. She kisses Mr. Arnette on the top of the head, presses her lips into his hair for a long time, until he moves away.

"What was that for?" he asks. He really wants to know, I can tell.

"It doesn't have to be for anything, does it?" she says. She smiles at me, lingers for a moment as if she has something to add but cannot remember what it could have been, and then she leaves.

Mr. Arnette swings the rocking chair around and faces me. "You don't have to go," he says. "Imagine me here, all by myself."

"You'll do O.K.," I say. "Come visit."

He nods, picks up the poetry book from the coffee table where my mother has left it, absently flips through it.

"She didn't even think to take it along," he says.

"She doesn't try so hard anymore," I say. "To fool anybody."

He stops on a page, squints at it, puts on his glasses. "Here's one you'd like," he says, smiling. "*Some say the world will end in fire, others say in ice.*" He stops, looks up at me, and raises his eyebrows.

"I'd like to see them," I say. I hear my mother's car start up in the driveway. "Just one time, see them together. Be a fly on the wall."

"We can be flies together," he says.

It is not a long drive, only a few miles, much too close as far as I'm concerned, for something that seems like it must be another world.

Mr. Arnette stays a few cars behind her, then drives past the motel after she pulls into the lot. He drives around the block twice, then three times.

"What are you waiting for?" I ask him.

"A reason not to do this," he says. He presses down the accelerator and we speed past the motel again. We drive around the city, looking at closed-down stores, empty streets. We don't talk, act as if we really have nowhere to go. He finally makes his way back to the motel, and this time he pulls into the lot. We park at the far end and walk along the row of empty spaces, toward my mother's car. The motel is nearly empty, but the room next to her car is occupied. The shade on the window is up a couple of inches. Mr. Arnette squats down, then reaches for me.

I close one eye and look inside. The bathroom light is on, the door open, and I can see my mother gingerly applying her eyeshadow in front of the mirror. There is a man in the bed, sitting up, yawning. He stretches his skinny arms. He is nearly bald but has a small mustache under his pointed nose. It is a stranger, no one I have ever seen before.

"He looks a lot different from the pictures," Mr. Arnette whispers.

"It's not him," I say, but as soon as I say this I know that it is.

Mr. Arnette looks at me. "Sweetheart . . ." he says.

My mother shuts off the bathroom light, and I can see her silhouette move to the edge of the bed. She sits down and touches the man on the chest, running her finger from his throat to his waist. He takes her hand and puts the finger in his mouth. It is like watching shadows. She says something I cannot make out. Is it about me? Of course, I realize, it is not.

I shiver in the cold. Mr. Arnette takes off his sweater and sets it around my shoulders.

The man begins to put his clothes on, slowly. Next to me, I hear Mr. Arnette's breath catch.

"What is it?" I whisper. I wonder if he can be jealous, if he cares that much.

He only shakes his head. "Chilling," he whispers.

"What?" I say.

"What happens to people."

They are sitting on the edge of the bed together. My mother

fumbles for her purse, takes out a pack of cigarettes, gives one to my father and takes one for herself. She lights them both.

"Where will we go?" Mr. Arnette whispers.

"What?" I say.

They are holding hands on the bed. The shadow of smoke drifts above them, the tiny circles of fire all that light the room.

"Where will we go?" he says again. I lean in against him. He is warm.

Inside the room is quiet. Together the man and the woman raise the cigarettes to their mouths. For a moment, the faces of my parents glow in the darkness. Then Mr. Arnette takes me by the arm and actually lifts me off the ground.

"Wait," I say. "Wait." But I don't fight him. I want him to take me away, finally. I have seen enough.

We are three blocks from the motel before he remembers to turn on his headlights.

"Slow down," I say. "You're gonna kill us both." I take out a cigarette and push the car lighter in.

"Jesus Christ," he says. "What would she do then?" For a moment he is insane, so much more than I ever could have hoped to be.

There are lights up ahead. Music. It is the carnival, its last night, in full swing. The car wildly spits up gravel as Mr. Arnette rumbles across the lot. He jumps out of the car, dashes forward a few feet, then turns and slams his fist into the hood. Then he is perfectly still. He looks straight at me, and I am afraid to move. The cigarette lighter clicks out. A father rushes his children into the back of the station wagon next to us, where they look at us through the big back window, mouths open.

I pull the lighter out, touch my fingers close enough to the middle to feel the raw heat. Then I light my cigarette and blow smoke into the windshield. Mr. Arnette watches me. I know now that he will never go back to my mother, will probably never lay eyes on her again. Something about seeing them, even though he knew. Something about seeing them.

He turns and starts walking toward the ticket booth. I get out of the car and follow him, stand behind him smoking while he buys two tickets.

"Ferris wheel," he says, turning to me. He smiles slightly. "None of those puke rides. Slow. Slow rides tonight."

We get into a car that I'm sure is broken. It swings differently from the others, crooked somehow. I start to say something, but a girl with yellow teeth and matching hair closes the bar over us and we are suddenly moving in a great lurch forward.

"Hey, hey!" Mr. Arnette says, squeezing the bar and looking down onto the park.

"These things are dangerous," I say.

"Bullshit," he says. "We're safer up here than anywhere else in the world."

We screech to a halt near the top, for the loading of passengers into the cars below us. We swing crookedly over the game booths, and I can see us crashing down into the middle of the ring toss. So many ways to buy it, so few to stay alive.

"I've always liked the looks of Canada," Mr. Arnette says. He is smiling pleasantly, innocent as the dawn.

We start moving again. The motion is hypnotizing, and I no longer feel sick but only strange, detached.

"Nice night for driving," I hear myself say.

He doesn't answer. He is looking at my hands, which are open, palms up on my lap, as if I am waiting for something on this ride. He reaches into his sweater pocket and takes out his pack of gum. He sets it in my hand, and my fingers close around it.

We swing around again. Below me, I see a circle of teenagers standing around a small bonfire, warming their hands. Sparks pop around them and die in the grass as the flame reaches higher. The Ferris wheel whips us toward it, and then away again, up into the night.

LYNNE SHARON SCHWARTZ

The Trip to Halawa Valley

FROM SHENANDOAH

THE WEDDING was over, and its residue showed the pleasing signs of success. The guests had been bedecked with leis — now the orchard of mango and lemon trees was strewn with white ginger petals. Coconut shells and half-eaten papayas, wet and succulent, dotted the grass. The tables held the leavings of a feast; the air kept the echo of strumming music and afterimages of hula dancing. Tomorrow the bride and groom would be off for an unknown destination.

"Where do you take a brief honeymoon if you already live in Hawaii?" Jim asked Lois. "Besides which, it's twenty-five hundred miles from anywhere." They sat on lawn chairs, exhausted, watching their oldest son, Paul, and his new wife and her cousins cleaning up. At twenty-four, to his parents' amazement, Paul had made an enormous sum of money after just two years in a Wall Street brokerage firm and rewarded himself with a surfing vacation. On impulse, he bought a lush orchard on the island of Molokai, an instructional manual, and remained. Paradise, he scrawled on his postcards.

"I imagine they're going to one of the other islands. To be alone for a while."

"Alone?" He gave an amused frown. "They've been living together for eight months."

Lois answered in kind, a wry glance from their old elaborate language of glances, recalled now like a mother tongue. They had married even younger than Paul and Kiana, with a vision of the road broadening before them, unfurling its adventures.

"Well, if it's privacy they want," Jim said, "then they shouldn't have me on the couch in the next room tonight. I ought to sleep in the cottage with you."

"Sleep with me?" She turned to him lazily. "Shouldn't that be illegal or something?"

"For convenience," he said. "A small courtesy."

"To them, you mean? Or to you?"

He laughed out loud, a man with flashes of charm all the more effective because of his usual somberness. Beneath that he was warm-hearted, aggrieved, delicate. The wedding had made him sentimental, thought Lois. He wanted to hold someone, or something, in his arms. A stuffed toy might do as well.

"Ask me later, okay?"

The wedding had softened her too, but differently. She missed having more family present. Above all, she missed their son Eric, who called two days ago to say he couldn't attend. A close friend had died of AIDS. He had to speak at the funeral. When Paul, disappointed, announced the news to the family gathered in the living room, a cousin of Kiana's said, "Too bad. Molokai's a hangout for drag queens. A lot of them work as waiters. In the inn in town, you'll find them."

"Eric is not a drag queen," Jim had said loudly, half rising from his chair, while Lois put a hand on his arm. The cousin's remark barely touched her. How close, she was wondering. How close a friend?

She missed Suzanne, who would have been seventeen. But that feeling was nothing new. She missed Anthony, Eric's twin; that missing was spiked with anger.

At night she relented — sharing the cottage was a small enough courtesy. They sat side by side in its one bed like married people, though they had been divorced for four years. "So, how about reading to me? Is that the guidebook you're holding? Read about this place Paul said we should go to tomorrow. What is it, Halawa Valley?"

"The *w* is a *v*," he said, and repeated it correctly.

"You've been studying up." She felt a stab of remembered admiration. An eager traveler, he always arrived ready, knowledgeable, his mind attuned.

"Sure." He riffled through the pages. "The hike is rated Hardy Family."

"As in Hardy Boys?"

"No. Hardy Family as opposed to Experienced Adults or Easy Family." There was a heavy pause. "Okay, first the road. 'It's a good paved road. The only problem is there's not enough of it. In places, including some cliff-hugging curves, it's really only wide enough for one car and you'll need to do some serious horn tooting.' But it's supposed to be an incredibly beautiful drive."

Lois slid lower on the pillows and yawned. Reading was one of the games they used to play. When she couldn't fall asleep, Jim would read to her from the newspaper, a sure soporific. Next morning he would quiz her, affecting sternness, to see at what point she'd dropped off. "Fill in the blanks, Lo. 'The mayor lashed out at the members of the blank committee. He proposed a blank percent increase in the number of police.'" Or they'd make up excursions for vacations never taken. "Those fjords, weren't they fantastic? The rushing water, the cliffs . . . ," Jim murmured for weeks after their trip to Scandinavia had to be canceled because he was fired. He did sound effects for films. Nowadays, with horror and violence in fashion, he was in no danger, was even overworked. Back then, the two-year layoff had been harrowing. Plus the twins were sickly, and Lois's assistant in the dress shop robbed her blind and disappeared. All very unnerving — Lois acquired the habit of seeing every mishap as the start of a series. Could they be jinxed?

"So much for the road. The hike itself is Molokai's most popular trail, they say, though it's a bit difficult to follow. You'll need sturdy walking shoes — did you bring some? 'The one-hour walk up is neither steep nor particularly strenuous, but it is often muddy and slippery.'"

"Oh, muddy and slippery? Sounds great."

"Lush vegetation, fruit for the picking, mangoes, papayas, blah blah. Keep an eye on the disappearing water pipe. Voracious mosquitoes. Come on," he said as she groaned. "It's an adventure. Let's think positive."

The very words he had used when Suzanne first got the frightening symptoms. A brain tumor, they were soon told. She was eleven. It had taken six months and toward the end there was no question of thinking positive. Better not to think at all, just do what the nurses taught them to do. Not long after her death, Anthony joined the Hare Krishnas at eighteen, recruited at the airport on his way to college. Seen in the right light, Jim remarked acidly, that might make a great farce. Their living room was not the right light. When Anthony visited with shaved head, peach-colored robe, and dirty laundry, asking for a contribution, Lois became ill and Jim went out to run, tripped, and gashed his knee, requiring nine stitches.

"Go on, read some more." He had new reading glasses with steel rims, more stylish than the old. He still slept naked. His chest hair was grayer.

"You have to ford a stream by stepping across the stones. They can be 'deceptively slippery.' Or you can wade. But if you wade, it says, 'choose your footing carefully. Water depth can go from ankle-high to knee-high in one step.' After a heavy rain it's almost impossible to cross safely."

Physical challenges held no intrigue for Lois. Jim was the hiker, skier, swimmer. He favored sports where you covered ground. Took flight. Sometimes he'd go out to run in the middle of the night after hours spent sitting up in bed side by side with her, talking until the words became a dull catechism. Maybe if we hadn't moved . . . ? The power lines? The food? The strain on Anthony . . .

How have we sinned? In no way commensurate with the results. How to continue? Acceptance, humility, move forward. But that next step balked them. They were too alike, they agreed, something stubborn and immutable in their natures. They should have taken turns mourning and soothing, but like cranky children, each one wanted to be It: grief's target.

The litany was enervating; energy seeped away with each predictable word. Sooner or later bile would come up. "It's a good thing we had a lot of children," Lois said near the end. "Like peasants. So no matter what happens there are some left to work the land and take care of the parents." Jim glanced over, pained at her levity. "On the contrary, maybe we should've stopped while we were ahead." His form of humor was worse. "Why?" she shot back. "Eric? He's okay. I can live with that." "Sure, I can live with it all right too," Jim said. "But can he? He could get sick any minute. He could be HIV-positive right now. Don't tell me you don't think about it all the time." When Eric had called from college to announce that he was gay, they took it well. After all. And gay couldn't hold a candle to the Hare Krishnas — there was no talking to Anthony since his mind had been colonized. Eric was more than eager to talk about his life. Share, as he put it. They listened. In return for their sophistication, he gave affection and details. "Be careful," Lois said each time he phoned, and when she hung up, moaned into the pillow, "This is not turning out as I pictured it."

"Once you cross over," Jim went on, "the trail parallels the stream, but you can't always see it. There's that water pipe to follow, but it comes and goes."

"We'll probably get lost and starve in the woods. Remember on the news the other night, they found a hiker in the woods after a week? He looked half-dead. Paul and Kiana won't be back for days, and no one will think of looking for us."

He still found her amusing, apparently. "It takes longer than that to starve, Lois. Besides, there's all that fruit to pick — mangoes, guavas, whatever."

"We could be washed away in a tsunami. Didn't Kiana say it was a tsunami area?"

"Yes, there was a huge one in 1946, it says here, which took all the taro farms and most of the people. Then another in 1957. There are only seven families left in the valley."

"We could visit the leper colony instead. It's not catching. Nobody shuns the lepers anymore."

He didn't laugh this time. Intent, hard-muscled, dark, he was absorbed in the guidebook propped on his raised knees. Friends had found his somberness intimidating, but not Lois. She saw it as a form of concentration, of rootedness in his life. No wonder he needed the running, skiing, swimming. When they finally parted, it was not in anger or antipathy but rather in exhaustion and defeat. If it had not turned out as they pictured it, at least they had completed jointly, as best they could, an assigned task, arduous, demanding. With Eric and Paul grown and in college, they could rest. Being together was not a rest. A reminder.

He was inches away. She focused on her body like a scanner but could find no urge to touch him. Right after Suzanne's death she couldn't bear to touch and suspected he felt the same. The touch and the desire it called forth felt toxic. No more, was all she could think. No more. Of course that madness had soon passed. She wouldn't mind, now, when he wrapped his arms around her to cling in the dark, as he surely would. A reflex.

He looked up, smiling belatedly. "Don't worry. We'll have a fine time. When you get to the falls there's a large pool — that must be the swimming Kiana mentioned. 'Partly because the pool is so deep in the center, the water is shockingly cold.'"

"I can hardly wait."

"You'll like it. You'll be hot from the climb." He seemed to grow more eager as he read. In another age he might have rushed off to join the French Foreign Legion. "The water is red. 'Moaula — that's the falls — translates as "red chicken," and fittingly, the water appears red.' Probably iron in the rocks."

"Or the blood of previous tourists."

"Listen to this. 'If you plan on taking a dip here, it's best to first place a ti leaf in the water. Legend has it that a *mo'o,* a giant lizard-like creature, resides in the pool. If the ti leaf floats, she welcomes company and it's okay to swim. If it sinks, it's a warning she wants no visitors.'" Abruptly, he shut the book and curled onto his side, staring at her. He turned to pluck a petal from the vase on the night table and rested it carefully on the sheet covering her. "What about you, Lois?"

"I want no visitors."

She inched around yet another hairpin turn, peering sideways through the windshield for a broader view, then slowed almost to a halt as a battered pickup clattered by from the opposite direction. She was the steadier driver. Jim was given to fits of rashness or caution that made her close her eyes. Once, driving to the hospital to see Suzanne, he hit a truck. No one was hurt; the police took them the rest of the way.

"Look out there on the right," she said. A sweep of blue sea and surf came into view below the sheer drop of rock, and in the distance, the islands of Maui and Lanai rose green and hazy, low tufty clouds dappling them with shadow. She glanced up to see more clouds amassing in a pale gray sky. It was risky to take her eyes off the road even for an instant, though. She tooted around another absurdly narrow curve. Jim seemed far away, gazing up at outcroppings of jagged black rock like half-finished sculptures.

Pain brought some couples closer and divided others. This was the sort of wisdom purveyed on the back pages of the daily paper, deduced from academic studies. Lois read the articles the way a mutilated veteran might read a textbook account of his battle — *Sure, tell me about it.* A friend who had found Buddhism lectured her about having no expectations. But how could you live without them? If you weren't a monk or a saint. The world ran on effort and reward, action and results, investment and return. Was it unreasonable to expect your daughter to grow up?

Soon the road headed downhill, ending in a valley walled by bulbous mountains that embraced a jigsaw-puzzle shoreline. Lois parked near the beach and rubbed her tense neck. "Okay. Muddy and slippery rocks, disappearing path, shockingly cold water — here we come."

"You forgot the voracious mosquitoes." He led the way to the tiny green church where the road began. According to the book, they were to proceed for half a mile past several houses, and at the last house to find a footpath.

They found a chain stretched across the road and a misspelled hand-lettered sign nailed to a post. "Road Closed. Keep Out. No Acess to Falls." They were slanting block letters crudely drawn, crammed close together as they neared the right-hand edge.

"What's this all about?" He stiffened, as though he might stamp his foot in anger. "That can't be an official sign. If they were serious, they'd block the road." He stepped over the chain. "Come on."

"It says it's closed. Maybe there's flooding. It could be dangerous. Anyway . . ." She looked up at the graying sky.

"We can always turn back. How bad can it be? It's a major tourist spot."

"But there are no other tourists."

A jeep appeared in the clearing in front of the church and Jim charged over. The driver, a middle-aged Hawaiian man wearing an Aloha shirt and a baseball cap, answered his questions in a lilting pidgin accent. No, there was nothing wrong with the trail and no flooding. But the road was on private property — those seven families awaiting the next tsunami, Lois thought — and the local people weren't happy about visitors going up and back. Specifically, they didn't want to be held liable for injuries that might occur on the trail. They couldn't afford liability insurance.

"But the path and the falls — that's not private property, is it?"

"No, but see? You pass by the houses . . ."

"I'm sure nothing's going to happen to us. And if it did, we certainly wouldn't sue any of the homeowners." Jim gave a winning smile, a new smile she was not familiar with. He probably used it on new women. Sunny, guileless, quite unlike the sky, which darkened as they spoke.

The man regarded them kindly. "You like go — go. If you see any locals, you tell 'um you understand the situation, 'kay?"

"Thanks very much." Jim took her arm firmly and led her back to the chain.

"Don't you feel it?" She rubbed drops off her bare arms. "Didn't it say crossing the stream is dangerous in the rain?"

"After a heavy rain. This is nothing." And he beckoned from the other side of the chain.

The first house, on the left, was a ramshackle wooden cottage with a refrigerator outside the front door and cut-off jeans hanging on a line. A rusty pickup stood moldering in the front yard. No people in sight. As they neared the second house, it began to pour. They turned and ran, leaping over the chain and making a dash for the car, where they waited briefly until the outburst settled into a dreary patter. At the car rental window four days ago, a man ahead of them had complained, "With the kind of rain you get here, you need wipers that work. You ought to check them out first." Lois started up the winding road into the mountains, praying that the wipers would work. Her prayers were granted.

"I'll sleep in the cottage. I'm used to it," she said that night when Jim invited her to join him in the empty main house. But she went over for breakfast the next morning. As they ate papayas from the orchard, he urged her into a second attempt at the falls. "Why not, Lo? It's a perfect day." He drove so Lois could enjoy the views. Enduring his last-minute hesitations at each curve, then his heart-stopping dashes forward was almost worth it: the mountains, remains of ancient volcanoes, were deeply scored as if by the tines of a giant fork. A lacework of surf spread out on the shore below, and the neighbor islands appeared untouched, sparkling, mythical. No hints of rain — they'd have to go through with it: muddy, slippery stones, perilous stream crossing, voracious mosquitoes, shockingly cold water.

Again they stepped over the chain. "Ready?" he asked with the new smile.

The shabby houses and yards along the road were brightened by frangipani and plumeria, whose mingled scents rose like a fragrant mist. After a few minutes Lois could see where the dirt road ended and the narrow path began. Good. Anything was better than her anxious anticipation. Suddenly from the yard of the last house came ferocious barking. Three large black dogs leaped about, then bounded toward the open fence.

"Dobermans," she said.

"One of them is lame. Look, he can't run very fast."

"Fast enough. They're heading straight for us. This is too much." She wheeled around. "They can keep their falls."

Jim didn't put up a fight. He'd been bitten by a stray years ago and needed a series of rabies shots. "Okay, but don't run. If we go slow they'll stop chasing."

They took long strides, trying to cover ground while appearing casual. At first the dogs were close behind, then they must have slackened — the barking grew less intense, but Lois was afraid to look back and check. By the time they stepped over the chain, the barks were intermittent. She turned to see the panting dogs some yards off, standing poised, on guard, then slinking away as if disappointed.

"Do you think we gave up too easily?" she said from a safe distance. "They might have backed off." Other people, she did not add, might have known how to calm the dogs, even befriend them.

"Dobermans? No! What a nerve. It's one thing to discourage tourists, but this is an outrage."

He was still fuming as Lois drove back. Going round the bends, they met several pickup trucks with young Hawaiian men piled in the back, laughing and talking loudly. Perhaps they lived in the ramshackle cottages. One of them might even own the Dobermans.

She headed for the café at the town's single hotel, where they sat facing the sea. Lois studied the horizon. Somewhere out in that vastness were Paul and Kiana. Even farther, Eric. But where, exactly?

"There was a meeting last night about closing the road." Jim was leafing through the island's thin paper. "Exactly what the fellow told us — they claim they're in danger of being sued and can't take the financial risk. Nothing about setting dogs on people, though."

"All right, look, it's over. It's just one sight we didn't see. Like the fjords."

Oh, those magnificent fjords, she wanted to hear him say. Unforgettable. The wind in our faces, the rushing water, the raw fish we ate on the boat. Instead he said, "It's the principle of the thing. It's all political, you know. The liability issue is just a front." He rattled the paper. "They don't come right out and say it, but it's there between the lines. They don't like tourists, they don't like whites traipsing over their land. You can hardly blame them after the atrocious history." He reminded her of how Hawaii came to be a territory — a gruesome account of missionaries turned exploiters and entrepreneurs, of brutal plantation owners, culminating in a sneaky takeover by the Marines a century ago that rankled more, not less, as years passed. "Paradise — hah!" he grumbled. It was a story of trust betrayed, of bitter disillusion, of promise turned to ash. The facts were vaguely familiar to Lois from a few pages in the guidebook, but Jim obviously knew more than could be learned from a guidebook. He had read up about the fjords too.

"With all that," he wound up, "we still have a right to see the falls."

"Right or not, it doesn't look as if we will. Jim, that waitress. Over there." The waitress was navigating between tables, balancing a heavy tray on her upraised arm. "You think she could be a man?"

"Oh, the drag queens." He took off his reading glasses.

"Please. Cross-dressers." They both grinned. Eric, who worked at a left-wing magazine, could be relied upon to teach the latest in proper terminology. He had told them months in advance about Oriental becoming Asian and black becoming African American. Even "queer" was being resuscitated, but he said they needn't go that far.

The waitress was striking, tall and slender, with a strong tanned face and shoulder-length dark hair. She wore a long print dress slit up the center that showed off her legs.

"She has very narrow shoulders, though."

"Lots of men have narrow shoulders." Jim scrutinized with the air of a connoisseur. "And she's kind of flat-chested."

"Lots of women are flat-chested."

Their eyes were following the waitress serving a group of Japanese tourists when just behind her appeared the Hawaiian man of the day before, who had encouraged them to take the path. He spotted them too and headed over.

"You keep following me or what?" he said with a broad smile.

"This must be one small island. So how was your trip? You wen hike through the valley and see the falls? One nasty storm, eh? Lucky when stop fast." When they told him about the Dobermans, he offered to call the dogs' owner and see that they were locked up the next day, if they cared to try again.

They exchanged a private glance in the old language. "Thank you," said Lois, "but we'll be leaving tomorrow. Anyway, twice up and back on that road is enough."

"Okay, then. I hope your stay stay good." He turned away to hail the waitress. "Hey, Tiny. What's up?" They shook hands energetically.

Instead of going out for dinner, they cooked together in Paul and Kiana's kitchen, then watched the local news. After the weather and surfing reports, Lois heard herself saying, "Listen, what the hell? The giant lizard welcomes visitors."

Jim looked surprised but not baffled. He remembered. His face changed — not mere courtesy, she hoped. No, it modulated to a familiarly dreamy, subtle expression, while his body grew more alert. "That's a terrific idea." He stood over her, extending a hand. "Your place or mine?"

"Yours. Since I'm here already."

But in the morning she was sorry. He was an adroit lover, always had been. After years apart they made love with the excitement of strangers, the tantalizing sense of discovery mellowed by trust. Strangers who knew their way around. Some frozen place in her, shockingly cold, had thawed a bit, and its tenderness was not welcome or comfortable.

A twelve-seater plane skimmed low over the sea to bring them to the Honolulu airport. They would fly to Los Angeles, where Lois would change for Seattle. A long time together, she'd thought when she made her plans. Still, it wasn't as if they didn't get along or couldn't bear each other's company.

"The wedding went well, didn't it?" he said, settling in for the long trip. Lois agreed. Here was a new and better litany. How happy the young couple appeared. How beautiful the island was. How lucky Paul was to have found the orchard, to have found Kiana.

There was a rich satisfaction in their words, which they felt equally and could feel only with each other. It was as if, in reciting Paul's good fortune, they were congratulating themselves: yes, they had done this part of their task well. And yet they knew — they had been over this ground so often — that pride was as misplaced as guilt. They had labored in the dark, through a mystery, their part in it infinitesimal. Far greater forces laid claim to their children. To themselves.

They knew, but knowing could not erase — and why should it? — that rich satisfaction, so fine and pure it might even be called love. Why could it not be enough? she wondered. Along with the night before, in bed. Did others, the ones whom pain brought closer, have something more? Know something more? Were she and Jim weak not to hang on? Or strong, seeing the inevitable and yielding with grace?

"A good visit, all in all." His voice, sly and intimate, penetrated her musings. "But I think the most memorable part was the trip to Halawa Valley."

"Halawa Valley? That fiasco?"

"The one-hour walk up wasn't really too strenuous, even though it was muddy. Luckily, we had sturdy old sneakers with us."

It was a moment before she could respond. It had been easier to take him into her body. "The path was pretty hard to follow . . ." She hesitated while his eyes held steady, urging her on. "But we kept alongside the water pipe. You were a good guide."

"Those stones crossing the stream were deceptively slippery too. I'm glad we decided to wade across instead. And we chose our footing carefully."

"It was pretty scary when the water went from ankle-high to knee-high in one step. It was almost impossible to cross safely. But we managed."

"And remember the fruit? Wasn't it delicious?" he asked.

"Yes, though I didn't care much for the voracious mosquitoes." She laughed and scratched her shoulder, even as she felt the tears rising.

"Well, me neither."

"The falls was even more beautiful than we expected."

"Yes," he replied. "Eric would have loved it. A pity he couldn't come."

"But that water! I still shiver when I think of it. Shockingly cold."
The mystery of it all did make her shiver, right there in her seat.
"And red," he added. "Don't forget, red. I'm glad the ti leaf
floated, though, aren't you? So we could swim."
"The giant lizard welcomed us."
"The *mo'o.* Yes, often she wants no visitors, but I guess she was in
a good mood. Or she just liked us."
The plane landed with ease in Los Angeles. They kissed goodbye
lightly, then Jim went to find a cab and Lois hurried off to make her
connecting flight. The airport was shockingly cold, especially after
the warmth of the island that had seeped into her skin. Again she
shivered, and again.

AKHIL SHARMA

If You Sing Like That for Me

FROM THE ATLANTIC MONTHLY

LATE ONE JUNE AFTERNOON, seven months after my wedding, I woke from a short, deep sleep in love with my husband. I did not know then, lying in bed and looking out the window at the line of gray clouds, that my love would last only a few hours and that I would never again care for Rajinder with the same urgency — never again in the five homes we would share and through the two daughters and one son we would also share, though unevenly and with great bitterness. I did not know this then, suddenly awake and only twenty-six, with a husband not much older, nor did I know that the memory of the coming hours would periodically overwhelm me throughout my life.

We were living in a small flat on the roof of a three-story house in Defense Colony, in New Delhi. Rajinder had signed the lease a week before our wedding. Two days after we married, he took me to the flat. I had thought I would be frightened entering my new home for the first time, but I was not. I felt very still that morning, watching Rajinder in his gray sweater bend over and open the padlock. Although it was cold, I wore only a pink silk sari and blouse, because I knew that my thick eyebrows, broad nose, and thin lips made me homely, and to win his love I must try especially hard to be appealing, even though I did not want to be.

The sun filled the living room through a window that took up half a wall and looked out onto the concrete roof. Rajinder went in first, holding the heavy brass padlock in his right hand. In the center of the room was a low plywood table with a thistle broom on top, and in a corner three plastic folding chairs lay collapsed on the floor. I followed a few steps behind Rajinder. The room was a white rectangle. Looking at it, I felt nothing. I saw the table and broom, the window grille with its drooping iron flowers, the dust in which we left our footprints, and I thought I should be feeling something — some anxiety, or fear, or curiosity. Perhaps even joy.

"We can put the TV there," Rajinder said softly, standing before the window and pointing to the right corner of the living room. He was slightly overweight and wore sweaters that were a bit large for him. They made him appear humble, a small man aware of his smallness. The thick black frames of his glasses, his old-fashioned mustache, as thin as a scratch, and the fading hairline created an impression of thoughtfulness. "The sofa before the window." At that moment, and often that day, I would think of myself with his smallness forever, bearing his children, going where he went, having to open always to his touch, and whatever I was looking at would begin to waver, and I would want to run. Run down the curving dark stairs, fast, fast, through the colony's narrow streets, with my sandals loud and alone, until I got to the bus stand and the 52 came, and then at the ice factory I would change to the 10, and finally I would climb the wooden steps to my parents' flat and the door would be open and no one would have noticed that I had gone with some small man.

I followed Rajinder into the bedroom, and the terror was gone, an open door now shut, and again I felt nothing, as if I were marble inside. The two rooms were exactly alike, except the bedroom was empty. "And there, the bed," Rajinder said, placing it with a slight wave of his hand against the wall across from the window. He spoke slowly and firmly, as if he were describing what was already there. "The fridge we can put right there," at the foot of the bed. Both were part of my dowry. Whenever he looked at me, I either said yes or nodded my head in agreement. We went outside and he showed me the kitchen and the bathroom, which were connected to the flat but could be entered only through doors opening onto the roof.

From the roof, a little after eleven, I watched Rajinder drive away on his scooter. He was going to my parents' flat in the Old Vegetable Market, where my dowry and our wedding gifts were stored. I had nothing to do while he was gone, so I wandered in and out of the flat and around the roof. Defense Colony was composed of rows of pale two- or three-story buildings. A small park, edged with eucalyptus trees, was behind our house.

Rajinder returned two hours later with his elder brother, Ashok, and a yellow van. It took three trips to bring the TV, the sofa, the fridge, the mixer, the steel plates, and my clothes. Each time they left, I wanted them never to return. Whenever they pulled up outside, Ashok pressed the horn, which played "Jingle Bells." I was frightened by Ashok, because, with his handlebar mustache and muscular forearms, he reminded me of my father's brothers, who, my mother claimed, beat their wives. Listening to his curses drift out of the stairwell each time he bumped against a wall while maneuvering the sofa, TV, and fridge up the stairs, I felt ashamed, as if he were cursing the dowry and, through it, me.

On the first trip they brought back two suitcases that my mother had packed with my clothes. I was cold, and when they left, I changed in the bedroom. My hands were trembling by then, and each time I swallowed, I felt a sharp pain in my throat that made my eyes water. Standing there in the room gray with dust, the light like cold, clear water, I felt sad and lonely and excited at being naked in an empty room in a place where no one knew me. I put on a sylvar kamij, but even completely covered by the big shirt and pants, I was cold. I added a sweater and socks, but the cold had slipped under my skin and lingered beneath my fingernails.

Rajinder did not appear to notice I had changed. I swept the rooms while the men were gone, and stacked the kitchen shelves with the steel plates, saucers, and spoons that had come as gifts. Rajinder and Ashok brought all the gifts except the bed, which was too big for them. It was raised to the roof by pulleys the next day. They were able to bring up the mattress, though, and the sight of it made me happy, for I knew I would fall asleep easily and that another eight hours would pass.

We did not eat lunch, but in the evening I made rotis and lentils on a kerosene stove. The kitchen had no light bulb, and I had only the stove's blue flame to see by. The icy wind swirled around my feet. Nearly thirty years later I can still remember that wind. I could eat only one roti, while Rajinder and Ashok had six each. We sat in the living room, and they spoke loudly of their family's farm, gasoline prices, politics in Haryana, and Indira Gandhi's government. I spoke once, saying that I liked Indira Gandhi, and Ashok said that was because I was a Delhi woman who wanted to see women in power. My throat hurt and I felt as if I were breathing steam.

Ashok left after dinner, and Rajinder and I were truly alone for the first time since our marriage. Our voices were so respectful, we might have been in mourning. He took me silently in the bedroom, on the mattress beneath the window with the full moon peering in. When it was over and Rajinder was sleeping, I lifted myself on an elbow to look at him. I felt somehow that I could look at him more easily while he was asleep. I would not be nervous, trying to hide my scrutiny, and if the panic came, I could just hold on until it passed. I thought that if I could see him properly just once, I would no longer be frightened; I would know what kind of a man he was and what the future held. But the narrow mouth and the stiff, straight way he slept, with his arms folded across his chest, said one thing, and the long, dark eyelashes denied it. I stared at him until he started flickering, and then I closed my eyes.

Three months earlier, when our parents introduced us, I did not think we would marry. The neutrality of Rajinder's features, across the restaurant table from me, reassured me that we would not meet after that dinner. It was not that I expected to marry someone particularly handsome. I was neither pretty nor talented, and my family was not rich. But I could not imagine spending my life with someone so anonymous. If asked, I would have been unable to tell what kind of man I wanted to marry, whether he should be handsome and funny. I was not even certain I wanted to marry, though at times I thought marriage would make me less lonely. What I wanted was to be with someone who could make me different, someone other than the person I was.

Rajinder did not appear to be such a man, and although the fact that we were meeting meant that our families approved of each other, I still felt safe. Twice before, my parents had sat on either side of me as I met men found through the matrimonial section of the Sunday *Times of India*. One received a job offer in Bombay, and Ma and Pitaji did not want to send me that far away with someone they could not be sure of. The other, who was very handsome and drove a motorcycle, had lied about his income. I was glad that he had lied, for what could such a handsome man find in me?

Those two introductions were also held in Vikrant, a two-story dosa restaurant across from the Amba cinema. I liked Vikrant, for I thought the place's obvious cheapness would be held against us. The evening that Rajinder and I met, Vikrant was crowded with people waiting for the six-to-nine show. We sat down and an adolescent waiter swept bits of sambhar and dosa from the table onto the floor. Footsteps upstairs caused flecks of blue paint to drift down.

As the dinner began, Rajinder's mother, a small, round woman with a pockmarked face, spoke of her sorrow that Rajinder's father had not lived to see his two sons reach manhood. Ashok, sitting on one side of Rajinder, nodded slowly and solemnly at this. Rajinder gave no indication of what he thought. After a moment of silence, Pitaji, obese and bald, tilted slightly forward and said, "It's all in the stars. What can a man do?" The waiter returned with five glasses of water, his fingers dipped to the second joint in the water. Rajinder and I were supposed to speak, but I was nervous, despite my certainty that we would not marry, and could think of nothing to say. We did not open our mouths until we ordered our dosas. Pitaji, worried that we would spend the meal in silence, asked Rajinder, "Other than work, how do you like to spend your time?" Then, to impress Rajinder with his sophistication, he added in English, "What hobbies you have?" The door to the kitchen, a few tables from us, was open, and I saw a cow standing near a skillet.

"I like to read the newspaper. In college I played badminton," Rajinder answered in English. His voice was respectful, and he smoothed each word with his tongue before letting go.

"Anita sometimes reads the newspapers," Ma said, and then became quiet at the absurdity of her words.

The food came and we ate quickly and mostly in silence, though all of us made sure to leave a bit on the plate to show how full we were.

Rajinder's mother talked the most during the meal. She told us that Rajinder had always been favored over his elder brother — a beautiful, hardworking boy who obeyed his mother like God Ram — and how Rajinder had paid her back by being the first in the family to leave the farm in Bursa to attend college, where he got a master's, and by becoming a bank officer. To get to work from Bursa he had to commute two and a half hours every day. This was very strenuous, she said, and Rajinder had long ago reached the age for marriage, so he wished to set up a household in the city. "We want a city girl," his mother said loudly, as if boasting of her modernity. "With an education but a strong respect for tradition."

"Asha, Anita's younger sister, is finishing her Ph.D. in molecular biology and might be going to America in a year, for further studies," Ma said slowly, almost accidentally. She was a short, dark woman, so thin that her skin hung loose. "Two of my brothers are doctors; so is one sister. And I have one brother who is an engineer. I wanted Anita to be a doctor, but she was lazy and did not study." My mother and I loved each other, but sometimes something inside her would slip, and she would attack me, and she was so clever and I loved her so much that all I could do was feel helpless.

Dinner ended and I still had not spoken. When Rajinder said he did not want any dessert, I asked, "Do you like movies?" It was the only question I could think of, and I had felt pressured by Pitaji's stares.

"A little," Rajinder said seriously. After a pause he asked, "And you, do you like movies?"

"Yes," I said, and then, to be daring and to assert my personality, I added, "very much."

Two days after that Pitaji asked me if I would mind marrying Rajinder, and because I could not think of any reason not to, I said all right. Still, I did not think we would marry. Something would come up. His family might decide that my B.A. and B.Ed. were not enough, or Rajinder might suddenly announce that he was in love with his typist.

The engagement occurred a month later, and although I was not allowed to attend the ceremony, Asha was, and she described everything. Rajinder sat cross-legged before the pandit and the holy fire. Pitaji's pants were too tight for him to fold his legs, and he had to keep a foot on either side of the fire. Ashok and his mother were on either side of Rajinder. The small pink room was crowded with Rajinder's aunts and uncles. The uncles, Asha said, were unshaven and smelled faintly of manure. The pandit chanted in Sanskrit and at certain points motioned for Pitaji to tie a red thread around Rajinder's right wrist and to place a packet of one hundred five-rupee bills in his lap.

Only then, as Asha, grinning, described the ceremony, did I realize that I would actually marry Rajinder. I was shocked. I seemed to be standing outside myself, a stranger, looking at two women, Anita and Asha, sitting on a brown sofa in a wide, bright room. We were two women, both of whom would cry if slapped, laugh if tickled. But one was doing her Ph.D. and possibly going to America, and the other, her elder sister, who was slow in school, was now going to marry and have children and grow old. Why will she go to America and I stay here? I wanted to demand of someone, anyone. Why, when Pitaji took us out of school, saying what good was education for girls, did Asha, then only in third grade, go and re-enroll herself, while I waited for Pitaji to change his mind? I felt so sad I could not even hate Asha for her thoughtfulness.

As the days until the wedding evaporated, I had difficulty sleeping, and sometimes everything was lost in a sudden brightness. Often I woke at night and thought the engagement was a dream. Ma and Pitaji mentioned the marriage only in connection with the shopping involved. Once, Asha asked what I was feeling about the marriage, and I said, "What do you care?"

When I placed the necklace of marigolds around Rajinder's neck to seal our marriage, I brushed my hand against his neck to confirm the reality of his presence. The pandit recited Sanskrit verses, occasionally pouring clarified butter into the holy fire, which we had just circled seven times. It is done, I thought. I am married now. I felt no different. I was wearing a bright red silk sari and could smell the sourness of new cloth. People were surrounding us, many people. Movie songs blared over the loudspeakers. On the ground was a red-and-black-striped carpet. The tent above us had the same stripes. Rajinder draped a garland around my neck, and everyone began cheering. Their voices smothered the rumble of the night's traffic passing on the road outside the alley.

Although the celebration lasted another six hours, ending at about one in the morning, I did not remember most of it until many years later. I did not remember the two red thrones on which we sat and received the congratulations of women in pretty silk saris and men wearing handsome pants and shirts. I know about the cold only because of the photos showing vapor coming from people's mouths as they spoke. I still do not remember what I thought as I sat there. For nearly eight years I did not remember Ashok and his mother, Ma, Pitaji, and Asha getting in the car with us to go to the temple hostel where the people from Rajinder's side were housed. Nor did I remember walking through the long halls, with moisture on the once white walls, and seeing in rooms, long and wide, people sleeping on cots, mattresses without frames, blankets folded twice before being laid down. I did not remember all this until one evening eight years later, while wandering through Kamla Nagar market searching for a dress for Asha's first daughter. I was standing on the sidewalk looking at a stall display of hairbands and thinking of Asha's husband, a tall, yellow-haired American with a soft, open face, who I felt had made Asha happier and gentler. And then I began crying. People brushed past, trying to ignore me. I was so alone. I was thirty-three years old and so alone that I wanted to sit down on the sidewalk until someone came and picked me up.

I did remember Rajinder opening the blue door to the room where we would spend our wedding night. Before we entered, we separated for a moment. Rajinder touched his mother's feet with his right hand and then touched his forehead with that hand. His mother embraced him. I did the same with each of my parents. As Ma held me, she whispered, "Earlier your father got drunk like the pig he is." Then Pitaji put his arms around me and said, "I love you," in English.

The English was what made me cry, even though everyone thought it was the grief of parting. The words reminded me of how Pitaji came home drunk after work once or twice a month and Ma, thin arms folded across her chest, stood in the doorway of his bedroom and watched him fumbling to undress. When I was young, he held me in his lap those nights, his arm tight around my waist, and spoke into my ear in English, as if to prove that he was sober. He would say, "No one loves me. You love me, don't you, my little sun-ripened mango? I try to be good. I work all day, but no one loves me." As he spoke, he rocked in place. He would be watching Ma to make sure she heard. Gradually his voice would become husky. He would cry slowly, gently, and when the tears began to come, he would let me go and continue rocking, lost gratefully in his own sadness. Sometimes he turned out the lights and cried silently in the dark for a half-hour or more. Then he locked the door to his room and slept.

Those nights Ma offered dinner without speaking. Later she told her own story. But she did not cry, and although Ma knew how to let her voice falter as if the pain were too much to speak of, and her face crumpled with sorrow, I was more impressed by Pitaji's tears. Ma's story included some beautiful lines. Lines like "In higher secondary a teacher said, In seven years all the cells in our body change. So when Baby died, I thought, It will be all right. In seven years none of me will have touched Baby." Other lines were as fine, but this was Asha's favorite. It might have been what first interested her in microbiology. Ma would not eat dinner, but she sat with us on the floor and, leaning forward, told us how she had loved Pitaji once, but after Baby got sick and she kept sending telegrams to Beri for Pitaji to come home and he did not, she did not send a telegram about Baby's death. "What could he do," she would say, looking at the floor, "although he always cries so handsomely?" I was dazzled by her words — calling his tears handsome — in comparison with which Pitaji's ramblings appeared inept. But the grief of the tears seemed irrefutable. And because Ma loved Asha more than she did me, I was less compassionate toward her. When Pitaji awoke and asked for water to dissolve the herbs and medicines that he took to make himself vomit, I obeyed readily. When Pitaji spoke of love on my wedding night, the soft, wet vowels of his vomiting were what I remembered.

Rajinder closed and bolted the door. A double bed was in the center of the room, and near it a small table with a jug of water and two glasses. The room had yellow walls and smelled faintly of mildew. I stopped crying and suddenly felt very calm. I stood in the center of the room, a fold of the sari covering my head and falling before my eyes. I thought, I will just say this has been a terrible mistake. Rajinder lifted the sari's fold and, looking into my eyes, said he was very pleased to marry me. He was wearing a white silk kurta with tiny flowers embroidered around the neck and gold studs for buttons. He led me to the bed with his hand on my elbow and with a light squeeze let me know he wanted me to sit. He took off the loose shirt and suddenly looked small. *No, wait. I must tell you,* I said. His stomach drooped. What an ugly man, I thought. *No. Wait,* I said. He did not hear or I did not say. Louder. *You are a very nice man, I am sure.* The hard bed with the white sheet dotted with rose petals. The hands that undid the blouse and were disappointed by my small breasts. The ceiling was so far away. The moisture between my legs like breath on glass. Rajinder put his kurta back on and poured himself some water and then thought to offer me some.

Sleep was there, cool and dark, as soon as I closed my eyes. But around eight in the morning, when Rajinder shook me awake, I was exhausted. The door to our room was open, and I saw one of Rajinder's cousins, a fat, hairy man with a towel around his waist, walk past to the bathroom. He looked in and smiled broadly, and I felt ashamed. I was glad I had gotten up at some point in the night and wrapped the sari on again. I had not felt cold, but I had wanted to be completely covered.

Rajinder, Ashok, their mother, and I had breakfast in our room. We sat around the small table and ate rice and yogurt. I wanted to sleep. I wanted to tell them to go away, to stop talking about who had come last night and brought what, and who had not but might still be expected to send a gift — tell them they were boring, foolish people. Ashok and his mother spoke while Rajinder just nodded. Their words were indistinct, as if coming from across a wide room, and I felt I was dreaming them. I wanted to close my eyes and rest my head on the table. "You eat like a bird," Rajinder's mother said, looking at me and smiling.

After breakfast we visited a widowed aunt of Rajinder's who had been unable to attend the wedding because of arthritis. She lived in a two-room flat covered with posters of gods and smelling of moth-balls and old sweat. As she spoke of how carpenters and cobblers were moving in from the villages and passing themselves off as upper-castes, she drooled from the corners of her mouth. I was silent, except for when she asked me about my education and what dishes I liked to cook. As we left, she said, "A thousand years. A thousand children," and pressed fifty-one rupees into Rajinder's hands.

Then there was the long bus ride to Bursa. The roads were so bad that I kept being jolted awake, and my sleep became so fractured that I dreamed of the bus ride and being awakened. And in the village I saw grimy hens peering into the well, and women for whom I posed demurely in the courtyard. They sat in a circle around me and murmured compliments. My head and eyes were covered as they had been the night before, and as I stared at the floor, I fell asleep. I woke an hour later to their praise of my modesty. That night, in the dark room at the rear of the house, I was awakened by Rajinder's digging between my legs, and although he tried to be gentle, I just wished it over. His face, flat and distorted, was above me, and his hands raised my nipples cruelly, resentful of being

cheated, even though I never heard anger in Rajinder's voice. He
was always polite. Even in bed he was formal. "Could you get on all
fours, please?"

So heavy and still did I feel on the first night in our new rooftop
home, watching Rajinder sleep on the moonlight-soaked mattress,
that I wanted the earth and sky to stop turning and for it always to
be night. I did not want dawn to come and the day's activities to
start again. I did not want to have to think and react to the world. I
fell asleep then, only to wake in panic an hour later at the thought
of the obscure life I would lead with Rajinder. Think slowly, I told
myself, looking at Rajinder asleep with an arm thrown over his eyes.
Slowly. I remembered the year between my B.A. and my B.Ed.,
when, through influence, I got a job as a typist in a candle factory.
For nearly a month, upon reaching home after work, I wanted to
cry, for I was terrified at the idea of giving up eight hours a day, a
third of my life, to typing letters concerning supplies of wax. And
then one day I noticed that I no longer felt afraid. I had learned to
stop thinking. I floated above the days.

In the morning I had a fever, and the stillness it brought with it
spread into the coming days. It hardened around me, so that I did
not feel as if I were the one making love or cooking dinner or going
home to see Ma and Pitaji and behaving there as I always had. No
one guessed it was not me. Nothing could break through the stillness, not even Rajinder's learning to caress me before parting my
legs, or my growing to know all the turns of the colony's alleys and
the shopkeepers calling me by name.

Winter turned into spring, and the trees in the park swelled green.
Rajinder was thoughtful and generous. Traveling for conferences
to Baroda, Madras, Jaipur, Bangalore, he always brought back saris
or other gifts. The week I had malaria, he came home every lunch
hour and cooked gruel for me. On my twenty-sixth birthday he
took me to the Taj Mahal and arranged to have my family hidden in
the flat when we returned in the evening. What a good man, I
thought then, watching him standing proudly in a corner. What a
good man, I thought, and was frightened, for that was not enough.
I knew I needed something else, but I did not know what. Being his
wife was not so bad. He did not make me do anything I did not want

to, except make love, and even that was sometimes pleasant. I did not mind his being in the flat, and being alone is difficult. When he was away on his trips, I did not miss him, and he, I think, did not miss me, for he never mentioned it. Summer came, and hot winds swept up from the Rajasthani deserts. The old cows that wander unattended on Delhi's streets began to die. The corpses lay untouched for a week sometimes; their tongues swelled and, cracking open the jaw, stuck out absurdly.

The heat was like a high-pitched buzzing that formed a film between flesh and bone, so that my skin felt thick and rubbery and I wished that I could just peel it off. I woke at four every morning to have an hour when breathing air would not be like inhaling liquid. By five the eastern edge of the sky was too bright to look at, even though the sun had yet to appear. I bathed both before and after breakfast and again after doing laundry but before lunch. As June progressed and the very air seemed to whine under the heat's stress, I stopped eating lunch. Around two, before taking my nap, I would pour a few mugs of water on my head. I liked to lie on the bed imagining that the monsoon had come. Sometimes this made me sad, for the smell of wet earth and the sound of the rain have always made me feel as if I have been waiting for someone all my life and that person has not yet come. I dreamed often of living near the sea, in a house with a sloping red roof and bright blue window frames, and woke happy, hearing water on sand.

And so the summer passed, slowly and vengefully, until the last week of June, when the *Times of India* began its countdown to the monsoon and I awoke one afternoon in love with my husband.

I had returned home that day after spending two weeks with my parents. Pitaji had had a mild heart attack, and I took turns with Ma and Asha being with him in Safdarjung Hospital. The heart attack was no surprise, for Pitaji had become so fat that even his largest shirts had to be worn unbuttoned. So when I opened the door late one night and saw Asha with her fist up, ready to start banging again, I did not have to be told that Pitaji had woken screaming that his heart was breaking.

While I hurried a sari and blouse into a plastic bag, Asha leaned against a wall of our bedroom, drinking water. It was three. Rajinder, in his undershirt and pajama pants, sat on the bed's edge and stared at the floor. I felt no fear, perhaps because Asha had said the heart attack was not so bad, or perhaps because I just did not care. The rushing and the banging on doors appeared to be the properly melodramatic behavior when one's father might be dying.

An auto-rickshaw was waiting for us downstairs, triangular, small, with plasticized cloth covering its frame. It seemed like a vehicle for desperate people. Before getting in, I looked up and saw Rajinder. He was leaning against the railing. The moon was yellow and uneven behind him. I waved and he waved back. Such formalities, I thought, and then we were off, racing through dark, abandoned streets.

"Ma's fine. He screamed so loud," Asha said. She is a few inches taller than I am, and although she too is not pretty, she uses makeup that gives angles to her round face. Asha sat slightly turned on the seat so that she could face me. "A thousand times we told him, Lose weight," she said, shaking her head impatiently. "When the doctor gave him that diet, he said, 'Is that before or after breakfast?'" She paused and added in a tight whisper, "He's laughing now."

I felt lonely sitting there while the city was silent and dark and we talked of our father without concern. "He wants to die," I said softly. I enjoyed saying such serious words. "He is so unhappy. I think our hopes are made when we are young, and we can never adjust them to the real world. He was nearly national champion in wrestling, and for the past thirty-seven years he has been examining government schools to see that they have the right PE equipment. He loves eating, and that is as fine a way to die as any."

"If he wants to die, wonderful; I don't like him. But why is he making it difficult for us?"

Her directness shocked me and made me feel that my sentimentality was dishonest. The night air was still bitter from the evening traffic. "He is a good man," I said unsteadily.

"The way he treated us all. Ma is like a slave."

"They are just not good together. It's no one's fault."

"How can it be no one's fault?"

"His father was an alcoholic."

"How long can you use your parents as an excuse?"

I did not respond at first, for I thought Asha might be saying this because I had always used Ma and Pitaji to explain away my failures. Then I said, "Look how good he is compared with his brothers. He must have had something good inside that let him be gentler than them. We should love him for that part alone."

"That's what he is relying on. It's a big world. A lot of people are worth loving. Why love someone mediocre?"

Broken glass was in the hallways of the hospital, and someone had urinated in the elevator. When we came into the yellow room that Pitaji shared with five other men, he was asleep. His face looked like a shiny brown stone. He was on the bed nearest the window. Ma sat at the foot of his bed, her back to us, looking out at the fading night.

"He will be all right," I said.

Turning toward us, Ma said, "When he goes, he wants to make sure we all hurt." She was crying. "I thought I did not love him, but you can't live this long with a person and not love just a bit. He knew that. When they were bringing him here, he said, 'See what you've done, demoness.'"

Asha took Ma away, still crying. I spent the rest of the night dozing in a chair next to his bed.

We fell into a pattern. Ma usually came in the morning, around eight, and I replaced her, hours later. Asha would take my place at three and stay until six, and then Ma's brother or his sons would stay until Ma returned.

I had thought I would be afraid of being in the hospital, but it was very peaceful. Pitaji slept most of the day and night because of the medicines, waking up every now and then to ask for water and quickly falling asleep again. A nice boy named Rajeeve, who also was staying with his father, told me funny stories about his family. At night Asha and I slept on adjacent cots on the roof. Before she went to bed, she read five pages of an English dictionary. She had been accepted into a postdoctoral program in America. She did not brag about it as I would have. Like Ma, Asha worked very hard, as if that were the only way to live and one needn't talk about it, and as if, like Ma, she assumed that we are all equally fortunate. But sometimes Asha would shout a word at me — "Alluvial!" — and then look at me as if she were waiting for a response. Once, Rajinder came to drop off some clothes, but I was away. I did not see him or talk with him for the two weeks.

Sometimes Pitaji could not sleep and he would tell me stories of his father, a schoolteacher, who would take Pitaji with him to the saloon, so that someone would be there to guide him home when he was drunk. Pitaji was eight or nine then. His mother beat him for accompanying Dadaji, but Pitaji, his breath sounding as if it were coming through a wet cloth, said that he was afraid Dadaji would be made fun of if he walked home alone. Pitaji told the story quietly, as if he were talking about someone else, and as soon as he finished, he changed the subject. I could not tell whether Pitaji was being modest or was manipulating me by pretending modesty.

He slept most of the day, and I sat beside him, listening to his little green transistor radio. The June sun filled half the sky, and the groundskeeper walked around the courtyard of the hospital in wide circles with a water bag as large as a man's body slung over one shoulder. He was sprinkling water to keep the dust settled. Sometimes I hummed along to Lata Mangeshkar or Mohammed Rafi singing that grief is no letter to be passed around to whoever wants to read.

There were afternoons when Pitaji became restless and whispered conspiratorially that he had always loved me most. Watching his face, puffy from the drugs, his nose broad and covered with blackheads, as he said again that Ma did not talk to him or that Asha was indifferent to his suffering, I felt exhausted. When he complained to Asha, "Your mother doesn't talk to me," she answered, "Maybe you aren't interesting."

Once, four or five days before we took him home, as he was complaining, I got up from the chair and went to look out the window. Beyond the courtyard was a string of yellow-and-black autorickshaws waiting under eucalyptus trees. I wanted desperately for Asha to come, so that I could leave, and bathe, and lie down to dream of a house with a red-tiled roof near the sea. "You must forgive me," Pitaji said as I looked out the window. I was surprised, for I could not remember his ever apologizing. "I sometimes forget that I will die soon and so act like a man who has many years left." I felt frightened, for I suddenly wanted to love him but could not trust him enough.

From then until we went home, Pitaji spoke little. Once, I forgot to bring his lunch from home and he did not complain, whereas before he would have screamed and tried to make me feel guilty. A few times he began crying to himself for no reason, and when I asked why, he did not answer.

Around eleven the day Pitaji was released, an ambulance carried Ma, Pitaji, and me to the Old Vegetable Market. Two orderlies, muscular men in white uniforms, carried him on a stretcher up three flights of stairs into the flat. The flat had four rooms and was part of a circle of dilapidated buildings that shared a courtyard. Fourteen or fifteen people turned out to watch Pitaji's return. Some of the very old women, sitting on cots in the courtyard, asked who Pitaji was, although he had lived there for twenty years. A few children climbed into the ambulance and played with the horn until they were chased out.

The orderlies laid Pitaji on the cot in his bedroom and left. The room was small and dark, smelling faintly of the kerosene with which the bookshelves were treated every other week to prevent termites. Traveling had tired him, and he fell asleep quickly. He woke as I was about to leave. Ma and I were speaking in whispers outside his bedroom.

"I am used to his screaming," Ma said. "He won't get any greasy food here. But once he can walk . . ."

"He seems to have changed."

"Right now he's afraid. Give him a few days and he'll return to normal. People can't change, even if they want to."

"What are you saying about me?" Pitaji tried to call out, but his voice was like wind on dry grass.

"You want something?" Ma asked.

"Water."

As I started toward the fridge, Ma said, "Nothing cold." The clay pot held only enough for one glass. I knelt beside the cot and helped Pitaji rise to a forty-five-degree angle. His heaviness and the weakness of his body moved me. Like a baby holding a bottle, Pitaji held the glass with both hands and made sucking noises as he drank. I lowered him when his shoulder muscles slackened. His eyes were red, and they moved about the room slowly. I wondered whether I could safely love him if I did not reveal my feelings.

"More?" he asked.

"Only fridge water," I said. Ma was clattering in the kitchen. "I am going home."

"Rajinder is good?" He looked at the ceiling while speaking.

"Yes," I said. A handkerchief of light covered his face, and faint blue veins, like delicate, almost translucent roots, showed through the skin of his forehead. "The results for his exam came," I told him. "He will be promoted. He was second in Delhi." Pitaji closed his eyes. "Are you hurting?" I asked.

"I feel tired."

I too felt tired. I did not know what to do with my new love or whether it would last. "That will pass, the doctor said. Why don't you sleep?"

"I don't want to," he said loudly, and my love drew back.

"I must go," I said, but made no move to.

"Forgive me," he said, and again I was surprised. "I am not worried usually, but I get frightened sometimes. Sometimes I dream that the heaviness is dirt. What an awful thing to be a Muslim or a Christian." He spoke slowly, and I felt my love returning. "Once, I dreamed of Baby's ghost."

"Oh."

"He was eight or nine and did not recognize me. He did not look like me. I was surprised, because he was my son and I had always expected him to look like me."

I felt exhausted. Something about the story was both awkward and polished, which indicated deceit. But Pitaji never lied completely, and the tiring part was not knowing. "God will forgive you," I said. But why should he? I thought. Why do people always think hurting others is all right, as long as they hurt themselves as well?

"Your mother has not."

I placed my hand on his, knowing that I was already in the trap. "Shhh."

"At your birthday, when she sang, I said, 'If you sing like that for me every day, I will love you forever.'"

"She loves you. She worries about you."

"That's not the same. When I tell Asha this, she tells me I'm sentimental. Ratha loved me once. But she cannot forgive. What happened so long ago, she cannot forgive." He was blinking rapidly, preparing to cry. "But that is a lie. She does not love me because," and he began crying without making a sound, "I did not love her for so long."

"Shhh. She loves you. She was just saying 'Oh, I love him so. I hope he gets better, for I love him so.'"

"Ratha could have loved me a little. She could have loved me twenty for my eleven." He was sobbing.

"Shhh. Shhh. Shhh." I wanted to run away, far away, and be someone else.

The sleep that afternoon was like falling. I lay down, closed my eyes, and plummeted. I woke as suddenly, without any half-memories of dreams, into a silence that meant that the power was gone, and the ceiling fan was still, and the fridge was slowly warming.

It was cool, I noticed, unsurprised by the monsoon's approach — for I was in love. The window curtains stirred, revealing TV antennas and distant gray clouds and a few sparrows wheeling in the air. The sheet lay bunched at my feet. I felt gigantic. My legs stretched thousands of miles; my head rested in the Himalayas and my breath brought the world rain. If I stood up, I would scrape against the sky. But I was small and compact and distilled too. I am in love, I thought, and a raspy voice echoed the words in my head, causing me to panic and lose my sense of omnipotence for a moment. I will love Rajinder slowly and carefully and cunningly, I thought, and suddenly felt peaceful again, as if I were a lake and the world could only form ripples on my surface, while the calm beneath continued in solitude. Time seemed endless, and I would surely have the minutes and seconds needed to plan a method of preserving this love, like the feeling in your stomach when you are in a car going swiftly down a hill. Don't worry, I thought, and I no longer did. My mind obeyed me limply, as if a terrible exhaustion had worn away all rebellion.

I got up and swung my legs off the bed. I was surprised that my love was not disturbed by my physical movements. I walked out onto the roof. The wind ruffled the treetops, and small gray clouds slid across the cool, pale sky. On the street eight or nine young boys played cricket. The school year had just started, and the children played desperately, as if they must run faster, leap higher, to recapture the hours spent indoors.

Tell me your stories, I would ask him. Pour them into me, so that I know everything you have ever loved or been scared of or laughed at. But thinking this, I became uneasy and feared that when I actually saw him, my love would fade and I would find my tongue thick and unresponsive. What should I say? I woke this afternoon in love with you. I love you too, he would answer. No, no, you see, I really love you. I love you so much that I think anything is possible, that I will live forever. Oh, he would say, and I would feel my love rush out of me.

I must say nothing at first, I decided. Slowly I will win his love. I will spoil him, and he will fall in love with me. And as long as he loves me, I will be able to love him. I will love him like a camera that closes at too much light and opens at too little, so his blemishes will never mar my love.

I watched the cricket game to the end. I felt very happy standing there, as if I had just discovered some profound secret. When the children dispersed, around five, I knew Rajinder would be home soon.

I bathed and changed into new clothes. I stood before the small mirror in the armoire as I dressed. Uneven brown aureoles, a flat stomach, the veins in my feet like pen marks. Will this be enough? I wondered. Once he loves me, I told myself. I lifted my arms and tried to smell the plantlike odor of my perspiration. I wore a bright red cotton sari. What will I say first? *Namastay* — how was your day? With the informal "you." How was your day? The words felt strange, for I had never before used the informal with him. I had, as a show of modesty, never even used his name, except on the night before my wedding, when I said it over and over to myself to see how it felt — like nothing. Now when I said "Rajinder," the three syllables had too many edges, and again I doubted that he would love me. "Rajinder, Rajinder," I said rapidly several times, until it no longer felt strange. He will love me because to do otherwise would be too lonely, because I will love him so. I heard a scooter stopping outside the building and knew that he had come home.

My stomach was small and hard as I walked onto the roof. The dark clouds made it appear as if it were seven instead of five-thirty. I saw him roll the scooter into the courtyard and I felt happy. He parked the scooter and took off his gray helmet. He combed his hair carefully to hide the growing bald spot. The deliberateness of the way he tucked the comb into his back pocket overwhelmed me with tenderness. We will love each other gently and carefully, I thought.

I waited for him to rise out of the stairwell. The wind made my petticoat, drying on the clothesline, go *clap, clap*. I was smiling rigidly. How was your day? How *was* your day? Was your day good? Don't be so afraid, I told myself. What does it matter how you say hello? Tomorrow will come, and the day after, and the day after that.

His steps sounded like a shuffle. Leather rubbing against stone. Something forlorn and steady in the sound made me feel as if I were twenty years older and this were a game I should stop or I might get hurt. Rajinder, Rajinder, Rajinder, how are you?

First the head: oval, high forehead, handsome eyebrows. Then the not so broad but not so narrow shoulders. The top two buttons of the cream shirt were opened, revealing an undershirt and some hair. The two weeks had not changed him, yet seeing him, I felt as if he were somehow different, denser.

"How was your day?" I asked him while he was still in the stairwell.

"All right," he said, stepping onto the balcony. He smiled, and I felt happy. His helmet was in his left hand and he had a plastic bag of mangoes in his right. "When did you get home?" The "you" was informal, and I felt a surge of relief. He will not resist, I thought.

"A little after three."

I followed him into the bedroom. He placed the helmet on the windowsill and the mangoes in the refrigerator. His careful way of folding the plastic bag before placing it in the basket on top of the refrigerator moved me. "Your father is fine?" I did not say anything.

Rajinder walked to the sink on the outside bathroom wall. I stood in the bedroom doorway and watched him wash his hands and face with soap. Before putting the chunk of soap down, he rinsed it of foam, and only then did he pour water on himself. He used a thin washcloth hanging on a nearby hook for drying.

"Yes," I said.

"What did the doctor say?" he asked, turning toward me. He is like a black diamond, I thought.

She said, I love you. "She said he must lose weight and watch what he eats. Nothing fattening. That he should rest at first and then start exercising. Walking would be best."

I watched Rajinder hang his shirt by the collar tips on the clothesline and suddenly felt sad at the rigorous attention to detail necessary to preserve love. Perhaps love is different in other countries, I thought, where the climate is cooler, where a woman can say her husband's name, where the power does not go out every day, where

not every clerk demands a bribe. That must be a different type of love, I thought, where one can be careless.

"It will rain tonight," he said, looking at the sky.

The eucalyptus trees shook their heads from side to side. "The rain always makes me feel as if I am waiting for someone," I said, and then regretted saying it, for Rajinder was not paying attention, and perhaps it could have been said better. "Why don't you sit on the balcony, and I will make sherbet to drink?"

He took a chair and the newspaper with him. The fridge water was warm, and I felt sad again at the need for constant vigilance. I made the drink and gave him his glass. I placed mine on the floor and went to get a chair. A fruit seller passed by, calling out in a reedy voice, "Sweet, sweet mangoes. Sweeter than first love." On the roof directly across, a boy seven or eight years old was trying to fly a large purple kite. I sat down beside Rajinder and waited for him to look up so that I could interrupt his reading. When Rajinder looked away from the paper to take a sip of sherbet, I asked, "Did you fly kites?"

"A little," he answered, looking at the boy. "Ashok bought some with the money he earned, and he would let me fly them sometimes." The fact that his father had died when he was young made me hopeful, for I thought that one must suffer and be lonely before one can love.

"Do you like Ashok?"

"He is my brother," he answered, shrugging and looking at the newspaper. He took a sip of the sherbet. I felt hurt, as if he had reprimanded me.

I waited until seven for the power to return; then I gave up and started to prepare dinner in the dark. I sat beside Rajinder until then. I felt happy and excited and frightened being beside him. We spoke about Asha's going to America, though Rajinder did not want to talk about this. Rajinder had been the most educated member of his and my family and resented the idea that Asha would soon assume that position.

As I cooked in the kitchen, Rajinder sat on the balcony and listened to the radio. "This is Akashwani," the announcer said, and then music like horses racing played whenever a new program was about to start. It was very hot in the kitchen, and every now and then I stepped onto the roof to look at the curve of Rajinder's neck and confirm that the tenderness was still there.

We ate in the living room. Rajinder chewed slowly and was mostly silent. Once he complimented me on my cooking. "What are you thinking?" I asked. He appeared not to have heard. Tell me! Tell me! Tell me! I thought, and was shocked by the urgency I felt. A candle on the television made pillars of shadows rise and collapse on the walls. I searched for something to start a conversation with. "Pitaji began crying when I left."

"You could have stayed a few more days," he said.

"I did not want to." I thought of adding, "I missed you," but that would have been a lie, and I would have felt embarrassed saying it, when he had not missed me.

Rajinder mixed black pepper with his yogurt. "Did you tell him you would visit soon?"

"No. I think he was crying because he was lonely."

"He should have more courage." Rajinder did not like Pitaji, thought him weak-willed, although Rajinder had never told me that. He knew Pitaji drank, but Rajinder never referred to this, for which I was grateful. "He is old and must remember that shadows creep into one's heart at his age." The shutter of a bedroom window began slamming, and I got up to latch it shut.

I washed the dishes while Rajinder bathed. When he came out, dressed in his white kurta pajamas, with his hair slicked back, I was standing near the railing at the roof's edge, looking out beyond the darkness of our neighborhood at a distant ribbon of light. I was tired from the nervousness I had been feeling all evening. Rajinder came up behind me and asked, "Won't you bathe?" I suddenly doubted my ability to guard my love. Bathe so we can have sex. His words were too deliberately full of the unsaid, and so felt vulgar. I wondered if I had the courage to say no and realized I didn't. What kind of love can we have? I thought.

I said, "In a little while. Comedy hour is about to start." We sat down on our chairs with the radio between us and listened to Maurya's whiny voice. This week he had gotten involved with criminals who wanted to go to jail to collect the reward on themselves. The canned laughter gusted from several flats. When the music of the racing horses marked the close of the show, I felt hopeful again, and thought Rajinder looked very handsome in his kurta pajamas.

I bathed carefully, pouring mug after mug of cold water over myself until my fingertips were wrinkled and my nipples erect. The candlelight made the bathroom orange and my skin copper. I washed my pubis carefully to make sure no smell remained from urinating. Rubbing myself dry, I became aroused. I wore the red sari again, with a new blouse, and no bra, so that my nipples would show.

I came and stood beside Rajinder, my arm brushing against his kurta sleeve. Every now and then a raindrop fell, and I wondered if I was imagining it. On balconies and roofs all around us I could see the dim figures of men, women, and children waiting for the first rain. "You look pretty," he said. Somewhere Lata Mangeshkar sang with a static-induced huskiness. The street was silent. Even the children were hushed. As the wind picked up, Rajinder said, "Let's close the windows."

The wind coursed along the floor, upsetting newspapers and climbing the walls to swing on curtains. A candle stood on the refrigerator. As I leaned over to pull a window shut, Rajinder pressed against me and cupped my right breast. I felt a shock of desire pass through me. As I walked around the rooms shutting windows, he touched my buttocks, pubis, stomach.

When the last window was closed, I waited for a moment before turning around, because I knew he wanted me to turn around quickly. He pulled me close, with his hands on my buttocks. I took his tongue in my mouth. We kissed like this for a long time.

The rain began falling, and we heard a roar from the people on the roofs nearby. "The clothes," Rajinder said, and pulled away.

We ran out. We could barely see each other. Lightning bursts would illuminate an eye, an arm, some teeth, and then darkness would come again. We jerked the clothes off and let the pins fall to the ground. We deliberately brushed roughly against each other. The raindrops were like thorns, and we began laughing. Rajinder's shirt had wrapped itself around and around the clothesline. Wiping his face, he knocked his glasses off. As I saw him crouch and fumble around helplessly for them, I felt such tenderness that I knew I would never love him as much as I did at that moment. "The wind in the trees," I cried out, "it sounds like the sea."

We slowly wandered back inside, kissing all the while. He entered me like a sigh. He suckled on me and moved back and forth and side to side, and I felt myself growing warm and loose. He sucked on my nipples and held my waist with both hands. We made love gently at first, but as we both neared climax, Rajinder began stabbing me with his penis and I came in waves so strong that I felt myself vanishing. When Rajinder sank on top of me, I kept saying, "I love you. I love you."

"I love you too," he answered. Outside, the rain came in sheets and the thunder was like explosions in caverns.

The candle had gone out while we made love, and Rajinder got up to light it. He drank some water and then lay down beside me. I wanted some water too, but did not want to say anything that would make him feel bad about his thoughtlessness. "I'll be getting promoted soon. Minaji loves me," Rajinder said. I rolled onto my side to look at him. He had his arms folded across his chest. "Yesterday he said, 'Come, Rajinderji, let us go write your confidential report.'" I put my hand on his stomach, and Rajinder said, "Don't," and pushed it away. "I said, 'Oh, I don't know whether that would be good, sir.' He laughed and patted me on the back. What a nincompoop. If it weren't for the quotas, he would never be manager." Rajinder chuckled. "I'll be the youngest bank manager in Delhi." I felt cold and tugged a sheet over our legs. "In college I had a schedule for where I wanted to be by the time I was thirty. By twenty-two I became an officer; soon I'll be a manager. I wanted a car, and we'll have that in a year. I wanted a wife, and I have that."

"You are so smart."

"Some people in college were smarter. But I knew exactly what I wanted. A life is like a house. One has to plan carefully where all the furniture will go."

"Did you plan me as your wife?" I asked, smiling.

"No. I had wanted at least an M.A., and someone who worked, but Mummy didn't approve of a daughter-in-law who worked. I was willing to change my requirements. Because I believe in moderation, I was successful. Everything in its place. And pay for everything. Other people got caught up in love and friendship. I've always felt that these things only became a big deal because of the movies."

"What do you mean? You love me and your mother, don't you?"

"There are so many people in the world that it is hard not to think that there are others you could love more."

Seeing the shock on my face, he quickly added, "Of course I love you. I just try not to be too emotional about it." The candle's shadows on the wall were like the wavery bands formed by light reflected off water. "We might even be able to get a foreign car."

The second time he took me that night, it was from behind. He pressed down heavily on my back and grabbed my breasts.

I woke at four or five. The rain scratched against the windows and a light like blue milk shone along the edges of the door. I was cold and tried to wrap myself in the sheet, but it was not large enough.

JEAN THOMPSON

All Shall Love Me and Despair

FROM MID-AMERICAN REVIEW

SCOUT LIKED THE NEEDLE. He liked it almost as much as the high. The tidy way the needle slipped beneath the skin, took its discreet bite, then the thread of pure amazement feeding into you. He liked the precision of it. "What does it feel like?" Annie asked him, back when she still wanted to know such things, when there was still a horrid glamour to it all. "Like something grows inside you," said Scout. "All at once, like a Jack-in-the-Beanstalk vine, leaves and stems and purple curling flowers, and it fills you up to your fingers and toes. It's like your head is an organ, and someone plays a chord."

But that was a long time ago, in the good part of the bad old days, and Annie's through with pretty words for ugly things. She doesn't want anything in her life that has to be tricked out in poetry, explained away. She's walking on a beach in Oregon, watching the sun go down. There's a thin watery layer of clouds that diffuses the pink-orange light, spreads it as evenly as butter from one end of the sky to the other. The beach is broad white sand, also smooth enough to reflect light, so that Annie walks in glory without having to think of names for it.

There are other people out on this fine evening, strolling along the soapy edge of the advancing tide or grilling hot dogs over driftwood fires, and here is a young man exercising his cockatiel. He runs along the sand waving a towel, with the cockatiel flapping behind him. Annie's seen him a few times; they greet each other. "Birdie surfing," the young man calls it. The bird is perfectly tame and won't fly off, but he has to keep an eye out for seagulls. Seagulls are worrisome. This is what Annie wants her life to be now: a procession of ordinary delights.

There's a cliff marking the edge of the beach, with stairs at intervals, and on this cliff edge the town is built up thickly. There are motels and restaurants and houses on minute lots, all of them shouldering each other for space, all of them built of the same weathered cedar or painted pine. The town has strict building codes, aimed at controlling development and preserving a casual beach-shack ambiance. The motels all have names like the Gray Whale and the Cove. The shopping district has stores devoted to pottery, seascapes, woven ponchos, hammered brass jewelry, and the like. You can buy jams and honey, locally produced and put up in gold-labeled jars. You can buy soapstone carvings of whales, bleached sand dollars, fudge, pizza by the slice, cookies, and ice cream cones. There are rentals for roller skates and beach tricycles, and two kite shops. Scout has a job in a bookstore. Annie makes sandwiches in a deli. They've been here two months, just long enough to say *tourist* about other people.

The ocean is no certain color. Steel and slate, gray and blue, reflecting light like metal or lapping up perfectly clear at Annie's feet. It's always too cold to swim in, even now, in August, unless you're a little kid. Up the beach a couple of miles is a cove where people in black rubber wetsuits windsurf and kayak. Annie thinks it's something she might like to try sometime, one of those violent ocean sports, just because it would be so unlike her. She imagines herself encased in a sleek rubber skin, jaunty and exhausted, her hair a shipwreck of snarls, lungs efficiently exchanging CO_2 and oxygen.

Scout, of course, jeers at the whole idea. "Buy me a thrill," he says. "All that equipment. It's the MasterCard high." Annie knows the ocean scares him. It's too large and indifferent, he can't get his mind around it. He has to find a way of dismissing it. Annie allows him this because he needs something to despise, as a substitute for dignity.

The trip from Chicago is something Annie can uncover like a scar on her body when she wants to remind herself that she can do anything. She drove every mile of the way. Even at the end, when Scout was well enough to sit up and look around him, she was the one who drove. Her shoulders, spine, and pelvis fused into one unit. She was a machine for driving. The car fed its energy into her, and she powered them on. Her fingertips drew in every mile of road. Her feet tickled. The road became her drug. Iowa was black night, and Nebraska sunrise. Headlights pricked out of the darkness, then just as suddenly extinguished themselves. They made Annie start, although she knew perfectly well this was paranoia, mental gymnastics, a trick she used to fuel them across the country of black wings. No one knew where they were. No one would know where they were ever again.

She muscled the accelerator down. In the back seat Scout moaned and sweated. Annie brought him cartons of milk, milkshakes, and jelly doughnuts, the only things he could eat. Even then he puked a couple of times, so the back of the car was full of wet, sour paper. At gas stations Annie pulled Scout to his feet and made him use the bathroom. She waited under the banks of humming lights at convenience stores. The lights reflected ten thousand cellophane-wrapped surfaces with crazed precision. Rows and rows of hygienic, appalling food. Sugar highs, caffeine highs, preservative highs. It was a place where you might find yourself reasonably contemplating armed robbery, or dying. Annie thought, *I could drive away right now. Somebody else will come along and take charge of him if he sits there long enough, the police, somebody, it won't matter, finally, who it is.* But she waited until Scout appeared, looking if anything a little worse, smelling a little more, his junkie's breath, his poisoned sweat, his rash-bearing skin, all of him collapsing into nothingness and bad air. Annie opened the back-seat door for him and they drove off.

Scout is twenty, Annie twenty-one. Scout is small, like a jointed puppet, an assemblage of stick arms and legs. So small that once, in high school, he found a Cub Scout uniform in the Goodwill bin, complete with neckerchief and hat, and it fit him. So did the name, which stuck. Scout has a mouse's face and little intelligent mouse eyes behind his wire-rimmed spectacles. Annie is half a head taller than Scout, but thin, and when they stand together they might be brother and sister, or at least members of the same brittle species.

Is Annie pretty? She doesn't think so, particularly. And she's not the kind of girl who gets told it very often. Sometimes, though, she leans close enough to the mirror to see, just out at the edge of her vision, not her reflection but a kind of shadow cast by her face. She sees a landscape of pale and dark in the liquid shine of her eyes and the grain of her cheek, distorted, mysterious, beyond beauty. Like looking at the moon through a telescope, or an eggshell under a magnifying glass. When she pulls back from the mirror, it's only a face, common and clumsy, no cause for marveling or delight. One reason she loves Scout is that he doesn't notice or care about people's faces.

Back in Chicago, in the good part of the bad old days, they used to walk down to Belmont Harbor to look at the boats. It was always windy, or that's how Annie remembers it, windy gray or windy blue, wind ruffling the water, shivering the well-tended strips of grass, making them dig their hands in their pockets and hunch their shoulders. Scout said the lake was nothing, just a big cold bathtub. It couldn't take you anywhere. What was the point of a boat if it always came back to the same place? (He hadn't yet seen an ocean, hadn't had the chance to be disheartened by one.) The lake was small potatoes. A poisoned fishbowl, an industrial sink. They should reverse the plumbing and flush it all clean. They should blast a hole in the ass end of Superior. Like those crazy old explorers who tried to get to India by way of Duluth. Another crazy thing was ore barges. Tons and tons of rock, floating on water.

Annie let him talk, though she didn't agree with what he said: the lake was bottomless and shoreless and seemed fearsome enough to her. When Scout talked, she made small noises in her throat as a kind of acknowledgment, so she didn't have to pay close attention or pretend one thing he said followed from another. Scout was the most intelligent person she knew, even when he said stupid things. Ideas kept coming out of him, everything he saw got turned into ideas. She was flattered that he talked to her. She knew Scout better than anyone else in the world did, because he talked to her so much. He imprinted himself on her, until his ideas took up space in her head and her own voice always seemed to be asking a hopeful, anxious question. In bed when he locked his body into hers, gulping air and crying out, tears came to her eyes. The tears had nothing to do with pleasure or pain, only the closeness, their two red hearts keeping exact time. She thought being in love was the most important thing she could ever do.

When Scout was high, he stopped talking. His thoughts were too slick and elegant, his ideas too big, like the slow turn of a planet on its axis. Annie wouldn't touch junk. Never. It scared her more than not doing it scared her. It was another thing without boundaries or measurable depths. When she felt herself wanting to do it, it was to keep from being lonely, and so Scout couldn't smile and tell her she didn't know anything: "Junk ain't no tea party, toots." Annie suspected he liked her not doing it. He wanted to have something he withheld from her, something too big and bad and sad for her.

Whenever she didn't want to do it, she felt guilty and dishonest. It meant a part of her was still not in love and wouldn't follow where he led. Because there is that about her. Something stubborn and mutinous and impatient, or perhaps merely practical, that makes her think *Yes, but* when he talks. Something that will not love him without judging him. Just last week, walking on the Oregon beach, Annie found the clean bleached skull of a seagull. Wedged at the back of its throat was a tight metal spring, of the sort used in mousetraps. She thought the part of her that refused to be in love was like that spring, like the sounds she made in her throat instead of words. Something that wouldn't go up or down, just got caught in her.

The first time they walked out on the beach they were timid, as if someone might shoo them away, smell the city or the fear on them and determine they had no right to be there. People were flying kites in the buoyant air, wonderful kites, kites stacked on kites, ingenious flying cantilevers made of geometric Mylar shapes in neon and black and paintbox colors, trailing cellophane ribbons. There were kites that suggested bats or spaceships or dinosaurs, others that resembled nothing at all, only some idea of flight given whimsical form. Annie laughed out loud at them. The laugh sounded odd, squawking, as if she'd swallowed a bird that was now squeezing its way out. It embarrassed her. "Aren't they something," she said rapidly, to cover up. "I mean, there must be all these people who work day and night just thinking about . . . kites."

She meant it was wonderful that people engrossed themselves in something so innocent. It seemed hopeful to her. She thought of all the kites that hadn't been invented yet, or even imagined. She thought that in this new life she might become a water conservation officer, or a mapmaker, or something just as blameless, just as absorbing.

Scout looked solemn and confused. He gaped up at the sky, then at the ocean. His hair was still damp from the shower, combed thinly across his skull, and he'd put on a clean shirt. Shabby, convalescent, scrubbed, he didn't belong there. You might as well take a pigeon out of its concrete roost. Annie didn't want to feel sorry for him; it would be one more weakness in him. "We could get us a kite," she said in a coaxing voice. "One of those big ones, with all the strings, like driving a team of horses."

Scout was still looking out at the ocean, as if he expected it to stop moving eventually. She touched his arm. "Scout?"

"Jesus," he said in a quiet, flattened voice. He rubbed at his nose with the back of his hand, then turned away, his eyes averted and noncommittal. Annie's heart sagged. He didn't like it and she couldn't fix it for him, not a whole ocean.

But then he reached out and spun her by the shoulders. Annie squealed. The sand made them stagger crazily. The wind blew Annie's long hair into both their mouths. Scout whooped. "We'll get a big goddamn mutha kite. It'll eat all the other kites."

Annie wanted to say that wasn't the point of a kite, but she was out of breath from laughing. Then Scout loosed her and sprinted away. Dizzy, she squinted after him. The sky tilted into the ocean. Scout was running straight into the water, arms outstretched. Ankle-deep, knee-deep, with his pants legs sogging and his shoes weighted down, legs pumping, getting nowhere, as if mere stubbornness could turn the ocean floor into a sidewalk. A green wave slid toward him and hit him waist-high. "Hey," called Annie. "Hey, dummy." It was important that she be there for him to ignore.

Finally he waded out again. He was grinning. His fingernails were blue and pinched. "You're nuts," said Annie. He looked pleased with himself, perhaps because he'd alarmed her. He peeled out of his wet shirt and swung it around his head, like a stripper. "Glad you're feeling better," she said mildly, which was her way of reminding him where they'd come from, and why.

Annie stooped and dug up a sand dollar, the flat cracked portion of one. She was glad she had something she could use to ignore him back with. She wondered what the thing that lived inside looked like, and how it grew this pleasing cool flat shape. She liked the delicate fossil print, resembling a blossom, or a five-pointed star, or an outstretched hand. She supposed there was some biological reason for the pattern, but she preferred to think it was pure whimsy, like the stripes on a kite. She said, hefting it, "This is great. This place. Everything about it. The cops ride bicycles. They look like kids whose parents buy them fancy bikes."

Scout didn't answer. They were laboring back up the cliff. The sand slowed them. Scout's bare chest was covered with big knobby goose bumps. The glee had worn off and he was sullen and shivering and glum, as if someone else, probably she, was to blame for his being wet. Annie wanted him to say he liked it here. She wanted him to say anything at all. It wasn't fair that she had to keep doing and saying everything, waiting not to be ignored, calling him back from deep water.

When they reached the top he brightened, as if he'd only wished to punish her for enjoying something on her own. "We did it, cupcake. We discovered the Pacific Ocean."

"Uh-huh."

"What's with you?"

"Nothing." The only thing she could openly accuse him of was running into the ocean, and that didn't seem like a real grievance.

"You worry too much," Scout pronounced. It was what he always told her. They were the same people in a new place. It had been stupid to think anything else.

"Come on, lighten up." Scout's hand in hers was colder than cold. Kissing, she tasted salt on him. It tasted like tears, only cold. She hugged him hard. His bones were shivering and electric. What was the difference between too much worry and too much love?

The needle always looked clean, no matter where it had been. Nothing could be cleaner than its thin bright nakedness, its silver eye, its spike. Scout let it fall to the floor. His eyes rolled back in his head like heavy silver pinballs. A piece of indifferent Chicago sky hung in the window. The room smelled of gas and sugar, a closed, wintertime smell. There was a color television and a beanbag chair and a sofa. The chair was dark orange tweed with black welting. Annie hated that chair. It was the single ugliest thing she knew. It absorbed every stink and puddle. It was an altar to ugliness. The needle lay in a fold of its orange hide.

"Scout," she said. A giggle slid out of him. The television was on, a tiny idiot noise, bathing the room in garish candy colors. When Scout's eyes opened again, the colors reflected off them. "Scout?"

After a while he turned toward her. His teeth were scallops of dim light. "Yaas," he said. "Speaking."

"You O.K.?"

His eyes were sugar yellow. His mouth made an O, for O.K. When his eyes closed again, Annie turned the television off. She sat and watched the piece of sky grow black. In the kitchen the gas stove and burners were turned on for heat. She could hear the blue gas whispering. She heard the city noises, traffic and catastrophe, muffled by distance, like a lion's yawn. This was Annie's secret: she liked these times. Because it was just the two of them, and he couldn't get away. Because he couldn't say things with his needle tongue, and she could say anything she wished. "I love you." She said it small, because there were already so many secrets filling up the room.

Scout said she worried too much. He only shot once in a moon. He could handle it. *Yes but.* The *why* of it kept itching her. Scout's real name is Edward. He grew up on the South Side, praying to the Polish saints. Their sweet faces were garlanded in roses and lit by candles in pink glass holders. It was the wrong kind of heaven for him, too grave and pastel, smelling too strongly of his mother's handcream. He wanted more commotion and sweat. He liked alleys and brick dust and gravel and old paint cans, he liked streetlights and the politics of sidewalks. Heaven got turned upside-down for him, as it does for a lot of people, and he was curious, bored, resentful. His father drove a bakery truck and the house was always full of stale or staling bread, stacks of butter cookies, doughnuts, coffeecakes dyed a staring yellow. Wasting food was a separate category of sin, involving thrift and ingratitude. Annie thinks Scout is always angry, or at least never very far from it. Like he's been cheated out of heaven and can't find anything important enough to take its place, and maybe that's what junk is. Junk lets you float right up there with those gilded antique saints and choirs of sugar angels, high and mighty. Junk turns all their fussy ribbons and their cotton-puff clouds into grandeur, junk is God. By the end, though, Annie doesn't think Scout's reasons are any smarter than any other junkie's. By the end it's no longer a matter of reasons.

In Oregon they live in the cottage, which is another way of saying converted garage, closer to the highway than the beach. It's a part of town that's home to the waitresses and grill cooks and garbage haulers, everyone making a summer living off the beach. The cottage is paneled in dark uneven boards. Moss grows at the base of the foundation slab. Ferns surround the garbage can. There's a matchbox kitchen, a loft for sleeping, and a shower stall with snails. Their jobs are simple and undemanding, time in exchange for money. On free afternoons they go to the laundromat and the grocery, like ordinary people. Scout brings home serious books by dead and living philosophers, inquiries into the nature of consciousness, or of politics. Annie brings home the ends of turkey rolls, avocados, and slices of cheesecake. They become friends with one of their neighbors, Phil, who delivers soft drinks to vending machines. Phil supplies them with Nehis and Dr. Peppers, and some evenings the three of them set chairs outside the front door and drink beer together.

"Say you like it here." Scout and Annie are in bed, and rain drills against the cottage walls. They are surrounded by water, like a ship at sea. Annie puts a finger in the corner of Scout's mouth to pry the words out. "Say it."

"Don't like all the rain. Being snail meat."

"You like the bookstore."

"I love selling cat cartoons to grandmas."

"Sco-ut." Annie sighs, a cinematic, exasperated sigh. She waits for one of them to get serious. After a minute Scout says, "You want me to say I like being straight."

They listen to the rain, its multitude of voices. "Well, do you?"

Scout's ribs expand and sink. Annie feels his breath in her hair. "I miss it sometimes. I miss the bigness of it. You know?"

Annie nods. Sometimes she misses her own holy pain. Saint Annie of the Spike. Our Lady of Dolours. The one thing she could always count on was that righteous misery. Who is she now? Somebody sadder but less miserable.

"I'm white bread," Scout says into her hair. "I floss my teeth. I watch *Wheel of Fortune*. I'm boring."

"So is dead boring?"

"You want me to say you saved my life. You think like that, don't you? Like an old-time movie."

She doesn't answer because he's right, he can always see through her. Scout goes on in a kindly, mocking voice, "Sure I like it here. I'll like anything you say. After all, you saved my life."

They are silent but the rain keeps talking, subtle and persistent, bubbling up from underneath, invading the house with fronds and jellied creatures, filling their dreams with water-words: *secrets, secrets, sleep.*

In the bad part of the bad old days the phone rang and rang. Annie said, Hello, hello? The phone was black and dense and listening. The ghost calls only came when Scout wasn't home. They scared her, and she got so she wouldn't answer at all, just cried and let the phone ring. The television was broken. Annie cried over that too, as if it were a pet. She thought it might be Scout on the phone, checking up on her. He was calling from junk heaven to tell her what it was like, saying ecstatic things in a frequency just out of her hearing.

Or maybe the caller wasn't Scout at all, but someone he owed money to or had stolen from, someone he'd brought around. The people Scout brought around were not friends. They were all involved in commerce and betrayal. They had faces like the dulled blades of knives. One day Scout brought home a man named Ace. Ace sat with his hands between his knees, picking at his fingernails, tapping his feet and grinning. "Ace has a car," said Scout. "We could go for a ride."

"Where to?" asked Annie. They didn't do things like go for rides.

"Anywhere. Or just you and Ace could go."

Ace kept grinning his grin. He could have been any age from thirty to fifty. Junkies all looked the same to Annie, like old newspapers. Ace glanced at Scout and wiggled his eyebrows. "Hell of a ride," he said.

Scout was edgy, keyed-up. "Come on," he said to Annie.

"Go yourself, if you're so excited about it." Annie got up and went into the bathroom and shut the door. She wanted to stay in there until Ace left. She didn't like him. He had a smell to him, a chicken-bone smell.

Scout opened the bathroom door. "Do you *mind,*" Annie said, but he wasn't paying attention to that. Scout's lips had a dark cracked rim around their inner surface, like someone with a fever. He said, "You got to help me."

Annie looked around the bathroom, thinking he meant something right in front of them, aspirin or a towel. "What do you need?"

"Help me with him."

"Help you what?" said Annie, but Scout just stood there, impatient, persistent, sly, like he was waiting for her to get an especially good joke. Then everything in front of her eyes changed, as if the light had cracked along with her comprehension, and she could not distinguish between the water running from the tap and the rust stain it followed like a river in its bed. "No," she said, then she screamed it, striking out at him.

Scout caught her hands in his. "Listen, I'm into him," he said, as if he had merely explained things badly. "I'm way into him. See?"

She screamed again and looked for things to throw. He backed out the door and she kicked it shut after him. "Jesus, this is *important*," he shouted. "Am I getting through to you? Huh?"

"I have the scissors in here," she announced, and waited. After a while she heard their feet receding down the stairs.

The phone rang. Annie opened the bathroom door and watched it ring. When it stopped she went into the bedroom and found a duffel bag and a backpack. She filled them with her things. She put a loaf of bread and three 7-Ups in a paper bag, thinking she must be forgetting something. She'd stopped crying by this time. All those tears. There were rust streaks beneath her eyes.

It was late, past midnight when she left. The sidewalk was lit with its pink streetlight moon. There were cars parked against the curb, pink and gleaming where the light hit them, shadowed below, lunar and motionless. She took two steps onto the pavement. Her own shadow swayed beneath her, then froze. Behind her in the closed apartment the phone was ringing. Her fingers shook in the locks. The door banged open. "Hello," she said to the silence.

She lay down on the bed to wait for daylight. *God god god.* Unlike Scout she had no childhood saints to beg or curse, and God was only a vague, woolly face, like an angry sheep. Then it was colorless dawn, and she opened her eyes to find Scout lying next to her. Dark thick strings stretched from the corners of his open mouth. Annie poked him and he swallowed.

"Get up," she said. She pulled the sheets from underneath him. They were flecked with the trails of old blood from his arms. "Get *up.*" Scout moaned and fell to his knees beside the bed. Something metal hit the floor. Annie stooped and picked it up.

Scout was doubled over, junk-sick. Annie shoved the keys under his nose. "What are these?"

"Car."

"What car? What did you do?"

The phone rang and kept ringing. Annie screamed and backed away from it. She pulled Scout up by his armpits. He retched and coughed. "What car, where?"

It was a little white Ford, the kind of car no one ever noticed or missed, a car she assumed had a long pedigree of theft. It had been new not so long ago. Now a puddle of bilge rocked on the floor, and the trunk was punched in at the lock. (It would get them as far as Umatilla, Oregon, where the engine seized up and they sold the tires for bus tickets.) Annie nudged the car along the city streets, then into expressway traffic. Moving, anonymous, observing all speed limits. She looked into the rearview mirror at Scout's bent knees, pointing up, then at her own stupefied eyes. Scout hiccuped. It was nine A.M. The Seagram's girl on the billboard above the Tri-State smiled her white-and-gold smile, like another kind of saint. "Goodbye," said Annie, which was as close as she could get to prayer.

Gift shops on the Oregon coast, the ones specializing in piety and bad taste, sell the Mariner's Prayer, wooden plaques decorated with nautical-looking ropes, and anchors formed into crosses. The prayer asks for calm seas and benevolent winds, guiding beams from the heavenly lighthouse. People here keep pleasure boats at the harbor marina or haul them on trailers down to the beach. Sometimes at an evening high tide you can watch half a dozen boats riding the surf in. They shoot out of the water and bump along the sand to the trailers, and it's a matter of skill for them to see how precisely they can aim. There are always little social groups of people around to assist and cheer, families driving off together in the dusk toward supper.

Their neighbor Phil has a brother who has a boat, an eighteen-foot skiff, the *Lazy Day*. On a clear evening, a sunset with a little scoop moon already in the sky, Scout and Annie walk down to the marina to see it. Annie is disappointed at how plain the *Lazy Day* is. No cabin, just a kind of hatch you can kneel into, an anchor on a winch, motor, fuel can, pump. Nothing else. Scout and Phil are having a serious conversation about draw and displacement, and Scout is nodding, like a man deciding whether or not to buy a car. "Taking her out this weekend," says Phil. "Come on along."

"Naw," says Scout, and Annie understands that the boat scares him just as the ocean scares him. "You and Annie can go if you want."

Annie glances at him sharply, but he's only poking around the boat slip, not looking at her, meaning nothing.

"It's not much of a boat," says Annie, just to be making conversation, as the two of them walk back home.

"It's a real boat. Not some bullshit floating RV. You ever hear of Thor Heyerdahl and the *Kon-Tiki*? The Polynesians? They sailed the whole damn ocean in canoes. Canoes."

"Mmm," says Annie.

"You know what would be cool? Staying out all night in a boat. Like the fishermen do. If we went up on a cliff right now, we could see their lights. The longer you look, the more you can see. Like stars."

"*Stella maris*," says Annie. "That's Latin. It means 'star of the sea.' I forget where I know that from. It just popped into my head."

Scout's still going on about fake-o cabin cruisers and the fake-os who own them. Annie watches the moon, thinking you could make a kite that looked like the moon, and says uh-huh, because she doesn't care one way or another. Boats are just something to talk about for her. They aren't things she has opinions about.

But Scout brings home books on navigation and shipbuilding and naval warfare. He talks knowledgeably about reefs and currents, riptides and swells. He spends a lot of time with Phil, tending to the *Lazy Day*, learning to talk like a sailor. He's disappointed when he finds out you need running lights and a radio to sail at night.

"Why don't you ever go out in the boat?" Annie asks him. "What's the point if you never go out?"

"I will when I feel like it."

"I mean, all you ever do is talk about stuff. Oh, never mind."

Scout is watching television, something with laughs in it, though his face is fixed and stony. Annie says, "I'm sorry if I hurt your feelings."

His face doesn't change. He's waiting for her to keep talking, apologize more, act interested. He's waiting to daunt her with some weary parade of facts. Annie looks at Scout and sees a sulky, big-headed child with glasses, his hair combed into an uneven peak, lower lip stuck out like a blister. He looks small and furious and absurd. She recognizes that she is seeing him without love. She recognizes this in the space it takes her not to speak.

Finally Scout says, "Oh for a life of deeds, not words. The smell of Old Spice. The swordfish mounted over the fireplace."

"Just for once don't talk that way. It's ignorant." Maybe she's never really loved him, only the image of her suffering self reflected in him.

"You know so much. Tell me one damn thing you know something about."

"You," says Annie. "I know you." She's just said a terrible thing: that she knows him and doesn't love him.

They're both quiet. Then Scout says, "Right. Me."

Sometimes she pretends that Scout keeps talking. *Don't sweat it. God's the only one who loves us perfect, and God isn't getting through on the phones. The rest of us love what gets us high. We end up hooked on all the wrong things. Gotta fly. Over and out.*

But of course he says nothing at all. Two days later Scout doesn't come home for dinner, and Phil, who gets stoned every morning before work, and collects beer cans, and who is bewildered to discover malice in anyone, comes to tell her the *Lazy Day* is missing.

So Annie walks in glory in the watery sunset, watching the incoming tide. Bits of kelp and clam shells rinse in and out. At the place where the sky meets the water is a star that looks like a boat, or a boat that looks like a star. They won't find Scout, he'll make sure of that. He will have worked out a way not to be found, just to prove to her that he knew what he was talking about. All along he needed her to prove things to, and to be afraid for him. Annie says, "Scout." Even his name will be buried at sea. Annie thinks he'd like the idea. In a little while she'll go home and be sad about everything, but not just yet.

MELANIE RAE THON

Xmas, Jamaica Plain

FROM ONTARIO REVIEW

I'M YOUR WORST FEAR.

But not the worst thing that can happen.

I lived in your house half the night. I'm the broken window in your little boy's bedroom. I'm the flooded tiles in the bathroom where the water flowed and flowed.

I'm the tattoo in the hollow of Emile's pelvis, five butterflies spreading blue wings to rise out of his scar.

I'm dark hands slipping through all your pale woman underthings; dirty fingers fondling a strand of pearls, your throat, a white bird carved of stone. I'm the body you feel wearing your fox coat.

I think I had a sister once. She keeps talking in my head. She won't let go. My sister Clare said, *Take the jewelry; it's yours.*

My heart's in my hands: what I touch, I love; what I love, I own.

Snow that night and nobody seemed surprised, so I figured it must be winter. Later I remembered it was Christmas, or it had been, the day before. I was with Emile who wanted to be Emilia. We'd started downtown, Boston. Now it was Jamaica Plain, three miles south. *Home for the holidays,* Emile said, some private joke. He'd been working the block around the Greyhound Station all night, wearing nothing but a white scarf and black turtleneck, tight jeans. *Man wants to see before he buys,* Emile said. He meant the ones in long cars cruising, looking for fragile boys with female faces.

Emile was sixteen, he thought.

Getting old.

He'd made sixty-four dollars: three tricks with cash, plus some pills — a bonus for good work, blues and greens, he didn't know what. Nobody'd offered to take him home, which is all he wanted: a warm bed, some sleep, eggs in the morning, the smell of butter, hunks of bread torn off the loaf.

Crashing, both of us, ragged from days of speed and crack, no substitute for the smooth high of pure cocaine but all we could afford. Now, enough cash between us at last. I had another twenty-five from the man who said he was in the circus once, who called himself the Jungle Creep — on top of me he made that sound. Before he unlocked the door, he said, *Are you a real girl?* I looked at his plates — New Jersey; that's why he didn't know that the lines, didn't know that the boys as girls stay away from the Zone unless they want their faces crushed. He wanted me to prove it first. Some bad luck once, I guess. I said, *It's fucking freezing. I'm real. Open the frigging door or go.*

Now it was too late to score, too cold, nobody on the street but Emile and me, the wind, so we walked, we kept walking. I had a green parka, somebody else's empty wallet in the pocket — I couldn't remember who or where, the coat stolen weeks ago and still mine, a miracle out here. We shared, trading it off. I loved Emile. I mean, it hurt my skin to see his cold.

Emile had a plan. It had to be Jamaica Plain, *home* — enough hands as dark as mine, enough faces as brown as Emile's — not like Brookline, where we'd have to turn ourselves inside out. Jamaica Plain, where there were pretty painted houses next to shacks, where the sound of bursting glass wouldn't be that loud.

Listen, we needed to sleep, to eat, that's all. So thirsty even my veins felt dry, flattened out. Hungry somewhere in my head, but my stomach shrunken to a knot so small I thought it might be gone. I remembered the man, maybe last week, before the snow, leaning against the statue of starved horses, twisted metal at the edge of the Common. He had a knife, long enough for gutting fish. Dressed in camouflage but not hiding. He stared at his thumb, licked it clean, and cut deep to watch the bright blood bubble out. He stuck it in his mouth to drink, hungry, and I swore I'd never get that low. But nights later I dreamed him beside me. Raw and dizzy, I woke, offering my whole hand, begging him to cut it off.

We walked around your block three times. We were patient now. Numb. No car up your drive and your porch light blazing, left to burn all night, we thought. Your house glowed, yellow even in the dark, paint so shiny it looked wet, and Emile said he lived some-where like this once, when he was still a boy all the time, hair cropped short, before lipstick and mascara, when his cheeks weren't blushed, before his mother caught him and his father locked him out.

In this house Emile found your red dress, your slippery stock-ings. He was happy, I swear.

So why did he end up on the floor?

I'm not going to tell you; I don't know.

First, the rock wrapped in Emile's scarf, glass splintering in the cold, and we climbed into the safe body of your house. Later we saw this was a child's room, your only one. We found the tiny cowboy boots in the closet, black like Emile's but small, so small. I tried the little bed. It was soft enough but too short. In every room your blue-eyed boy floated on the wall. Emile wanted to take him down. Emile said, *He scares me.* Emile said your little boy's too pretty, his blond curls too long. Emile said, *Some night the wrong person's going to take him home.*

Emile's not saying anything now, but if you touched his mouth you'd know. Like a blind person reading lips, you'd feel everything he needed to tell.

We stood in the cold light of the open refrigerator, drinking milk from the carton, eating pecan pie with our hands, squirting whipped cream into our mouths. You don't know how it hurt us to eat this way, our shriveled stomachs stretching; you don't know why we couldn't stop. We took the praline ice cream to your bed, one of those tiny containers, sweet and sickening, bits of candy frozen hard. We fell asleep and it melted, so we drank it, thick, with your brandy, watching bodies writhe on the TV, no sound: flames and ambulances all night; children leaping; a girl in mud under a car, eight men lifting; a skier crashing into a wall — we never knew who was saved and who was not. Talking heads spit the news again and again. There was no reason to listen — tomorrow exactly the same things would happen, and still everyone would forget.

There were other houses after yours, places where I went alone, but there were none before and none like this. When I want to feel love I remember the dark thrill of it, the bright sound of glass, the sudden size and weight of my own heart in my own chest, how I knew it now, how it was real to me in my body, separate from lungs and liver and ribs, how it made the color of my blood surge against the back of my eyes, how nothing mattered anymore because I believed in this, my own heart, its will to live.

No lights, no alarm. We waited outside. Fifteen seconds. Years collapsed. We were scared of you, who you might be inside, terrified lady with a gun, some fool with bad aim and dumb luck. The boost to the window, Emile lifting me, then I was there, in you, I swear, the smell that particular, that strong, almost a taste in your boy's room, his sweet milky breath under my tongue. Heat left low, but to us warm as a body, humid, hot.

My skin's cracked now, hands that cold, but I think of them plunged deep in your drawer, down in all your soft underbelly underclothes, slipping through all your jumbled silky woman things.

I pulled them out and out.

I'm your worst fear. I touched everything in your house: all the presents just unwrapped — cashmere sweater, rocking horse, velvet pouch. I lay on your bed, smoking cigarettes, wrapped in your fur coat. How many foxes? I tried to count.

But it was Emile who wore the red dress, who left it crumpled on the floor.

Thin as he is, he couldn't zip the back — he's a boy, after all — he has those shoulders, those soon-to-be-a-man bones. He swore trying to squash his boy feet into the matching heels; then he sobbed. I had to tell him he had lovely feet, and he did, elegant, long — those golden toes. I found him a pair of stockings, one size fits all.

I wore your husband's pinstriped jacket. I pretended all the gifts were mine to offer. I pulled the pearls from their violet pouch.

We danced.

We slid across the polished wooden floor of your living room, spun in the white lights of the twinkling tree. And again, I tell you, I swear I felt the exact size and shape of things inside me, heart and kidney, my sweet left lung. All the angels hanging from the branches opened their glass mouths, stunned.

He was more woman than you, his thick hair wound tight and pinned. *Watch this,* he said, *chignon.*

I'm not lying. He transformed himself in front of your mirror, gold eyeshadow, faint blush. He was beautiful. He could have fooled anyone. Your husband would have paid a hundred dollars to feel Emile's mouth kiss all the places you won't touch.

Later the red dress lay like a wet rag on the floor. Later the stockings snagged, the strand of pearls snapped and the beads rolled. Later Emile was all boy, naked on the bathroom floor.

I'm the one who got away, the one you don't know; I'm the long hairs you find under your pillow, nested in your drain, tangled in your brush. You think I might come back. You dream me dark always. I could be any dirty girl on the street, or the one on the bus, black lips, just-shaved head. You see her through mud-spattered glass, quick, blurred. You want me dead — it's come to this — killed, but not by your clean hands. You pray for accidents instead, me high and spacy, stepping off the curb, a car that comes too fast. You dream some twisted night road and me walking, some poor drunk weaving his way home. He won't even know what he's struck. In the morning he'll touch the headlight I smashed, the fender I splattered, dirt or blood. In the light he'll see my body rising, half remembered, snow that whirls to a shape then blows apart. Only you will know for sure, the morning news, another unidentified girl dead, hit and run, her killer never found.

I wonder if you'll rest then, or if every sound will be glass, every pair of hands mine, reaching for your sleeping son.

How can I explain?

We didn't come for him.

I'm your worst fear. Slivers of window embedded in carpet. Sharp and invisible. You can follow my muddy footprints through your house, but if you follow them backward they always lead here: to this room, to his bed.

If you could see my hands, not the ones you imagine but my real hands, they'd be reaching for Emile's body. If you looked at Emile's feet, if you touched them, you could feel us dancing.

This is all I want.

After we danced, we lay so close on your bed I dreamed we were twins, joined forever this way, two arms, three legs, two heads.

But I woke in my body alone.

Outside, snow fell like pieces of broken light.

I already knew what had happened. But I didn't want to know.

I heard him in the bathroom.

I mean, I heard the water flow and flow.

I told myself he was washing you away, your perfume, your lavender oil scent. Becoming himself. Tomorrow we'd go.

I tried to watch the TV, the silent man in front of the map, the endless night news. But there it was, my heart again, throbbing in my fingertips.

I couldn't stand it — the snow outside; the sound of water; your little boy's head propped on the dresser, drifting on the wall; the man in the corner of the room, trapped in the flickering box: his silent mouth wouldn't stop.

I pounded on the bathroom door. I said, *Goddamn it, Emile, you're clean enough.* I said I had a bad feeling about this place. I said I felt you coming home.

But Emile, he didn't say a word. There was only water, that one sound, and I saw it seeping under the door, leaking into the white carpet. Still I told lies to myself. I said, *Shit, Emile — what's going on?* I pushed the door. I had to shove hard, squeeze inside, because Emile was there, you know, exactly where you found him, face down on the floor. I turned him over, saw the lips smeared red, felt the water flow.

I breathed into him, beat his chest. It was too late, God, I know, his face pressed to the floor all this time, his face in the water, Emile dead even before he drowned, your bottle of Valium empty in the sink, the foil of your cold capsules punched through, two dozen gone — this is what did it: your brandy, your Valium, your safe little pills bought in a store. After all the shit we've done — smack popped under the skin, speed laced with strychnine, monkey dust — it comes to this. After all the nights on the streets, all the knives, all the pissed-off johns, all the fag-hating bullies prowling the Fenway with their bats, luring boys like Emile into the bushes with promises of sex. After all that, this is where it ends: on your clean wet floor.

Above the thunder of the water, Clare said, *He doesn't want to live.* Clare stayed very calm. She said, *Turn off the water, go.*

I kept breathing into him. I watched the butterflies between his bones. No flutter of wings and Clare said, *Look at him. He's dead.* Clare said she should know.

She told me what to take and where it was: sapphire ring, ivory elephant, snakeskin belt. She told me what to leave, what was too heavy: the carved bird, white stone. She reminded me, *Take off that ridiculous coat.*

I knew Clare was right; I thought, Yes, everyone is dead: the silent heads in the TV, the boy on the floor, my father who can't be known. I thought even you might be dead — your husband asleep at the wheel, your little boy asleep in the back, only you awake to see the car split the guardrail and soar.

I saw a snow-filled ravine, your car rolling toward the river of thin ice.

I thought, You never had a chance.

But I felt you.

I believed in you. Your family. I heard you going from room to room, saying, *Who's been sleeping in my bed?*

It took all my will.

I wanted to love you. I wanted you to come home. I wanted you to find me kneeling on your floor. I wanted the wings on Emile's hips to lift him through the skylight. I wanted him to scatter: ash, snow. I wanted the floor dry, the window whole.

I swear, you gave me hope.

Clare knew I was going to do something stupid. Try to clean this up. Call the police to come for Emile. Not get out. She had to tell me everything. She said again, *Turn the water off.*

In the living room the tree still twinkled, the angels still hung. I remember how amazed I was they hadn't thrown themselves to the floor.

I remember running, the immaculate cold, the air in me, my lungs hard.

I remember thinking, I'm alive, a miracle anyone was. I wondered who had chosen me.

I remember trying to list all the decent things I'd ever done.

I remember walking till it was light, knowing if I slept, I'd freeze. I never wanted so much not to die.

I made promises, I suppose.

In the morning I walked across a bridge, saw the river frozen along the edges, scrambled down. I glided out on it; I walked on water. The snowflakes kept getting bigger and bigger, butterflies that fell apart when they hit the ground, but the sky was mostly clear and there was sun.

Later, the cold again, wind and clouds. Snow shrank to ice. Small, hard. I saw a car idling, a child in the back, the driver standing on a porch, knocking at a door. Clare said, *It's open.* She meant the car. She said, *Think how fast you can go.* She told me I could ditch the baby down the road.

I didn't do it.

Later I stole lots of things, slashed sofas, pissed on floors.

But that day, I passed one thing by; I let one thing go.

When I think about this, the child safe and warm, the mother not wailing, not beating her head on the wall to make herself stop, when I think about the snow that day, wings in the bright sky, I forgive myself for everything else.

Contributors' Notes

ALICE ADAMS was born in Virginia and grew up in Chapel Hill, North Carolina. She graduated from Radcliffe College and since then has lived mostly in San Francisco. Last year she published her hundredth story and her ninth novel, *A Southern Exposure*. Of her next novel, *Medicine Men*, she says, "It is very mean-spirited and, I hope, funny — all about doctors."

▪ I have almost no clear sense of how or why I came to write this story — less, that is, than I usually do. I have not been personally involved with eating disorders; I've never been excessively thin, nor for that matter fat. However, the images of these three people from somewhere presented themselves to my mind: the skinny young girl, who is vain and smart and silly; the middle-aged failed painter, in love with his wife and his woods and fields; and that wife, fat and sexy and generous, a super cook, who could sing.

Recently, which is to say long after I wrote that story, I went to a Gladys Knight concert; she was marvelous, beautiful and so at ease with herself, not to mention such a great voice, and a beat. But thinking about Ms. Knight and about this story, I did see that there had always been such an admired and envied figure somewhere in my mind, a big woman happy in her flesh. In fact, after the Gladys Knight concert I told a friend that I thought I would try to gain twenty pounds or so, but she pointed out, "No use, you still won't look like Gladys Knight." So perhaps I do, after all, feel a little like young Nan, left out and wanting to be Mary.

As I got into the story, I was also interested in how little Nan is aware of the Travis-Mary bond, its complexity and its strength — their complicity. She of course has her own much weaker and much more evil complicity with the minister who stalks and touches her.

And it now occurs to me that in this story I was working backward from the title; I liked the idea of a very small group of people, each complicitous in ways unknown to the others.

RICK BASS lives in northwest Montana with his wife and daughters. He is the author of several books of fiction and nonfiction, including an essay collection about Montana's imperiled Yaak Valley, *The Book of Yaak*. In 1997 Houghton Mifflin will publish a collection of novellas entitled *The Sky, the Stars, the Wilderness*. Rick Bass is currently working on a novel, *Where the Sea Used to Be*.

▪ I wanted to see if I could write a story about a character with some internal illness without ever mentioning this fact — to see what the story would do, with those internal biological changes unacknowledged: to see what would come out of the subconscious. At first it seemed to me that there were cyclic rhythms of alteration reflected by the changes at all levels: the snowshoe hares, like blood cells, turning from brown to white; forests being scorched (and then growing again) by fire; the comings and goings of geese, and the pseudo illness itself, like the hedgehog, coming and going at unknowable, unpredictable times. But I soon realized that Glenda had no such illness, that her disease, like the narrator's, was simply the primal fear of giving up territory — of loving and being loved.

I wrote an earlier draft of this story with Gordon Lish, for his magazine, *The Quarterly*, and then when the story was about to be included in a story collection, *In The Loyal Mountains*, my editors Camille Hykes and Larry Cooper helped me do some more stuff with it, and we published it again, changing the ending slightly.

Not long after reworking the story, I read the following passage from the essayist and naturalist Terry Tempest Williams, which reminds me, indirectly, of Glenda and the narrator: "If I choose not to become attached to nouns — a person, place, or thing — then when I refuse an intimate's love or hoard my spirit, when a known landscape is bought, sold, and developed, chained or grazed to a stubble, or a hawk is shot and hung by its feet on a barbed-wire fence, my heart cannot be broken because I never risked giving it away. A man or woman whose mind reins in the heart when the body sings desperately for connection can only expect more isolation and greater ecological disease. Our lack of intimacy with each other is in direct proportion to our lack of intimacy with the land. We have taken our love inside and abandoned the wild."

JASON BROWN grew up in Maine, received his M.F.A. from Cornell University, and is currently a Wallace Stegner Fellow at Stanford University. His work has appeared or will appear in the *Georgia Review*, the *Mississippi Review, TriQuarterly*, and *DoubleTake*.

▪ I wrote this story when I was twenty-two, living in Portland, Maine, in a condemned building with no heat and working for a company, believe it or not, called Bits and Pieces Delivery. They delivered many things. Body parts were a small part of their business. I had the night shift, which is when, for some reason, the parts needed to be delivered. I would lie back in bed next to my kerosene heater and wait for my beeper to ring. Then I'd rush to the hospital for a case of eyeballs or whatever to be taken down to Logan Airport. I guess I knew that every time my beeper went off, some person with a donor card had just been creamed on the highway, and I had to quit the job after a short time. The story for me was about trying to hold it all together. I think writing the story helped me to hold it together.

ROBERT OLEN BUTLER has published seven novels (*The Alleys of Eden, Sun Dogs, Countrymen of Bones, On Distant Ground, Wabash, The Deuce,* and *They Whisper*) and a volume of short fiction (*A Good Scent from a Strange Mountain*), which won the 1993 Pulitzer Prize for Fiction. His stories have appeared in such publications as *The New Yorker, Harper's, GQ,* the *Hudson Review,* the *Virginia Quarterly Review,* and the *Sewanee Review* and have been chosen for inclusion in four annual editions of *The Best American Short Stories* and five annual editions of *New Stories from the South.* His works have been translated into a dozen languages, including Vietnamese, Thai, Korean, Polish, Japanese, and Greek. A recipient of both a Guggenheim Fellowship in fiction and a National Endowment for the Arts grant, he also won the Richard and Hinda Rosenthal Foundation Award from the American Academy of Arts and Letters. His forthcoming book of short fiction, *Tabloid Dreams,* is being developed into a series for Home Box Office, a project that he is coproducing. He has recently written screenplays for Twentieth Century Fox, Warner Brothers, and Paramount. He teaches creative writing at McNeese State University in Lake Charles, Louisiana, where he lives with his wife, the novelist and playwright Elizabeth Dewberry.

▪ This parrot, like a dozen other characters whose voices I've recently been hearing and recording, was inspired by the headlines in the supermarket tabloids and will become part of a book of stories called *Tabloid Dreams.* As a society, our embrace of popular culture is becoming more and more impassioned as the millennium comes to an end, and I decided to listen for the serious words of yearning whispered beneath that ardor. Not incidentally, after I'd read this story for the first time in public at a writers' conference summer before last, I wrote a proposal of marriage on the manuscript and gave it to Elizabeth Dewberry just before her reading. We had fallen in love reading each other's books on our respective book tours that previous winter, even before we'd met, and she said yes.

LAN SAMANTHA CHANG is a graduate of the Iowa Writers' Workshop and a former Wallace Stegner Fellow at Stanford University, where she now teaches creative writing. She has received a Michener-Copernicus fellow-

ship and a Transatlantic Review prize. She is completing a collection of
short fiction, which includes stories that have been published in *Greensboro
Review, The Atlantic Monthly, Story,* and *The Best American Short Stories 1994.*

▪ Although ghosts appear frequently in Chinese folk literature and su-
perstitions, my knowledge of them is limited to the works I've read in
translation and to the occasional comments of my father, who, despite his
scientific education, maintains a healthy respect for the irrational. Other
sources for this story are American. In the Iowa City Public Library, I
found collections of rural ghost tales, which, like their Chinese counter-
parts, concerned themselves with haunted houses, unhappy love affairs,
and people who died unsatisfied. Both Chinese and Iowan ghosts reminded the living of unfinished business, of human stories so potent they
did not end with death. Perhaps ghosts remind us of people or things we
may want to forget but cannot, because they are such powerful parts of our
lives that to exorcise them would be to deny our own stories. This paradox
started me thinking about a question that still preoccupies me and my
work: is ordinary love not a kind of burden, stifling and terrifying in the
choices and responsibilities it forces on us? And yet we yearn for it, suffer
for it, define ourselves by our experience of it, cannot live without it.

DAN CHAON was raised in rural western Nebraska and attended Northwestern and Syracuse universities. He is the author of a collection of short
stories, *Fitting Ends and Other Stories,* published in November 1995, and his
work has appeared in such journals as *TriQuarterly, Ploughshares, American
Short Fiction,* and *Story.* He is a visiting instructor at Ohio University.

▪ Writing stories, for me, is something like putting together a jigsaw
puzzle. I write hundreds of pages of fragments every year and put them in
folders together, hoping they will mate. But it's generally a long process,
and this story was no exception. I had a folder three inches thick, full of
jottings on the quarreling brothers Del and Stewart, which I thought
might be a novel. In another folder, I had descriptions of "Pyramid," a
dream version of the village I grew up in, and that grain elevator, an icon of
my childhood, which (honestly) a tornado whisked away in 1986, while I
was in college. In yet another I had a junked-up ghost story, a mock of the
True Ghost Stories I loved as a child. During my first year teaching composi-
tion, a student wrote an essay about the Outward Bound program, which
moved me, and which helped me to understand the character of Del in a
way I hadn't before.

Still, I am always groping in the dark when it comes down to actually
fitting pieces of these fragments together, and the lights I find are usually
through reading the work of writers who inspire me. In this case, I learned
a lot from Sherwood Anderson's "Death in the Woods," that granddaddy
of self-reflective narrative; from Alice Munro, whose brilliant structures

and meditations on time and loss in such collections as *The Progress of Love* filled me with awe; from my teacher, Tobias Wolff, whose stories taught me about the power of narrators who do the wrong thing; from Liz Rosenberg's poem "Ghosts"; and . . . well, from a great number of others. Part of the process of wanting to write, for me, is having a switch in my brain flipped on by some wonderful story or poem.

Finally, I suppose, the story came together for me because of a quote from Wright Morris's book *A Cloak of Light:* "It is the writer's nature and his talent to restore to the present much assumed to be lost. The emotions generated in this act of repossession may also exceed those he felt at the time, evidence that the past is never so much a part of the present as at this moment of recovery." The ghost that haunts the story comes from that quote.

The story should be dedicated to my father, who died in February of 1996, and who told me when he read the story that he didn't much care for the last line. "There's always something worth becoming," he said. "You'll learn that later."

PETER HO DAVIES's work has appeared in *Agni, Antioch Review, Greensboro Review,* and *The Best American Short Stories 1995.* His collection of stories, *The Ugliest House in the World,* will be published in 1997. Born and brought up in Britain, he has been a fellow at the Fine Arts Work Center in Provincetown and currently teaches at Emory University in Atlanta.

▪ I had been waiting to write "The Silver Screen" for two or three years, ever since working in Malaysia in 1989. That was the year the remaining communists still in the jungle finally left their camps on the Thai border, effectively ending the conflict begun in 1948. I was living with my mother's family at the time, too homesick to appreciate their hospitality but with enough sense to listen to their stories of the Japanese occupation and the postwar years. I knew this was strong material, but even after I left Malaysia I kept putting off writing about it to do more research. Some of this was invaluable (I'm especially indebted to Noel Barber's richly anecdotal history of the conflict, *The War of the Running Dogs*); much of it was stalling. I was both in love with and wary of the material, knowing it to be wonderful but afraid of not doing it justice. I might have gone on prevaricating for several more years if I hadn't faced a series of workshop deadlines at graduate school that forced me to finally stop "saving" material. As it was, I wrote the "The Silver Screen" essentially in a morning, pouring everything I knew (although certainly not everything there is to know) about the Emergency into a few thousand words. At the time, it was quite different from anything I'd produced before — a case, I hope, of new material shaping and changing me as a writer.

Incidentally, a common response to the story has been that it would make a wonderful novel (a slightly backhanded compliment, I have to feel), and there have been times — those miserable days wondering where the next story will come from — when I've wished I had husbanded my material better, wrung more pages out of it. Yet, rereading "The Silver Screen," I find the story's crazy profligacy with material — that sense of stretching at the seams — one of my favorite things about it.

JUNOT DÍAZ was born in Santo Domingo, the Dominican Republic, and later immigrated to New Jersey. His fiction has appeared in *Story, The New Yorker, Glimmer Train, TimeOut New York,* and *Paris Review.* His first collection of stories, *Drown,* is forthcoming from Riverhead Books. He now lives in Brooklyn.

▪ A couple years ago I was in Santo Domingo for the summer. Trying not to feel too awkward and trying to see as much as the country as I could. My abuelos told me not to bother with the campo — nothing out there anymore, he said — but I went to visit friends and relatives anyway. Spent my nights playing dominoes by lamplight and my days walking around and dropping in on people. One afternoon I was heading down a path with a friend when we came on this monstrous pig, half buried in the landscape. The fucker scared the shit out of me, but he also reminded me of the boy in this story, of what had happened to him. The story didn't come together until later, when I was back in New York. I was standing on a streetcorner in Brooklyn and a small boy ran past me in a homemade mask. He was obviously disfigured but not unhappy and that's what did it for me. I knew then that I could write this story and a month later I did.

STEPHEN DIXON was born, raised, and educated in New York City. Since 1980 he has been teaching in the writing seminars at Johns Hopkins University. He has published about 350 short stories, ten story collections, and seven novels; a new story collection is forthcoming, and his eighth novel, *Gould,* will be published in 1997. His novel *Frog* was a PEN/Faulkner finalist and a National Book Award finalist. His most recent novel, *Interstate,* was a National Book Award finalist in 1995. Stephen Dixon lives in Baltimore with his wife and two daughters.

▪ "Sleep" started from a cold my wife had. You can say that instead of catching her cold I caught a story. It was a bad cold and her heavy breathing and coughing kept me up at night — I'm a light sleeper. My children and she have suggested I go to sleep wearing earplugs, but I'm always afraid I won't hear the smoke detector go off or some disaster going on outside the house if I wear them. During one sleepless period at night, while my wife slept fitfully and my children slept angelically, I got the idea for the story, projecting the worst that could happen from a wife's illness and how the narrator would react to it. Very often in my fiction I've used simple incidents in my family life to project the worst things imaginable that can happen to a family, and I've gotten stories from them that have affected me deeply. "Sleep," once the first draft was written, in a single sitting, was a tough one emotionally to complete, but it seemed a good story to do at the time and one I hadn't projected or written in this kind of way before, two of the main incentives to my working on a story.

Why a story comes, how it comes, what makes it come the way it comes and be written in the way it's written, has always been a mystery to me, something I've managed to keep a mystery for thirty-five years by not exploring. I've felt for my entire writing life — and for a reason I can't now discern I'm going to slip into metaphor — that if I try to discover why my well is always full, if not brimming over, another mystery will happen, and that's that the well will suddenly run dry. There's only one thing in life I prohibit myself from exploring in my fiction and head, and that's where my stories and styles come from. I know I don't like to repeat myself in my fiction, but of course there's much more than that. After I put away my manual typewriter, with no intention of ever using it again — if that ever takes place, though my feeling is I'll probably drop dead over my type-writer while writing a story — I'll try to dig into my creative process in a much deeper way, till I find out how and why I wrote those things and where they came from and why the well never ran dry.

STUART DYBEK is the author of two collections of stories, *Childhood and Other Neighborhoods* and *The Coast of Chicago,* and a collection of poems, *Brass Knuckles.* He has received numerous awards for his work, including a PEN/Malamud Award for lifetime excellence in the short story form in 1995. He teaches in the writing program at Western Michigan University.

▪ Anyone who has listened to fiction writers or poets introduce their own work at readings knows that there are frequently stories behind stories, and stories behind poems. Sometimes, especially with poems, the stories behind them can be longer than the work itself. But there are certain pieces that come, if not out of silence, then out of a fog or a blur, and "Paper Lantern" is one of those for me. I do recall that, like at least half of the stories I've written, it began as something totally different from its final form. Instead of a story with a relationship at its heart, "Paper Lantern" started out — I almost want to say started out *innocently enough* — as a two-page prose poem about writing prose poems. The original tone was whimsical. However, as I've never been a fan of poems about writing poems, or prose poems about writing prose poems, for that matter, I junked that notion after looting the imagery of the laboratory, the snowy night, and Chinese food. How I got from that start to everything that happens in the story is where the blur comes in. Sometimes, of course, a writer knows in entirety the story he's writing before committing the first word to paper. But often the process of writing is analogous to a songwriter composing at the piano, stringing chords and phrases together until a song seems to emerge from the keys themselves rather than as a transcription of some melody the composer heard in his mind while taking a shower or driving in his car. I know painters who describe the process of painting as "moving paint around the canvas" until a painting emerges, as opposed to painting from a model or the memory of a model. In that sense, "Paper Lantern" is a story that emerged from moving the words around on the page.

DEBORAH GALYAN is at work on a novel in Provincetown, Massachusetts, where she lives with her husband and five-year-old son. She won the *Missouri Review's* 1995 Editors' Prize for her story "The Incredible Appearing Man." In recent years, her fiction and essays have also appeared in the *North American Review,* the *Chicago Review,* and several anthologies. She is grateful for a fellowship she received from the Illinois Arts Council in 1995, without which this story could not have been written.

▪ I wrote "The Incredible Appearing Man" at a time in my life when I was looking over my shoulder at the disappearance of a whole continent I knew I could never touch again — the casual intellectual smorgasbord of college, graduate school, and urgent late-night study groups on the death of capitalism, the impulsive road trips with their nonstop conversations begun on a dare, perhaps in a bar in Denver and concluded days later in a diner in Austin? New Orleans? over a plate of eggs — in short, the land of my self-absorbed twenties. So noisy and full of joy at the time, later they struck me as obsessed with loss and the One Big Love that never worked out but wouldn't go away, either.

That life was drifting away from me, a few inches at a time. It belonged to another tectonic plate. In my mid-thirties, I had hopped aboard a different continent entirely. Riding with me were a husband and a toddler; I also had a day job and the ongoing battle to keep writing, which I fought the way one struggles inside a collapsing tent. In the midst of it all, I wanted to do something to salute that other continent before it drifted so far off that I couldn't recall the natural features of its terrain, its indigenous wildlife. I felt guilty whenever I thought about the obsessive love that drove me to extremes in my twenties: I found that I didn't want to do the one thing that late-twentieth-century psychotherapy had to recommend. I didn't want to let go, relearn, repent. I didn't want to become disentangled or unenmeshed. I wanted to build a shrine to it. I wanted to honor it, to give it a marker in my new land. I wanted to mythologize it. This is one of the great privileges that writers enjoy, the act of making myth out of private experience. Perhaps the therapists are right when they recommend we burn the bridges behind us and go on, save ourselves. But I believe a writer's potency lies in the strength — weakness? — of mind it takes to go back into the deluge, when no one else would or should.

So this story is my shrine to the lost continent of my twenties. Some of that terrain was as gorgeous as the northern California setting of the story, full of dense deciduous forests and shimmering curtains of light. And much of it was gnarled and impassable. But broken love deserves a shrine, even if it is only a few cheap mirrors, smoking candles, and a scrap of colored tinfoil.

MARY GORDON was born on Long Island, grew up in Queens, and was educated at Barnard College, where she is now the McIntosh Professor of English. She has published four novels — *Final Payments, The Company of Women, Men and Angels,* and *The Other Side* — and a collection of stories, *Temporary Shelter,* as well as numerous essays and articles. Her most recent book is *The Shadow Man,* a memoir. She lives with her husband and two children in New Paltz, New York.

▪ For three years I read Proust every morning; it was the first thing I did after coffee, my first language after the language of dreams. One day when I was reading it I came upon the words "summer house." And, in an instance of life imitating art, the words set off a train of Proustian association. I thought of my grandmother, my Irish immigrant grandmother, than whom no one could be less Proustian, I thought. I decided to put my eminently practical grandmother in a place where there was no place for her: the world of Proust. To my astonishment, she fit there. Or fit somehow. And that placement is this story.

DAVID HUDDLE's books include *Tenorman, Intimates, The High Spirits, Only the Little Bone, The Nature of Yearning, Stopping by Home, Paper Boy,* and *The Writing Habit.* He teaches at the University of Vermont and the Bread Loaf School of English.

▪ As I wrote for the issue of *Story* where "Past My Future" was first published, "Marcy, the narrator . . . appeared as a college student and then a middle-aged woman in the story I wrote immediately before this one. She was like an actress who steals the show: even though she was a minor character, I kept on having to say more and more about her. When I finished that piece, Marcy was still requiring my attention. I'd have been a fool not to give her a story of her own."

Now that I've had a couple of years away from "Past My Future," I've been able to discern some of the literary ingredients that went into the making of it. I was strongly affected by Michael Ondaatje's *The English Patient* — and inspired by the disparate lives of the characters who were so intimately and convincingly set forth in Ondaatje's prose. The stories of

Amy Bloom's *Come to Me* also cast a spell on me with their plucky way of waltzing into unsavory sexual subject matter. I've admired Andre Dubus's cross-gender writing (in stories like "The Pretty Girl," "The Fat Girl," and "Graduation") for a number of years, and his "A Father's Story" sets a high standard for fiction that challenges its reader in moral and ethical terms. Finally, a conversation I had with the novelist and story writer Joyce Kornblatt showed me something I had missed — Marcy's rage — in my early drafting of the story.

ANNA KEESEY was raised in Oregon, taught high school in Seattle, and earned an M.F.A. in Iowa City. Now she lives in Portland, Oregon, and teaches writing at Willamette University in Salem. She has held fellowships from James Michener–The Copernicus Society and the Fine Arts Work Center in Provincetown, and recently won the Nimrod/Hardman Katherine Anne Porter Prize for her story "One Girl's Blues." She is the only one in her family who is not a psychologist, except for her brother, who flies planes.

▪ A friend said to me, in passing, "You should write a story about the people who sat in the fields waiting for God to take them to heaven." He was talking about the followers of William Miller, who believed Miller had deciphered from the Bible the precise date of Christ's return to earth. I imagined the faithful waiting that night — how lonely they would be, how hopeful. That was one part of the story.

About a year later the Branch Davidian compound burned. I hadn't known how interested I had been in that long conversation between the government and the people barricaded inside until I heard the place was in flames. I felt certain — perhaps romantically — that what had happened to those people was pure religious persecution, a grotesque failure of the world to allow for disruptive, dissenting belief. I was moved then to begin reading about the Millerites and found that they were themselves reviled, expelled from their churches, humiliated in the press. In 1843, with the continent still to be claimed, no one wanted to hear that Christ would return to earth on an ordinary day in March. I felt for the Millerites in their alienation and longing, and also for the people who found them an incomprehensible threat. I'd hope we would learn something from these sorts of collisions of belief, but maybe we don't. It's possible that we write letters to the air, and the air doesn't answer, and we are left only with a little more self-definition, a renewal of awe.

I also remember, as I write this, a British or West Indian man I saw on television during the Waco fire. His ex-wife and several children had perished. I'm sure I was thinking of his loss.

JAMAICA KINCAID is the author of *Annie John*, *A Small Place*, *Lucy*, and, most recently, *The Autobiography of My Mother.* Her first book, a collection of stories titled *At the Bottom of the River,* received the Morton Dauwen Zabel Award of the American Academy and Institute of Arts and Letters and was nominated for the PEN/Faulkner Award. Born and educated in Antigua, she now lives with her husband and two children in Vermont.

WILLIAM HENRY LEWIS was born in Denver, where his family still lives, but his significant growing-up years were spent in Washington, D.C., and Chattanooga. He received his M.F.A. from the University of Virginia. His fiction has appeared in *Ploughshares* and *Speak My Name: Black Men on Masculinity and the American Dream* and has been honored by the Zora Neale Hurston/Richard Wright Foundation, the only organization in America founded primarily to support the accomplishment and growth of African American undergraduate and graduate writers. His first collection of short stories, *In the Arms of Our Elders,* was published in 1995. He designed and codirected the Reynolds Young Writers Workshop, a ten-day summer program for high school writers, at Denison University. He teaches at Mary Washington College.

▪ "Shades" was originally a section from a larger story I had been working on for quite some time, but I could not manage its emotional size. I first tried to complete it by writing more, thinking that I was headed into a novel. But the more I worked on draft after draft, the more I realized that it was the power of *absence* that fascinated the narrator and intrigued me. The story is about many things, but I let go of the larger piece because I wanted to deal with larger unknowns in a smaller space; that which *isn't* present was what remained irresistible and haunting for me. The scorching moment of high summer mired in seemingly endless heat and the threshold of manhood on which this boy teeters came from this focus. Whether it is the heat that issues forth image and illusion or the shades of becoming and being, what feels legitimate is something less than solid — stifling and ever-present, but far from clear. And in the midst of all of this drifts the narrator's father, like so many other things that cannot be placed with certainty. What remains to be more certain is the blurred reality that the boy has come to behold, like some old photograph in which only the edges of the image remain discernible. There are several moments that guided me, but when I visualized the moment when the boy realizes that perhaps the father does not recognize his own son, I knew more precisely the layering of conflict, and I knew that much of it would thrive in reduction. To capture this with resonance, I needed less story to infer more of that void; one doesn't need too many words to tell the tale of what isn't there. The narrator's need to fulfill his wishes was very much in line with my need to write the story: to come to terms with that which couldn't be grasped, and through the passage of the story perhaps to bring closer together something that is tangible and that which is evanescent even as it becomes understandable.

WILLIAM LYCHACK was born and raised in Putnam, Connecticut, and is a graduate of Connecticut College and the University of Michigan. In the past few years he has worked as a bartender, apartment caretaker, editor, teacher, children's book author, and Mister Softee ice cream man. He currently lives with his wife in St. Paul, Minnesota, where he works as a freelance writer. His stories have appeared in *Ascent, Quarterly West, Seattle Review, The Sun,* and *Witness.*

▪ For a short time I was associate editor of *New England Review,* and I took the opportunity to ask William Maxwell if he would send us any of his work. He kindly did. Perhaps it will be arcane, but I was so moved with joy and admiration over the tales he sent that I wanted to find a way, if possible, into the tones and compassions that he and writers such as Italo Calvino, Gabriel García Márquez, and Sylvia Townsend Warner conveyed to me. The single image I brought to the little story was that of the old woman putting her things in order. The rest — with the help of that most magic of spells, "Once upon a time" — somehow sprang open around her. It was like play.

JOYCE CAROL OATES is the author of a number of works of fiction, poetry, and criticism, most recently the story collection *Will You Always Love Me?* and the novella *First Love.* She is a recipient of the National Book Award, the 1996 PEN/Malamud Award for lifetime achievement in the short story, the Rea Award, and the Bobst Lifetime Achievement Award, among others; her stories have been reprinted in previous volumes of *The Best American Short Stories, Prize Stories: The O. Henry Awards,* and the *Pushcart Prizes.* Since 1978, she has been on the faculty at Princeton University, where she is the Roger S. Berlind Professor in Humanities.

▪ "Ghost Girls" is one of those stories that originated not in an idea, concept, or theme but purely out of an image: the small country airport with its rotted windsock slapping in the breeze and a single dirt runway between cornfields. Such airports were part of my childhood in upstate New York; my father and certain of his friends flew small airplanes like the ones described in the story (including, in fact, the romantic old Vultee basic trainer). The child Ingrid, her attractive momma, and the absent, possibly malevolent daddy are as vivid to me as my own memories of the past, but are wholly fictional. Ingrid's fascination with the mysterious lives of her parents mirrors my fascination with my parents' lives — the child's fascination with an adult world that surrounds her, entirely out of her control and even her comprehension. After "Ghost Girls," there came to me a related story, also narrated by Ingrid, titled "See You in Your

Dreams"; then came "Easy Lay"; then "Gorgeous"; eventually "Man Crazy" — when I came to see that the stories constitute a single story, a novel built of images and episodes titled *Man Crazy*. Its genesis is the image of the "airstrip at Marsena."

ANGELA PATRINOS was born in Milwaukee, Wisconsin, in 1963. She received an M.F.A. in modern dance and choreography from Case Western Reserve University in Cleveland, Ohio. There, she began writing fiction under the guidance of Lee K. Abbott. She lives in Brooklyn, New York.

▪ I'd wanted this to be a complex and awesome story about divinity, nakedness, and exile, but I wilted and almost dried up under my desires. As an instructor, I was ridiculous. Also, I was anxious about my ability to entertain. After eleven or twelve drafts, I had to say *fuck you* to myself. Just walk where the two people walk. So I did. Thankfully, I was able to keep an eye outside for the sake of form.

SUSAN PERABO is a native of St. Louis and holds an M.F.A. from the University of Arkansas, Fayetteville. Her work has appeared in *TriQuarterly*, *Black Warrior Review*, *Missouri Review*, and *New Stories from the South*. She currently teaches fiction at Dickinson College in Carlisle, Pennsylvania.

▪ I started this story with the image of the narrator and Mr. Arnette crouched outside that hotel room and the simple notion that as many times as a person might narrowly miss whatever he or she needs to make it possible to face the day, it's only fair that there must be at least a few times when he or she smacks right into it. Kierkegaard once told a story about a church full of ducks. The ducks all waddled into church on Sunday morning and squatted down in their pews and the duck minister went to the pulpit and shouted, "We are ducks, and ducks have wings!" And all the ducks shouted "Amen!" The minister shouted, "We are ducks, and ducks can fly!" And all the ducks shouted "Amen!" The minister shouted, "We can soar to the clouds!" And all the ducks shouted "Amen!" The minister shouted, "We are ducks, and we have wings!" And all the ducks shouted "Amen!" Then the duck minister closed the service and all the ducks waddled home. This little parable clarifies for me why, at the end of the story, the narrator and Mr. Arnette are off the ground.

LYNNE SHARON SCHWARTZ's most recent book is *Ruined by Reading: A Life in Books*. Her earlier books include the novels *The Fatigue Artist*, *Disturbances in the Field*, *Rough Strife* (nominated for a National Book Award), *Leaving Brooklyn* (nominated for a PEN/Faulkner Award), and *Balancing Acts*, as well as two story collections, *The Melting Pot and Other Subversive Stories* and *Acquainted with the Night*. Ms. Schwartz has taught fiction writing

in many graduate programs and has received grants from the John Simon
Guggenheim Foundation, the National Endowment for the Arts, and the
New York State Foundation for the Arts.

▪ A story comes from the same place as a dream. And while we've
become adept at analyzing both the surface and the subterranean elements of a dream, we shall never know why or how those elements arranged themselves in that particular configuration on that particular
night. The place that gives birth to fantasy, sleeping or waking, is only
dimly accessible; its strategies and purposes are an enigma. I think that is
for the best.

In keeping with the nature of their source, stories and dreams turn up
unaccountably, like unlooked-for gifts (though some gifts, and some
dreams, are unwelcome); the writer simply performs a service, using craft
and language to redesign the gift and pass it along. If she is especially
diligent and fortunate, she may even glimpse its obscure origins.

Some dream images are easily accounted for — the newspaper article
we read that morning, the delivery man's bicycle chained to a lamppost,
the hat of the supermarket clerk. They are not the real dream, though,
only the furnishings of the room, so to speak. The real dream is the texture
of the air in the room — its smell and its density, its temperature, memories and omens. As far as "The Trip to Halawa Valley" goes, I can easily
account for its "furniture."

I lived and worked for several months in Hawaii; I visited the island of
Molokai; I read the guidebook; I saw, or attempted to see, the sights. I
came home with my senses bedazzled. It was inevitable that the flowers, the
fruits, the water, all the standard elements of postcard scenery, would find
their way into my writing, along with the history I learned.

I am also wildly amused by certain kinds of ritualized and formulaic
language — the language of instruction manuals, of recipes, of catalogues,
and so on. Thus my characters' pleasure in repeating phrases from their
Hawaii guidebook, and my own in mischievously putting those innocent
phrases to a quite somber and unintended use.

But the real story? How it came to be written? On that I am wordless.
What can be told has been told. The story belongs to its readers now, and
my private sources to me.

AKHIL SHARMA writes: "My family left India and came to Queens, New
York, when I was eight. After some time we ended up in New Jersey. I went
to Princeton, the best $100,000 in debt I ever took on. Then I went to
Stanford and was poor for a while. Now I'm at Harvard Law School taking
'Secured Transactions' to protect my vast future holdings.

▪ I wrote the first draft of the story as a freshman in college. It was three
pages long and about a Jewish woman. Back then I used to start all my

stories with a hook: "On Tuesday I died" sort of thing. For some reason I was not as dazzled with this story as I was (and still am) with most everything I write. (I have a hard time resisting reading aloud everything I write to everyone I know.) I rewrote it seventeen times. I sort of remember there being an eighty-page draft at some point. But that could be a manifestation of the horror I feel when I remember the literally years (an hour or two a day) I worked on "If You Sing Like That for Me." I finished it when I was a senior in college. (I have never read it all the way through since then.)

I sent this and several other stories to an agent, who, after collecting two rejection letters for me, stopped returning my calls.

After college I went to an M.F.A. program and tried writing a novel. I began getting odder and odder. I put garbage bags over my windows. Most of the day, if I wasn't working, I was lying on the piece of foam packing that was my bed and giggling to myself as I read Shakespeare and ate day-old muffins.

In a lurch toward sanity, I sent "If You Sing Like That for Me" to five nationals. Four rejected me within a week. *The Atlantic Monthly* didn't respond. I thought the bastards had kept the stamps on my SASE.

Several months later, I got an acceptance from *The Atlantic,* a contract that said sign at X and return. I called my agent to gloat and the shameless wretch promptly asked for her commission. I said no. For the next two weeks she periodically called and talked about money. When I repeated my no, she would remain on the phone but wouldn't say anything. (All this over a $250 commission.)

At that point I decided to go to law school.

This story is for Carolyn Wilsker Green: beautiful, kind, gallant.

JEAN THOMPSON lives in Urbana, Illinois. She is the author of two novels and two collections of short fiction. Her stories have appeared in *The New Yorker, Mademoiselle, TriQuarterly, American Short Fiction, Ploughshares, New England Review,* and *The Pushcart Prizes XIX.*

▪ Scout and Annie are the literary ghosts of a couple I knew (vaguely, peripherally, that is, not well enough to prevent me from transforming them into fiction) circa 1970. At that time they seemed both appealing and sinister. Looking back, I would probably find them a little ridiculous as well.

Nothing remains of them except the impression that they lived on some fringe of the normal world, and the first line of the story, which reached me as a rumor. I was interested in the pathology not just of drugs but of unwholesome relationships, where love does indeed equal despair. Scout's imperfect and angry yearning for God functions as another sort of addiction.

Once the story took shape, what propelled me through it was language.

I wanted language to be heightened, nearly extravagant, yet with the control of emotion remembered. I wanted the story to hinge or unify itself with a series of repetitions and interlocking images: water, birds, flight, God, sugar, junk, and so on. It's something of an artistic contrivance to have Scout kill himself, and in such a romantic fashion. Strict realism would keep him grubbily alive, and still doing damage.

MELANIE RAE THON is the author of two novels, *Meteors in August* and *Iona Moon*, and a collection of stories, *Girls in the Grass*. A new collection, *First, Body*, will be published in 1997. Last summer her work was included in *Granta's* "Best of Young American Novelists" issue. She is originally from Kalispell, Montana, and has lived in Arizona, Michigan, Massachusetts, and New York. She now lives in Columbus, Ohio.

▪ This story is the middle piece of a triptych called "Nobody's Daughters." It took me months to hear Nadine's voice clearly enough to write the first section; but once I did hear her, she wouldn't leave me. Still I struggled, as I always do, with the question of whether or not this was truly *my* story to tell. That's the challenge of first person: I wonder, do I have the right to speak in this person's voice? For me, it's not an artistic question, it's a personal one. I have to be sure I feel close enough to my people to imagine what they see and how they talk about their lives. So I was thinking, *Do I know her?* but I was too busy to write. Then one night I dreamed I was Nadine. I'd broken into a house. I touched everything there. I saw everything. I woke at four that morning. The power was out. I lined up all my candles along the windowsill and wrote until dawn.

100 Other Distinguished Stories of 1995

Selected by Katrina Kenison

HURSTON, ZORA NEALE
Black Death. *Oxford American,*
March/April.

JERSILD, DEVON
Eggs. *Ploughshares,* Vol. 21, Nos. 2
& 3.
JIN, HA
New Arrival. *Chicago Review,* Vol. 41,
No. 4.
JONES, THOM
Nights in White Satin. *Harper's
Magazine,* May.
Superman, My Son. *The New Yorker,*
February 13.

KIDD, SUE MONK
In the Graveyard of Afterbirth.
TriQuarterly, No. 92.
KIRN, WALTER
Thumbsucker. *The New Yorker,*
January 9.
KLAM, MATTHEW
The Royal Palms. *The New Yorker,*
December 4.

LATTIMORE, STEVE
Jarheads. *Mississippi Review,* Vol. 24,
Nos. 1 & 2.
LEEBRON, FRED
Baby Girl. *TriQuarterly,* No. 93.
LE GUIN, URSULA
Olders. *Omni,* Winter.

MARDER, NORMA
Getting to Know You. *Georgia
Review,* Vol. 49, No. 3.
MARTINEAU, THERESE
Sister Zita. *Calyx,* Summer.
MASON, BOBBI ANN
Proper Gypsies. *Southwest Review,*
Vol. 31, No. 4.
MATTISON, ALICE
Pekko's Boat. *North American Review,*
September/October.
MCNALLY, T.M.
Skin Deep. *Yale Review,* July.

MOORE, LORRIE
Beautiful Grade. *The New Yorker,*
December 25 & January 1.
MOSLEY, WALTER
Double Standard. *GQ,* August.
The Thief. *Esquire,* July.

NELSON, ANTONYA
Irony, Irony, Irony. *TriQuarterly,*
No. 94.
NELSON, KENT
What Shall Become of Me.
Gettysburg Review, Vol. 8, No. 1.

OATES, JOYCE CAROL
The Vision. *Michigan Quarterly
Review,* Vol. 24, No. 1.
OROZCO, DANIEL
The Bridge. *Story,* Autumn.

PAINE, TOM
General Markman's Last Stand.
Story, Summer.
PIETRZYK, LESLIE
The Invisible Hand. *Iowa Review,*
Vol. 25, No. 3.

REICH, TOVA
The Lost Girl. *Harper's Magazine,*
August.
ROBERTUS, POLLY
Brothers and Sisters. *American Short
Fiction,* No. 17.

SCHULMAN, HELEN
The Revisionist. *Paris Review,*
No. 135.
SCHUMACHER, JULIE
Dummies. *The Atlantic Monthly,* April.
SCHUTT, CHRISTINE
Metropolis. *Mississippi Review,* Vol.
24, Nos. 1 & 2.
SCHWARTZ, ADAM
Dancing with Earl. *DoubleTake,* Vol.
2, No. 1.
SHIELDS, CAROL
Mirrors. *Prairie Fire,* Vol. 16, No. 4.

Editorial Addresses of American and Canadian Magazines Publishing Short Stories

When available, the annual subscription rate, the average number of stories published per year, and the name of the editor follow the address.

African American Review
Stalker Hall 212
Indiana State University
Terre Haute, IN 47809
$24, 25, Joe Weixlmann

African Voices
270 West 96th Street
New York, NY 10025
$10, 12, Carolyn A. Butts

Agni Review
Creative Writing Department
Boston University
236 Bay State Road
Boston, MA 02115
$12, 13, Askold Melnyczuk

Alabama Literary Review
Smith 253
Troy State University
Troy, AL 36082
$5, 21, Theron E. Montgomery

Alaska Quarterly Review
Department of English

University of Alaska
3211 Providence Drive
Anchorage, AK 99508
$8, 28, Ronald Spatz

Alfred Hitchcock's Mystery Magazine
1540 Broadway
New York, NY 10036
$34.97, 130, Cathleen Jordan

American Letters and Commentary
Suite 56
850 Park Avenue
New York, NY 10021
$5, 4, Jeanne Beaumont, Anna Rabinowitz

American Literary Review
University of North Texas
P.o. Box 13615
Denton, TX 76203
$10, 14, Scott Cairns, Barbara Rodman

American Short Fiction
Parlin 108
Department of English
University of Texas at Austin

Austin, TX 78712-1164
$24, 32, Joseph Krupa

American Voice
332 West Broadway
Louisville, KY 40202
$15, 20, Sallie Bingham, Frederick
Smock

American Way
P.O. Box 619640
DFW Airport
Texas 75261-9640
$72, 50, Jeff Posey

Analog Science Fiction/Science Fact
1540 Broadway
New York, NY 10036
$34.95, 70, Stanley Schmidt

Another Chicago Magazine
Left Field Press
3709 North Kenmore
Chicago, IL 60613
$8, 16, Sharon Solwitz

Antietam Review
82 West Washington Street
Hagerstown, MD 21740
$5, 8, Suzanne Kass

Antioch Review
P.O. Box 148
Yellow Springs, OH 45387
$30, 11, Robert S. Fogarty

Apalachee Quarterly
P.O. Box 20106
Tallahassee, FL 32316
$15, 4, Barbara Hamby

Appalachian Heritage
Berea College
Berea, KY 40404
$18, 6, Sidney Saylor Farr

Ascent
P.O. Box 967
Urbana, IL 61801
$9, 8, group editorship

Asimov's Science Fiction Magazine
Bantam Doubleday Dell

1540 Broadway
New York, NY 10036
$39.97, 27, Gardner Dozois

Atlantic Monthly
745 Boylston Street
Boston, MA 02116
$15.94, 12, C. Michael Curtis

Baffler
P.O. Box 378293
Chicago, IL 60637
$16, Thomas Frank, Keith White

Bellowing Ark
P.O. Box 45637
Seattle, WA 98145
$15, 7, Robert R. Ward

Big Sky Journal
P.O. Box 1069
Bozeman, MT 59771-1069
$22, 4, Allen Jones, Brian Baise

Black River Review
855 Mildred Avenue
Lorain, OH 44052
12, Jack Smith

Black Warrior Review
P.O. Box 2936
Tuscaloosa, AL 35487-2936
$11, 13, Mitch Weiland

Blood & Aphorisms
P.O. Box 702
Toronto, Ontario
M5S ZY4 Canada
$18, 20, Hilary Clark

BOMB
New Art Publications
10th floor
594 Broadway
New York, NY 10012
$18, 6, Betsy Sussler

Border Crossings
Y300-393 Portage Avenue
Winnipeg, Manitoba
R3B 3H6 Canada
$23, 16, Meeka Walsh

Boston Review
Building E53
Room 407
Cambridge, MA 02139
$15, 6, editorial board

Boulevard
P.O. Box 30386
Philadelphia, PA 19103
$12, 17, Richard Burgin

Briar Cliff Review
3303 Rebecca Street
P.O. Box 2100
Sioux City, IA 51104-2100
$4, 4, Phil Hey

The Bridge
14050 Vernon Street
Oak Park, Ml 48237
$8, 10, Helen Zucker

BUZZ
11835 West Olympic Blvd.
Suite 450
Los Angeles, CA 90064
$14.95, 12, Renee Vogel

Callaloo
Dept. of English
Wilson Hall
University of Virginia
Charlottesville, VA 22903
$25, 6, Charles H. Rowell

Calyx
P.O. Box B
Corvallis, OR 97339
$18, 11, Margarita Donnelly

Canadian Fiction
Box 946, Station F
Toronto, Ontario
M4Y 2N9 Canada
$34.24, 23, Geoffrey Hancock

Capilano Review
Capilano College
2055 Purcell Way
North Vancouver,
British Columbia

V7J 3H5 Canada
$25, 12, Robert Sherrin

Carolina Quarterly
Greenlaw Hall 066A
University of North Carolina
Chapel Hill, NC 27514
$10, 13, Brenda Thissen

Century
P.O. Box 150510
Brooklyn, NY 11215-0510
$33, 10, Robert J. Killheffer

Chariton Review
Division of Language & Literature
Northeast Missouri State University
Kirksville, MO 63501
$9, 6, Jim Barnes

Chattahoochee Review
DeKalb Community College
2101 Womack Road
Dunwoody, GA 30338-4497
$15, 21, Lamar York

Chelsea
P.O. Box 773
Cooper Station
New York, NY 10276
$11, 6, Richard Foerster

Chicago Review
5801 South Kenwood
University of Chicago
Chicago, IL 60637
$15, 20, Andy Winston

Christopher Street
P.O. Box 1475
Church Street Station
New York, NY 10008
$27, 50, Tom Steele

Cimarron Review
205 Morrill Hall
Oklahoma State University
Stillwater, OK 74078-0135
$12, 15, Gordon Weaver

Cities and Roads
P.O. Box 10886

Greensboro, NC 27404
$15.75, 20, *Tom Kealey*

Colorado Review
Department of English
Colorado State University
Fort Collins, CO 80523
$15, 8, *David Milofsky*

Columbia
404 Dodge
Columbia University
New York, NY 10027
$13, 14, *Ken Foster,*
   Justin Peacock

Commentary
165 East 56th Street
New York, NY 10022
$39, 5, *Neal Kozodoy*

Concho River Review
English Department
Angelo State University
San Angelo, TX 76909
$12, 7, *Terence A. Dalrymple*

Confrontation
English Department
C. W. Post College of Long Island
   University
Greenvale, NY 11548
$8, 25, *Martin Tucker*

Conjunctions
Bard College
Annandale-on-Hudson, NY 12504
$18, 6, *Bradford Morrow*

Cream City Review
University of Wisconsin, Milwaukee
P.O. Box 413
Milwaukee, WI 53201
$10, 30, *Brian Jung,*
   Matt Robertson

Crescent Review
P.O. Box 15069
Chevy Chase, MD 20825-5069
$21, 23, *J. Timothy Holland*

Critic
205 West Monroe Street, 6th floor
Chicago, IL 60606-5097
$20, 4, *Julie Bridge*

Crucible
Barton College
College Station
Wilson, NC 27893
12, Terence Grimes

Cut Bank
Department of English
University of Montana
Missoula, MT 59812
$12, 20, *Ed Skoog*

Denver Quarterly
University of Denver
Denver, CO 80208
$15, 5, *Bin Ramke*

Descant
P.O. Box 314, Station P
Toronto, Ontario
M5S 2S8 Canada
$20, 20, *Karen Mulhallen*

Descant
Department of English
Texas Christian University
Box 32872
Fort Worth, TX 76129
$12, 16, *Stanley Trachtenberg, Betsy*
   Colquitt, Harry Opperman

DoubleTake
Center for Documentary Studies
1317 West Pettigrew Street
Durham, NC 27705
$32, 10, *Robert Coles, Alex Harris*

Eagle's Flight
P.O. Box 832
Granite, OK 73547
$5, 10, *Rekha Kulkarni*

Elle
1633 Broadway
New York, NY 10019
$24, 2, *John Howell*

Epoch
251 Goldwin Smith Hall
Cornell University
Ithaca, NY 14853-3201
$11, 23, Michael Koch

Esquire
250 West 55th Street
New York, NY 10019
$17.94, 12, Rust Hills, Will Blythe

event
c/o Douglas College
P.O. Box 2503
New Westminster, British Columbia
V3L 5B2 Canada
*$15, 18, Christine Dewar, Maurice
  Hodgson*

Fantasy & Science Fiction
143 Cream Hill Road
West Cornwall, CT 06796
$26, 75, Edward L. Ferman

Farmer's Market
Elgin Community College
1700 Spartan Drive
Elgin, IL 60123
$10, 18, Rachael Tecza

Fiction
Fiction, Inc.
Department of English
The City College of New York
New York, NY
$7, 15, Mark Mirsky

Fiction International
Department of English and
  Comparative Literature
San Diego State University
San Diego, CA 92182
$14, Harold Jaffe, Larry McCaffery

Fiddlehead
UNB Box 4400
University of New Brunswick
Fredericton, New Brunswick
E3B 5A3 Canada
$16, 20, Don McKay

Florida Review
Department of English
University of Central Florida
P.O. Box 25000
Orlando, FL 32816
$7, 14, Russell Kesler

Folio
Department of Literature
The American University
Washington, D.C. 20016
$10, 12, Elisabeth Poliner

Four Quarters
LaSalle University
20th and Olney Avenues
Philadelphia, PA 19141
$8, 10, John J. Keenan

Frank
Association Frank
32, rue Edouard Vaillant
93100 Montreuil, France
$38, 6, David Applefield

Free Press
P.O. Box 581
Bronx, NY 10463
$25, 10, J. Rudolph Abate

Geist
1062 Homer Street #100
Vancouver, Canada
V6B 2W9
$20, 5, Stephen Osborne

Georgetown Review
400 East College Street, Box 227
Georgetown, KY 40324
$10, 5, Leslie Peitrzyk

Georgia Review
University of Georgia
Athens, GA 30602
$18, 10, Stanley W. Lindberg

Gettysburg Review
Gettysburg College
Gettysburg, PA 17325
$18, 22, Peter Stitt

Glimmer Train Stories
812 SW Washington Street
Suite 1205
Portland, OR 97205
*$29, 40, Susan Burmeister, Linda
   Davies*

Good Housekeeping
959 Eighth Avenue
New York, NY 10019
$17.97, 7, Arleen L. Quarfoot

GQ
350 Madison Avenue
New York, NY 10017
$19.97, 12, Lisa Henricksson

Grain
Box 1154
Regina, Saskatchewan
S4P 3B4 Canada
$19.95, 21, Connie Gault

Grand Street
131 Varick Street
New York, NY 10013
$40, 20, Jean Stein

Granta
2-3 Hanover Yard
Noel Road Islington
London, England N1 8BE
$32, 12, Ian Jack

Great River Review
211 West 7th Street
Winona, MN 55987
$12, 8, Pamela Davies

Green Mountain Review
Box A 58
Johnson State College
Johnson, VT 05656
$12, 23, Tony Whedon

Greensboro Review
Department of English
University of North Carolina
Greensboro, NC 27412
$8, 16, Jim Clark

Gulf Coast
Department of English
University of Houston
4800 Calhoun Road
Houston, TX 77204-3012
$22, 10, Marsha Recknagel, Merrill Greene

Gulf Stream
English Department
Florida International University
North Miami Campus
North Miami, FL 33181
$4, 6, Lynne Barrett, John Dufresne

Habersham Review
Piedmont College
Demorest, GA 30535-0010
*$12, David L. Greene, Lisa Hodgens
   Lumkin*

Harper's Magazine
666 Broadway
New York, NY 10012
$18, 9, Lewis H. Lapham

Harvard Review
Poetry Room
Harvard College Library
Cambridge, MA 02138
$12, 6, Stratis Haviaris

Hawaii Review
University of Hawaii
Department of English
1733 Donaghho Road
Honolulu, HI 96822
*$15, 40, Robert Sean MacBeth, Kalani
   Chapman*

Hayden's Ferry Review
Matthews Center
Arizona State University
Tempe, AZ 85287-1502
*$10, 10, Eric Chilton,
   Genevieve Hangen*

High Plains Literary Review
180 Adams Street, Suite 250
Denver, CO 80206
$20, 7, Robert O. Greer, Jr.

Hudson Review
684 Park Avenue
New York, NY 10021
$24, 8, Paula Deitz, Frederick Morgan

Hyphen
3458 W. Devon Ave., No. 6
Lincolnwood, IL 60659
$12, 8, Matthew Adrian, Margaret Lewis

Image
3100 McCormick Ave.
Wichita, KS 67213
$30, 12, Gregory Wolfe

Indiana Review
316 North Jordan Avenue
Bloomington, IN 47405
$12, 13, rotating editorship

Ink
P.O. Box 52558
St. George Postal Outlet
264 Bloor Street
Toronto, Ontario
M5S 1V0 Canada
$8, 10, John Degan

Innisfree
P.O. Box 277
Manhattan Beach, CA 90266
$20, 100, Rex Winn

Interim
Department of English
University of Nevada
4505 Maryland Parkway
Las Vegas, NV 89154
$8, A. Wilber Stevens

International Quarterly
P.O. Box 10521
Tallahassee, FL 32302
$22, 20, Van K. Brock

Iowa Review
Department of English
University of Iowa
308 EPB
Iowa City, IA 52242
$18, 20, David Hamilton

Iowa Woman
P.O. Box 680
Iowa City, IA 52244
$18, 15, Marianne Abel

Iris
Box 323 HSC
University of Virginia
Charlottesville, VA 22908
$8, 4, Kristen Staby Rembold

Italian Americana
University of Rhode Island
College of Continuing Education
199 Promenade Street
Providence, RI 02908
$15, 6, Carol Bonomo Albright

Jewish Currents
22 East 17th Street, Suite 601
New York, NY 10003-3272
$20, 8, editorial board

Journal
Department of English
Ohio State University
164 West 17th Avenue
Columbus, OH 43210
$8, 5, Kathy Fagan, Michelle Herman

Kairos
c/o Language Studies
Mohawk College
P.O. Box 2034
Hamilton, Ontario
L8N 3T2 Canada
$5, 3, Royston Tester

Kalliope
Florida Community College
3939 Roosevelt Blvd.
Jacksonville, FL 32205
$10.50, 12, Mary Sue Koeppel

Kansas Quarterly
Department of English
Denison Hall
Kansas State University
Manhattan, KS 66506
$20, 8, Ben Nyberg, John Rees, G. W. Clift

Karamu
English Department
Eastern Illinois University
Charleston, IL 61920
$6.50, 8, Peggy L. Brayfield

Kenyon Review
Kenyon College
Gambier, OH 43022
$22, 18, Marilyn Hacker

Kiosk
English Department
306 Clemens Hall
SUNY
Buffalo, NY 14260
$6, 9, Lia Vella

Laurel Review
Department of English
Northwest Missouri State University
Maryville, MO 64468
$8, 20, Craig Goad, David Slater,
William Trowbridge

Lilith
250 West 57th Street
New York, NY 10107
$16, 4, Susan Weidman

Literal Latté
Suite 240
61 East 8th Street
New York, NY 10003
$25, 12, Jenine Gordon

Literary Review
Fairleigh Dickinson University
285 Madison Avenue
Madison, NJ 07940
$18, 10, Walter Cummins

Louisiana Literature
Box 792
Southeastern Louisiana University
Hammond, LA 70402
$10, 8, David Hanson

Lynx Eye
1880 Hill Drive

Los Angeles, CA 90041
$20, 12, Pam McCully, Kathryn Morrison

McCall's
110 Fifth Avenue
New York, NY 10011
$15.94, 6, Laura Manske

Madison Review
University of Wisconsin
Department of English
H. C. White Hall
600 North Park Street
Madison, WI 53706
$14, 8, Andrew Hipp, Richard Gilman

Malahat Review
University of Victoria
P.O. Box 1700
Victoria, British Columbia
V8W 2Y2 Canada
$15, 20, Derk Wynand

Manoa
English Department
University of Hawaii
Honolulu, HI 96822
$18, 12, Ian MacMillan

Massachusetts Review
Memorial Hall
University of Massachusetts
Amherst, MA 01003
$15, 6, Mary Heath, Jules Chametzky,
Paul Jenkins

Matrix
1455 de Paisonneuve Blvd. West
Suite LB-514-8
Montreal, Quebec
H3G IM8 Canada
$15, 8, Terence Byrnes

Michigan Quarterly Review
3032 Rackham Building
University of Michigan
Ann Arbor, MI 48109
$18, 10, Laurence Goldstein

Mid-American Review
106 Hanna Hall

Department of English
Bowling Green State University
Bowling Green, OH 43403
$12, 11, Rebecca Meacham

Minnesota Review
Department of English
State University of New York
Stony Brook, NY 11794-5350
$12, 10, Jeffrey Williams

Mirabella
200 Madison Avenue
New York, NY 10016
$17.98, 2, Kathy Medwick

Mississippi Review
University of Southern Mississippi
Southern Station, P.O. Box 5144
Hattiesburg, MS 39406-5144
$15, 25, Frederick Barthelme

Mississippi Valley Review
Dept. of English
Western Illinois University
Macomb, IL 61455
*$12, 16, John Mann,
    Tama Baldwin*

Missouri Review
1507 Hillcrest Hall
University of Missouri
Columbia, MO 65211
$15, 23, Speer Morgan

Modern Words
350 Bay Street #100
San Francisco, CA 94133
$20, 10, Garland Richard Kyle

Ms.
230 Park Avenue
New York, NY 10169
$45, 7, Marcia Ann Gillespie

Nassau Review
English Department
Nassau Community College
One Education Drive
Garden City, NY 11530-6793
Paul A. Doyle

Nebraska Humanities
Suite 225
215 Centennial Mall Square
Lincoln, NE 68508
8, Jim Cihlar

Nebraska Review
Writers' Workshop, ASH 212
University of Nebraska
Omaha, NE 68182-0324
$10, 10, Art Homer, Richard Duggin

New Delta Review
Creative Writing Program
English Department
Louisiana State University
Baton Rouge, LA 70803
$7, 9, Mindy Meek

New England Review
Middlebury College
Middlebury, VT 05753
$18, 16, T. R. Hummer

New Letters
University of Missouri
4216 Rockhill Road
Kansas City, MO 64110
$17, 21, James McKinley

New Orleans Review
P.O. Box 195
Loyola University
New Orleans, LA 70118
$18, 4, Ralph Adamo

New Quarterly
English Language Proficiency
    Programme
University of Waterloo
Waterloo, Ontario
N2L 3G1 Canada
*$14, 26, Peter Hinchcliffe,
    Kim Jernigan, Mary Merikle,
    Linda Kenyon*

New Renaissance
9 Heath Road
Arlington, MA 02174
$11.50, 5, Louise T. Reynolds

New Yorker
25 West 43rd Street
New York, NY 10036
$32, 45, Tina Brown

Nimrod
Arts and Humanities Council
of Tulsa
2210 South Main Street
Tulsa, OK 74114
$15, 10, Francine Ringold

North American Review
University of Northern Iowa
1222 West 27th Street
Cedar Falls, IA 50614
$18, 13, Robley Wilson, Jr.

North Dakota Quarterly
University of North Dakota
P.O. Box 8237
Grand Forks, ND 58202
$15, 13, William Borden

Northeast Corridor
Department of English
Beaver College
450 S. Easton Road
Glenside, PA 19038-3295
$10, 6, Susan Balee

North Stone Review
D Station, Box 14098
Minneapolis, MN 55414

Northwest Review
369 PLC
University of Oregon
Eugene, OR 97403
$14, 10, Hannah Wilson

Notre Dame Review
Department of English
University of Notre Dame
Notre Dame, IN 46556
$15, 8, Valerie Sayers

Oasis
P.O. Box 626
Largo, FL 34649-0626
$22, 14, Neal Storrs

Ohio Review
Ellis Hall
Ohio University
Athens, OH 45701-2979
$16, 10, Wayne Dodd

Omni
1965 Broadway
New York, NY 10023-5965
$24, 20, Ellen Datlow

Ontario Review
9 Honey Brook Drive
Princeton, NJ 08540
$12, 8, Raymond J. Smith

Other Voices
University of Illinois at Chicago
Department of English
(M/C 162) Box 4348
Chicago, IL 60680
$20, 30, Sharon Fiffer,
Lois Hauselman

Oxalis
Stone Ridge Poetry Society
P.O. Box 3993
Kingston, NY 12401
$18, 12, Shirley Powell

Oxford American
115½ South Lamar
Oxford, MS 38655
$16, 12, Marc Smirnoff

Oxygen
Suite 1010
535 Geary Street
San Francisco, CA 94102
$14, 10, Richard Hack

Pangolin Papers
P.O. Box 241
Nordland, WA 98358
$15, 6, Pat Britt

Paris Review
541 East 72nd Street
New York, NY 10021
$34, 14, George Plimpton

Paris Transcontinental
Institut du Monde Anglophone,
  Sorbonne Nouvelle
5, rue d'École de Médecine
75006 Paris, France
$20, Claire Larriere

Parting Gifts
3006 Stonecutter Terrace
Greensboro, NC 27405
Robert Bixby

Partisan Review
236 Bay State Road
Boston, MA 02215
$22, 4, William Phillips

Passages North
Kalamazoo College
1200 Academy Street
Kalamazoo, MI 49007
$10, 8, Michael Barrett

Pikeville Review
Humanities Division
Pikeville College
Pikeville, KY 41501
$4, 4, James Alan Riley

Playboy
Playboy Building
919 North Michigan Avenue
Chicago, IL 60611
$24, 23, Alice K. Turner

Ploughshares
Emerson College
100 Beacon Street
Boston, MA 02116
$19, 20, Don Lee

Potpourri
P.O. Box 8278
Prairie Village, KS 66208
$12, 20, Polly W. Swafford

Pottersfield Portfolio
The Gatsby Press
5280 Green Street, P.O. Box 27094
Halifax, Nova Scotia

B3H 4M8 Canada
$18, 12, Ian Colford

Prairie Fire
423-100 Arthur Street
Winnipeg, Manitoba
R3B 1H3 Canada
$24, 8, Andris Taskans

Prairie Schooner
201 Andrews Hall
University of Nebraska
Lincoln, NE 68588-0334
$20, 20, Hilda Raz

Prism International
Department of Creative Writing
University of British Columbia
Vancouver, British Columbia
V6T 1W5 Canada
$16, 20, Annabel Lyon

Provincetown Arts
650 Commercial Street
Provincetown MA 02657
$9, 4, Christopher Busa

Puerto del Sol
P.O. Box 3E
Department of English
New Mexico State University
Las Cruces, NM 88003
$10, 12, Kevin McIlvoy

Quarry Magazine
P.O. Box 1061
Kingston, Ontario
K7L 4Y5 Canada
$22, 20, Mary Cameron

Quarterly
650 Madison Avenue, Suite 2600
New York, NY 10022
$30, 210, Gordon Lish

Quarterly West
317 Olpin Union
University of Utah
Salt Lake City, UT 84112
$11, 6, Darin Cain,
Jeffrey Vasseur

RE:AL
School of Liberal Arts
Stephen F. Austin State University
P.O. Box 13007
SFA Station
Nacogdoches, TX 75962
$8, 10, Dale Hearell

The Recorder
991 Fifth Avenue
New York, NY 10028
4, Christopher Cahill

Red Cedar Review
17 Morrill Hall
Department of English
Michigan State University
East Lansing, MI 48823
$10, 12, Tom Bissell

Redbook
959 Eighth Avenue
New York, NY 10017
$11.97, 10, Dawn Raffel

River Styx
Big River Association
14 South Euclid
St. Louis, MO 63108
$20, 30, Jennifer Tabin, Richard Newman

Room of One's Own
P.O. Box 46160, Station G
Vancouver, British Columbia
V6R 4G5 Canada
$20, 12, collective editorship

Rosebud
P.O. Box 459
Cambridge, WI 53523
$10, 20, Roderick Clark

Salamander
48 Ackers Avenue
Brookline, MA 02146
$12, 10, Jennifer Barber

Salmagundi
Skidmore College
Saratoga Springs, NY 12866
$15, 4, Robert Boyers

San Jose Studies
c/o English Department
San Jose State University
One Washington Square
San Jose, CA 95192
$12, 5, John Engell, D. Mesher

Santa Monica Review
Center for the Humanities
Santa Monica College
1900 Pico Boulevard
Santa Monica, CA 90405
$12, 16, Jim Krusoe

Saturday Night
Suite 400
184 Front Street E
Toronto, Ontario
M5V 2Z4 Canada
$26.45, 4, Robert Weaver

Seattle Review
Padelford Hall, GN-30
University of Washington
Seattle, WA 98195
$9, 12, Charles Johnson

Sewanee Review
University of the South
Sewanee, TN 37375-4009
$16, 10, George Core

Shenandoah
Washington and Lee University
P.O. Box 722
Lexington, VA 24450
$11, 17, R. T. Smith

Shooting Star Review
7123 Race Street
Pittsburgh, PA 15208
$10, 12, group editorship

Short Fiction by Women
Box 1276 Stuyvesant Station
New York, NY 10009
$18, 20, Rachel Whalen

Sinister Wisdom
P.O. Box 3252
Berkeley, CA 94703

$17, 15, Akiba Onada-Sikwoia,
Kyos Featherdancing

Snake Nation Review
110 #2 West Force Street
Valdosta, GA 31601
$20, 14, Roberta George

Sonora Review
Department of English
University of Arizona
Tucson, AZ 85721
$10, 12, Becky Hagenston

So to Speak
4400 University Drive
George Mason University
Fairfax, VA 22030-444
$7, 10, Colleen Kearney

South Carolina Review
Department of English
Clemson University
Clemson, SC 29634-1503
$10, 8, Frank Day,
Carol Johnston

South Dakota Review
University of South Dakota
P.O. Box 111 University Exchange
Vermillion, SD 57069
$15, 15, Brian Bedard

Southern Exposure
P.O. Box 531
Durham, NC 27702
$24, 12, Eric Bates

Southern Humanities Review
9088 Haley Center
Auburn University
Auburn, AL 36849
$15, 5, Dan R. Latimer, Virginia M.
Kouidis

Southern Review
43 Allen Hall
Louisiana State University
Baton Rouge, LA 70803
$20, 17, James Olney, Dave Smith

Southwest Review
Southern Methodist University
P.O. Box 4374
Dallas, TX 75275
$20, 15, Willard Spiegelman

Stories
Box 1467
Arlington, MA 02174
$18, 12, Amy R. Kaufman

Story
1507 Dana Avenue
Cincinnati, OH 45207
$17, 52, Lois Rosenthal

Story Quarterly
P.O. Box 1416
Northbrook, IL 60065
$12, 20, Margaret Barrett, Anne
Brashler, Diane Williams

Sun
107 North Roberson Street
Chapel Hill, NC 27516
$30, 30, Sy Safransky

Sycamore Review
Department of English
Heavilon Hall
Purdue University
West Lafayette, IN 47907
$9, 5, Michael Manley

Talking River Review
Division of Literature
Lewis-Clark State College
500 8th Avenue
Lewiston, ID 83501
$10, 10, group editorship

Tamaqua
Humanities Department
Parkland College
2400 West Bradley Avenue
Champaign, IL 61821
$10, 5, Neil Archer

Thema
Box 74109

Metairie, LA 70053-4109
$16, Virginia Howard

Threepenny Review
P.O. Box 9131
Berkeley, CA 94709
$16, 10, Wendy Lesser

Tikkun
5100 Leona Street
Oakland, CA 94619
$36, 10, Michael Lerner

Trafika
Columbia Post Office
Box 250413
New York, NY 10025-1536
$35, 27, Dorsey Evans

Treasure House
Suite 3A
1106 Oak Hill Avenue
Hagerstown, MD 21742
$15, 11, J. G. Wolfensberger

TriQuarterly
2020 Ridge Avenue
Northwestern University
Evanston, IL 60208
$20, 15, Reginald Gibbons

Turnstile
175 Fifth Avenue, Suite 2348
New York, NY 10010
$12, 24, group editorship

University of Windsor Review
Department of English
University of Windsor
Windsor, Ontario
N9B 3P4 Canada
$19.95, 12, Alistair MacLeod

Urbanite
P.O. Box 4737
Davenport, IA 52808
$13.50, 6, Mark McLaughlin

Urbanus
P.O. Box 192561
San Francisco, CA 94119
$8, 4, Peter Drizhal

Venue
512-9 St. Nicholas Street
Toronto, Ontario
M4Y 1W5 Canada
$26, 4, Jane Francisco

Vignette
4150-G Riverside Drive
Toluca Lake, CA 91505
$29, 4, Dawn Baille,
Deborah Clark

Virginia Quarterly Review
One West Range
Charlottesville, VA 22903
$15, 14, Staige D. Blackford

Wascana Review
English Department
University of Regina
Regina, Saskatchewan
S4S 0A2 Canada
$10, 8, J. Shami

Weber Studies
Weber State College
Ogden, UT 84408
$10, 2, Neila Seshachari

Webster Review
Webster University
470 East Lockwood
Webster Groves, MO 63119
$5, 2, Nancy Schapiro

Wellspring
770 Tonkawa Road
Long Lake, MN 55356
$8, 10, Maureen LaJoy

West Branch
Department of English
Bucknell University
Lewisburg, PA 17837
$7, 10, Robert Love Taylor,
Karl Patten

Western Humanities Review
University of Utah
Salt Lake City, UT 84112
$20, 10, Barry Weller

Whetstone
Barrington Area Arts Council
P.O. Box 1266
Barrington, IL 60011
$6.25, 11, Sandra Berris

Whiskey Island
University Center
Cleveland State University
2121 Euclid Avenue
Cleveland, OH 44115
$6, 10, Kathy Smith

William and Mary Review
College of William and Mary
P.O. Box 8795
Williamsburg, VA 23187
$5, 4, Forrest Pritchard

Willow Springs
MS-1
Eastern Washington University
Cheney, WA 99004
$8, 8, Heather Keast

Wind
RFD Route 1
P.O. Box 809K
Pikeville, KY 41501
$7, 20, Quentin R. Howard

Witness
Oakland Community College
Orchard Ridge Campus
27055 Orchard Lake Road
Farmington Hills, MI 48334
$12, 24, Peter Stine

Worcester Review
6 Chatham Street
Worcester, MA 01690
$10, 8, Rodger Martin

Writ
Innis College
University of Toronto
2 Sussex Avenue
Toronto, Ontario
M5S 1J5 Canada
$8, 7, Roger Greenwald

Writers Forum
University of Colorado
P.O. Box 7150
Colorado Springs, CO 80933-7150
$8.95, 15, Alexander Blackburn

Xavier Review
Xavier University
Box 110C
New Orleans, LA 70125
$10, Thomas Bonner, Jr.

Yale Review
1902A Yale Station
New Haven, CT 06520
$20, 12, J. D. McClatchy

Yankee
Yankee Publishing, Inc.
Dublin, NH 03444
$22, 4, Judson D. Hale, Sr.

Yellow Silk
P.O. Box 6374
Albany, CA 94706
$30, 10, Lily Pond

ZYZZYVA
41 Sutter Street, Suite 1400
San Francisco, CA 94104
$28, 12, Howard Junker